her way

her way

NICCI HARRIS

also by nicci harris

Copyright © 2021 by Nicci Harris

All rights reserved.

No part of this book may be reproduced in any form or by any electronic or mechanical means, including information storage and retrieval systems, without written permission from the author, except for the use of brief quotations in a book review.

ISBN ebook: 978-1-922492-07-4

ISBN print: 978-1-922492-08-1

ISBN print: 978-1-922492-10-4

Edited by Writing Evolution. @writingevolution. www. writingevolution.co.uk

Internal graphics by Nicci Harris

Cover design by Books & Moods

Nicci illustration holding kindle by @lamdin.designs

This is a **work of fiction**. Names, characters, businesses, places, events, locales, and incidents are either the products of the author's imagination or used in a fictitious manner. Any resemblance to actual persons, living or dead, or actual events is purely coincidental.

to a crazy group of authors and readers

—*my people—The Ricers.*

To my sweet friend Natalie, who helped me find Bronson when he didn't want to be found. When he refused to show me his vulnerabilities.

To my partner in this business and dear friend Holly, who believed in me and attempted to control my unrealistic expectations. See how I said 'attempted.' She's not a miracle worker.

To the Official Butcher Girls for pushing me, for cheering me on, for loving The Butcher Boys.

her way

song list

Her Way

1. The Pretender – Foo Fighters
2. Paper Walls – Yellowcard
3. Jekyll and Hyde – Five Finger Death Punch
4. All of Me – John Legend
5. Seize the Day – Avenged Sevenfold
6. Always Remember Us This Way – Lady Gaga
7. Riot – Hollywood Undead
8. This City – Sam Fischer
9. Someone You Loved – Lewis Capaldi
10. Crawling – Linkin Park
11. Without Me – Halsey
12. Headstrong – Trapt
13. I'm On Fire – Bruce Springsteen
14. Blow – Ed Sheeran, Chris Stapleton, Bruno Mars
15. Wicked Game – Theory of a Deadman
16: Fuel —Metallica
17: Seven Nation Army —White Stripes

Go to Spotify to listen.
Her Way

"loss is a lonely place.

—*For it is so personal, as no one is like you. Like me. Like us. No one will fill the emptiness that seems to occupy so much space inside me."*

CHAPTER ONE
bronson

Present day

AS I STAND on the edge of the jagged cliff, pissing into the estuary, the dense hot air strokes my cock. "You know, you always were my favourite," I say to the dead corpse to my right. The sound of my piss permeating the rippling water and the shuffling of rocks moving beneath my boots are the only sounds for miles. "Fuck, it's peaceful here. Not a bad place to die." The dome above me twinkles, the clusters of stars so fucking clear, they illuminate the whole environment —reflecting in the water, creating another dimension within its dark depths.

I shake my cock before stuffing it back into my jeans and pulling the zipper up. Twisting to face Salvatore, his big brown eyes still wide with shock, horror, and betrayal, I release a long, rough breath. "At least I shot you quick." I nod to myself. "Mate, it was painless. Don't look at me like that."

I take a few steps to kneel by his side. The scent of his blood and urine invades my senses. Poor bastard. I study him. Good looking lad. Total dickhead but not a bad mug on him. I lightly slap his cheek in a playful gesture, a kind of acknowledgement. I'll miss him. "Goodnight, cuz." I lean down and press my lips to his forehead.

My heart swells. It's not from remorse nor even guilt. Not today. For them, I'd kill my cousin again in a heartbeat. It's something else entirely. A moment of clarity. Of sadness. A reminder of mortality in all its grim certainty.

"Do you remember that time we stole Jimmy's Lamborghini? We went over that fucking bump and its guts fell out. He locked us in his basement for a week, fed us nothing but fucking rice. Good times." I laugh to myself.

Sal laughs too —wherever he is.

I'm sure of it.

He was scared-as-shit when it happened, but eventually, he laughed about it.

Patting him on the shoulder, I stand and get to work.

I grab the chicken wire from beside me. Red dirt flicks over Sal's body, sticking to the viscous fluids oozing from the two gaping holes in his chest. I shot him at close range. We were eye to eye, chatting about his fucking glorious adventures in India.

He had just got back.

I lay the wire down beside him. Grabbing his shoulder and his hip, I roll his limp, sluggish body onto it. The wire protests as I wrap it over him, blanketing his whole body. I kneel on him and pull the other side of it up, creating a tight cage around him. I fix it together with cable ties.

Standing, I stare down at my handiwork. That corpse won't be floating anytime soon. As bodily gasses release, the body will bloat, but the wire will shred his flesh, opening pockets of his skin, allowing the air to escape. Fish will eat him.

It's the circle of life, really. Beautiful in a way. And then, after a while, all that will be left in that cage will be his bones.

The quiet is suddenly interrupted by the chiming of my phone, alarming me to the exact time. Smiling, I consider my options. I really should just fucking get him in the water, sink him quick, and walk away —get going.

But instead, I grab my burn phone, punch in the number —a number I know by heart —and wait to hear *that* voice. I've been in Darwin for a few weeks now and I'm going fucking crazy without seeing her. The dial tone drops, and her sweet, high-pitched cadence massages my ear, dragging me away from the ominous scene at my feet.

"Daddy said bad word."

I gasp in a mock display of shock. "He what? What word did he say, Outlaw?"

"The F one," Kelly says, sounding so serious, her voice as curt as a three-year-old's can be. I can imagine her with a crazy pile of golden-blonde hair on her crown, shuffling her little pink bunny slippers on the glossy marble tiles. Imagine Cassidy warming up a glass of milk for her. Max watches them as though they are both feathers balancing on the wind, their presence so fragile and precious. He still doesn't believe he deserves them. He's a damn fool; my beautiful brother deserves all the happiness in this magnificent world. All the love a woman like Cassidy can offer. The love my little outlaw gives freely and without judgment —just like her mummy.

I tilt my head as if she can see me. "You mean *frog*?"

She giggles, the lovely sound pulsing my heart, provoking it to beat hard and fast. I thought I understood love. I've loved hard. I've loved to the point of blinding pain.

And I love my brothers.

But the day my stunning, gentle sister-in-law walked into our house with a bundle of pink blankets in her arms and a baby tucked protectively inside, I loved harder still.

Fuck me.

Kelly... the third great love of my life.

"No, not that one," she sings.

Laughing, I kick Sal's body, rolling it towards the cliff, towards his wet, salty grave. "Froyo?"

She giggles harder. "*No.*"

I kick again. "Oh, I know the one." I pause for dramatic effect. "Fox."

"*No.*" She lowers her voice with caution. "*Fuck.*" I can hear her double-dimpled smile, a cheeky curve to her lips that usually accompanies something she deems as naughty.

After I kick the body the last few metres, it balances right on the lip of the rocks. "I don't know that word," I say, looking down into the pitch-black water.

"It's a swear."

"Like a pinkie swear?" I ask, making the sign of the cross on my chest, wordlessly offering my own respects, before lightly pushing my boot into the wire, finishing the job. The body hits the estuary with a soft splash.

"*No*, not a pinkie swear."

Stuffing one hand into my pocket, I make my way through the low, dry shrubs, and towards the grey rental car parked on the side of the dirt road. I cringe at it, missing my bike. "What story did you read tonight?"

"*Um*, the pigeon one."

"*Don't Let the Pigeon Drive the Bus*? That's a goodin. Did you let him?"

"He'll crash, Uncle Bronson."

"I know. I know. But he looks so sad." Gripping the door handle, I pause to inhale the scent of salty water and feel the hot air tapping my face. Humid and dense, and in every way a classic night in outback Australia. Sicily is similar in many ways. It's in my blood to be in this heat, near the sea. "Hey, I just called to say goodnight." I look up at the sky. Those glowing white dots twinkle akin to the way her star projector does on the ceiling in her room. The image of her at my funeral, all in black, hammers behind my eyes, unwelcome and self-indulgent and pointless. But tonight will go just fine. "Miss your face," I say. "Have sweet dreams."

"I miss face *too*," she says, playing with the *too* for a while.

I laugh, opening the car door and placing one foot inside. "This ugly mug?"

"Not ugly." She tsks. "Handsung"

"Handsome?" I grin, her word filling me with pride. "Where'd you learn that word?"

"Mummy," she squeaks cheerfully.

"Well shucks, thanks, Outlaw." I feel my body stiffen as the moment to bid her goodnight looms, feel a roll of tension moving its way up my back, reminding me once again how risky my next plan will be. That maybe it isn't the best idea, not the only way, maybe —Nah. I got this. I force a wide grin so she can hear it. "Do me a favour, kiss your beautiful mummy and daddy for me. Right on the lips."

"I will."

"Nighty night."

I hang up the phone, stuff it into my pocket, and slide in behind the wheel.

While heading straight towards the other side of the

river, to a long underpass that connects directly onto the highway, I switch on some beats.

The White Stripes.

The need for a cigar before my imminent dose of adrenaline beckons me. I lean over, fumbling with the glove box, and retrieve the tin. Driving with my knees, I spark the bitch up and suck on it, the smoke swirling into my mouth. I lean my elbow on the door, watching the black road rush by.

After pulling under the pass, between the water and the cement column, I park up and enjoy the last few puffs of my cigar. Flicking the cigar butt from my car, I grab my gun and phone and step from the vehicle. It's go time.

CHAPTER TWO

bronson

Fourteen years old

I WATCH from under the slowly swaying tree as Jimmy, my dad, and four 'uncles' converse in loud burly tones. Sat around the outdoor table with their drinks, cards, and chips all spread across the wooden top, they look as though they are entertaining one another with wit, humour, and reminiscing kind of tones. What sits heavily around them, though, is an invisible entity that is powerful and greedy.

Jimmy always has a smile for us smoothly set into his tanned Sicilian face. He smiles at everyone, in fact. But no creature is more dangerous than the unreadable man who can just as easily smile at a person as he can slice their stomach open and watch their innards pile up at his feet.

One look and there is no mistaking that Jimmy Storm, with his unhurried movements and black suit, completely crease-free and impeccable, is a powerful motherfucker.

I idolise that man.

I've been working for him, the Family, in a casual way for over four years. Usually, that means breaking things when debts are overdue. It isn't personal. I usually check on them the next day; I even help clean up the rubble.

But I love my job.

Fucken ay, I'm fourteen and above the goddamn law.

I turn my gaze out over the lush green lawn to watch as my brother Max jogs back and forth with a fucking leather rugby ball clutched in his grasp like it's the Holy Grail. He is obsessed with that game. And well, *fuck*, my beautiful brother is talented. Ambitious. That level of commitment, of interest, is foreign to me. I've never found anything I care about...

At least not more than my brothers.

Xander runs after him, only ten and too fucking clever for his own good. He is always jumping into one of our shadows when he should be lighting his own path.

Turning back to Jimmy and my dad, I observe them in awe as they eye my mum, who is approaching them like a fly hovering too close to their meals. Despite the abuse she inflicts on us, I haven't managed to hate her yet.

Not like Max does.

But I do imagine her death.

Often.

She mutters something and attempts to sit on my dad's lap. He holds a hand out to stop her. Jimmy grins easily at her but waves her away. Tight-lipped, my mother fights her predisposition to scowl at the dismissal, and I smile so wide, my cheeks hurt.

Powerful men like these are elitists with whom they share their conversation.

Their respect.

These men have earned it.

I will too.

As I turn to join my brothers, Jimmy grabs the back of Uncle Gio's neck and slams his face down onto the wooden table, clattering their short whiskey glasses. A howl and a hiss escape Gio as his nose spills open, leaking dark red fluid all over the wood. It happens quick. Blood now glitters the table.

"*Shit,*" I mutter under my breath.

Jimmy's eyes shoot to me and hold me hostage.

Unable to get out of the snare of those brown irises, I simply stare back. My uncle is groaning, gripping the bridge of his nose as his wife rushes around cleaning up the mess. The other men seem unfazed, if not a little inconvenienced. I'm not sure how long we stare at each other, but suddenly, I'm drawn from his eyes by my mum as she pulls me away from them.

"Stop staring! Are you slow?" she snaps, tugging me by the arm.

"Leave the boy," I hear Jimmy call out to her, and I laugh at the red-painted lips now sneering at me. "In fact, Vicky, bring him a chair. I believe your boy has something he would like to say to me."

Holy fucking shit.

If looks could kill, my mum would have exploded my face. I saunter over to Jimmy, waiting to sit on the chair being positioned beside him at the table.

I glance around, first at the men now eyeing me with approving smirks and then at Gio as he stuffs his nostrils with tissues, his blood seeping into the thin mesh, dying it pink.

Jimmy picks up a card and cleans the blood off it by wiping it across my uncle's forearm. "Why were you watching me?" he asks smoothly, not glancing in my direction.

I swallow my nerves down, knowing there is no place for them at this table. "I don't know."

He doesn't look at me as he sorts the cards in his hand, arranging the queen and king and ace, placing them in order. "Do you want to know why I did that?"

Glancing at my uncle Gio, I try not to appear shocked and confused by the altercation nor the fact that Gio is still sitting here, tending to himself and none the more irritated. "Yeah," I admit.

Jimmy places his cards face down on the table before fixing me with a serious expression. "Because your uncle forgot himself." His eyes stay locked on mine, but he directs his words to Gio. "Didn't you?"

I dart my gaze to him as he says, "Yes, Jimmy."

My wide blue eyes flashback to the dark-brown ones cutting through me like a knife peeling an onion. "Don't let anyone forget themselves in your presence, my boy. Not even once. For the second time they do, they'll have made a fool out of you." I look over at my dad, who is watching our inter-action with that cool analytical gaze of his. His irises are sharp and clear-blue, like Xander's are, but his hair is grey-ing, and his face is far sharper edged and adorned with scars from his years as a professional boxer. Still, I've often seen women throw themselves at him, desperate for just one night with The Legend, Luca—The Butcher—Butcher or as he goes by now, simply, Butch. He is always the neutral man in the room, playing the game with every bit of skill Jimmy does. "What do you want?" Jimmy pauses on a thought. "What do you love?"

Usually, a question like this would have me smirking and making a silly comment, but Jimmy Storm demands truth and respect when he offers his attention and he does so with little effort. He demands without demanding and that is mesmerising to me.

I sit up straighter and say, "My brothers."

Jimmy nods slowly, scrutinising me contemplatively, all the wisdom in the world playing behind his eyes. "Then you are vulnerable," he states plainly. "Make sure you hide this vulnerability. Hide this behind your smile, *se?*"

I clear my throat. "I do."

"I know you do." He turns back to face the table. "You can leave now," he says, picking up his cards. As soon as he does, all the men begin to converse as though I have faded into non-existence.

Standing, I have every intention of leaving, but instead, my feet refuse to move while my mouth refuses not to. "What do you love, Jimmy?"

Silence falls around the table, and I take a big breath in. Jimmy smiles at his cards, then places them back down, turning to acknowledge me with a new look on his face. One I can't read, but it's badarse. "I care for a great many things, my boy. But love... only myself. Only ever myself."

CHAPTER THREE

shoshanna

Present day

WHEN I ENTER Gwendoline's room, she is sitting on the cushioned ledge beside her hospital window. Her arms are raised, and her palms are pressed together, making a pyramid over her head. She is completely oblivious —more like in denial —to the fact that resting should take precedence over her evening yoga.

I stop by her bedside, letting out a long sigh. "Why are you out of bed?"

"You weren't here when they all came in," she says, her voice cranky, her eyes shut as she pretends to meditate. "They talk about me like I'm an animal."

After my night in Emergency and a full day on the floor, they left me to sleep in the on-call room during rounds this evening. I force down the reasons they didn't wake me up, a consideration Residents are rarely offered, even after a heavy night shift.

But Perry is Attending today.

"They don't do that," I state, gripping both hips, trying to ignore the contractions in my stomach, the gnawing of what little food is present. I'd love to sit down with her and steal a moment. Meditate with her. I wish I wanted that, but the hospital race is one I've been training for my whole life, and being left out of it only works to agitate me.

I've given medicine seven years of my life.

Given up important things to be here...

"They do," she grumbles, dropping her hands and opening her eyes to reveal her cutting brown irises. The sun slashes lines of white across the silver mop of hair on her head, showcasing her wild violet tips. Her scowl is all nuisance and moxie. "I know what I want."

"*Yes.* But want and need are two different things."

"You're a baby." She scoffs. "What do you know about either?"

"I know that if you don't rest," I take a measured step towards her, "you'll die soon."

She bursts into laughter, and I purse my lips hard at her flippant attitude.

"That's why I like you," she says, crackling. "No fucking bullshit with you, Natalie."

Still with this Natalie Wood stuff...

I raise a brow at her smile. "Do you kiss your grandsons with that mouth?"

"They kiss me with worse," she admits with an adamant nod of her head. Rolling my eyes, I sigh. *They do.* When they actually make the effort to visit her, they spend most of the day discussing their inheritance. The rest, insincerely asking me questions as though I don't notice the smug looks on their faces. Don't notice the silent conversation they share as they glance at each other. Or the way their eyes move around my body.

A young female doctor.

The interruptive sound of the voice-over fills the room and hall behind me. "Code."

I suck in a sharp breath.

"Omega."

Severe blood loss.

Quickly, I pull out my pager. It vibrates against my palm, flashing the code and my initials. *Omega SA*. My pulse quickens, and I stuff the device back into my blue scrubs.

"Get back into bed, Gwen," I call over my shoulder as I rush down the corridor towards the trauma ward. My mind goes into overdrive, calculating the multiple sequences of action. First in the room. TPR. Fluids. Blood transfusion. O-Neg. Am I expected to run this room? Is that why Perry let me sleep? The first—and second-year residents flow from their stations like fish joining downstream, and we all fall into a meaningful stride together. I push open the prep room door and am met by Nurse Mandy.

Rushing over to the sink, I scrub up. After a few minutes, I twist to face her, and she instantly slides on my gown. I hold my clean hands out, not touching anything. Despite my nerves, I peel my surgical gloves on, precise in my application of them. As she slides my mask on, I suck recycled air back into my lungs; the feeling used to bother me, but now I'm used to it.

I push the doors open and enter the theatre room, ignoring the beady-eyed med students behind me while focusing on the monitors and displays. I note that the patient's oxygen saturation level is below eighty-five—he is hypoxic. Then it all happens so fast. Their voices come at me like sirens. Their eyes set seriously over masked noses and lips.

"Tension pneumothorax in the right lung due to a gunshot wound."

"Tachyonic"

"Trachea has deviated."

"Obstructive shock."

"Circulatory issues."

I jolt to work. "Get me a sixteen-gauge angi," I state, ignoring Perry at the foot of the bed as he measures and studies my every move. I pretend he's not there, not ready to jump in and save the situation at any moment.

Pretend *I'm* The Attending.

I'm in control.

The angi is placed in my hand.

As I lean closer to the patient, my eyes are suddenly snagged on a bright red blade tattoo that follows the contours of his ribcage. The beeping, the breaths, the shuffling —all the sounds slow. I drop the angi. Reaching out to touch the delicate red lines, I trace them with my finger. An action so natural to me, so familiar—

"Dr Adel?"

Startled, I snap my wide-eyed stare up to the patient's face and—

The room whirls around me.

I hear my name again, but it is floating in the air.

In the distance.

"Dr Adel?"

I'm drawn to that face like gravity. A whole facet of myself, previously lost and forgotten, now awoken inside me, and once again wearing my skin.

My breathing becomes shallow.

His perfect face.

Was he always so perfect?

Frantically, I stare at the wound. I wince. My heart fucking twists as though a massive fist is using it as a stress ball, pumping panic into it, each pulse reducing seven years of medical training to absolutely nothing.

Vibrating uncomfortably, my eyes find the monitors again. *His oxygen levels.*

He could die.

And while my mind screams at me to act, my muscles seize up under the immense pressure of having him on my table. Of having him need me again. Of having my entire body rendered utterly useless when it should be anything but.

Anything but useless!

Feeling a warning hand squeeze my wrist, I'm unsure how much time has just passed. A second. A minute. I don't know. My wrist suddenly aches within the band of someone's palm, throwing me back to the now.

"*Get. Out,*" Perry hisses.

His tone should bother me, but his opinion doesn't matter right now. I'm still. My ambitions are still, my need to prove myself to him and the world —*still*. Caught somewhere between reality and flashes of my past, I recognise Mandy escorting me from the theatre room.

The door shuts.

Pressing my back to it, I slide down until my bum hits the cold, hard floor. I press my palm against my stomach as a sinking feeling settles in.

I exhale his name. "*Bronson Butcher.*"

CHAPTER FOUR

shoshanna

Thirteen years old

"THEY SHOULDN'T BE HERE," Jessica whispers in my ear, her lips nearly touching me. I roll my shoulder up to encourage some space between us, but don't tear my eyes away from the three Butcher boys that have just sauntered into the party as if they own the goddamn place and all the people in it.

"*You* shouldn't be here," I mutter angrily as the girls to my side coo and giggle.

After having tried for nearly an hour to study in my room, I grumpily came down to lie by the poolside. If you can't beat them, join them... and all that shit. I settled down on the lawn beside the only other thirteen-year-olds invited—my big sister's little minions. Well, not the only thirteen-year-olds now that the young Butchers have made an appearance.

"They are going to get into a fight. I'm sure of it. They piss off the senior boys. They always do."

"It's because Clay is here. He's seven years older than them."

"Is Clay Butcher here?"

"I heard they are part of some kind of gang."

I flip onto my stomach, returning my attention to the textbook in front of me. I lick my finger and flip the page. A new chapter title mocks me with its significance —The Respiratory System. Someone bellows beside me, and a few girls gasp, but I focus on the intricate graphic now haunting me —two apple slice-like shapes connected by a channel and entwined with red string-like lines. *Fuck.* It is the most important part of the body. Most people say that the heart is, but my father says the lungs are. Even a small amount of oxygen deficiency can cause insanity-like symptoms. When the heart stops beating, it is the lack of oxygen being carried around that ultimately causes organ failure. Oxygen to our cells is like—

"Someone just got nailed in the face, and you didn't even look up." A masculine voice cuts through my internal thought process, dragging me unwillingly back to the party and the boy now lying beside me. I don't look over at him. Instead, I let out a slow sigh, lick the pad of my index finger, and use it to turn to the next page.

A rumble comes from his chest, but I try to ignore it.

"Do that again."

I frown at the page, attempting to focus, not wanting to give him any reason to stick around. In my peripheral vision, I can see a cool smile and dark hair, and it is taking all my strength not to peer over and catch a better glimpse of him. Heat prickles my cheek from his piercing gaze; it scorches the side of my face with dominance and arrogance that is uncomfortable.

"You have great hair."

As a few loose dark strands are suddenly swept from my cheek, I feel him move in close, hear him inhale deeply.

What the fuck!

When I twist on my elbows to glare at him, I'm instantly hit with the smirking, wide smile of Bronson Butcher. I've never seen him up close before. He has eyes like the sea, blues and greens shifting and sparkling as though his irises are adorned with their own mood gems. Strong chocolate-brown brows cut straight above thick black lashes.

I want to roll my eyes at how beautiful he is. My teeth lock together to stop myself from smiling nervously at him.

His mouth drops open in a ridiculous feigned expression of shock, his eyes still smiling with an annoying and endearing intent. "Woah, you have beautiful eyes." He pokes his tongue out through his renewed grin and kicks his heels into his backside, mimicking me, making a show of being a cocky, teasing arsehole.

"And skin," he confirms. "Great skin. Tanned, like mine. What ethnicity are you? Spanish or something?"

I still my legs, not having realised I was kicking them.

"Are you retarded?" I snap.

He laughs so loudly and grins so hard, a dimple indents his left cheek. "No. Why? Are you?"

I groan, ready to just pack up and leave, but where would I go? "Hints lost on you?"

An elbow from Jessica knocks me lightly in the rib. "You're being rude."

"Hint? *Why,* whatever do you mean?" he asks playfully, ignoring Jessica and the minions who I can hear whispering and giggling.

My eyes narrow on him, and he studies my scowl as if amused.

"Why are you looking at me like that?" I snap.

"'Cause you're ugly," he says, his tone dropping a few decimals.

"Good!" I spit out. "Then stop looking at me."

"Aren't you a bit young to be at a party like this?" I hear a snigger and peer up quickly to see Max and Xander Butcher standing beside Bronson's lounging body. I drop my line-of-sight back to Bronson and his annoying face.

I scoff, well and truly over this Butcher bully bullshit. They may run the halls and have the teachers wrapped around their fingers, but not here. "It's my house, brainiac. It's my sister's party. What's your excuse? High school kids at a college party? You're like thirteen."

Bronson frowns. "Fourteen—"

I glance up at Xander, who I think is ten. "Shouldn't your brother be in bed?"

"He's fine—"

"*Oh wait.* Let me guess. Your *nanny* came in here to get laid and left you three in the car, and you thought no one would notice how *tiny* you are?"

His right eyebrow twitches. "You are the ugliest girl with the dumbest fucking hair and the plainest eyes."

He grins again, as if an insult is somehow going to drive home his dominance. He can't intimidate me. I relax my face, then lather my tongue over my lower lip before nibbling at it slightly. Bronson fixates on my mouth like a cat does a mouse.

"Really?" I purr, edging a slither closer to him, ignoring the way my body wants to feel the heat of his. How it wants to taste those smirking lips. "So you *don't* want to kiss me then?"

One of his brows rise, expressive and full of hubris. He swipes his nose over mine, breath hitting breath. My heart pounds in my ears, but I try to drown it out, not wanting him to hear it. It is that fucking loud.

Finally, he breathes words against my lips. "I wouldn't kiss you if you were the last girl on earth."

His scent floats all over me —a medley of male pheromones and soap and sweat. And my whole body wants to rock towards his, but as our lips brush, I pull back and snort. "You're dreaming, Bronson Butcher."

"*Oh shit*," I hear Xander mutter.

In one second, Bronson's face goes blank. The next, it switches, dark and unidentifiable —he may as well have shape-shifted. He grabs the nape of my neck, pushing me quickly towards him and mashing our lips together. As I try to get free, he invades my mouth's wet center with his tongue. Slapping at him, at his shoulder, at his chest, I try to fight him off. I squeal into his mouth. A tongue like a whip lashes at me, mixing aggression with passion, moving in and around my lips.

My whole body sets on fire.

Finally, he releases my neck, my mouth, and I gasp for air. Growling, I swing my palm into the side of his cheek so hard the sting radiates up to my elbow. Hissing low, I try to hide the sounds of pain leaving my throbbing limb.

Everything is suddenly on mute. Slowed. My actions have shocked me just as much as they seem to have shocked him. He stares at me as though I have just sprouted another head. With his mood-gem eyes drilling into my soul, he lifts his hand to work his jaw and cheek, rubbing the place I hit with all my might. For a second, I can't breathe. Unsure of what he'll do next. What I'll do next. What even just happened.

Then a slow cocky-arse smile slides across his lips, and he mouths, "*I love you.*"

I clench my teeth to stop smiling because it's not funny. He's not funny. I'm not amused. Why do my lips want to curve? Fight the fucking curve; this is not cute.

This behaviour is disgusting.

I slam my book shut, needing to get as far away from him as possible. I jump to my feet and nearly stumble. Feeling his eyes follow me as I walk around the pool, I shoulder guests twice my size out of the way. For reasons unknown, my feet stop suddenly mid-stride. My neck and back are blanketed in heat, like hot flames licking around me in search of oxygen. I take two big breaths before twisting my torso to see him again. His trained gaze makes my heart leap into my throat, so I spin back around and run through the house to my bedroom.

When I enter, I slam the door behind me and crawl into bed, pull the blankets up like I used to do when I was a kid, and hide under them.

I blink at the lightly luminescent fabric of my comforter over me. My ceiling globe creates a glow behind it.

What the fuck was that shit?

My lips are still humming, so I lift my fingers and stroke them gently, feeling the skin he just invaded, took, and licked without a care in the world. My heart whips around inside me, caught in a vortex of confusion and annoyance. Am I annoyed?

I picture his eyes on me, examining me in an indecent and primal way. Completely cool and cocky, and who the fuck looks at a stranger like that anyway? I feel a wave of something moving through me, down my body, and settling between my thighs. I squeeze my legs shut. This is not happening. I am not interested in a bad-mouthed, over-privileged Australian with a silver spoon up his arse and a chip on his shoulder. No way. I part my lips to help myself breathe adequately, feeling dizziness and annoyance duel in my mind.

The commotion outside is a welcome interruption to the unwelcome thoughts swarming through my head like a plague of wasps.

Bottles smash somewhere.

Boys yell at each other.

I roll onto my side and face away from the window. A picture of my father and mother in Cairo for their anniversary captures my gaze. They left us here. I was only nine. Akila, thirteen.

As I study the photo of my mother wrapped in a traditional kaftan and my father looking dapper in his, I'm reminded of how proud they were to bring us to Australia. How many times I heard that everything they did was to give us the best opportunities. The sacrifices they made to give me and Akila a new life. I've felt humbled my entire childhood.

In debt to them.

If our dad had any idea that Akila was throwing parties every time he left, he would have us both deported back. She is already not getting the grades she needs to get into a pre-medicine course, and so the weight has shifted to my shoulders, moved so easily, and fitted so tightly I didn't even see or feel the confines of it until it was too late.

The smile on my mother's face stiffens my brows as I wonder what she had to be so happy about. Wonder how it's possible she could smile with such candour when two months after this photo was snapped, she left my father.

Left us too.

Another howl from a boy radiates through the glass of my window.

I throw the blanket off and step from the bed. Wandering over to the window, I draw back the thin sheath of purple fabric and stare through the glass at a brawl taking place around the pool.

Two boys are holding back two other boys. Smaller boys... *Max and Xander.*

My heart hits the back of my throat.

I search for Bronson through the dense crowd. Everyone is hovering around, watching the chaos unfold, blocking my view. I can see Max taking swings at people, but the boys holding him back are older and larger, restraining him most of the time. I wince when an older boy throws a fist into Max's stomach. Suddenly, my eyes dart to catch Xander as he wriggles free from his captors and makes a break for it.

The poor kid is so young; he must be scared shitless.

At the sight of Bronson, I nearly swallow my tongue. He is submerged in the water; his head being held under by someone. The stranger's bicep vibrates as they fight Bronson's resistance. Fight his desperate need to break the surface, to draw in air, fight his body as it gyrates around on the side of the pool edge.

I can't breathe.

Can't think.

Just as his body goes lax, giving up its fight for life, and I think I'm going to hurl through a scream, I see Clay Butcher bursting through the crowd, tailed by little Xander.

Clay brandishes a bat over his shoulder, a crazed look in his eyes. Without hesitation, he swings the bat into the boy holding Bronson underwater. The impact throws the boy backwards. His body flies through the air. Blood sprays the crowd. The sound of his howl is so loud I want to cover my ears. My eyes dart back to Max and Xander, who are now dragging a lifeless Bronson from the pool.

No.

I spin around and race from my room.

As I shoulder my way through the crowd, observing Max and Xander as they lay Bronson's sluggish body down on the concrete, I chant the sequence of CPR in my head. By the time I drop to my knees beside his body, his face is ashen, making his brown hair a dark contrast against his cheeks. The lips I kissed only a few minutes ago are now pale.

I mean, he kissed me.

I didn't kiss him.

I reach for him, my attention solely focused on the lifeless young man on the pavers. Someone grabs my wrist before I can check his pulse, gripping my flesh tightly, warningly.

When I look up, Max is scowling at me. "Don't fucking touch him!"

Xander cries out to their big brother. "Clay!"

I tug my wrist away from Max, feeling venom hit my tongue. "You need to call an ambulance!" I bounce my gaze from brother to brother, wondering why they are hesitating, feeling agitated and desperate for them to move. *Make a move. Do something!* "Call triple zero now!"

"Should we call Jimmy?" Xander asks, his voice a vibrating mess.

"Call a fucking ambulance, not Jimmy!" Max growls.

"Stop arguing. Who is going to perform CPR?" I bite out at them, noticing a twitch of discomfort in Max's jaw, a subtle sign that he's not in control and ready to snap.

"You know how?" Max glares at me. His eyes have the power to slice a person in two, dislocating their strength from their form, making them puddles of weakness. My breathing shakes violently, but I try to disguise it.

Clay drops down beside his brothers, his large powerful body towering over us. "You know CPR?"

I stare straight at him, hoping he'll trust me to help save his brother's life. It is clear in their narrowed, scrutinising eyes that they don't trust me. Perhaps they trust no one with each other. "Yes."

"Do it," Max barks.

What am I doing? I've only ever done this on dolls.

I reach a trembling hand up and touch two fingers to Bronson's wet neck. The thrumming of his pulse is evident but weak. His lashes lay flat against his cheek, weighted by water. Shuffling in closer to him, knowing that his life could be in my hands, I try to remain calm. My whole body vibrates violently as I open his mouth, tilt his head back, and check his airway. His tongue is in a strange position, so I try to flatten it before going straight to work. Pinching his nostrils together, blocking any air from entering or exiting, I lean over him and enclose his entire mouth with mine. Blowing into his lungs, I feel his chest rise slightly and know I have successfully filled his lungs with air. I do this twice and then entwine my fingers and press down on his sternum.

"Count with me," I say, my voice squeaking out. "I need you to count with me to thirty." The pressure of trying to count while my body is trembling so viciously is terrifying.

Chest compression. "One," we all say in unison.

Chest compression. "Two."

"Three... Four... Five ... Six—" We count up to thirty.

God, he's still not moving. Ignoring Xander as he swears

and cries beside me, I lean down and block Bronson's nose, breathing into his mouth again with all my energy. My arms tremble from fatigue and from fear and—Did he just move?

Pulling back from his mouth, my eyes widen, frantically searching for a sign he's coming to... but he's still unresponsive. Lunging back to take his mouth, I block his nose and press my lips to his again.

Warm air strokes across my tongue, but it isn't my own. Relief floods me. His face twitches against mine. I hear a murmur. Suddenly, a hand grabs the nape of my neck, holding me down, forcing me harder against his mouth as his tongue plunges into the depths of my widely spread lips. He licks the roof of my mouth, and heat hits my ears, burning up the panic and relief and replacing it with sheer anger.

Fucking prick!

I shove at his chest and he lets me go, weaker than he was the first time he pulled this crap. Instinctively, I raise my palm to slap him again, but Max catches my wrist this time.

"Fuck you!" I scream, ripping myself free of him.

Xander lets out a broken sigh of relief. Gripping his brother's shoulder, he squeezes lightly. "Bron?"

Clay strokes Bronson's hair. Bloodied fingers shaking with emotion comb through his wet strands. Lots of blood. Not his own, I presume. "Buddy, stay still."

And none of the boys even acknowledge that I exist. That their brother just assaulted me while I tried to save his life. I jump to my feet. Storming off, I will myself not to look back at them, will myself to leave these arrogant arseholes to their own precious company.

Stupid.

Jerk.

Fucking perverted... dickhead.

"Wait! What's your name?" I hear Bronson cough the words out from behind me.

Rushing away from him, I have no idea why I answer, but my name growls from between my pursed lips. "Shoshanna!"

CHAPTER FIVE
shoshanna

Present day

I RACE into the scrub room to catch Perry as he exits the theatre. "Perry!"

He stills, slowly turning to fix his narrowed hazel-coloured eyes on me. His blond brows are tightly woven across his forehead. He is so handsome in an incredibly wholesome way, with his high cheekbones and perfectly smooth jawline. His blond hair, which is shorter on the sides than it is on top, creates a small styled crown. Not a single tattoo decorates his body, but he has lean muscles and an athletic physique created by daily runs down the coast. So why is my heart yearning for a different body to hold me?

"What the fuck happened in there, Shosh?" he bites out before he has time to calm himself, his eyes flickering around for witnesses. He never bothers to hide his anger at home. Never hesitates to tell me how I've messed up.

My heart thunders in my ears, my focus on something else. "Br—" I halt the word. "The patient. Is he okay?"

Perry tilts his head at me as though that isn't a perfectly reasonable question to ask. "Yes. He'll be fine. Let's talk about why you couldn't hack it in there, yeah? You freezing up like that is not good for you. Or us."

I breathe out in a rush, letting the nerves and tension leave me in that one small action. He's okay. That fucking lunatic is alive. Again. Nodding, I try not to let my lips curve into a smile at the thought of him. Of his constant antics. Of his ability to live this fast, hard, crazy existence because he has all these lives. I want to burst into laughter. Hysterical laughter. That is how he makes me feel.

The emptiness in my stomach grows.

We got to stop meeting like this, nutcase.

I nod, trying to appear in the present. "I know."

His face tightens. "Why are you smiling? Now is not the time to be playing around."

"I smile when I'm nervous, Perry!" I spit out, raising my hands to rub my cheeks, pleading silently with them to stop rising. But I can't help feeling elated that he's alive and still so beautiful to look at. That he is so close. That I could walk in that room and touch him.

My heart drops.

I shouldn't see him, though. The thought saddens me, but it would be kinder, for him, to not see me again after what I did to us.

"I let you sleep in," Perry says, pulling me away from my past demons. "I'm trying to support you here. Prove to everyone you can do this. But then you pull this crap. It is not just your career on the line. It is mine. I'm vouching for you." Shaking his head slowly, he says, "You embarrassed me in there, Shoshy." His mouth touches my ear, his breath hits me, chilling my spine. "Do you need a break?"

Clenching my teeth together, I lock out all thoughts of Bronson. Perry is who matters to me. I should be thinking of him. He loves me and my sister. Without him, I wouldn't be the person I am today. Wouldn't be a doctor. Wouldn't have the safe, easy life I have now.

He straightens and scrutinises me, his eyes still soft on my face but not overly kind. It is a practised show of kindness, of tenderness, a patronising tilt to his lips. "Look, I'll take care of this for you. I always do, don't I? No one needs to know. Just go home. Have a nap. I'll see you for dinner tonight."

And with that, he turns and leaves me standing there like a scolded child. I remind myself that he is right. This is his career too. He's sticking his neck out for me. And being a woman, I'm at a disadvantage in our field already. Mainly, that when a woman shows emotion in a field such as ours, shows anger or acts impulsively, it is seen as either hormonal or overly emotional. But when a man does it, it is always simply a show of passion.

Wandering back down the hall, I still feel like I'm in the twilight zone. I haven't seen Bronson for... ten? No, eleven years. I have no idea what he would say if he sees me because the last words we shared... *God.* The very last conversation we had *killed* me.

My arms go around my stomach, just like they did that day in the park, supporting myself against the memories that want to rise. My throat tightens as I see the pain in his eyes. Hear the roar of anguish as it leaves him. Hear the distant growl of his bike as he leaves me. *Oh God*, he won't want to see me.

Eleven years apart and not a single sign he ever looked

for me. Never tried to drag me back like he would have done if he cared. Like he would have done moments before our last conversation.

"WHAT IF THEY *don't let us?" I ask.*
He grins. "Then I'll kill them."

BUT HE DIDN'T.

And that speaks volumes about how he feels about me.

Pull yourself together!

Lowering my hands to my sides, I breathe deeply through my nose, channelling calm, fighting the pain. I pretend this is just a normal day in the hospital and stride past the nurses' desk, heading towards the changing rooms to remove my scrubs and grab my bag. I need to head home. Need to get away from here, even though I can feel myself being ripped down the middle. One half is desperate to leave. The other, desperate to go to him...

With that thought, I think about telling Perry. He has been my confidant. My partner in life. I should just tell him... Well, not *everything*. Bronson's presence in this hospital is palpable to me.

But the thought of telling Perry about Bronson makes my stomach gnaw at itself. In fact, both names bouncing around in my head, wrap me in guilt. They exist in very different worlds, the blending of which would be catastrophic. One is a world of responsibilities and commitments. The other... of intensity and madness and childish ignorance to the way the world really works.

As I enter the changing room, I'm met by Mandy and

Katie. They both share glances back and forth before scrutinising me. *Fuck.*

I roll my eyes at them, hoping they can't see what I don't want to address. I move over to my locker to grab my things. "Don't start."

"What was that all about then?" Katie asks in her usual salacious tone. Her creamy-blonde hair is pulled tightly off her face, making her small, delicate features appear even more so. We do not get along. She likes to tell me and everyone else exactly how she sees things. Strangely, it is the one thing I *don't* despise about her; I know exactly where I stand. She doesn't manipulate or lie. She doesn't like me, though. But at least she never pretends to. "You're looking a little flushed," she teases contemptuously.

I tug my scrub shirt off over my head and stand in front of her in my bra. "I know him. That's all."

She smiles, a scandalous tilt to the corner of her mouth. A twitch to her arched blonde eyebrow. "Know him? Who? The patient?"

I groan at her expression. "Why are you looking at me like that? Don't you have anything better to do? Like your job?"

"Better than this? No. He doesn't look like the type of man I imagine you *ever* knowing," she drawls.

I wished that were true.

Many times...

Then I never would have hurt him.

I shake my head. Turning from her, I tug my pants off each leg and pull on a pair of denim skinny jeans. Faded at the thighs and cut at the knees, they show little slithers of my bare skin between the slashes of material. I pull on a white tank top and tuck it in. When I turn back to the girls, Mandy is staring at me curiously and Katie is smirking.

"What now?"

Mandy eyes me thoughtfully, tucking her brown hair behind her ear. Her pretty blue eyes are big and round, a contrast to her pointed nose and sharp cheekbones. "Did you tell Perr—"

"How *well* do you know him?" Katie cuts in. "Curious minds are inquiring."

"We were just childhood friends," I lie. It is the biggest fucking lie I have ever told because nothing could be further from the truth. We were never *just friends*. We couldn't have been even if we wanted to, which we never did.

"I'd like to be childhood friends with him," Katie purrs.

"God, Katie!" I slam my locker door shut. "He could have died in there, and you were checking him out? Talk about professionalism." My heart jumps into my ears again, and I have no idea where that anger came from. If Mandy's wide-eyes and Katie's excited grin are anything to go by, then they have no idea either.

I rub my temples, shaking the irritation out, the discomfort.

"*Meow*," she sings with a scathing laugh. "And *excuse me*, but it's kind of hard not to notice the patient is tall, muscular, and covered in tattoos."

Mandy stares at me unblinking. "What's gotten into you? Does Perry know about this?"

"What are you, his spy or something, Mandy?" Katie laughs, folding her arms over her chest and leaning on one hip. "You gonna go report something to him?"

"No," she says with a little smile that makes me nervous. My brows weave. I know her deal. I've seen the way she looks at Perry. Witnessed the little touches. She's run to him with gossip more times than I can count. She's basically his trained and tagged carrier pigeon. Mandy motions towards me, looking at Katie. "Look at her. She's exhausted."

"*She*!" I growl. "Is standing right here." I take a big breath in and exhale it slowly. "I'm not exhausted," I state. I'm fucking hurt! I'm scared of what to do! But knowing it'll make them back the hell off, I concede. "Maybe..." I hate these words. "Maybe I *am* tired."

I walk off towards the door, pushing it open and entering the hospital halls once again. I refuse to ask Mandy not to tell Perry. That'll only make her more suspicious.

And maybe I am just tired.

As I make my way outside, towards my bike, the thick Australian air envelops me, and for a moment, I wonder why it's so dense. The District is never this humid. Then I remember where I am.

What the hell is he doing in Darwin anyway... bringing this bullshit up here? A gunshot wound. Of fucking course. So, nothing has changed. He's still working for Jimmy.

Jimmy...

I knew he was powerful, but I never knew just how powerful until that day at the park. If only I had known, things might have been different...

The sinking feeling in my stomach starts up again. Pulling my bike from the rack, I ignore it. I swing my leg over and take off down the street towards the aqua-blue shoreline. The sound of the wind whipping past my ears and the nattering and splashes coming from the popular tourist beach to my left remind me why my father chose to relocate here.

The other reason, impossibly, happens to be lying in a hospital bed with a puncture in his chest.

That thought is interrupted when I ride down our driveway and notice the letterbox is still full. I stop briefly beside it to pull the letters, junk mail, and a magazine out. My sister hasn't been outside today. She loves it outside.

I swing my leg over the bike and walk up the driveway, making my way inside to find her. She is sitting by the window, her torso swaying forward and back, her dark hair in a ponytail, the long strands tumbling down the back of her wheelchair. She is still in her nightgown. I reach her and kneel at her side, staring up into a vacant, lost gaze.

"I'm home, honey," I say with a small chuckle. "Let's go outside." Rising, I lay the mail on her lap and kiss her forehead. I grip the chair handles, kick the wheels' safety off, and manoeuvre her around the house, making our way out the front door. Pushing her onto the lawn, I park her under a big palm tree and kneel beside her. The grass cushions my legs, the thin blades tickling the bare skin between my ripped denim jeans.

I sit down and pull the Food and Wine magazine off her lap. She has had a subscription since she was twenty. She loves all things culinary. I keep them all. Every subscription.

I scoff as I read the leading article aloud for her. "Life's a peach." I sigh. It most definitely is not. "This one is about peaches." I flick through it. "Peach deserts. Peach beer. Peach jam. Now, if I could cook at all, I'd give this one a go," I say, pointing at the peach tart on the page.

'I'll cook for you every night.' Seventeen-year-old Bronson's words tumble into my head. I clear my throat as it tightens up; not wanting her to hear how the words are strained. "So, weird thing happened today... You'll never guess what..." I rip the tart page from the binding and fold it, making an origami rose. Back in high school, whenever we would gossip about boys, we would make bouquets and swans. I only ever spoke about one boy.

"Bronson is in Darwin."

I gaze up at her, my fingers still working away through muscle memory. "I feel so strange," I admit. "I've barely thought about him... Not for a long time anyway. I think I even forgave myself."

Of course, I'm met with silence. On a good day, I can get a sigh or a scoff, sometimes a chuckle, but I'm not sure that they aren't just sounds. Not attached to any sentiment or feeling. Just sounds her mouth sometimes makes. Either way, her chuckles make me smile.

"Girl, he was angry with you. He didn't want you after what you did," I say for her. "And it was forever ago. You don't even know him anymore."

I groan at my inner Akila. "*Fucksake.* I'm being ridiculous. I was a child. He was a child." My words add to that emptiness in my stomach. I rip at the grass blades, watching as they scatter in the gentle, tropical breeze. "He was so angry last time I saw him. And I feel this sinking feeling inside. Now, having to face him again. Maybe. I doubt he wants to see me anyway. Or maybe he just doesn't care at all. I mean, it's been eleven years."

"You know he'll care," I answer for her. "Hate is still a form of caring."

I wince, my Akila monologue grating on me.

"Hey!" someone calls out from behind me. The husky voice comes from Akila's carer —Mary. "I'm heading off. She had a good day but wouldn't let me take her pyjamas off. But I thought it wasn't worth upsetting her over."

"Sure. It's all good," I call back, not turning around because I'm annoyed, but it isn't worth the fight. Perry picked her and pays for her; nothing she does is ever wrong.

We owe him so much.

* * *

After blowing out the candles on the neatly set dining

table, I pick up both plates. The cold vegetables and steak slide around as I walk them to the trash and scrap the idea of an apology down into the lemon-scented rubbish bag.

Another cold meal.

Another night eating alone.

Strolling up the stairs to our bedroom, I pull off my navy-blue dress and heels and chuck them into the dressing room. I pull out my earrings. I wipe off my makeup. Slide onto the bed, feeling all kinds of restlessness.

Rolling around, I flip from side to side and then lay flat on my back to stare at the ceiling. The fan above me hums as it moves warm air around, the humidity affecting me more now than it ever has. And I thought tonight would help me dissolve the confusion I feel over having *him* so close.

Help me highlight to Perry how *fine* I actually am.

But my efforts have fallen into the trash along with the overcooked steak and undercooked vegetables.

Blinking into the dark, my breathing picks up pace as an ache shifts between my thighs. I squirm around, groaning at how uncomfortable it is.

Closing my eyes, I imagine *his* hands trailing from my face towards my nipples. When I reach the tight aching nubs, I squeeze them to the point of pain and my pussy ripples. Groaning at the sensation so cruel and needy, I continue the descent of my fingers until they are between my legs. My folds are wet. I push a finger inside to elevate some of the yearning, the internal beckoning for a release. I move my fingers inside the way he used to. With steady, deep, meaningful thrusts. My ears and neck and face grow hot, prickling and perspiring in the surrounding humidity.

I picture the sweet agony on his face as he comes inside me. Picture the way his muscles would contort with restraint as he pounded into me. All those large muscles. They weren't that intimidating when he was seventeen. Now, though, they are very. Very. Intimidating. I can only imagine the way he could handle a woman in his bed.

At that thought, a burst of pleasure begins, and I don't even bite down on my lips, moaning his name to the world, feeling the beginning of something so needed bubbling through me.

Heat boils in my stomach.

I feel it coming on quick.

Rubbing myself hard, I chase it as it lingers just out of reach. My release teases me with tiny bursts of pleasure. My other hand finds my nipple again and I pinch it between my nails. A zap of pain rushes to the coiled nerves between my folds and I'm almost there.

Fuck.

The front door opens and then closes.

Whimpering, I pull my hand from between my legs and try to rein in the pain caused by my lack of release. My breath comes in and out fast as I stare into the dark, feeling admittedly hard fucking done by.

The croaking of frogs and the clicking of crickets are the only sounds besides his steps moving up the staircase.

Perry enters the room, moving straight into the bathroom and switching the faucet on. *God*, I can feel the disappointment in the air.

I face the wall and listen to the sounds of nocturnal outback Australia.

The door to the bathroom opens and steam fills the air, adding to the already dense atmosphere. The mattress sways beneath my body, an indication he's moving up the bed towards me.

"How are you feeling?" he asks, kissing his way up my arm to my shoulder.

I roll onto my back, and he now hovers just above me, kissing my jaw and cheeks, an obvious display of what he wants. It's what we had planned for the night, but I thought we might talk first...

Staring at blond hair, I drag my hands up through it and feel him shudder beneath my fingertips. It is shorter than when we met. I was twenty-one. And fuck, it was easy to fall in love with Perry Jackson then. He was handsome, clever, respected, and he made me feel like a future with him would be easy and safe. I needed that. *Easy. Safe.*

"Akila was still in her nightgown when I got home," I say delicately, hoping he's in a good enough mood to talk about her. He's dying for children, but every month that goes by, he seems to struggle more and more with Akila as his dependent. Even though he was so fucking eager to take us both on financially and legally. After the crash and losing our dad, I was in no state to manage her care. Or, I could have, but I would have had to quit medical school and work full time just to afford a slither of the lifestyle Perry provides for us.

I don't thank him enough for that.

Putting me through medical school, adopting Akila, and now trying to give me everything I've ever asked for. *I love him,* I think to myself as his blond strands slide through my fingers. *I do...*

I'm just not sure I'm *in* love with him anymore. Unlike my mother though, I won't be running off, because love is still love even when it's quiet and easy. *Right?*

"She probably put up a fight," he murmurs against my skin, rubbing himself into my leg. "Let's not talk about her right now, please."

"She doesn't put up a fight though," I say. "Not when I look after her."

He tenses around me. "Goddamn it, Shoshy, I'm tired. I

want my woman to help me relax and instead, you're nagging me about Akila again? Let's talk about this another day. Okay?"

Quickly, his mouth moves from my jaw to my lips, demanding my submission. When his tongue strokes the roof of my mouth, the image of the first boy who ever did that to me plays behind my eyes. Squeezing them shut, I look into beautiful green-blue irises.

Kissing me between pants, he thrusts into me, sliding in as I'm so wet. He dips his head into the crook of my neck, working himself in and out of me. "So wet for me."

I want to tell him to stop so that we can talk about Akila. "Perry. Please, can we discuss this?"

He shuts me up, swallows my words, bites my lower lip until I whimper, and then plays the entire action off as intimacy, kissing me softly again. I let the conversation lay. This is scheduled sex and if he doesn't finish, can't finish because I'm not into it, he'll be pissed off. And I'll feel guilty.

So I moan.

CHAPTER SIX

shoshanna

Present day

MY PEN VIBRATES on the desk as I struggle to concentrate on the forms in front of me, my attention drawn elsewhere. Through the glass screen overlooking the nurses' station, I can see them huddled together, chatting and giggling over who is going to check his vitals next.

They have never been so fucking efficient.

I should be glad they are taking his well-being so seriously, but I simply want to bitch slap every one of them at the exact same time. And I'm moody as all fuck because I'm ovulating; I hate this time of the month. It must be blatant in my posture or expression because no one has approached me since I sat down to fill in this stupid report. Either that or Perry has told everyone to leave me alone. That thought alone makes me feel ten years old.

I glance down at the words on the chart in front of me,

then back to his door at the sound of Nurse Jade entering his room. Inhaling a deep breath, I breathe out slowly as I watch the closed door intently, my eyes now glued to it.

At the sound of a giggle and a masculine voice, I jump up and press one palm to my chest, feeling my heart beneath all those layers of skin and bone, beat at an intense tempo. My pulse forces its way into my ears, like a drum, taking me back to that day at the park.

When I hear his chuckle, my knees suddenly go weak, the deep cadence damn near knocking my legs out from under me. *A fucking chuckle.* I couldn't remember the way that sounded even when I used to try so hard. To draw on happy memories. All that came up, all I could remember, was the pain. The hurt. I shouldn't be here. My fingers find the desk, gripping it tightly to steady myself. Glancing at the ground, I stare at my black Hush Puppies, shifting my weight as I try to gain some composure.

Balling my fingers in tight, I straighten and walk from the office, past the suddenly quiet nurses who are following my every step towards his door. I stop on this side and lean on the wall, listening to the inaudible words coming from within.

Jade pulls the door open, and in her shock at finding me on the other side, she gasps.

"Fuck. Dr Adel. Sorry." She laughs on an exhale. A light rouge paints her usually pale cheeks, provoking a frown from me that I can't mask for the life of me.

"What has you so flushed?" I ask, smiling stiffly and folding my arms across my chest, quite aware of the bitch face I'm sporting and hating myself for it.

"The patient is awake." She tries to fight her smile. "And he's..." She giggles once. "In good spirits."

Is he? I swallow hard. Jade's smiling eyes are suddenly

drawn back into the room. She gasps, moving quickly back inside. "You shouldn't be up, Mr Butcher."

Breath leaves me in a rush.

No. Don't get up.

I shuffle backwards, taking little steady steps.

You shouldn't be up, Bronson.

My heart is securely lodged in my throat as I turn and stride away, my spine aching from how stiff I feel. I hear heavy, meaningful footsteps quickly coming up behind me.

"You shouldn't be out of bed!" Jade calls out, her voice following me down the hall, indicating his presence mere steps behind mine. As if I need that sign.

I've always felt his presence.

But he hates me.

Tensing to prepare for his anger, I jump when he slides his hand around my waist, stilling my stride. Gripping my opposite hip, he twists me, walking me backwards until I am pressed against the hospital wall and staring at the hard wall of his body.

I open my mouth to draw air in as it's suddenly thick, and hard to find. His energy is so wild. It always was. Powerful. Unrestrained. Like a wildfire. Like Bronson Butcher. He's hot and dangerous and hard to control.

Unable to acknowledge what is happening, I just try to steady my racing pulse for the sake of the onlookers. Two palms press against the wall on either side of my head while large, tattooed arms bar me within the cage of his body. What are you doing?

God, he's gotten bigger.

More muscular.

And those tattoos... so many of them.

My mouth fills with saliva, and when I lick my lips, I hear the slightest growl rumble from deep in his chest.

And I hear... *'Do that again,'* in my head.

I fight the urge to look up. I can see his chest moving fast and can hear his breaths expelling fiercely, so I know his eyes will be smouldering pits of green and blue.

For a moment, there is no one else but us. His breath is heavy. Mine frantic. Raising his hand, he runs his fingertips gently down the contours of my face, gliding each digit down my forehead, over the tip of my nose, to my mouth, where he drags the swell of my lower lip down so I can taste the salty skin on his fingers. I stifle a moan. It's a gesture so familiar and melancholy, it's painful.

I squeeze my eyes shut, holding them like that.

To the feel of him.

To the feel of those memories.

He doesn't hate me?

God, I needed his touch eleven years ago.

"Shoshanna."

He purrs my name in his deep tone, in a voice sexy and gravelly with sentiment. It's an erotic sound that can make any girl boil from the inside out.

"Should we call someone?" I hear Jade ask nervously.

I manage to breathe the word out. *"No."* But her voice has worked like a blade, severing the invisible pull between us enough to snap me back to where I am —to who I am.

Slowly opening my eyes, I am struck by the sight of his searing gaze on my face. So close. His eyes are as green-blue as I've ever seen them.

Oh. God.

And now I can't tear my eyes away from his because there is this little freckle within his left iris that is neon emerald. And it means he's on a knife's edge of some emotion too powerful for him to handle. I used to call his eyes, 'his mood rings'.

They clearly still are.

Is he thinking about that last day?

The sinking hole in my abdomen starts to hollow me out, heart and all. For a moment, I think he might bite me or kiss me or growl. And that's always been him. The arousal of his passionate response, be it deadly and unpredictable or overwhelmingly intimate and gentle, is always moments away, hiding in that green speck.

I swallow hard and look down at his hospital gown. Somehow, I find enough sanity to say, "You need to get back to bed."

His warm breath rushes down my neck like a literal caress, my skin prickling awake in response. I squeeze my thighs together. "Well then," he mutters smoothly, emotion deepening his voice further. "You should probably take me back, Doc. Not sure I can make it on my own."

He pushes off the wall, stepping backwards twice, giving me my first real look at him. And I'm not a shallow person, but this man shouldn't be allowed to look so fucking gorgeous. It should be a crime. With a masculine jaw tight with emotion, colourful tattoos licking up from his neck and covering both arms entirely, being six foot five with a primal physique and ready to hunt and play and fuck and—

I clear my throat and begin walking towards his hospital room, desperately trying to ignore the feel of his eyes as they follow me. I can sense him stalking me up the hallway. Can see the nurses wide-eyed with shock.

Entering his room, I try to figuratively put my doctor hat on by pulling his chart off the foot of his bed.

A ridiculous move and stance, but what else can I do? He strides through the open door with the confidence and strength of a man who is infallible and invincible and wasn't just fucking shot in the chest. There must be so much pain flaring through his body right now, but he looks unaffected by it.

"Do you want me in bed?" he asks, a salacious purr to his words. *He's flirting with me?*

I don't answer. Can't. How can he be so damn calm, given our last conversation all those years ago? Does it not haunt him? Twist him up inside? Doesn't the sight of me remind him of what I did to him?

I focus on the chart, my eyes scanning the words, none of them making any sense, while my mind churns with nervousness. I swallow hard, fighting with myself not to say anything stupid to him. As though talking might remind him of what I did. Stupid woman.

As he makes his way over and sits on the mattress, my eyes dart to the cannula in his hand, ripped straight from the giving set. "I might need some help getting in," he jokes. And although he grins at me, his Butcher dimple pressing into the side of his cheek, I don't see contentment or happiness in his eyes. He's unpredictable right now, the glowing green in his irises telling me as much. I try not to notice, bouncing my eyes back to the chart, feigning a sense of nonchalance.

"Look at you," he says, relieving me of the silence. I finally cave, staring directly into his gaze as I wrestle to control my emotions.

You're not angry anymore?

Why are you here?

He drags his gaze down my body in an indecent way, causing my left leg to buckle beneath his piercing eyes. "I'm so proud of you, baby. All grown up and wearing your scrubs like armour."

As though he just reminded me that I'm a doctor —his doctor —my eyes find his wound, my throat tightening. "You were shot."

"I'm fine, baby. Don't you worry about me." He shifts his weight on the bed, nodding in my direction. "Are you happy with your life?"

God, that's a horrible question. Or maybe, maybe it's just one of those things you say to someone you haven't seen in eleven years. It is just like asking about the weather. I glance around the room, seeking a moment of peace from his cutting gaze. It's a simple question really, but impossible to answer. Do I try to explain myself again? Do I tell him that every happy memory we shared was drowned out by his anger that day? That all I can feel now when looking at him is sorrow and guilt?

That I'm not happy.

No.

"What are you doing here?" he asks.

Blinking at him, I mutter, "I live here."

"Since when?"

"This whole time."

He laughs, but it's not gentle or nice, and the reasons why twist at my stomach. "*This whole time*," he repeats. Standing up, he adds, "I think I need to get naked..." He winks at me, and I fight my cheeks' predisposition to blush. "Have a shower, that is. Should we get one of those nurses to help me or will my beautiful doctor be doing it?"

"Cute." The word slips out, an incarnation of a sixteen-year-old girl. A girl who loved him as if the last eleven years never happened. As if we didn't rip each other bare, shredding our hearts, our future, our promises, in that goddamn park.

"You always did think so." He pulls off his robe, dropping it onto the floor, baring his masculine body to me. More tattoos than I've ever seen on a man before wrapping themselves around muscles in a perfect way —weaving over defined curves, their colours vibrant and expressive just like him. A smirk plays on his lips when I drop my gaze to his thick tattooed thighs and the long semi-hard shaft hanging between them.

Jesus fucking Christ.

Nudity is a part of my job, but most people shuffle with nerves or cover their privates.

Bronson isn't most people.

I fight the urge to react. "I'll get Brian to help you shower if you'd like? He's strong enough to handle anything you need... *washed.*"

"Brian?" Bronson's eyes light up, and my heart breaks over that cool, affable grin. Another thing I couldn't draw from my memories. Not after the look of betrayal he left me with. He takes a step towards me, and I take a step back. "Is he hot?"

My lips twitch with a smile that has no place being there. "I'm not sure I ever noticed."

He takes another step towards me, and I crane my neck to hold his gaze. "You were always such a perv," he says. "I find that hard to believe."

"I'm a perv?" I say, my cheeks burning with the urge to let that smile set into my face. To let the good memories in and maybe, maybe finally get closure.

"Yeah. You couldn't keep your little hands off me, if I remember correctly."

"I don't think you remember correctly."

"Oh, Doc. I remember. *Everything.*"

The thread holding my heart together tears a little. He is so close to me now, I can feel his potent, masculine energy like a pulse against my skin. I lift a shaky hand and press my palm flat against his rock-hard abdominals, against a tattooed hourglass. Fighting the overwhelming desire to run my fingers over it, to feel the muscles it paints trembling against my touch, I ball my hand into a fist.

"Stop." I press back against his advances with my knuckles. "I work here. Don't do this."

His tone drops further, his smile in his voice, along with something else, something dangerous and him. "How do you want me to act, Shoshanna? Like I don't know the colour of your pussy? Like I don't know the way your sweat smells and tastes? Like I don't know you have a bite? Where's my crazy girl in there?" His dirty words flush through me like pure arousal being injected into my core. His strong arms hang by his sides, but his fingers rub the skin of his palms. I know he wants to use them. To grab me. "Who is this wound-up young lady I see in front of me?"

With that, I step backwards. "Don't talk to me like that here."

"Okay. Where then?"

I blink at him, trying not to look at his impressive physique, his smooth skin, tattoos, thick cock—"What?"

"Where are you taking me so I can talk to you like that? And I'm not a cheap date. I want romance, baby. Or I'm not putting out."

I let out a small laugh, and it's such a foreign sound, I barely recognise it, the bad memories fading for a slither of a moment. "You're incorrigible."

"It's been years," he says. "I'd like to know what you've been doing."

"Put some clothes on. I can't do this with you right now, Bronson." I turn towards the door, taking slow steps away from him. My body and heart duel, my heart clearly eager to stay and talk... To have that chance to say I'm sorry *again*. But he seems to have moved on? And he looks unaffected? Did he meet someone, maybe? Has she taken away his pain?

Taken away *me?* But all I say is, "I'm working. Get some clothes on. I'll send someone in to fix your giving set."

"I can't stay, baby. You know that. I have places to be," he states with a serious tone. Duty. It's his 'I have duties to uphold' voice. The words and tone still me. Because while my heart is breaking in two all over again, he's just eager to leave.

Growling, I whirl around and bark at him. "You stubborn dickhead. You have to stay! You just had a goddamn blood transfusion. Now get into the goddamn bed."

"There she is." He smirks and sticks his tongue out to lick his lower lip. "Now come here and give me a hello kiss."

Shaking my head at him, I'm finding his nonchalance more hurtful than his anger. "I have to go. I have patients to see." I stop at the door, having pulled it ajar. Glancing back at him, I find him the most glorious sight of masculinity —now with his cock hardening, his thighs and biceps clenching in a way that offers insight into his desire to lunge for me.

I swallow hard against an internal moan. "Stop looking at me like that."

His turquoise-coloured eyes pierce through me, daring me to walk away, knowing exactly the effect he has over me. "Like what, baby?"

I swallow hard, barely being able to get the words out. "Like I'm ugly."

Quickly, I turn my back to him and slip from the room.

CHAPTER SEVEN
bronson

Fourteen years old

SHE'S GOT to let me in soon.

It's been fucking hours.

So she slapped me, kissed me, and saved my life, and that was all before I even knew her name. What can I say? I like that in a girl.

I circle around the end of the cul-de-sac and pedal back past her house, whipping the handlebar around and then breaking hard, practising my nose wheelies. A few of her neighbours are pretending to water their lawns, when in fact they are scoping me out. The sun has just dropped past the rooftops, and I'm creeping down the street under the flickering lamps.

They must think I'm bad news.

Either that or they know I'm a Butcher, know I'm bad news.

Her house, a small red brick single story construction, is tiny compared to mine. She's got a great old-school pool though, outdoors and large. Unlike ours, which is inside and heated and just not the same as being under the rays. I nearly fucking drowned in her bowl of water a few weeks ago, so I feel a closeness to it. I hope she lets me swim in it with her one day.

She's still peering through the window, the sheer curtains partly covering her cute face. Strands of her glossy near-black hair float beside her cheeks. One amber-coloured iris narrows on me. She can pretend to hate my guts all she wants, but I know the truth. Doesn't she realise I can see her? Her girlfriends are taking it in turns on the opposite window to watch me. I give them a little show. Bunny hopping with my tire and grinning at them. I swear I can hear them giggling from here.

Finally, I see my opening. A pizza delivery guy pulls up onto her driveway and I pedal quickly towards him. Jumping from my bike before he can get to the door, I land on my feet. The bike slides across the grass, as I call out to him. "Hey, mate. I got it."

The guy looks confused as I take both pizza boxes from his hand. "You gonna pay?"

Grabbing my wallet, I pass him a fifty. "That should cover it. Keep the change."

The smell of pepperoni hits my nostrils, and since I've been out here for hours, I can really go for a feed. The front door opens and Shoshanna... *Shoshanna*. What a fucking name. Whenever I say it, I find myself playing with the sounds, the phonetics, the *shhhh. Shhhosh-anna*

I look at her. She looks pissed as hell, glowering at me as I hold her pizzas in my hands.

Smirking, I eye that tight little body, developing tits. She may have the best rack I've ever seen on a girl our age. "Got the pizzas, baby."

She grips both hips, drawing more of my attention to how full and womanly they already are. Her flat tanned belly flashes at me from between the top hem of her tight black jeans and the little white crop top she's sporting. I want to lick that part of her skin. One day, she'll let me. "Don't you think for one second that you're coming in here."

"Now, now, that's not very nice," I say, stepping towards her, tearing my gaze away from her belly button and up to her smouldering amber eyes. "I just bought you dinner. It's an official date."

She scoffs, and I grin. "It's not a date," she says. "I don't date thugs."

A smirk engulfs my face, but I gasp in a feigned display of offence. "Thugs?"

Clearly not buying my wounded ego, she confirms, "Yes."

Opening a pizza box, I grab a slice out and take a bite, humming enthusiastically. "You're really going to deny me your company?"

She nods. "Yes."

"Because I'm a thug?" I murmur around a bite of delicious cheese and pepperoni.

"Yes."

Stepping even closer, I get within an arm's length of her hot little body. "Thugs need hugs too."

Shoshanna bites her bottom lip, appearing to be fighting a grin. "That's not cute."

I laugh because she's trying so fucking hard not to show me any softness. "Tell your smile that."

She crosses her arms over her chest, puffing up her breasts a little, and I can't help but stare at those lovely mounds, can't help but burn a hole through the material covering them, imagining the tanned skin beneath. I am a tit guy... That is for fucking sure.

Immediately, she drops her arms to her sides. When I bounce my gaze back to meet hers, she is scowling even harder with a feigned look of disgust.

I like your tits, baby; it's not a crime.

She stiffens. "I have friends over."

Feeling pretty stiff myself, I feel the need to move. I step towards her, holding the pizza boxes out of the way with one hand, bringing me to a place where she has to arch her neck to see me. Where I can see straight down her white shirt and watch the heavy rise and fall of her breasts as her breathing picks up pace. Lowering my voice, I say, "And?"

Her throat rolls, and I love how that simple action shows her nervousness. I love how I make her nervous. And I reckon that means she likes me... at least enough to care what I think.

She matches me stare for stare. Her cutting amber eyes sit perfectly circled by ink-black lashes that bow up to her eyelids—perfect black fans. The kind my mum pays hundreds a week to have glued on hers.

"So if I let you in, it's not a date," she states adamantly.

Remembering the pizza slice in my other hand, I take another bite. "If you say so, baby."

"Don't talk with your mouth full!" She turns and I tail her in, groaning around the pizza at the sight of the gap just below her round arse, the one between her thighs. A little diamond-shaped gap. "And don't call me baby," she snaps.

The giggling girls sitting on the couch in their pyjamas draw my attention to the lounge room I have just entered. Five mattresses splay across the beige carpet. The television flickers in the dimly lit room as it plays some girly crap with that chick with the huge lips and red hair —Julia, I think.

"Slumber party, hey? Where are your folks?" I ask, smirking at the girls.

I take them all in, recognising two of them. One, I think, lives in my neighbourhood. They are all pretty. Shoshanna has hot friends.

The girl from my neighbourhood, petite brunette, eyes me timidly, darting her gaze to the floor as soon as I notice her.

I move over to the spot beside her, plop down onto the mattress, and place the pizza on the floor in front. Stretching my legs out to get comfortable, I say, "So, I brought my girls pizza."

They all giggle, but Shoshanna scoffs, and I think I like her scoff just as much as her concealed smiles. *God*, I want to kiss those lips. That scoff. I want to kiss it until I can't breathe.

"We're playing truth or dare," the pretty brunette says, smiling widely at me, flashing her white teeth. Her violet-coloured eyes blink fast as she peers at me over her shoulder, her brown hair making a curtain beside her face.

"And what's your name?" I ask.

"Nina."

"I'm Bron—"

"I know who you are."

"Oh? Has Shoshanna been talking about me?" I say, raising my gaze to watch my baby as she glares at me and her friend. And if I didn't know any better, I'd guess she is a little jealous of how close we are sitting. That thought makes me grin so fucking hard at her. "Whose turn is it next?"

Shoshanna raises a perfectly arched brow at me. "You're not playing."

Pouting a little, I ask, "What am I going to do while I'm here then, baby?"

"He can play," Nina says, twisting to face me, her knee lightly grazing mine. "Truth or dare."

I like this chick, so I indulge her, giving her my attention. "Dare."

Hearing a scoff coming from Shoshanna and the words, "Of course," I find myself beaming now.

Nina picks up a little bottle of liquor and smiles at me, her eyes somehow both coy and bold. "I dare you to drink the rest of this vodka."

"Vodka?" I say with a smirk. Glancing at the white liquor, I try not to cringe, not being a vodka guy really. Whiskey is what I was brought up on. I spare a glance at Shoshanna, who looks five shades of red; I love those colours on her cheeks. "Where are your folks again?"

"They are out of town, but don't get any ideas. Akila is upstairs with her boyfriend."

"Out of town a lot, aren't they?" I ask, tilting my head, catching her eyes in mine, wanting to study all the different colours of orange and amber in them. A flame. I see embers and sparks and she's just... *fuck.* Beautiful. I think about the first time we met, two weeks ago. Remembering her house party, a chaotic collection of morons and adolescents, and then her... young and alone. Trying to study.

My jaw tics.

I suddenly don't like that she is alone here despite the access it gives me to her. Actually, the thought seems to torch something in my guts, a deep internal boiling. It is just bubbling right now, but it's enough for her to shuffle on the carpet, so she must see my agitation. With my stare still locked on hers, I study her expression. She glances away as if holding my gaze is hard or uncomfortable. Am I scowling? I know I'm only fourteen; that fact is drilled into me on the daily. What do I know about responsibility? But I do know this... I know that a man needs to be present.

I know this to the depths of my marrow.

He needs to look after his family. Watch them. That is a fucking truth. If I had a sister, she'd never be left alone. I barely want to leave my little brothers in that fucking house without me. Something dark wraps around me and I feel uncomfortable, like I'm on the edge of losing time..."Your daddy leaves you alone a lot, baby."

She blinks a few times, as if considering her response.

Reaching for the vodka bottle, I chug it down. As the liquor slides down my throat, it leaves a scorching trail in its wake, but I'm intent on getting my turn.

I place the empty glass bottle down beside me. The girls are all staring at me wide-eyed, as if I did something more impressive than just down the remaining third of a bottle.

"My turn," I say with a grin, focusing on the prettiest girl in the room. She still hasn't sat down, standing and staring at me as if I'm the thing causing her discomfort. I suppose I am. That's not my intention. "Shoshanna. Truth or dare?"

Her eyes stay locked on mine, challenging me with their unwavering attention. "Dare."

"Kiss me."

"Truth then."

"Are your folks gone a lot?"

She breathes out fast.

"I don't want to play," she states, still holding my gaze but letting a bit of confidence slip away like a leaf in autumn, unable to fight the effect nature has on it.

"I'll kiss you," I hear someone say from beside me, but I can't pull my eyes from Shoshanna as she shifts her glare to her friend.

I can feel the girl's eyes on my profile.

See Shoshanna's on her's.

Quickly and without further thought, I turn to the redhead and mash our mouths together. She squeals in excitement as I cup her cheeks and deepen our kiss. Her lips fumble on mine in her inexperience, and it's adorable. She tastes like lollies. Just when I close my eyes, I'm dragged off her by someone not nearly as strong as they think they are. They pull at my collar, a fistful of my shirt in their hand.

I crack up laughing as my girl drags me from the room with an admonishing growl. I follow willingly, of course, letting her pull me by the shirt to the room at the end of the hallway, unable to stop laughing.

"Someone playing with your toy, baby?" I say, still laughing so hard. She slams her bedroom door, closing us both inside. Her room is decorated in purples and greys and, as I expected, it's tidy to the point of perfection. She has a light grey bedspread with silver, glittery flower patterns all over it. A floor to ceiling window beside her desk looks out over the pool that I first kissed her beside... Oh, and that I nearly drowned in. Good times. When she turns to face me, my sides stitch up at the sight of her brat-like scowl.

"Kiss me!" she bites out.

My smile falls.

With quick strides, I'm upon her with my lips on her lips and my tongue demanding entry into her mouth. I've already kissed a lot of girls, but never for anything more than fun. Never a girl I wanted to date. When she doesn't push away but instead brings her dainty hands up to my chest, stroking the spot where my heart shudders like a bird in a cage, I groan through the sensation her affection gives me. I walk her backwards.

The backs of her knees hit the mattress, buckling her legs and breaking our kiss for a brief moment. Eager and desper-

ate, I'm on her again before she can take a breath, manoeu-
vring us both up the bed until we are comfortably lying
beside each other. I slow our kiss down, enjoying the gentle-
ness of her lips as they learn how to move against mine.

She is sweet. In my arms. Not sure where that brat has
gone, but she's not nervously stroking my chest and kissing
me willingly with her eyes closed. Her lips are good. Really
good. I hope she hasn't had much practise at this with other
guys. The thought alone makes my insides boil again.

I lick the roof of her mouth, tasting everywhere inside.
Pulling away from her mouth, I slide lower, can't help
myself, even though I can tell she's nervous. Even though I'm
hiding the fact that I am. That I have no idea what I'm
fucking doing. The skin on her neck rises with little goosebumps as I chase her pulse down, eager to get to her chest.
My cock stirs as I take a handful of her right tit. *Fuck...*

She sits up abruptly, separating us completely as she
pants uncontrollably.

"Go out with me," I order, sitting up to be closer to her.

She touches her lips as though confused by the way they
feel on her face. "No."

I laugh out of total shock. "No?"

Fuck this shit.

Crawling off her bed, I make my way to the window. I
slide the glass across, push the fly screen out, and step onto
the sill. Noticing a downpipe, I grab hold of it and begin to
climb up to the rooftop.

"What are you doing?" she calls up to me.

Gripping the gutters, I haul myself up onto the blue clay
tiles covering the roof. They shuffle slightly beneath my feet,
making a tapping sound as they click together.

I open my arms wide, greeting the warm Australian
breeze as it tosses my shirt around my body, greeting the

moon and stars as they glow against the dark-blue night-time sky. Howling, I invite all the attention from any nosy neighbours. In fact, I'm counting on them. "Shoshanna Adel, go out with me!" I yell. Chuckling to myself, I imagine her face red with agitation. "I'm begging you. I want to be your boyfriend."

"Get down," I hear her plea from below me, a hint of panic pitching her voice higher.

I peek over the edge to find her hanging out of the window, bright crimson from embarrassment and anger. "Not until you agree to go out with me," I say, parting my grin with my tongue.

Her brows furrow, eyes turning to slits, drilling her annoyance right into me. "No."

I grin wider. Straightening, I yell even louder over the rooftops. "Shoshanna Adel, I need to be your guy! Kissing you is better than—"

"Oh my God! I'll go out with you!" I hear her screech and my heart doubles in size.

"What was that?" I say teasingly, peering down at her again, catching a smile on her face before she tightens her lips, concealing it from me. "I can't hear you."

"I will go out with you, you nutcase!"

"Oh. Alright." I laugh, sitting down on the side of the roof, and grin at her. "Whatever you want, baby."

CHAPTER EIGHT

bronson

Present day

"HE'S MISSING," I lie as the water pounds down onto the shower floor. Steam fills the room with thick clouds, and drops of condensation drip down the walls. I turn the tap on as well, intent on drowning out my conversation. In case hospital staff are nearby.

Hospital staff.

Grinning, I still can't believe that the universe brought her back to me. *Here is your woman, Bronson Butcher.* After years of searching for her. She's here, saving my life again. And my God, what a fucking stunner she has become.

When I had her pinned to the hospital wall, the surrounding energy was like a vacuum, fucking sucking everyone else into a vortex, leaving just her and me. I was moments away from tearing her scrubs from her flesh,

revealing her tight body with those voluptuous curves in all
the right places, and impaling her on my cock. Fucking the
past eleven years out of her, fucking them out of me, and
starting over. Saying sorry. And sorry again...

So, she's been here all this time, hiding away in stinking
hot Darwin, stealing years from us. I'd do just about
anything to go back to that day in the park. I feel uncomfortable heat move down my spine so I grin and thinking about
now, about taking action with her right fucking now.

It is a miracle I could rope in that desire; it is not something I am known for —restraint. That was restraint like no
other though. I had to remind myself that seventeen-year-
old Shoshanna had seventeen-year-old Bronson. She might
need a bit of warming up to take the current *me*.

I smile at the thought of what I will do to her to warm
her up. Starting with her tits.

God, I missed her tits.

"Bronson, my boy," Jimmy says calmly through the
speaker, shattering my image of Shoshanna with her tits out
and my cock between them.

What a cockblocker.

I splash water on my face. Stroking my beard, I try to
focus my attention on my boss. His tone was precise and
unaffected when it should have been anything but given his
nephew is missing. I've known Jimmy fucking Storm my
entire life though, and the question he is dying to ask sits just
on his well-mannered, manipulative tongue. "Take a
moment," he tells me, "and see what you can remember."

"We were shot at," I confirm, feigning a hint of agitation.
Of annoyance. I could have put it on thick and pretended I'm
in a state of panic, but he'd never buy that from me. "They
hit me in the fucking chest." I laugh once for good measure
because that seems like something I'd do.

Silence follows my chuckle.

Then finally he says, "Did you see the shooter?" This time, his words are expressed in a slow, meaningful cadence. His accent is thick as his emotions begin to bubble to the surface. "Ethnicity, *se*? Did he speak with you?" He doesn't give a shit about the gunshot wound in my chest, potentially cares very little that Sal is missing. *Ask the question, Jimmy. I can fucking hear it like a phantom moving through all your nonsense.*

"Not a fucking word, but the prick was Italian. I'm sure of it. Only a wop would have the Mother Mary tattooed on his neck like she'll save him from having his throat cut open. And I've tried Sal's phone. He isn't in the hospital. But I'm going to find him, Jimmy. I'll find him and open that Mother Mary up."

Even though I pretend I don't know the shooter, I know he does. Know he'll recognise that tattoo. It belongs to one of his own. One of his oldest and most trusted.

Letting out a long rough sigh, he states curtly, "A bullet for you is a bullet for me, *se?*"

Yes. That is the point.

I wipe condensation from the mirror, staring at my reflection for a moment before saying, "Who's got big enough nuts to go against you, Jimmy?"

A smile creeps across my face.

He clears his throat. "The diamonds?"

And there it is.

I grit my teeth, pretending to sound at least a little uneasy. "I don't know."

"No good!" he barks, then takes a moment of silence to settle that break in his resolve. Jimmy was raised in the Old Country by the Family. Raised to be unreadable. Lethal because of his apathy. He can project the pantomimes of any emotion with little ease, but he has a big fucking ego. It is by far his biggest weakness. Disrespecting him, stealing from him, making him feel as though there are things he cannot control, will slowly be his undoing.

"That is an unacceptable answer, my boy. You had one job to do. To collect Sal and the diamonds and get them over the border. You have lost them both, *se?* I should have sent Clay." Using my big brother's name was surely done to irk me, but I don't give a shit anymore. I gave my youth to Jimmy Storm. My life up until now. At seventeen, I took my vows in front of God and the head of the Family. I love Jimmy. Idolise him. Always have. Still do. He is a pillar of what a man should look like: powerful, unemotional, deadly.

I idolise him, yes. But I'll kill him anyway.

And I do not fail. For them, I never fail.

"Get back here immediately," he orders smoothly. "I'll send people to search for my nephew."

He kills the call.

And that is where he is wrong. I was never here to bring Sal back. To bring his diamonds across the border. I am here to be the rot inside his fatal flaw. His ego. After finding out that he's been lying to my family for over a decade, concealing a secret that claimed most of my brother's youth, that stole his childhood from him, only to hold leverage over my dad...

Keep your enemies close? Ay?

That is exactly what Jimmy has been doing all this time, making damn fools out of us. He's even wed his eldest daughter to Clay, my big brother. Cementing our families. Binding us. As though that will save his life one day.

It won't.

Because I'm not here for The Family.

I'm here on Butcher business.

Now I have to leave.

But not without her.

CHAPTER NINE

bronson

Fifteen years old

AFTER A QUICK SHOWER, I head downstairs while Shosh straightens her hair. I spend just as much time here as I do at my own pad, so it feels completely natural to wander around without her.

As I round the hallway, I see her sister, Akila, sitting at the dining room table. She lifts her gaze. Her eyes are swollen and pink as though she has been crying. My jaw locks up, but I grin anyway.

"Sleep well, sis?"

She rolls her eyes at my term of endearment. "One of these days, you're going to come down here and find our dad, and he will lose his shit."

"Good. I can have words with him about how unacceptable it is to leave his two daughters alone."

"You are such a chauvinist. We are quite capable of

looking after ourselves," she bites out, but her tone only works to spread my grin wider. When she stands, I move quickly to her side and grab the empty plate and coffee mug from her hands. She freezes, but lets me take them from her, lets me take care of her. Leaning in slightly, I whisper, "I know you are. But I believe you deserve to be looked after." That dipshit of a boyfriend of hers is on thin ice with me. She is always upset, and that is on him. It is his responsibility to keep her happy.

She spins around and leans on the table, her arse just balancing on the edge. I can feel her eyes on me as I stack the plates in the dishwasher. Akila is hot as fuck, curved like her sister, with shoulder-length dark-brown hair and beautiful olive skin that makes my heart thrash around whenever I see it.

But no one makes me feel the way Shosh does.

She sighs. "You know Shoshanna will never be allowed to be with you, right? This is just a high school romance until you two move on to more appropriate partners."

I chuckle because there is very little I can't have if I really want it, and I've never really wanted anything like I want Shoshanna. "I think I'll decide who is appropriate for your sister."

"No. You won't. We are not like your family. There are huge expectations of us. My dad is one of the best cardiothoracic surgeons in the country, ya know? Maybe the world. We are both going to study medicine. And no way would Shosh be allowed to date you. If our dad ever found out—"

"He will," I cut in, turning to face her, a smirk playing around my lips. Reaching for a glass, I fill it up with water and take a sip, thinking about piles of bloodied bodies. Bodies of people who try to take her away. No one is going to keep her from me. I'll die. I'll die before that happens. "He'll have to. I'm going to have babies with your sister. He'll want to know his grandchildren."

She laughs with derision, but my grin doesn't falter. "You're fucking insane."

"Not the first time I've heard that."

"Look, Bronson, I like you. I think you're annoyingly cute. But my sister means more to me than anything else in this world and I'm trying to save her the heartache... You two..." She shakes her through a sigh. "You move like magnets. When you are together, it's like—" Her eyes dart around, searching for words. "Like, no one else in the world exists to you. It's dangerous and unnatural."

I bite my bottom lip, eyeing her with a smirk. "I'm dangerous and unnatural."

"You need to be careful!" she snaps. "You will get her in trouble one day. Your dad puts people in hospital. Mine helps them get out."

At the mention of my dad, my business, the Family, my spine steels. A strange high-pitched cadence fills my ears, blistering and drowning out rational thought and consideration, leaving only the need to lash out and shut the flapping mouth of the person talking about my family.

My fist suddenly aches.

Looking down at it, I notice blood oozing from between my fingers. I squint at the red fluid, unsure of where it came from. Is it *my* blood? Tomato sauce? I open my palm and see pieces of glass embedded in my flesh, twisted in tight, moving and swaying, the crimson-coated shards glistening. I follow the blood down to the floor and see more pieces glittering on the tiles.

Well, fuck.

I peer back up to find Akila staring at me wide-eyed, face drooping from her gaping mouth.

"*Fuck,*" I mutter, dropping to my knees. I pick the shards up with my bare fingers. "Sorry, sweetheart. There must have been a hairline fracture in that bad boy, yeah? They break real easy when that happens." I pause and nod at the floor, still collecting the glass. This isn't the first time I've lost time.

I clean up the mess in silence, Akila having walked from the room without even finishing her lecture. Mulling over what she said, I find it pretty fucking rich that daddy has such a say in their lives but such a fleeting presence.

Reminds me of my own.

My fingers twitch around shards of glass.

In my peripheral vision, I see long legs and smooth olive skin. She is wearing denim high-waisted shorts that hike up at the side of her thick curvaceous thighs and a tucked-in black singlet.

I jump to my feet and grin. The sight of her erases the... whatever it was I was thinking about. Quickly, I rinse the blood from my hands, pulling out the little shards implanted in my palm. I feel her eyes scrutinising me. After washing most of the blood off, I hold my hand out for her.

"Shall we, baby?" I ask.

Glancing at my hand, still dotted with small amounts of crimson, she nods and takes it. Pressing her palm into mine tightly, she leads me from her house.

CHAPTER TEN

bronson

Present Day

MOVING from the bathroom and into the hospital room, I am met instantly by a cute blonde. I glance down at the name tag hanging from her pocket, but her fob watch blocks the first letter. She smiles sweetly, so I reach out and brush the watch to the side to reveal the hidden K.

Katie.

I watch her throat roll as the tips of my fingers brush her shirt. "Nurse Katie?"

"Yes," she says with a breathy exhale. "I came to check you, check *on* you. I mean, to mark off your pain. Um, to find out if you're in any pain."

"Don't be nervous around me, beautiful. I'm a teddy bear, really. I just need cuddles," I say, crossing my arms over my chest, grinning easily at her. She blushes hard. I imagine I make her nervous. I'm six-foot-five and completely covered in tattoos, standing in front of her in white cotton boxers. My cock is aching, so I know I'm slightly engorged. Shop talk gets me hard. Revenge gets me hard. Shoshanna gets me hard. And all three things are front and center in my mind right now.

"How's my patient?" A blond man walks in, his white, freshly ironed doctor's coat swaying with each step, his stethoscope bouncing around his neck.

The incline of my shaft halts, no longer interested in playing a part in this scene. Katie tries to cover her blushing cheeks but doesn't manage in time before Doctor Clean sees her and fixes her with a quick, tight smile.

Standing casually, I say, "I'm feeling fantastic, Doc." I point at the hole in my chest, which is neatly pinned together with stitching and glue. "Your handiwork?"

He grins at me, white teeth flashing with just a hint of condescension. I wonder where that came from. I'm a fucking charming guy. Who wouldn't want me as a patient?

"I'm Perry," he says, nodding towards the wound. "Yes, my handiwork. You were in a bit of trouble when you first came in. But you seem sprightly for someone who has just been through what you have."

"Sprightly," I repeat, and then wink over his shoulder at Katie. "That's me."

"Are you in any pain?"

"Nothing a whiskey can't cure..." I grin wider. "Or a cuddle."

He ignores my adorable comment, but Katie bites her lip, breathing hard. "I suggest laying off the alcohol for a few weeks and, ah–" He eyes me, rolling his gaze quickly over my tattoos, making assumptions about me that are probably fair. "Any strenuous activities too."

"Damn it." I let out a teasing sigh. "They'll miss me down at the country club."

He gives me a tight smile. "I am sure they will, Mr Butcher." Crossing his arms over his chest, he matches my stance but not my height or my build, so his attempt to be the big man in the room falls short. Just like him. If only his presence were larger. That falls short too.

He fixes me with a serious look while I try not to laugh at him, amused by the hostile attitude seeping from him despite his attempt at a professional demeanour. "I also hear you had a bit of an altercation in the corridor earlier today with one of my doctors."

My smile twitches. "*Your* doctors?" I lower my arms slowly to my sides. "Do you own them, Perry?"

He narrows his brown eyes on me. "This one, I do."

I. Stand. Very. Still. "Is that right?"

With my eyes now scorching a hole through his, I lock my teeth together. My grin spreads wider still, but it feels anything but pleasant. I hear that distant, high-pitched laughter again. The same laughter I always hear when I'm about to lose my mind. Stroking my palms with my fingers, I try not to imagine throwing him through the window behind me. Try not to imagine his body falling from the three stories and hitting the ground with a slap. It would definitely make a slapping sound at this height. All his bones snapping, his innards popping open, leaking out, marking the pavement with a bloody blotch.

"Tell me again who owns her," I demand smoothly, but just as I do, Shoshanna walks in. The three of us freeze. Perry doesn't even turn around, but he can sense her. Perhaps he's become accustomed to the scent of the strawberry shampoo she still uses, distinguishing it like a fucking bloodhound, knowing it well because it's probably left on his sheets after he fucks her. I'd know.

Glaring down at Doctor Clean, I'm surprised to see him craning his neck to match my glare. I'm not sure when I took a step towards him; his proximity to me sets a flame of unease in the pit of my stomach.

And this...

I feel something in my hand.

What is this?

I squeeze the object tighter to analyse the feel of it; it's cold and hard against my palm. Realising I've picked up the fork that was on my breakfast tray, I use my thumb to keep it hidden from view.

What were you planning on doing with this, Bronson?

"You two know each other," Perry states, eyeballing me.

Images of me removing all the parts of him that have ever touched her flash behind my eyes.

I don't release him from my gaze as I say, "Hey, baby. Just met your friend. He seems nice. Kinda dreamy if you ask me. Maybe we'll have a beer at the country club once I'm allowed to drink again."

"We went to school together," Shosh says, her voice hitching higher. She didn't exactly lie, now did she? Still, I'm filled with the need to fuck her in front of him so there is no mistaking who she really belongs to.

Moving quickly, she soon stands between us, pushing me backwards a few steps. I let her. She pretends to check the incision on my chest, but it isn't a smooth move.

It's sloppy.

He knows what you did, baby.

Did you press your hands to my chest to get me away from him... or to get him away from me?

I feel a hand on mine, but don't look down, already aware

she is taking the fork from me and placing it in her scrub pocket. How she knew... Of course she did.

Unable to tear my glare away from him, I measure him up again, this time as my girl's suitor. As the man who holds her in his arms every night.

Six foot, maybe. A lean looking guy with a clean outward appearance, gentle facial features, and a smooth, hairless jawline. Older than her. At least a decade older. She always did have daddy issues... I wonder what he uses to fuck her with. Staring down at his fingers, I now know they have been inside her, touching the tight coil of muscles that throb when stroked just right.

I clamp my teeth together, squashing the dangerous feelings inside me.

Doctor Fucking Clean and Wholesome.

How is she not bored?

Flaring his eyes at me, the clogs in his head move, showing him a slideshow of me, perhaps... with her. I hope it hurts a little knowing I've been inside her.

Looking down at her, her little fingers on my chest, the same ones that used to stroke my cock so eagerly, I notice a tan line around her ring finger. My heart halts to a gut-wrenching stop. My teeth lock. I hiss at the sight.

You didn't give her back to me.

You're taunting me with her.

I will myself not to move, not even an inch. If I do, I'm not sure what will happen. Carnage, I think and smile.

Her lovely lips are open, drawing air in fast. "It looks good," she mutters breathily.

I growl low into her ear. "You always did think so."

She closes her eyes, holding them pressed together for a few seconds. I watch as one of her heels rises, and I can picture her little toes curve within their confines. She's nervous. Or turned on. Or both.

Do I need to remind you how I can make you feel, baby?

Then she walks away from me.

She stops by Dr Clean's side. "Can I have a word?"

They leave.

And I still don't trust myself enough to move.

CHAPTER ELEVEN

bronson

Fifteen years old

THE SUN SHINES through the thin layer of skin over my eyes, forcing a half-conscious state I am dead set on fighting. Luckily, with it comes the scent of my girl's strawberry shampoo and the feel of her silky black hair as it brushes my cheek.

Tightening my grip around her, I feel her torso moving as her breathing shifts, indicating her broken slumber. I grab the pillow from behind my head and place it on the other side of hers, shielding her from the sun as it drills through the bullshit thin curtains at her window.

She squirms around, her perfectly plump arse brushing against my erection, forcing me to bite back a groan. I spend so many mornings with this throb of need inside me. This tension. A need for release. Morning glory is only fun if your girl jumps on it and gyrates around, but she isn't ready for such a ride.

I'm cool with that.

Slowly, I trail my fingers up her arms, awakening little bumps on her. She moans, and I long for that moan to feather against my lips. Gently, I encourage her to roll over in her sweet, sleepy state. Her perfect little nose touches mine and those lips, slightly pleated at the top, a few light brown beauty spots adoring the corners, skates across mine.

I bring my hand up to her face. Gently, I memorise every feature with my fingertips. I circle her closed eyes, her long, thick black lashes tickling me. Stroking between her brows, I move down the length of the most incredible nose, which is delicately tipped at the end. Placing my knuckles on her cheek, I stroke her soft skin.

I love touching this face.

Staring at it.

She is mine.

She was mine the moment I saw her five months ago.

She'll be mine 'til the day I die.

But I'll be hers for even longer.

Fuck, I'm a romantic dipshit.

"*Bronson*," she murmurs, her tongue dipping out of her mouth, licking the arid skin covering it. My gaze drops to her tits. More than a handful and in a white singlet, visible and plump and womanly. As my cock knocks against me like it has a mind of its own, thrumming for relief, my hand moves down to her chest. I squeeze her left breast, flicking the little bud on top that I know is a beautiful light shade of brown.

She winces slightly, and I frown in response. *Did I hurt her?* I let go of her tit, studying her face, seeing that her brows are furrowed. As her eyes bat open, orbs of amber stare up at me through long lowered lashes. Her arms suddenly go to her abdomen, cradling it protectively.

What the fuck?

I growl at the tension in her face. "What's wrong, baby?" She hides her face and curls in on herself. Unease rushes up my spine as I feel her pain in my bones, in my marrow. "Baby?"

Groaning her discomfort, she says, "What is it with you and growling. You got a fucking invisible lion with you at all times or what?"

"Don't deflect, baby." I cup her chin, tilting it up until I have her eyes on me. "What the fucks going on with your stomach?"

"Don't." She releases her stomach to quickly cover her face with her palms, groaning into them. "Just don't say anything. Forget you are seeing anything. I don't want to say."

My spine stiffens. "What the fuck happened?"

She drops her hands, glaring at me with exasperation. "Don't go getting all crazy. No one hurt me, Bron. I've just got... *cramps.*"

I frown. "*Like...*"

"From my period, idiot!"

I exhale fast. "Fuck." Shaking my head with relief, I grin at her. "Baby, don't be embarrassed about that." She groans again and I fucking hate it. "Take your shirt off."

She scrunches up her nose, adorable little wrinkles forming along the bridge. "No. I don't want to." Her cheeks glow pink, showing me just how vulnerable she is at this moment. How fragile. It is the best thing I could ever see in her. It is trust... but it's the worst thing she could ever see in me. It would mean I couldn't handle her trust, couldn't look after her.

"I promise I'll make you feel better," I assure her.

She sighs. Her long, elegant fingers find the hem of her singlet just above a soft flat stomach. I try not to groan my pleasure as she leisurely glides the material up over her head. Her breasts bounce free, the full size of them enough to make me ignite with heat.

"Oh my God." I grin at her and the dark hue of crimson coating her cheeks. She releases a stained giggle when I wiggle my brows. Desperate to take away her pain, I dip down to her abdomen and prop myself up on my elbows. I gently stroke her lower stomach, peppering kisses along it. She squirms at first but then starts to breathe deeper, seemingly allowing herself to relax.

She hums and I try to ignore how the sound resonates in my cock as much as it does in my heart. "That feels nice. It feels a little better. How can that be?"

As I tenderly stroke her soft tanned skin, I say, "Xander used to get these wicked migraines when he was younger. So I would massage his head sometimes. He said that the feeling took over the pain inside. Like, adding a pleasurable sensation right over the pain somehow dulled it. Is it working? I'll do this all day if you need."

A little chuckle leaves her through a sigh. "It is working... but I'm so embarrassed."

"Don't be. This is my job. It's my job to make you feel good," I state adamantly, peering up from her stomach to watch her tits rise and fall.

"You're a nutcase, you know that, right?" Her fingers find their way into my hair, feeding through the dark strands and mussing them around my crown.

As I watch her head drop back to the pillow, her eyes closing, her breaths steady, I'm in awe of everything she is. "I love you," I say before I care to think about it because it is true, so fuck it.

A little smile plays with a corner of her lips, and she lifts her head to stare at me again. "You love my *tits*."

I laugh, and she laughs too. "Yeah. They are fucking *magnificent*." I reach up and stroke the outer swells of one of them, the parts that hang over her frame because of the position she is in.

"I'm fat," she mutters softly, and those two words hit my forehead like a flaming bat, bursting heat behind my eyes, but I grin at her anyway.

"This–" I take a gentle but possessive hold of the flesh at her hips. "And this." I grab the thick skin of her thigh. "They are the best parts. I want them all around my face." She giggles, her tanned cheeks bunching above her smile, and my heart fucking melts. I like her like this. Loose. Easy. Letting me take care of her. She sits up and her tits drop slightly, forming the most perfect little mounds. I lick my lips and she snorts out a laugh, shaking her head as though I'm incorrigible.

"You have no idea—" I say, the words coiled tightly with a suppressed growl, knowing what I desire but can't have. I cup her breast again, lightly flicking its tight, pointed bud with my thumb. "What I want to do to this body."

She smirks, a cute cheeky curve to her lips. "I'm sure I'd be revolted."

I laugh. "I'm fucking positive you would be."

Leaning forward, I lick her nipple and she arches her back, lifting them further towards me. Only to fist my hair and try to drag my mouth away from her. The strands weaved between her fingers bite at my scalp as I resist. Enjoying the pain, I groan from deep within my chest. Reluctantly, I allow her to control my head, prying me from her nipple.

"We have school." She mashes our lips together in a quick but crushing kind of kiss. A kiss that screams she owns me. She does. She fucking owns me. I smirk at her and jump to my feet on the mattress so that her head is eye level with my erection. My blood boils when she stares at my cock. I wiggle my hips, swaying my cock at her, the weight of it almost painful but in a good way.

I chuckle. "He's waving at you. Say hello."

And holy fucking shit, she lifts her hand and wraps it around my cock. I nearly blow my load all over her. She shakes my cock like she would a hand and giggles again, the sound like nothing else I have ever heard. Somehow sweeter and more melodic with my cock in her grasp.

Is that a thing?

It is now.

"I have to shower and get some painkillers," she says to my crotch and then jumps off the bed, bounding away, her arse jiggling as she does.

"Can I come?"

"No!"

"*Fuck,*" I mutter, peering down at my cock. "I tried, buddy."

CHAPTER TWELVE

bronson

Fifteen years old

SHOSHANNA IS SITTING on my handlebars as I ride us to school. Even when I don't stay the night at hers, I always pick her up. No way is she walking to school alone. That just isn't happening. Not on my watch.

I pedal around the clean, thriving streets of Connolly. Shoshanna grips the handles, her body bouncing as I take us over curbs.

What a *beaut* day. Fucking stinking hot, but I love the look of perspiration on her thighs, the beads sliding down her smooth olive skin. I want to lick them off.

Everyone should just get fucking naked in this weather.

When we get to the bike racks, she jumps off. I thread the tire into the metal column before joining her as she wanders into the main building. Kids litter the space around us, their noises echoing in the halls. Excited nattering. Lockers shutting. Feet shuffling. Laying my arm over her shoulder, I revel in the way she moves into me, fitting snugly under my arm.

We stop at her locker. Leaning on the metal door beside hers, I watch her sort through the messy space. Once a pristine and obsessive area, it's now crammed with paper and books shoved in randomly. My doing. A little chaos hurt no one.

I chuckle at her concentration. Unable to pull my eyes from her, I watch her in awe. A beautiful brain in that stunning head and a perfect body and all fucking mine.

Well done, Bronson. You fucking legend.

She shuts her locker and leans one shoulder on it, mimicking my position, ending my fantasies about our babies being gorgeous and smart, just like her.

"Are you going to get your books, Butcher? Or are you going to stare at me all day?"

I open my mouth to speak, but the words are cut short by her suddenly startled expression as she peers over my shoulder. I frown at her discomfort, twisting to follow her line of sight and—

That fucking screeching hits my ears again.

A howling sort of current moves through me, the laughter inside my head follows in its wake.

As I watch my little brothers walk through the halls, one with a split on his forehead and the other with purple-blue marks painting his swelling jaw, my blood doesn't boil... it *fucking ignites*. The kids around me jostle each other and nod, believing they have it all figured out, while my fingers twitch to the images playing in my mind. Images of them eating their own gaping, judging eyeballs. They presume my beautiful brothers have been fighting in the streets, but I know what really happened.

Know who is really to blame.

Me.

For not being in that house to protect them.

I hear laughter

See black.

CHAPTER THIRTEEN

shoshanna

Fifteen years old

MY BREATH VIBRATES on an exhale at the shocking sight of his brothers. Feeling a shift in Bronson, I turn to focus on him. His mood gem irises are now two thin glowing turquoise rings around large pitch-black holes, making him look menacing. The anger radiating from him is not loud; it is quiet and eerie. I've never seen him angry before. It is like a complete stranger has pulled his skin on slowly. His usually grinning face has fallen, leaving no expression at all.

With long, unhurried, and yet meaningful strides, he heads towards them. I can feel his mood like a cold front moving through the ventricles of my heart.

I trail Bronson as he moves to meet his brothers in the centre of the hallway. Kids divert their gazes, focusing on their lockers as all three Butcher Boys share a strange silent interaction that I don't quite understand. As Bronson raises his hand up to touch the wound on Xander's forehead, Max scowls at me as though I am a voyeur, watching something incredibly personal.

Back off, Max.

I match his glare, noting the bruising and swelling along his jawline and the haemorrhaging on his forearm, which looks like it could have been caused by a thorough beating with a baseball bat. I'm not intimidated by him anymore. It's not just me that annoys him, but literally everyone at school bores him to the point we might as well all be invisible.

Placing my hand on Bronson's back, I let him know I'm here for him. Whoever they need to face, I'll face with him. His muscles roll against my palm, thick and strong, responding to my touch.

"She threw a glass at my head," Xander says, looking solemnly at the ground.

"And Dad?" I hear one of them say. Doing a double take, I realise it's Bronson, but he sounds so detached, I could swear... could swear I've never heard that voice before. I swallow so hard I can hear it in my ears. And as I dart my eyes between them, the information being shared settles into me like concrete, sinking to the bottom of my stomach, threatening to drag me to the floor like a puddle.

That fucking bitch!

My brain screeches with the need to lash out at her, to tear at her Gucci pencil dress, remove her status clad armour. How long has this been going on? Is she a drunk?

Xander sighs through a slow shake of his head. "In Sydney. He left yesterday. I doubt he'll be back for months; he took half his clothes."

"And Carter?"

"His night off," Max states curtly. I know Carter is Xander's bodyguard. I know a lot now about the boys that I shouldn't. That they need to be watched —guarded— because their dad is involved in some kind of bullshit that puts a target on all of them. Everyone always whispers about their family; hushed tones sharing gossip about the seedy underbelly of the District. That the Butcher Boys have affiliations with the Mafia.

At least, that is the rumour.

And all signs point to that rumour being real.

Bronson grips his brother's shoulder. "Maxipad took it for you, buddy?"

"He did. He stepped in front of the bottle. I think it broke his forearm. I just—" Xander's face contorts, and he stares at the ground again as though an eleven-year-old is supposed to hold his own.

My lips open on a question but snap closed just as quickly when I realise it doesn't matter. It doesn't matter what he did to make her so angry. I hate that the question even formed in my mind.

Taken by surprise, Bronson turns towards me, eyeing me thoughtfully for a moment. Then he grins, the chilling thing wearing his skin dissolving in an instant. That cool smile that makes each girl's legs turn to noodles moves across his cheeks, complete with his dimple, and he's back to himself again. "Fuck school. Let's all go get a feed."

My mind won't settle that easily though. There are too many questions about his mother. The bruises I've noticed on them often. Guilt hits me for not asking about them before. I presumed they were fighting other boys. My heart stutters on the feelings, the confuse—

"Your mind is far too impressive to be wasted on that thought," he whispers to me.

Then he takes my mouth with his.

It's a slow meaningful kiss, one that kicks the questions

and concerns out of my mind and replaces them with nothing but this moment. The gentle, dominant motion of his lips on mine, filling me with tingles. His tongue licks mine while our collective breath mingles and dances.

He breaks our kiss and I inwardly sulk. Without further thought, he threads our fingers together and the air around me gets even sweeter, the feel of his fingers like a shot of euphoria.

And I know he is my *first* love.

But looking at Bronson, as he steers me down the corridors and back outside towards the bike racks, his body strong and tall, his face chiselled in a beautiful way, I can't imagine not loving him. Not laughing with him. Not playing.

Before I met Bronson, I would have never skipped school. Never wasted my time with a boy like him. Never wasted my time at all. Now, though, I'd follow him almost anywhere.

I sit on his handlebars, and he takes off down the road. His brothers flank us on their bikes. Turning right out of the junction, in the opposite direction from our houses, we head towards the center of town.

As we near the little restaurant we frequently go to, a little place that his family owns, he suddenly hits the brakes. An arm bands around my middle like a belt, only just keeping me stationary as we screech and slide along the road.

"Oh fucking perfect," he sings from behind me, a hint of mischief lacing his voice. I drop from the bars just as he jumps off the seat. Swiftly, he picks up his bike and hurls it through the back windscreen of a parked red sports car. I nearly lose my footing, my eyes raking in the scene in utter shock.

"Bronson, no," Xander says, stopping his bike beside me. Max appears on the other side of me, making no attempt to jump off his bike and stop his big brother, appearing completely content with the scene in front of him.

Half of Bronson's bike now hangs out. The alarm bellows down the street, the whirling sound so close and loud, I cover my ears to protect them from what feels like tangible waves assaulting the delicate drum inside.

"What the fuck, Bronson?" I yell, peering around at the pedestrians. Some of them pull out phones, probably calling the police. I rush to Bronson, desperate to get away from the crime before anyone interferes, arrests him, or restrains him, but as I do, he pulls the bike from the window, separating an entire sheet of shattered glass from the frame. I freeze, not wanting to get in his way. He's so incredibly strong, making the screen and bike look feather-light. The glass panel hits the road, still in almost one piece. The entire street has fallen into a strange state of quiet, making the car alarm a perpetual echo.

He laughs. "That's a fucking good tinting job." Jumping on to the bonnet, he lifts the bike above his head and slams it through the front screen. I try to ignore the people at the beauty parlour opposite us, as they press their hands to the glass, watching us.

I gape at Bronson, unable to move or form words, overcome with shock. He nods triumphantly down at his handiwork.

Raising his line of sight, he grins sweetly at the onlookers. "Sorry for the interruption everyone."

As he jumps from the bonnet, the metal creaks, and I take a step back, unsure of what he'll do next. But he just strolls casually up to me and threads our hands together again. His palm is warm, his breathing a little faster, more uneven.

"Sorry, baby, we're gonna have to walk. Or you can ride with Max? Or I can carry you?"

I falter, assessing his cool, calm expression, his bright eyes as they sparkle with flecks of green in the piercing sunlight. I finally retrieve a few words. "Ah... What. The. Actual. Fuck?"

Studying my open mouth and blinking amber eyes, his dark-brown brows furrow in confusion. "Oh," his tight forehead relaxes with realisation, "the car? It's my mum's."

CHAPTER FOURTEEN

shoshanna

Present Day

"JESUS, Shoshanna! That is the kind of guy you used to date? No wonder your dad was so hard on you. God, I hope our kids don't get this rebellious side of you." Perry huffs, riffling through his top drawer, searching for his tie pin.

Our kids.

Blinking ahead, I think about Bronson. About what we promised each other so many years ago. About how often we spoke of having a big family one day. We would be better than our parents, present, and kind. We would fill our house with silliness and jokes and all our crazies.

My heart twists.

My stomach feels empty.

Shaking the thought away, I focus on Perry. I think about how much I want a normal life. Kids are normal. But... my egg production is working at the pace of a forty-year-old woman. The gynaecologist told us we'd still have a chance; though, however slim, we may get lucky.

A chance.

Luck?

Perry doesn't take chances. Doesn't believe in luck. He became more meticulous with when and how we make love. Knowing it may take years, he started the baby-making routine straightaway. And so, before we have even said our vows, sex has lost its pleasure. It is now filled with expectations, pressure, and fourteen days later, disappointments.

Lifting my foot up onto the mattress, I roll the soft, sheer black material of my stocking up to my knee. "We were young," I murmur to myself more than to him and it hurts.

Downplaying *us* hurts.

In truth, the moment the gynaecologist told me about my eggs, I remembered him.

When Perry initiated baby-making protocol too fast, I remembered him.

As much as I've tried to forget him, Bronson has been a shadow in my subconscious. In my heart.

As I continue to roll my leggings up, I graze my thigh lightly with my nail. Instantly, I close my eyes as the image of *his* teeth sliding up my leg washes through my mind. My head gets heavy for a moment, my breathing shallow. I press down harder, dragging the sharp ridge of my nail further up my thigh, leaving a burn in its wake. As I near my inner thigh, I stifle a moan.

I force my eyes open.

Take a big breath in.

Looking up, I find Perry standing closer to me than before, with a strange expression etched on his features. Studying that handsome, worldly face, I reach for a time when we had an easy, supportive kind of love story. When we weren't climbing the professional ladder. When we weren't all business. When we made love for fun rather than ticking off a step needed to make a baby. When we just... *were.*

I miss those days.

But it feels as though he is charging forward, dragging me with him, and all the while I'm stalling. Maybe I'm still at that park, holding myself together. So I go with the flow now.

Perry's flow.

Looking at him, in his black fitted suit, with the shadow of disappointment in his eyes, I'm surprised that the peaceful love we shared has become so stale. So mixed up with routine. I thought it was this kind of love that sailed steadily through the tests of time.

I blink at my fiancé, feeling a wave of unease beneath his measuring eyes. "What is it?"

"You kept this from me," he states, leaning back on his heels. "You knew who he was the moment you saw him. It's why you flipped out in the theatre room. Why would you keep this from me? I didn't think you were the kind of woman who kept secrets from her fiancé. Am I wrong?"

I shuffle my feet, guilt simmering inside me for no reason. I am allowed to process. Swallowing hard, I answer him honestly, hoping he'll understand, perhaps even relate. "I felt uncomfortable. Bronson and I had a very intense relationship." As I move to the other side of the room to slip my nude heels on, he follows my movements.

His blond brows draw in tight. "Do I need to be concerned about this little visit interrupting things between us? You know Akila is only getting worse as time goes by. She needs a calm environment but if you're feeling overwhelmed, then maybe we need to talk about putting her in a home."

Flattening my gold flapper-style dress down my stomach, I force back the panic wanting to rise. "You know I don't want my sister in a home."

"Well, she is *my* responsibility and I need to do what is best for her. And you're sleeping in while on call. You're running out during surgery—"

"What!? I didn't sleep in. You let me."

"You're shouting at nurses."

My mouth drops open. "I didn't shout at them. Fucking Mandy!" I growl. She's such a nark. "How can you talk to me like this? You know she has it in for me."

"Look at you, you're acting up right now. This isn't high school, Shoshy. No one has it *in* for you," he sneers, closing the gap between us and cupping my neck with his hand. "It's okay. I took care of it. But you're acting erratic. Maybe we need to bring the night nurse back on a permanent roster, yeah? So you can get more sleep."

"No. I can manage," I say through a clenched jaw. I hated it last time, but I was in medical school and couldn't juggle all my commitments. And I'm better now. I can handle this. Even though she can't say it, I still see it in her eyes; Akila just waits for me to be with her.

"I've already spoken to Brenda about staying on permanently for the night shifts. She is good with Akila, and Mary is more than happy to train her up for full-time night work," he says, narrowing his hazel eyes on my tense face. I try to hold his gaze, reminding myself that he may be my boss and my sister's guardian, but he doesn't *own* us...

And yet, he somehow shrinks me with his sharp stare, making my eyes dart to the floor. "Okay... *fine.* As long as I can keep Akila here. I don't want to have this conversation again. She is not going to a home."

Perry looks angry for a moment, then schools his expression and says, "Having him close isn't good for you. I can see that." He touches a piece of my hair, running the dark strands between his fingers. "Don't be like this," he whispers, leaning in to kiss my forehead. "I love you, Shoshy. I'm going to ignore this tone of yours. Lots going on. Lots going on in here." He taps my temple with his index finger, and I want to slap his hand away, but I don't, so used to the feeling of being patronised now that I'm not even sure if that's what he's doing. I'm not sure when this started happening. Or maybe he was always like this and I'm the one who has changed. Maybe it's having Bronson close that reminds me how love can make your heart skip and fly and scream with bliss.

I nod at him, smiling tightly. He smiles softly in response before turning to grab his car keys.

As he opens the door for me, he says, "So I can't imagine that guy has much going on upstairs. Whatever did you two have to talk about?"

Grabbing my clutch and elbow-length gloves, I rush out into the hallway, laughing the question off.

But the answer, of course, is ... *everything*.

* * *

On the drive to the theatre, Perry talks about his conference as I stare out the sheet of glass separating me from Friday night city life.

Akila *should* be fast asleep now.

Yeah, we'll see how Brenda goes, Perry.

A soft glow illuminates the interior of our BMW. I push aside my concerns, eager to enjoy tonight. To feel like myself again. Perry isn't perfect, but he is *good*. Honest. Hard-working. Respectable. And he took my sister in and made her his own. Who does that?

I reach for his hand, entwining our fingers on the gear stick. He smiles at me and then returns his gaze to the road, continuing to share his most recent insights.

Out the window, the world is alive. I love the almost organic movement of the city at night. Couples walk hand in hand on their way to an event or restaurant while suited men leaving work late head for the bus stop. Lights from cars flash and glow, their horns beeping in this strangely living environment.

Emptiness settles in my abdomen.

I miss The District; Darwin is tiny, barely a city at all in comparison.

The high beams of a motorbike closing in on us catch my eye. I stare in the side mirror at a black helmet, an ominous vision, a man with no face. He edges closer and closer to our back tyre. I cover my mouth as my breath halts at the back of my throat. He's going to hit us.

The rider flashes his headlights.

I frown at the bike.

What the hell?

"What a moron," Perry snaps, glaring into his rear-view mirror. "Organ donor right there."

Cars fill up the dual lane, so our black BMW moves out of the fast lane to let the red bike past. While it slowly moves to overtake us, my heart begins to flutter. When it gets to Perry's window, it slows to match our speed. The growling of the engine seems to penetrate the car.

A warm pool moves down to the place between my thighs, forcing me to press my legs together and ease that beckoning ache. My blood heats as the rider stares through the driver's window at us.

No, not us...

Me.

I have no idea how I know this, as I see nothing but a black visor twisted over a shoulder... but I can feel the eyes within its dark casing scorching a fiery trail across my face. As my pulse vibrates in my throat, I part my lips to breathe harder. I dart my eyes to the road and back again, silently yelling at him to watch the fucking traffic. Then, I'm too lost in the black helmet. The shiny surface fixed on me and I on it.

The rider turns back to the road.

Breaking my trance, he speeds off, filtering through the cars up ahead until I lose sight of him all together.

"What a loose cannon. You okay, Shoshy?"

No. I stare blankly for a few moments at the road before forcing a smile and nodding stiffly. *He wouldn't.* Slowly, I pull my phone from my clutch. When I see a message from Katie already flashing at me, my pulse moves from my throat to my ears.

> Katie: He left. He signed an early discharge form.

Fuck.

That stupid son of a bitch.

That confirms nothing. He'd struggle to ride a bike with that kind of injury to his chest. I feel the urge to rush back to the hospital only to watch in loss as the girls redress his bed, knowing that he's gone...

My heart aches, contracting uncomfortably as though it misses his being so close —a similar tug to the one all those years ago when he left me sobbing in that park.

He doesn't seem to care though. He probably has someone to get home to —his brothers, a girlfriend perhaps... I despise her already. And yet, there is this little part of me that whispers a truth between my ears —he isn't leaving town that easily. I hate how much I hold on to that little insight like my last breath. Like the last beat of my heart.

Realising we've arrived at the hotel, I will myself to not think about that bike. After Perry parks in the turning circle, we both step out of the car. The valet takes Perry's place behind the wheel and heads towards the undercover car lounge.

Perry grabs my hand, guiding me into the lobby. Guests flitter around in their 1920's style dresses. Most are cut straight across at the knee; some are adorned with delicate beading and braided trimmings. Feather boas are slung around shoulders playfully, while white pearls flash softly from various necks. Above, a banner saying, "The Great Gatsby. Live Tonight" hangs from the chandelier-lined ceiling.

I smile at the few people I recognise. Perry waves across the room at a few others. Suddenly, it feels like *Groundhog Day*.

Like I did this yesterday.

It all feels the same.

Even these people seem to be having the same boring conversations they always do —light chitchat with no substance so as not to offend anyone. Growing up with The Butcher Boys, they always said it as they felt it. I loved that.

I wonder if they still do...

Looking around the room, I remind myself that to a young girl fresh out of medical school, this is quite a scene to be a part of.

I'm just not sure it is *my* scene anymore.

Making our way into the ballroom, we head straight for

the bar. *Thank God for alcohol.* We grab a drink, a red wine for me and a boutique beer for Perry, and take our seat at a circular table a few places back from the stage.

I tap my nail on the crystal red wine glass as seats fill up around us and Perry converses with the waiter, ordering our meals. Trying to hide my discomfort, I force a smile, but unease seeps through my body. Shaking my head, I try to dislodge the person troubling me.

Bronson Butcher.

Perry glances at my nail as it vibrates on the glass. "Just the one wine tonight, Shoshy. Okay?" I take a big mouthful, the tart tannins and citrus acids flirting inside my mouth. He leans over and strokes the bare skin on my arm affectionately. "You love the opera. Let's just have an enjoyable night. I'm sorry about our little quarrel, beautiful." He squeezes my forearm until I look at him. "Are you?"

I take another enthusiastic sip of my wine. "I need the bathroom," I say, standing and grabbing my clutch. I lean down and kiss his cheek, but it feels wrong for some reason. Not waiting for his response, I head towards the corridors.

God, what is wrong with me?

Maybe I just need a moment in my own space, not having been alone since we left the hospital, since Bronson met Perry. And now surrounded by glitz, glam, and bullshit, I just can't settle my mind.

I head towards the glowing ladies room sign. The red carpet beneath my heels shimmers as though a bucket of glitter was dumped on it. A long mirror lines the entire length of the corridor, which is disorientating with the various doors opening and closing and my perception of depth seems to fail me.

My heart lurches into my throat when a hand wraps around my mouth. A large body presses against my back, dragging me quickly through one door and into a dark, quiet room.

I can't breathe.

My eyes bulge open as the door is kicked shut. I try to scream. But my sounds of panic are muffled behind a tight, merciless grip. Tears force their way out from the corners of my eyes.

"It's okay, baby. It's me."

God. My eyes squeeze shut as emotion overwhelms me; the exact reason for it, be it relief or fear, is too difficult to decipher right now. He pushes my chest against the wall as I begin to sob into his palm. The tears slide down my cheeks and pool at his hand.

He didn't leave...

All the adrenaline I was just hit with is now making rational thought a distant memory. The beads of tears balancing on my lashes bat out onto my cheeks as I slowly open my eyes to the dimly lit room. Soft possessive lips touch my ear, the warmth from them tumbling down my neck.

He cares...

"I can feel how wound up you are. Dr Clean hasn't been looking after my girl properly, has he?" I shiver as his words move through my body, awakening something primal and indecent within me. Something that is drawn to all the indecent parts of him.

With one of his hands still encasing my mouth, the other massages down my breasts. He lets out a groan so long and rough it rumbles through my spine. When I thrash to wrestle free, he only presses himself harder against me, pressing the entire length of my body against the wall, sandwiching me between his warm hands and powerful body.

There is no mistaking his arousal at this moment. The

length of him presses into my lower back, beating against me in obvious intention. *And warning.*

He kicks one of my heels out slightly, widening my thighs.

I need to see. We need to talk. The memory is eating me up every moment we ignore it. "Turn the light on," I plead, my words muffled against his palm.

"*No,*" he says softly. "You'll like sensory deprivation. You can hide in the darkness of my making. Relying on all your other senses. All the feelings I offer you because you deserve them. Because you're such a good girl. So grown up. So strong. So beautiful." He slides his hand away from my mouth slightly, allowing me to speak. "Have you been told that lately, baby?"

I shiver, fighting the emotion wanting to erupt behind my eyes. "I don't need to be told that. I'm not a child."

Covering my mouth again, he laughs. "No. But doesn't daddy call you that?" Heat floats down the skin on my neck, followed by his tongue lapping up the slender column, provoking a long moan from me that rumbles against his palm.

My heart flutters, begging him not to stop, while my mind screams for him to. I try to talk, but it's impossible; the words come out as desperate whimpers laced with need and fear. "I can smell how aroused you are, baby. I can almost taste you in the air." He growls as his hand dips between my legs. Lifting my dress up to around my waist, he grips me hard.

God, he's doing this.

Right here.

I stifle a sob, tears threatening to fall as guilt takes hold. "Don't make me cheat on him."

He spreads his fingers at my mouth, allowing me to speak. "What was that?"

"*Please*, don't make me cheat on him."

He tightens his grip around my mouth. His tone seems to have deepened as he whispers, "Each time you let him touch your skin, your hair." He cups me between the legs, and I press myself shamelessly against his palm. "This pussy, you have cheated on me. He owes me a debt, baby. As do you."

I stifle a moan, but it reverberates from within my throat anyway as two fingers press against the wet lace between my thighs. And I remember... I remember the first time he touched me between my legs. I remember the way he was in awe of me. I remember his smiles. His laugh. How we played. The pain of that day mingles with all the joyous times, and I embrace them. Because he isn't just angry with me. We are more than just that day. I cry, emotions erupting within me.

He rolls his fingers up between my folds, the material between them intensifying the feeling—a lace-like caress moving in long, firm strokes. He uses his entire palm to hold me to him, his fingers buried between my arse cheeks, his thumb beginning an assault on my clit —a grip that locks onto that part of my body in a possessive and protective way.

"What do you let him do to this body? *My body*? Do you let him run his tongue over it?"

He growls. Seemingly unsettled by his own words, he suddenly rips my knickers aside, sinking a long, skilled finger into me. I mewl against the ambush of his talented finger when it thrusts with a knowledge of my body, hitting all the sensitive spots with perfect precision. "I've got you, baby. You should remember how I can make you feel."

His mouth crashes against my neck, biting the bend where my collarbone meets my shoulder. His hand tightens around my cheeks and jaw, demanding I lift my chin to allow his lips and tongue and teeth full access to my throat. The fingers inside me speed up, fucking me hard against the wall, sliding in and out quickly, drawing sensations from me.

My head spins.

Somewhere in this confused, pleasured state, I hear a click, and then Bronson's hand leaves my pussy. The agony of his sudden absence is like torture. He twists me to face the door, where a burly man stands wide-eyed, staring directly at the barrel of the gun Bronson is pointing between his eyes.

Jesus Christ.

I grab at Bronson's hand, clawing for him to release my mouth.

Put the gun down!

The man raises his arms, swallowing hard, shaking even harder, a vibrating mass of lax muscles beneath a tailored suit.

"Get in here," Bronson states, his voice a smooth hoarse purr. Using the tip of the gun, he gestures him in. "Sit in the corner with your back to us. If you move, I'll use this gun on you and it won't be in the way you think."

The man swallows. "Are you hurting her?"

"Only in the way she likes."

The man does as he's told, sitting and facing the wall opposite us. Bronson kicks the door shut, leaving us in near darkness again. My pulse sounds through my entire body as Bronson shuffles around behind me, sliding the gun into the back of his pants.

"No one is going to take this from my girl. So you're now the luckiest man on earth. You get to listen while I make her come all over my fingers."

I attempt to loosen his hold on me, but it's weak and

half-hearted because I'm not sure I want to get free. My ears ring with the need to come undone. Every part of me is hot and tightly coiled. He walks me slowly towards a large shape in a corner, and as we near it, the lines and curves of a piano appear.

He bends me over. My breasts meet the cold dark wood, exposing my arse to him and the cool air.

Releasing his hold on my mouth, he says, "Don't do anything stupid, baby. Don't make too much noise. Let me fix this problem for you." When he moves his hand away all together, I instinctively want to scream.

But I don't.

I break my promises to Perry and myself in that one act of compliance.

Don't do this, Bronson.

Don't let him.

I press my cheek against the piano and breathe heavily, allowing him to slide my knickers down to my ankles. He grabs my arms, twisting them behind my back, pinning me down to the cool wood, leaving no room for me to move.

His total domination washes over me, leaving me a trembling mess, begging for release, making me forget the bad things left between us. We were so beautiful together. So intense. He knew my body. Knew when I wanted him. I try to forget about the man in the corner, although I can hear his breath tumbling out.

Forget about Perry.

As Bronson strokes my wet folds, he groans with desire. "Beautiful little pussy. You're so sexy. Sweet. The perfect combination of both. Why are you so wound up? Dr Clean not look after you?"

I don't answer. Can't.

Arching my back slightly, I lift further into his touch,

hoping he'll take that gentle invitation and give me what I'm desperate for. Guilt floods me; I don't want to cheat on Perry.

But I do... *want* this.

My pulse is rampant in my ears. My neck.

Excitement and fear pounds in equal measure.

"Alright, baby." He pushes two fingers inside me and then draws them out at an excruciatingly slow pace, activating every muscle that is already firing and twitching for something more. I moan against the wood as he works my body with those unhurried, meaningful thrusts. Each one deeper than the last. Both fingers circle to massage every inch of flesh enveloping them.

"*Bronson.*"

He growls. The fingers inside me, the hand pinning my arms behind my back, they twitch and tighten with unease. Then his fingers pick up pace.

I roll around to the onslaught of them fucking me hard.

"Remember that name tonight, baby," he growls from deep within his chest, and I'm so attuned to the sound, I can tell he is clenching his teeth. "When you spread your legs for him again, I dare you not to close your eyes and see mine staring down at you. Dare you not to feel my fingers working your cunt hard and fast just. Like. This." His rhythm becomes beautifully brutal, not giving up, stimulating the perfect spot to the point of near pain. I whimper. "Dare you not to pretend his cock is mine when he thrusts inside you. Dare you not to scream my name in your head when your muscles start to shake."

I grit my teeth as pleasure pounds down on me, beating against me in punishingly sweet waves that hurt and relieve and twist me inside out. I scream his name and he bites out, "I dare you not to think about me."

He slows his pace as I quiver on the piano, having come

completely apart, my entire body set free from the coiled state it's been in for eleven years. I pant against the wood, time meaningless for a few euphoric moments.

My breath is the only sound in this room.

As his fingers slowly slide from inside me, his hand releases its tight grip on my arms.

I slowly stand. My hair cascades wild around my shoulders and back. My underwear rest tight around my ankles. His tall, shadowed body is all I can see in the dark. His steel-like pose has me shuffling nervously in place. My legs, weak from that orgasm and the intensity of that moment, give out, but he catches me. Bringing my head to his chest, he feeds his hands through my hair, holding me close for a moment as if he's genuinely afraid I'll dissolve within his grasp. I can hear his heart racing on the other side of flesh and bone, betraying his chillingly quiet demeanour. Unsure what else to do now, I choose not to fight it anymore. Wrapping my arms around his middle, I fist his shirt behind his back. *Bronson.*

I'm so sorry, nutcase.

I'm sorry.

His spine stiffens, and he drops his hands. Slowly pulling my arms from around him, he lifts them between our bodies to inspect.

I can't see his eyes in the dim light, but I can feel a dangerous shift in him. When he runs his thumb slowly over the diamond on my ring finger, I freeze. A chill sweeps around us, provoking my nervous system to attention. He presses his lips to my hand, then kisses each finger, and I want to cry. I refuse to, biting back soft helpless sobs from the sixteen-year-old version of myself who loved him so immensely, that the love swallowed her whole.

A fire, once so intense, it burnt us both up. Now, embers

lay between us. There's no longer a flame, but what's there is just as ready to scorch our flesh should we dare touch it. I can't let that happen.

Bronson wraps his mouth around my pinkie finger, sucking on it, then around my ring finger. My heart twists as my body duels between singing or weeping. I revel in the feel of his tongue and then-

He suddenly bites down.

A bolt shoots through me, dragging me from my pleasured state to what he is doing. Grating my skin, he slides the ring from my finger with his teeth.

I blink.

No!

Ripping my hand away from him, I swing at his jaw or cheek and it is too dark to tell which, but pain flares through my palm when it meets something hard.

"Give it back!" I snap, anxiously searching his hands in the dim for my engagement ring. I force each one open to find them...empty.

Then I hear him swallow.

My eyes dart up to his shadowed face.

My mouth drops open. "*No.* You didn't."

"You'll get it back," he says, amusement in his voice. "It's my last night in Darwin and I'm staying upstairs. You'll need to join me up there, for say... twelve hours?"

"Oh. My. God. Did you concentrate in anatomy at all?"

I can almost see his smirk. "*Your* anatomy."

"It can take five days sometimes, Bronson!"

"Bummer. Guess you're gonna have to come back to the District with me."

Bending down, I grab my underwear and slide them up, wriggling to get the lace over my backside. My cheeks heat, humiliation and anger both lighting the flame beneath my skin.

Stupid emotional woman!

What was I even thinking?

I ball my fists by my sides. When he chuckles at my huffs of annoyance, I bark, "This is not funny! You didn't swallow it. Give it back."

I hear his smile when he says, "I hope it doesn't hurt later. I may need a doctor. That was rather sharp on the way down."

My ears and neck burn. "You drive me crazy! I have a life, you know? That I love! This is just like you to swoop in and take whatever you want without thinking about the consequences. You always do this!"

His head tilts, his face, a dark perfectly masculine oval, looks down at me. The darkness only allows for the slightest of outlines, yet still displays the hints of a mischievous grin. "I always do what?"

"Whatever you want!" I bite out and then cover my face, breathing into my palms fiercely the way I do now. To calm myself down.

"Did you not want that?" he whispers, his tone hinting at a hiss. "Did you not feel that?"

Dropping my palms to my sides, I try not to cry. "I feel... *lots*. I feel so much —I need my ring back," I say, shaking my head fast from side to side as the image of Perry asking me where it is beats into my mind. "Or Perry will have another reason to—"

"To what?"

"He looks after me. He knows me."

"Fill in the gaps then, baby," he says. "What does Dr Clean know that I don't?"

I lose all sense. All control. I feel as though my orgasm

and his words have somehow ripped my armour down. I hate Bronson for bringing this out of me. Hate him for making me feel this volatile. "He has been here for me for the past six years! Supporting me! He gets the world I am in now. Knows how hard I'm going to have to work to make it as a cardiothoracic surgeon. I can't fucking take any chances. Can't act crazy. I have responsibilities. I'm going to be the only fucking female cardiothoracic surgeon in the state, Bronson! And he knows what I need. What my weaknesses are. How broken I am—" Words just stop in my throat as the truth rises and holds them hostage. "I can't take care of things alone," I whisper to myself more than to him. "Nothing I do is good enough."

There is a long pause.

Silence is never nice when sharing a room with the charismatic Bronson Butcher. A man who loves to tease and play and—"Need me to kill him?"

I burst into laughter even though I shouldn't, the endorphins and adrenaline skipping through my veins like a drug. As he chuckles softly with me, he reaches up both hands to cup the sides of my face. Feeding his big palms down my hair, he slides his fingers through the soft strands, forcing me to close my eyes and enjoy his crazies. Mine too.

But I have to go.

"I have to go." I rush towards the door, but Bronson grabs my hand. Pulling it up to his lips, he kisses my knuckles, and I close my eyes and breathe in the sensation of his lips, trying to stop the thin tethers of my resolve from snapping, from throwing me into his arms. I don't have time to indulge in this anymore. Can't let it consume me. I won't. "I have to go."

"Your ring, baby."

I pause, looking at his silhouette.

There are too many emotions swarming through me. I'm

too confused. My head hurts. My heart aches. My body hums. I want to talk to him. We need closure, need to say all the things we never did. We need to...

"Okay. I'll come see you," I say, barely recognising the voice attached because it's breathy and shaky. My mind swarms with guilt, but it doesn't seem strong enough to control my actions. "What room?"

"You know the number."

I do.

Twenty-three.

I turn my back to him, my fingers slowing slipping from his. The feel of his eyes on me is almost painful and piercing. Glancing at the black shape in the corner, at his trembling back, I nearly laugh again. *Absolute nutcase.* "What about him?"

"Sorry, mate," Bronson says with a little laugh. "Won't be long now. You can leave after we do."

And so I walk away from him and out into the bright lights of the hotel, more confused than when I was dragged in. More confused, yeah, but also content and excited.

Avoiding my reflection as it follows me down the corridor, I smooth my clothes down. Make my way back to my fiancé.

And prepare to feign nausea.

CHAPTER FIFTEEN

shoshanna

Sixteen years old

CARRIED ACROSS THE OCEAN, the warm breeze sweeps sand up and lightly taps it against my cheeks. I catch sight of the moon as it peeks from behind a low-lying cloud. It's a beautiful pink hue. The sun's descent slowly dips below the horizon.

It's pretty.

Wrapping my hands around the balcony balustrade, I daydream about owning a house like this one day.

On the beach.

With a boat and a big peppy tree that has a resident possum we have named.

With Bronson.

Maybe he can feel peace alongside the ocean —something as deep and mysterious as him. Maybe he'll let it sweep his demons out to sea, drag them clawing from his body and into its depths, swallowing them forever. The ocean has that kind of effect on people.

"Hey?" A young guy approaches me, leaning next to me with his back to the ocean. I glance at him sideways, noting the hubris slant to his lips. He clearly thinks a lot of himself with his neatly swept sandy-brown hair and confident posture. He eyes me. "How do you know the birthday girl?"

Unwavering from the glistening water ahead, I mutter, "Why are you looking at me when you could be looking at the ocean?"

"Why would I want to look at the ocean when I could look at you?"

"Flattery will only get you a broken nose."

He laughs. "Wow, you're kind of a badarse."

"That is the only kind of *arse* you'll get from me."

He laughs again, as if this is my version of flirting. As he edges closer to me, I frown, annoyed at the interruption. I was enjoying the company of the ocean. "You're funny," he says. "Has anyone ever told you that before?"

"My boyfriend tells me that all the time. Among other things." The sound of Bronson's Ducati suddenly hits my ears, growing in volume as it approaches from the side of the house. "In fact, that's him there." I stop talking when I see he has a girl sitting behind him, her arms wrapped around his middle, *my* purple and grey helmet on her head, her long black hair flowing down her back.

Nina.

She wants him. Reminding myself that she lives next door to him, that this is just a ride to the party, I rein in my irrational thoughts. My jaw still aches as I inadvertently clench it, trying not to show my irritation to the stranger studying me intently.

When Bronson parks the bike, Nina hops off. He leans it

on its stand. Swinging his leg over, he dismounts with the gracefulness of a man who is equally agile as he is strong. I frown as he helps her remove *my* helmet. Bile rises to the back of my throat when his newly tattooed fingers graze her chin.

Ugh.

But I find myself shuffling and biting my bottom lip at the sight of him. *God, he's gorgeous.* Even from this distance, I can see that cool grin. Can identify those broad muscles below his black leather jacket. Thick, strong thighs covered in denim and black boots that stomp when he walks, creating a soundtrack to his every move. Bronson Butcher is every bit a man, already over six foot and growing, with a roguish easy grin and telling green-blue eyes that sing of mischief and indecency. My Bronson Butcher. My nutcase.

Not hers.

"Well, he seems to be pretty cosy with that girl. Are you sure you're not just trying to avoid talking to me?"

Bronson disappears below the roofline, and I pull out my phone to text him I am out on the balcony when the guy next to me snatches it from my grasp. I whirl to face him, ready to flog him raw. "What the fuck?"

Gazing at me, he chuckles easily. "It's really rude to use your phone when having a conversation with someone." His flippant attitude only makes it harder to control the slow simmer in my blood.

"Conversations go two ways, moron," I snap. "You were having a conversation with yourself. Give me back my fucking phone."

"Why are you such a rude bitch? I was being nice to you. You're all alone. I pitied you."

"Please save your pity. I just don't conv—" My words are cut off at the sight of Bronson striding towards me, towering over the other people scattered around the balcony, a wide grin etched across his deadly handsome face. I blink at him and he stares at me as though I'm lit from behind like an angel.

It's his love look.

He gets within a few steps of us, his eyes never leaving mine, and for a moment all I feel is the intense fluttering of my heart. Then he lowers his shoulder and flips the guy I was talking to over the balcony.

The world stills.

My vision spins in front of my eyes. I scream through a hard hit of panic.

Gasps leave the spectators.

As people rush to peer over the side and down the two storeys where the guy lies groaning on the grass, I'm frozen in disbelief.

"Hey, baby," Bronson says, leaning down to kiss me, but I shove him away.

"Oh my God!" I grip the balustrade as if it's able to stop me from plummeting, my legs suddenly like jelly. That didn't just happen. "What the fuck did you do?"

He peers over the edge, inspecting the situation with indifference. "Friend of yours?"

"Why did you do that?"

"Not sure." He grins at me. "He looks fine. Wanna go check on him?"

Suddenly, the attention of everyone on the balcony shifts to us. Each person appears ashen with shock. No one says anything.

Not a word.

They somehow even breathe quietly, but if it's possible to scream with your whole body, that is what they are doing right now.

An ominous shiver rushes down my spine.

"He'll be fine." Bronson lets out a cool chuckle, and I snatch his hand, pulling him along the balcony, towards the sliding door, shouldering people out of the way. One thing is on my mind. Damage control. Protect my man. Dragging him out the front, I rush over to his bike. "We have to go."

"Why? I just got here. Let's go dance. I wanna see that sexy arse shaking," he says, swaying his hips playfully as though he didn't just throw a guy off the second-floor balcony.

"Because someone is going to call the cops!"

He looks around, catching the eyes of those swarming the lawn, surrounding the guy who is slowly sitting up. People bend to talk to him, assessing his injuries.

"You okay, mate?" Bronson calls over to him with a smooth and even voice. "Need an ambulance?"

"You're fucking insane!" the guy growls, gripping his crippled arm with a shaky fist. "Get your bitch and get the hell away from me."

Bronson lets out the loudest laugh I've ever heard from him, forcing my blood to become like ice in my veins. It is anything but a cheerful sound. He legs it towards the guy. Throwing his boot into the man's head, he snaps it backwards. The guy's body flops into a coma-like-state on the lawn.

My heart beats like a drum, but where I should feel more guilt, I only think, *'I did tell you that flattery would get your nose broken.'*

"*Fuck,*" I mutter to myself more than anyone else.

Quickly, I run towards Bronson's bike as he strides back over to me.

He grabs my helmet, the one Nina had on a few minutes ago, and slides it over my head. "Where to, baby?" Swinging his leg over and shuffling along the vinyl seat, he waits for me to jump on, then says, "Yeah. Probably best that we leave now, baby. Sorry I ruined your night."

"Just go, nutcase."

As the bike takes off, I revel in the feel of the humming below my thighs. I close my eyes and allow the sensation and motion of the bike to thrust me through the air, around the streets, gliding.

Bronson's Ducati is my favourite sound. If freedom had a soundtrack, it'd be made up of the rumbles and growls of a motorbike engine, hinting at danger and excitement and possibilities. But the freedom I feel right now doesn't just come from the bike's ability to take us anywhere, but from the connection we share. The bike only manifests this single entity we become when we share it. We could go anywhere *together* on this bike.

Just the two of us.

No one else will fit.

No one else is needed.

I'm reminded of Nina and how she sits here too, provoking possessiveness like a ball of fire in my stomach. My fist closes around Bronson's shirt, clenching over his hard sculptured abdomen.

We circle a big Norfolk Pine I recognise. Knowing we are about to head down a gravel track toward the shore, I grip him tighter. Although I know how competent he is on his Ducati, having spent more hours riding it than not, each bump still provokes an exciting little jolt to my heart.

The headlights flick through near blackness, spotlighting shrubbery and waves as we careen over the sand.

The bike slows as it approaches our little lookout, one we created for ourselves two years ago. His BMX takes us thirty minutes to get here. The Ducati, five.

I bounce off and walk straight towards the trail leading up the dunes. The sand crumbles away beneath my feet as I climb the steep incline, heading towards the overhanging wooden platform. Two steps forward, one back —it's a workout.

"Someone has their panties in a twist. Can I see?" His laugh only stokes my frustration.

"You and Nina!" I snap.

His laughter increases and I hate how much I love the sound. "Not the fact I threw a guy over the balcony?"

"Why was she on your bike?" I call back to him, sweeping the pendulous shrubbery aside and trying to control my breathing, the fatigue of the climb having unsettled my voice.

"She didn't play with your toy. She just used some of the accessories."

I huff some more, the pathetic jealous tone so familiar now. I don't want to share him. Not a single smile. Not a sweet cheeky comment. I want them all. "You're not funny." We reach our lookout. Lookout twenty-three. It is the furthest away. The hardest one to get to.

Which is why we love it.

I stare over the ocean. The moon's reflection creates a blanket of glitter across its dark rippling surface. "Why did you throw him off the balcony?"

"Because I wanted to," he says from just behind me.

The heat from his body moves into me like an impenetrable force. I spin to find him close. "You can't just do things like that, Bronson. You're not above the law. Even though... Well, I know what you do for your family, but—"

He smirks. "You don't know what I do for my family."

I stare up at him, through his incredible gem-like eyes. "Yes, I do. I know who Jimmy Storm is. I know everything."

My eyes flutter shut when he lifts his hand and touches my face, the way he often does —a memorising kind of caress that sends me into a spin with its gentle possessiveness.

"I killed a boy today," he whispers.

I snap my eyes open. "What?"

"He witnessed something he shouldn't have," he says, watching my expression and his fingers as they feather against my skin. "I killed him for them." My skin prickles with a chill, his words somehow dominating the external humidity. "I didn't intend on killing him, baby. It just happened."

"I don't understand," I murmur just as his lips meet mine. Demand mine. Demand I take it all away for him, even when he wears his cloak of indifference.

I break our kiss, not allowing his soft, needy lips to seduce me. "Are you okay?"

"I'm fine," he says before his mouth finds my jaw, becoming a little frantic. Hurried. Messy.

"Do you feel anything for that boy?" I say, trying to focus on the conversation. But my body wants to moan, to let go. "Bronson?" I try to shrug him off, but he refuses to relent his assault on my neck and jaw, eating at my skin with desperation. "Bronson!"

He stills and then mutters, "I don't even know him... How can I feel anything for him?"

I pull back to study his eyes; the greens shining brighter like the embers of truth, unable to stay hidden despite the flame lying dormant. "You're lying. You do care."

He grins. "You just hope I do, baby."

Shaking my head slowly, I say, "No. Your eyes are green. You care."

"That's because I'm in love with you," he says, brushing

my hair over my shoulder, his hands finding any reason to touch me. "My beautiful Egyptian princess. My eyes are green for you."

"That's bullshit," I state adamantly. "It's because you feel guilty."

He smiles sweetly, and it chills my blood. "I took the family flowers."

"Bronson, this conversation is insane." I lean back against the wooden fencing. My lower back presses into it as I try to catch his gaze, to anchor him to me. "Tell me what happened?"

As he takes a step back, I prepare myself to listen intently.

"I tied him to a tree," he admits, shoving his hands into his pockets. "I beat him up. I left him there for the night... The next morning, I brought him a coffee and a bagel. He's a chubby kid. Was a chubby kid. Well, he probably still is chubby. Anyway, I thought we could make peace with a bagel. But, ah, see it rained last night. Remember?"

I swallow hard. "*Yes.*"

"Well, after I beat him up, I pulled his shirt over his head, so his stomach was showing. Guess I was being a prick about his weight. But it rained so much, the material filled up with water and... I guess he fucking suffocated."

Covering my mouth, I whisper through my palm. "*Fuck.*" Moving towards him, I reach up to stroke his beautiful face, which is lightly adorned with neat stubble. "Are you going to get in trouble?"

"No. Jimmy took care of it." He pauses for a moment, deep in contemplation. "I do feel a little guilty. I think that is what this feeling is. How did you know?"

A sad smile forms on my lips. "I know *you*, nutcase."

He reaches down and wraps his hands around the backs

of my thighs, lifting me up to straddle him, before walking us over to the hammock we set up the last time we were here. He lays me down inside it and settles on top of me, his lips moving around my skin. Tasting. Teasing.

I want him to get lost in me.

To let himself just be real.

"Tell me about it. What was it like when you hurt him?" The words tumble out at the same time as the thought arises, giving me no time to analyse them. I just want to be closer to him, I think. Connected to his dark mind and accepting of it.

I reach for his hand and push it beneath my shorts, guiding his finger between my folds, working my pussy together. He lets out a long groan and wastes no time diving deeper inside me, obviously excited I'm letting him touch me.

I am too.

I wonder if he likes the way I feel. Pulling my hand out, I let him take over. As he rocks my pelvis back and forth with each inward thrust and outward pull, I grip his shoulders.

"When I hurt people..." He leans up and stares down at me as I pant beneath him. The blazing pools of green and blue watch me intensely while his fingers set a steady rhythm inside me. I try not to blush, hoping he likes this as much as I do.

I lift into his touch.

Fight to hold my eyes open.

A tingle grows within me as he explores. When pleasure prickles along my skin, I wriggle and moan. Learning as my body responds to him, he slows down and focuses his attention on the right places. I breathe through a moan that seems to go on and on. "When I threw that guy off the balcony, baby, because he was talking to you, because he was rude to you, I heard something. Like a high-pitched laugh. But it was far away. It's not the first time I've heard it." His words scare me, but the thrusting of his fingers only redirects those spikes of adrenaline towards feverish unrelenting pleasure.

My head spins.

Feels so good.

Sounds so bad.

Why is this turning me on so much?

His eyes ensnare me as I start to quiver.

"Do you like it when I fuck you with my fingers? Does it turn you on that I would kill for you, baby? That I'll protect you? Never leave you alone to fend for yourself?"

God. It comes on fast.

My abdomen clenches as a wave of euphoria crashes down on top of me, sinking me further into the hammock with its intense pressure. His words scare me as his fingers make me come, and I'm delirious in both pleasure and confusion. Both send me spinning. "I got you, baby. Let it all go." He groans when I clench around him, coming hard, a constant pulse that massages his fingers.

"Fuck, this is hot. You're hot. Your body. The way it works," he murmurs in awe, his fingers circling slowly.

After a few moments, my senses settle. My body stops humming. I look up at him to find a curve to his lips. I laugh a little at the insanity of him. *Of us.*

"I don't like that you hurt that boy," I confirm.

"Me neither," he finally admits.

I cup the back of his neck. "But we're in this together."

He buries his head at the base of my throat, and I hold him close as he says, "Okay, baby."

Bronson Butcher.

In all his madness and shadows, he is the only person who gives me the confidence to be myself. I always thought that a good relationship was when two people made each other better versions of themselves... but it's not. It's when they are content enough together to let all their crazies shine.

And maybe he is mad.

Me, a little crazy.

But we are mad in love and crazy about each other.

CHAPTER SIXTEEN
shoshanna

Present day

I SPEND most of the day at home, pretending to be unwell. It's actually really nice to sit outside with Akila and talk and talk. Now, though, I need an excuse to not be in our bed when Perry finishes his shift. So, grimacing, I call Katie.

I dislike the bitch.

But she isn't a nark like Mandy.

She picks up instantly. "Well, well. If it isn't perfect Shoshanna Adel. Feeling better?" Katie sings through the speaker, her sideways smirk somehow visible, even through the phone.

I nod at the Uber driver as I exit his car, shut the door, and make my way into the hotel foyer. Lowering my head as I pass the doorman, I wrap a hand around my waist as if to protect myself somehow.

"Yeah..." I lie. In more ways than she knows.

Sweat slides down my chest and between my breasts, the

tiny beads seeping into my low-cut white shirt, turning the material opaque.

I make my way towards the elevator, passing people who don't know me but whom I still avoid as guilt plays out across my face. A preliminary walk of shame. Not that anything is happening tonight.

Maybe.

Probably.

Just that I shouldn't be here in the first place... But the circumstances are unique. "So I need a favour. I need you to say I'm with you tonight." Perry would never suspect I'd lower my chin to ask a favour from her, which is exactly why it is the perfect lie. Some lies drag you down with their weight. Others liberate you.

This one does both.

She clicks her tongue. "This has to do with Mr Tall, Tattooed, and Fucking Delicious, doesn't it?"

I know that if I just admit it, she'll think she has won and might let it go. "Yes."

"You know, you're a lot more interesting since he came to town. This side of you I might even like."

Stepping into the elevator, I press the level two button, lean back onto the railing, and turn to watch the door close with the loyal and honest version of myself on the other side.

In here, I'm surrounded by mirrors reflecting the girl who has followed me for over a decade. I try not to look at the sixteen-year-old inside me, the one who begs me to steal this moment of freedom with him.

Akila is fine.

"No. You won't," I say.

"Yeah, you're right." She pauses, the silence teasing without the injection of her voice. "Okay. But... what do I get out of it?"

I let out a long sigh as the elevator chimes and then opens, revealing a long cream carpeted hallway with a few trays scattered outside of various doors. Striding out, I say, "I'll do anything, Katie. Okay? I'll get you better shifts."

I hear her scoff. "You don't have that kind of power."

"I'm your resident. I could request things for you," I say, stopping abruptly at room twenty-three. Shaking my head, I think about how crazy this is. I spin to stride back to the elevator, but the girl inside spins me back around and stations me right in front of it. Akila used to say, 'You two are like magnets'. I seriously feel that pull now.

"Not my boss, though, so I doubt you'll have any effect over my shifts," Katie cuts into my thoughts.

"Fine!" I snap, glaring at the number two and the number three as though all my answers lay there, which they do and they don't. "What do you want?"

"I want you to convince Perry to let me scrub in with you."

Rolling my eyes, I lean my shoulder on the hallway wall. "He doesn't like you."

"I don't like him. But for some reason he *loves* you."

"He doesn't trust you," I point out.

"I'm a better nurse than Mandy," she bites out. "That sly bitch. You know she has big eyes for him."

Sighing, I work my forehead with my fingers, knowing it'll be a hard sell to Perry because Katie is all attitude and I'm supposed to hate her. I mean, I do hate her. "She told him about our chat the other day. You know, when I snapped at you guys in the bathroom."

"Yeah. You were interesting that day too." She laughs. "I liked it."

I almost smile. "Just, if I do this, you know you have to follow directions. Be quick. Take criticism. Don't backchat."

"Fine. I will," she moans.

"Well, fine, I will ask Perry then."

"Cool."

I hear something come from within the suite —music and something else. "So, I'm with you right now?" I confirm. "And you needed to talk to me about... *what?*"

She doesn't skip a beat. "My closest friend was in an accident and is in a wheelchair. I'm struggling emotionally. I thought you could help me squash all my personality and happiness so that I can cope with this new drama and responsibility."

My stomach rolls, and I want to claw off the smirk I can hear in her voice. "You're a bitch."

"I know."

I nod, knowing Perry would never think I'd stoop that low if it wasn't true. "That works though."

"I know." She laughs triumphantly. "Now go be a slut."

"*Ugh.* Bye, Katie." I hang up and slide the handset into the back pocket of my denim short shorts. I adjust the white singlet I have on, smoothing it down my stomach and checking it is nicely tucked into my shorts. I peer down at my black ankle boots, adorned with little studs up the inside.

I shouldn't be doing this.

But we never got to say goodbye.

Tonight is our closure. One night to acknowledge something that was cut short before we were ready to let it go. This is a hello. I hope you are well. I wish you well. I'm sorry. I'm *so so* sorry for my part in it... And finally, our long-awaited *goodbye.*

I tap the door with my knuckles while my heart double taps in my chest. The music from within lowers. Footsteps approach. I shuffle my stance, listening as he walks —steady and confident, almost in a swagger.

The door opens, and I'm momentarily deafened by the droning pulse in my ears.

In casual attire, standing in the full light of the room, he gives me my first true glimpse at twenty-seven-year-old Bronson Butcher. I take him all in.

Jesus Christ.

He stands with that signature Bronson charm, which both welcomes the universe to be his friend and reminds them how everything is on his terms. He stares down at me with a devouring gaze, his indecent thoughts apparent within his searing turquoise-coloured eyes.

Annoyingly cute and yet still clearly dangerous, with mussed dark-brown hair and colourful tattoos licking up every inch of exposed skin. A short, neat dark-brown beard shapes his strong masculine jaw, creating a stark contrast against the whites of his teeth.

The notorious Butcher dimple all but taunts me like a shiny light leading its prey into a false sense of security. And those muscles... Defined, they fill out his blue shirt. Over his shoulder, he has a tea towel with a smear of red on it.

Is he cooking?

He licks his thumb and forefinger slowly before running his tongue along his lower lip, tasting something that was on them. I raise a brow at him, knowing the little games he plays, knowing the effect he has on women.

On me.

His sweet grin spreads further across his cheeks. "Are you lost, Doc?"

I hold my hand up. "Shush. Don't be cute. Don't say anything. Just listen, as hard as I know that is for you."

As he folds his arms over his chest, the true mass of each bicep is revealed. I can imagine how easily he could manhandle a woman to his heart's content. Shifting my eyes to his, I lock on to those mood ring irises surrounded by thick black lashes that shouldn't be allowed on a man.

"I don't know what you're talking about," he says.

"You're a flirt," I say, trying not to smile. "You can't help yourself. Just stop with the face thing."

He raises a brow at me. "The face thing?"

"The smirk," I say with exasperation. "The thing you're doing right now with your dimple."

"I don't control my dimple." He laughs. "But I do know he'd like to be rubbing against your inner thigh right now."

My legs feel that sentence settle into the flesh between them. "I. Said," I say through a strangled breath. "Not a word. Okay?"

He nods, amusement all over his lovely features. "My dimple and I comply."

"Tonight, I'm going to pretend..." I reach for what I want to express. Need to. I force it out. "Pretend that I'm not engaged. And I want us to talk." I try to stop my breath from shuddering out as I speak. "Be honest with each other."

He slowly lowers his arms to his sides. "Just tonight?"

"There is only tonight," I mutter, my voice shaking with each painful word, as they are neither strong nor fierce, but hesitant and sorrowful.

I have Akila to think about.

He runs his gaze over the length of my body. If his eyes could lick me from my foot to where my heart beats frantically within my chest, they would. "My dimple and I object."

"Object to what?"

"Just tonight."

"Bronson, please. No joking."

"I'm not a joking kind of guy."

That's the most inaccurate statement ever uttered. I

strangle a giggle, focusing on getting this part of the evening out of the way. "Do as you're told, Bronson Butcher!"

He raises his hands, a smirk still firmly in place. "Okay, baby. No jokes."

I nod. A heavy breath pushes past my unsteady smile. Bronson steps aside, holding the door open for me as I walk into the rich, comforting space of his suite. "Jesus, this is a nice place."

Watching me closely, he tracks my movements around the hotel suite. "My dimple is not humble."

Making my way into the kitchen, I see a pot on the flame simmering away. Fresh leafy greens cut up on a wooden chopping board, sliced tomatoes tossed with salt and pepper and feta, and two wine glasses sit on the shiny granite kitchen counter. Sadness seeps through me. I breathe in fast. Out. In.

"I'LL COOK *dinner for you every damn night. We'll never eat in front of the TV. We'll sit at the table and talk about our day.*"

"YOU'RE COOKING FOR ME?" I say, sliding on to a black stool. His presence strokes my spine as he moves past me into the kitchen.

"I cook every night, baby. I said I would."

My throat tightens. Fighting back emotions, I watch all six-foot-five inches of tattooed masculinity work in the kitchen with ease. He spins to face me, that knowing smirk on his face.

"Checking me out?"

I try not to blush too hard. "I'm hungry."

He slowly licks his lower lip, eyeing me with obvious

intent. His gaze dances around the heavy rise and fall of my breasts, and time, for a moment, is still. Very still. The sound of the water slowly rising to a boil builds the tension between us. Just as the water steams and bubbles, becoming more volatile and scorching, so does the environment. The simmer of water is a suspenseful sound that seems to grow as the quiet lingers.

My insides simmer to its melody.

It dares me not to feel it.

His gaze arrows into me. "Careful with the way you look at me, baby. Or you'll get that pretty little mouth stuffed with something besides risotto."

Jesus Christ.

Clearing my throat, I force myself to ask something, anything, needing to deflect the feelings he is throwing at me; a virile kind of energy that affects me from my ears to the tips of my toes. "What happened to your chest?" I ask, steadying my breaths on that question. "How did you get shot? You're still fucking around with your brothers and Jimmy Storm, I take it?"

Jimmy —the great and powerful Jimmy Storm.

All those years ago, I was supposed to keep Bronson from falling further into that world. Into Jimmy's clutches. I was supposed to be his something else...something honest and normal. It is what we discussed. What I promised his brother. Yet another way, I failed him.

When he turns back to the kitchen, I take that moment to close my eyes, holding them for a moment of peace. Opening them again, I observe him stirring the pot of risotto and then spinning the dial until the flame dies out.

The simmering stops.

I know he hates when people discuss his business, but

we never had secrets between us. He always told me point blank who he was. Is.

What he does.

And why.

For them.

I think I'm the only one who gets the truth when others find a cocky answer muddled with half-truths and jokes.

"A lot has changed since you left me, Shoshanna," he says, turning to face me. A cocky grin plays with the corner of his mouth while pride flashes in his eyes. "Clay is a councillor now. My beautiful Max is City Architect, controlling basically every new commercial project. We are inside the bitch now. Jimmy and Dad have tenders over half the District and my little Xander is going to take the bar next year. Kid's got a brain the size of a planet. There isn't much they won't control soon enough."

Once again, he leaves himself out. "And you?"

He grins harder, a mischievous tick to his lips. "I make sure things don't get in the way of their happiness. Of their opportunities."

"Your brothers' happiness. Your brothers' opportunities?"

He tilts his head, still amused by my inquisition. "Of course."

"What about your fucking happiness?" I bite out. "Your opportunities?" My heart hammers in my chest, slamming into bone, trying to claw its way out of my skin. I need to hear he is happy. That what I did didn't destroy him like it did me. That he was okay after I left. That I didn't kill not just what was between us, but him as well.

"Not much of a scholar, remember? I was somewhat distracted by a beautiful girl in high school."

Shaking my head, not buying these excuses, I say, "Don't

blame me. You were *very much* distracted by Jimmy Storm and that world."

Scooping up a small amount of risotto onto a fork, he strolls over to me with slow, predator-like strides. I open my mouth instinctively, letting him place the spoon in between my lips like he used to. The warm metal heats my tongue. The flavour of chorizo and minted peas burst to life in my mouth. He stares at my lips as I work the food inside them and the blacks of his eyes grow; the shiny rings of blues and greens are incredibly thin —a glimpse of light banding dangerous black vortexes.

He strokes my face with his gaze, reining in his heated desires. "You have been my distraction from the moment I saw you by the pool, baby. On your belly. With that slip of olive skin between your jeans and your shirt. From the moment I open my eyes in the morning to when I close them again at night, you are my beautiful distraction."

My heart rushes up my throat.

He drags the spoon out slowly and smears the juices from my saliva and the sauce across my cheek. My breathing becomes uneven. Leaning down, he laps his tongue from my jaw to the corner of my lips, tracing the flavours of me and his food. He stops by my mouth, leaving me a panting mess, wanting to turn my cheek and accept his tongue inside me.

He hums his enjoyment and then leaves me sitting there, my legs shaking violently. Strolling back to the stove, he prepares two bowls, sprinkling the fresh greens on top. He places one bowl in front of me and pours two glasses of wine.

All I can do is watch as the sadness I felt a few minutes ago crawls back into me, settling in deep. He never mentioned his happiness.

Playing with my food, I build up the courage to ask him again. "And your happiness?" I choke out. My breath hitches.

"If my brothers are happy, then I am happy," he says smoothly as he eats a spoonful of risotto. "You know this, baby."

My stomach drops. My heart stops.

A lie.

I can see it in his eyes. He loves his brothers. He's happy they're happy. But he's not fucking happy. He wasn't okay. He wasn't okay, and it was because of me. Too many emotions run through me. Pain and guilt at the forefront, driven by the knowledge that I hurt this beautiful man, but followed quickly by elation and fury and confusion.

On the brink of tears, I pick up a spoonful of risotto and catapult it onto his shirt. The food glides down the fabric and slops on to the table.

He looks up at me, a slow grin drawing his lips out. "You don't like it, baby?"

He isn't happy. But he didn't look for me? I stayed away from him. I wrote letter after letter, text after text, only to throw them away and delete them... I settled—I settled for easy and safe, but he isn't happy anyway! Heat hits my ears. "Then why didn't you come for me?" I mutter, my eyes dancing around his tattoos. To the butcher bird on his hand. To the word 'Butcher' in cursive writing, which traces the cords of muscles running the full length of his neck. Vibrant colours. So much love and loyalty for his family. But I was his fucking family! We were family! "Why didn't you come for me?" I say louder this time, and when I find his face again, his smile has slipped. "Why didn't you come for me!" I scream through a strangled sob that makes his eyes gloss over and his jaw tic. "I thought you hated me." My breath shakes violently as he stands up and walks back around the counter. I barely manage to gaze up. Can't quite bring myself to meet his eyes. "I thought—"

"You think I didn't try?" he says smoothly, raising his hand to stroke my face. Closing my eyes, I allow a few tears to slide out. "Shoshanna," he purrs. "You think I didn't try to hunt you down, baby? You think I'd just let you leave me?"

He tried to find me...

I open my eyes, peering up through lashes beaded with tears. "You still loved me?"

His eyes are pools of pain masked by cool detachment. "Did you think I'd just stop?"

"I don't know." I breathe out hard. "I don't know."

"Yes," he says, lifting my chin with his finger. "I still *love* you. I never stopped. Not for a second."

Emotions overflow, my heart aching for the sixteen-year-old girl who loved him more than life. Craved him more than her next breath.

It's too late now.

It's too late.

Tears burst from my eyes, and within seconds, he is sweeping me into his arms. I give myself to him willingly, wrapping my legs around his waist, circling my hands around his thick, strong neck. His arms band my whole frame and his mouth finds mine in a completely devouring kiss.

It's rough.

Bruising.

He growls his emotions against my lips, and I sob mine against his. Because it is too late. I don't know where the time went or how I learnt to breathe without him, but I can't start over again. Can't go through that perpetual grief. That loss.

This is goodbye.

It has to be.

His tongue tastes me as he walks us into a wall, crushing me against it until I can barely breathe. Then he moves to the door.

Squeezing his hips with my thighs, I rub my core against his stomach, ignited by the anticipation of him inside me... again. He carries me into the master bedroom. Climbing onto the bed, he drags me with him.

Our kisses are messy.

Frantic.

His movements are beautifully jarring and exhilarating, his lips perfectly rough. His hands find my bra strap behind my back, skilled fingers unclipping them with ease.

Breaking our kiss, he pins my hands above my head, then lifts my bra and shirt up in quick succession, leaving them knotted around my elbows. Clawing at the pillow above my head, I keep my arms up, letting the shirt and bra restrain me.

He is back on my mouth again, biting and growling and losing control. And I want it.

Teeth graze down my jawline, scoring a line to my breasts. He sinks his teeth in to one of my nipples. My back arches on a whimper as pain flares through me, gravitating directly to the swelling skin between my legs. I thrash around as he applies more pressure to that sensitive hard bud before moving to the other breast, taking that one with just as much passion. Just as much dominance.

The mattress shifts as he slides down my stomach, his tongue licking me in a primal way, tasting my skin. My sweat. His breath trails heat as he approaches my shorts. He unbuttons them with his teeth.

Planting my feet on either side of him, I lift my bum up so

he can wriggle my clothes over my arse, leaving me in my black-coloured underwear.

I'm suddenly painfully aware of all the lights above me, illuminating my body. Every dip. Every curve. I slip into a place of self-conscious thoughts, plagued by the clouds of his past lovers. Women far more beautiful than me. How many has he had? Did he love any of them?

Before I can sink too far into that thought, he spreads my knees, pushing them up and pinning them to the mattress. He exposes my pussy and arse, displaying me to him, spread eagle and only partly covered by the lace of my underwear. Nerves and arousal ignite across my skin.

Nuzzling down my core, his nose and lips both rub the silk-covered flesh between my thighs. Teasing me with what is coming, he sends me out of my mind with urgency. I lift into him, eager for more.

"Do you have a greedy little pussy?" He growls. "You let that dickhead touch you? Tell me. Tell me what you let him do to you." His words chaff my ears; all the while, the laps of his tongue against my knickers blanket me in pleasure. "Tell me, does he kiss you here?"

Sliding my knickers aside with his teeth, he starts to lick the valley between my lips in long, deliberate laps.

Tasting.

Groaning.

Long.

Slow.

Fuck.

When I spasm on a wave of sensitivity, he forces my thighs into the mattress harder and plunges his tongue into me. He suddenly gets feral and rough.

The friction from his short beard is deliciously stimulating, while the licks of his tongue feel like pure ecstasy. One demanding that I am his and the other reminding me he is mine. Both awakening something. "Answer me."

When he bites down on my clit, I yelp. "Yes!" My leg kicks out instinctively as currents rupture through me, stimulating my rippling coil of nerves. But he doesn't let my sensitive bud go, flicking it with his tongue while it's pinched tightly between his unyielding teeth.

Mewling and panting, I'm a mass of trembling limbs. My hands swing down to grab his hair, tugging at the strands, knotting them in tight. Hissing, he kneads the flesh of my legs, pushing them further into the mattress. My pelvis rises instantly into his devouring mouth.

"Are you thinking about him now? Do you wish he was between your legs?"

I wince at his words, but I'm still unable to concentrate on my dislike of them while he accosts my clit with intense punishing pleasure. So good. It feels so good.

Heat pools in my abdomen.

"Do you?" he demands.

Releasing one thigh, he slides two fingers deep into the soft depths of my pussy.

I hurtle over the edge. "No! I think of you!"

My hips jolt off the bed. I scream his name as I come; the sensation wrapping around me, suffocating me, wringing pleasure from me. And I can't feel anything besides the flow of my orgasm as it moves through my muscles and out all over his eager tongue and working fingers.

I feel so wet.

So wet. But he licks me from my opening to my clit, cleaning all the moisture with his tongue.

As my head rolls on the pillow, I release my death grip on his hair. Melting into the mattress like a puddle, having lost all my strength, I vaguely register him slide from the bed. As my ears ring with the aftershock of that painful pleasure, I close my eyes and inhale deeply, hoping it relents.

When I hear a zipper, I open them again. At the sight of him bare chested and sliding his pants down his strong, tattooed legs, I lick my lips. The wound in his chest clearly does nothing to weaken him and is almost unnoticeable within the lines of his tattoos.

He stalks towards me, his thick hard cock pulsing as he moves, bobbing with its own devious warning. He is so much more beautiful than any man I have ever seen —a six-foot-five god with muscles that palpitate with his desires, and tattoos that offer a glimpse into his heart.

He is on the bed again. Slowly crawling up my body, he slides his tongue along my skin in a sweet, healing way.

Reaching my lips, he leans on one elbow, holding his weight off me. Feeding a hand through my hair, he dips his mouth to take mine, but this time, he is slow and soft, dancing to the ballad of meaning and loss. His tongue laps inside my mouth, stroking the roof of it and all around. He always wanted to taste everything. This man enjoys every part of my body. Always has.

As a warm hand moves from my knee to my thigh, he wraps my leg around his back. I bring the other leg up too. My eyes meet his and I'm nervous. As his cock meets the soft entrance between my legs, I draw a sharp breath in. He's so much bigger than Perry. I must have known, but it's been years since I've had him.

"I want you," I plea, tears forcing their way out of my eyes as emotions erupt. Time has been cruel to me since the last day I saw him. All my crazies had to die. To cope with the loss of him. They had to die.

I missed him so much.

He catches my tears on his thumb and licks them from his finger. "Mine. Every part of you, baby."

Tonight. Only tonight.

It's too late now.

I close my eyes in anguish over those devastating truths. Bronson positions himself, slowly nudging at my folds, dipping in shallow. I open my eyes to find him staring at me with a possessiveness that damn near scares me.

"Mine," he growls, pushing all the way in, sliding his long thick cock to the hilt and pushing harder still, stretching the fragile tissue inside. I whimper at the invasion, at the feel of being filled so thoroughly.

He groans and bares his teeth as he starts to thrust, dragging his cock against the tight soft vice of my pussy and pounding back in. Out and in. "Such. A. Tight. Little. Pussy."

I grip the nape of his neck and our noses slide together, our lips caressing gently with each rock of his body against mine. "I'm going to claim every part of this body. Remind you who you belong to." He suddenly rears up, still pumping his hips at a steady pace, shaking with the ecstasy of the feeling of us together. His expression is one of agony and anguish.

Abruptly, he grabs hold of my throat, squeezing until my eyes widen with uncertainty. Pumping his hips faster, my body becomes overwhelmed by the rhythm of his.

And he's rougher than I remember. Fucking me with all the hate he has for me and what I did all those years ago.

Our bodies become slick with perspiration. His eyes blaze, locked on my face. "*Shoshanna*," he hisses, broken and guttural. "I'm not coming without you, baby."

He rolls his hips against me, the thick length of him stimulating the muscles inside me that beg to be rubbed. Just like that. Hard. Fast. Fierce.

He has it.

Just there.

God...

Brushing his pelvis against my clit, he tickles my over-worked nerves. My brain turns to mush over the sensation. I close my eyes and moan low in my throat as heat boils up inside me. The hand around my throat squeezes as my sounds of pleasure vibrate within it. I can only just breathe.

Just enough.

While his tight grip around my throat draws out fear and adrenaline, his methodical thrusts push in pleasure, and I'm lost in it. My pussy pulses around him violently with each inward stroke, grabbing hold of his cock, begging it to stay deep.

"*Fuck*," he hisses. "I'm coming, baby."

"*God*, Bronson. That. *God*."

"*Shoshanna*."

My body is a shuddering mess beneath him now, useless and lethargic and his to handle as I plummet into a frisson of pleasure. A violent growl erupts from him as he beats his hips harder, coming with a feral need to fill me. To claim me. To not waste a drop of what he wants me to take.

Eventually, his hips slow, but he stays deep.

My body hums from being fucked so thoroughly.

When he presses his forehead to mine, we breathe together in the whirl of bliss and melancholy. I squeeze my eyes shut, feeling overwhelmingly heartbroken and raw. All those years apart... We will never get them back.

Rolling his forehead against mine, I feel his brows tighten in anguish. "I'm so sorry, baby," he chokes out, his voice hoarse and deep and-

I gasp as something punctures my neck. It's so quick, I

can barely process the sensation. He pulls back. I see the needle in his fist. *Fuck.*

I stare up at him wide-eyed. "What have you..." My voice falters as my tongue swells in my mouth, becoming heavy and thick and useless. My lashes... like lead, bat slowly, dropping like curtains over my vision. "*Done?*"

A rush of nausea takes me.

My head rolls on the mattress as a dark abyss crawls up my body, consuming my senses. My body becomes heavy, my head swarms in a thick haze.

"I'm so—"

I hear him, but the words are drifting away from me.

"Fucking sorry."

He roars, but it's not loud like it should be. The mattress shakes violently. Over and over. My neck sways with each thud. He is pounding it with his fist, I think. There is so much pain in his tormented growls. I want to hold him, but I can't lift my arms and I've forgotten why. My legs flop, muscles loosen, and his cum slides slowly out from between my legs.

I feel his forehead meet mine again, and tears stream down my cheeks, but they aren't mine.

Breath cascades across my face. "I ... can't... let ... you ... leave... me ... again."

CHAPTER SEVENTEEN

bronson

Six years old

I SIT IN THE BATHTUB.

It's cold. So cold... it hurts.

My body feels strange. Slow. Like I'm asleep. But I'm wide awake. I play a game. Breathing out, forcing the smoke from my body, watching it float through the surrounding air.

It's getting hard to play this game.

Breathing is getting hard.

I look down at the painful water, the ice cubes that knock into each other. It looks deep.

Something moves. I look up at my brother's blue lips. He is shorter than me, so his shoulders sit just above the surface. He looks strange. Smaller than he normally is. A different colour, too. A different expression on his face. Still.

I don't think I like the way he looks.

Max is such a good boy. I thought little brothers were annoying. But he isn't. He's quiet. Every night, he cleans up his toys. But sometimes he forgets to close the drawers.

She doesn't like that.

He eats all his food, but sometimes he drops bits on the floor.

She doesn't like that.

I can see that he tries.

Why doesn't she see?

And my little brother, Xander. He is naughty. Naughty but *so so* funny. I see him making everyone laugh. Even Max. I'm glad he isn't in the water. I'm glad he's naughty because she locks him away in a cupboard. She doesn't like his screams. I think the cupboard is better than the water. But I'm not sure.

I think that if I had to choose my brothers, I would choose Max and Xander. I like them. I don't know what love really means, but I think I know how it feels. It feels like always. Like you want them to be near you always. I think I love my brothers.

As I focus on Max again. His eyes are very still. And I wish he wasn't my brother today. Wish he didn't leave the drawer open. Wish he didn't drop his food.

Then he wouldn't have the blue on his eye.

Then he wouldn't have the hurt on his stomach.

I don't like the way he looks right now. Not at all.

I look at our mum. She is looking at her nails. They are pink. I think she is pretty. But... she is not pretty too in a different way. I blink at her. I squeak. My voice is little. More little than normal. She doesn't look up.

I look at Max.

I look at my mum.

I look at the bath.

Why am I the only one looking?

And I know... I need to protect them. Max doesn't look right, and she isn't looking at all. *Mum? Why don't you look, mum?* ... My heart hurts... She. Doesn't. Like. Us...

When I look back at Max, his eyes are closed. My heart feels fast. It makes me feel dizzy. "Max. Max. Don't close your eyes, Max." I think I spoke. I tried to speak, but no one was looking, and now I'm watching him slide down into the water. My throat burns. My heart burns. My head burns.

I start to laugh.

I laugh so loud, and it won't stop. A sound that rips through me and it nearly hurts. I feel tears fall down my face. Hot tears. They burn. It all burns.

Max...

I laugh.

Then she looks, looks and starts to yell at me. For laughing. My laughing made her look. She stands and walks towards me. Something hot hits my cheek. Her hand. And again. It's warm. I like it. Mum is mad. She puts her hands on my shoulders and pushes me under the water... it isn't deep. It isn't cold anymore either. She lets me go, and I float under the water for a while, laughing.

Then I see Max.

Under the water opposite me.

His eyes are closed.

Mine are open.

I'm looking. I burst up. Mum is gone, but I'm looking. I drag Max up. He is heavy. But I pull him out of the bathtub. Out of the water. I grab the towels. All of them. I wrap them around us. Max needs to be warm. I hold him. I've stopped laughing now, but I can still hear it echoing in my head. I think I broke my brain in the water, but I was still looking.

I was looking, Max.

I'll keep looking after you.

CHAPTER EIGHTEEN

bronson

Present day

I FINISH the bottle of whiskey. Placing it on the carpet, I watch it roll onto its side, a small pool of brown liquor collecting on the underside.

Despite the hour, the overhead downlights are bright. And although I'm not alone, I've never felt more so. I can't drag my eyes from her body for long. The clicking of the clock keeps an ominous tab on the moments that pass, on the silence that her state and my madness bring.

Leaning forward to rest my elbows on my knees, I focus on the subtle movements of her lovely naked form flopped across my mattress like it used to be. But this time... she...

My eyes narrow on her.

She doesn't have anyone to blame but herself. *My baby...* She knows me better than this. Did she really think I was going to let her go back to him?

Bitch.

I growl at the word, despising its simple definition, its inadequacy, everything about it. Especially how it popped into my head while watching her deep in drugged slumber. She's not. She's not a bitch. Fuck no. She is the most incredible creature to ever indulge me. And all this time away from me, she's been festering with that last day... with the way I treated her.

But I hate that she didn't come back to me. She knew where I was. Anger surges through me. And I laugh cruelly because she is right... I am angry with her.

But not for what she did...

For her absence.

For her presence.

For letting him touch her.

For flaunting the thing I want more than anything in front of me, like I wouldn't tie it up and keep it.

I want to keep it.

My beautiful distraction.

She shone hope on my existence. I liked being someone else with her. How I became more... But without her, I don't want to be more. Without her, I have a place. Beside them. Protecting them. Making their lives better.

When my eyes fixate on the tan line on her ring finger, I clench my teeth to the point of pain.

Fuck.

I jump up, heading to the second bathroom. A whimper from the other side sounds as I turn the knob.

I open the door slowly and grin at the Italian fuck lying in the bathtub, bound with rope and gagged with black cloth. He flips around like a slug, trying to glimpse at me. Like he doesn't know exactly what I look like or what is going to happen. They must all know by now. Does my reputation not proceed me? I take a step inside, letting the door click closed at my back.

All I can think about are her curves as they wriggled beneath me when I fucked her deep. Fucked him out of her. She let me. Wanted it like that, I think. Now I can smell her perfect scent on me. And mine will be all over her.

I blink at him, not sure why I'm in this room right now. Tears have dried on my cheeks, leaving tight salty tracks in their wake.

I lower my head, glaring at him through my lashes, feeling tight and volatile. I sniffle, eyes trained on him.

The Italian fuck in the tub starts to whimper, eyeing me. The state I'm in. I bet... I bet it's terrifying. Deranged. I bet... I bet she was fucking terrified when I pierced her neck with that needle while her pussy still clung to my cock.

Another tear slips from my eye.

Grabbing a chair from beside the vanity, I drag it along the charcoal-coloured tiles to the side of the tub. As I twist it to sit on it backwards, hanging my arms over the backrest, he shuffles to face me. He stares at me like I'm the devil personified, begging with the whites of his eyes for a chance, for mercy.

I look from his wide eyes to the Mother Mary tattoo that wraps around his throat and remember how much I wanted to open The Mother up.

"You know the thing that makes the Butcher bird more deadly than other birds of prey is their ruthless pursuit when protecting their family. I get that. Protecting my family is what makes my blood pump... I have four brothers. You know me. *Us*," I say to him, my gaze glossy, my eyes red from the tears I shed over that moment in the bedroom. I look straight through him. "One of my brothers I have only just met. Missed his childhood. I'll never get that back." I point at him and wave my finger. "You might know him actually. His name is Konnor Slater. Your boss used to call him *son*. A long time ago. Then, get this, he paid to have him kidnapped. The only reason that makes sense is if he knew he wasn't his. A bastard boy with Butcher blood. We don't know if he knew that for sure... but we can't be sure he didn't either. So my beautiful brother spent four years locked in a sick fuck's basement. On your boss's orders. Any of this ringing a bell?" I glance towards the door, still being pulled back to her. I should tuck her in.

Hold her.

His muffled words draw me back to him.

I shake my head. "No. You don't talk. Just listen. I also have a sister. A beautiful, gentle sister-in-law. She is fucking sunshine, and she brings my family so much peace and joy." I lean towards him, feeling heat crawl up my neck, ready to take over and bring carnage. "Your boss hurt her. Now, if you think I'm messing around, I'm disappointed. If you think that when I remove your gag, I will listen to the slightest bullshit, that I am going to spare you pain, then consider this. In the room across the hall, I have drugged the love of my life. And I plan on dragging her sweet arse across the country with me. I plan on keeping her until she forgets I took her against her will. Until she forgives me for it. And if she doesn't forget, forgive, I'm keeping her anyway. If I can do that to her... what do you think I can do to you?"

I eye him for a long, patient moment.

"*Now*." I sit up straighter and lock eyes with him, ignoring the need to be beside her. To pretend she is holding me willingly in her sleep. Being my beautiful distraction from the beautiful world and its ominous place for me. "Where is Dustin Nerrock?" I ask. When I'm met with silence, I glare into his wide panicked eyes that scream a message. I dart my gaze to the gag in his mouth. I laugh coldly. "Sorry." Grabbing the black gag, I rip it from his mouth. "You were saying?"

"Jimmy will never approve of this!" He coughs the words out with a mouthful of spit and bile. "I have worked for Dustin for years. For Jimmy. I know Dustin and Jimmy are having a few issues, but they are family! We all are"

I grin, leaning back and folding my arms across my chest. Dustin and Jimmy are having issues, ay? Even though Jimmy played the whole attack on Cassidy down, the fact that Dustin disappeared after it always seemed off to me. If I was Jimmy, I'd have removed a finger and made everyone kiss and make up. He must have been unimpressed enough to banish Dustin... My grin grows at the thought. I bet Dustin hated that. "You aren't family though, are you?" I laugh. "Jimmy and I are. And, ah, well, the old boy doesn't like you very much at the moment, mate."

"What?" He blinks in a panic, and it's annoying that Jimmy's disappointment strikes more fear in him than mine. "I haven't done anything! Tell him."

I shrug, grinning harder now. "He thinks you took his diamonds and killed his nephew."

"The diamonds? Sal? *Madonna Mia*. Sal is dead? I didn't kill him! Fuck, Bronson. I didn't! You must believe me. I swear, I love Jimmy. I'd never do this."

I nod. "I believe you."

He stares blankly at me. "What?"

"I believe you," I say smoothly, but he's no fool. He knows that's not a good thing, given I bound him in a bathtub.

"I don't understand," he says, and I watch his throat roll slowly. "Wha—Why?"

"I know you didn't do it," I say, tilting my head. "Because I know who did it."

Tears burst from his eyes, knowing this is it. He's probably already concluded that I've gone rogue, but he's just waiting for the words. The words that will sign his death note. Because he knows I'd never let him live with this information. "*Who?*"

Still smiling, I announce, "I did."

His face turns ashen, my words having drained it completely of the crimson glow of living things. He doesn't even try to beg for his life at this point. He doesn't disrespect my intelligence by promising his silence, his loyalty. I like that. An honourable quality, indeed.

His eyes float to the wall over my head as if he can see the reaper appear, waiting for his moment and to the only definite of life —death. Brown terrified eyes move back to mine. "And my family?"

"Safe. If you tell me where Dustin is hiding out. You see, since he attacked my sister a few years ago, he's been like a ghost. We had people on him for a while. Last place we saw him... was here... with *you*."

He nods slowly, understanding or no longer listening. My stomach lurches. For a moment. I feel sadness for him. "Will you make it quick?" he asks, his voice hollow in his hopelessness.

I look over at the door, the image of her body on the other side flashing into my mind. "*Ish.*"

Reaching into my jeans pocket, I retrieve my cigar tin. "Cigar?" I say, displaying the content of the tin to him. "Romeo y Julieta?"

He nods. "Please."

I draw one out, place it in his mouth, and light it up. The ember flares as he sucks on it hard. Biting down on the cigar, he mutters around it, "He's back in the District. He's been hiding out in Stormy River. He's been importing, running his own scheme from the docking yard there —guns."

I stare blankly at him as my mind swarms with that message. *Back in the District...* How he got past our watchers, I have no idea. How he got past Jimmy's... "Without Jimmy?"

"Jimmy knows," he says, sucking the cigar smoke into his lungs enthusiastically.

We should know everything that happens in that city. How Dustin is importing without Clay's knowledge is damn near unbelievable... I smile in thought, not liking the scene being painted with betrayal and lies. Unless... my beautiful big brother *does* know...And his need for Dustin's political pull outweighs his responsibilities to us.

I soften my smile before it becomes too manic. "Why are Dustin and Jimmy having issues?"

He shakes his head. "My family... you guarantee they are safe?" he says, and I nod. "Dustin's pride was hurt when Jimmy sent him away. He's pissed Jimmy always favours Luca and you boys over him."

"It's because we're so pretty," I say, feeling content with the information he's shared. It's going to be even easier to turn them against each other, given their friendship is already on a knife's edge. Slowly, I get to my feet and pull the vanity drawer out. I grab the stainless-steel barber blade from within, flicking it open. "Any last words?"

He raises his eyes to meet mine, refusing to give the blade much of a look, fighting the urge to wallow. Something flickers in them, a hit of adrenaline that the loom of the blade stokes, perhaps. "Yes," he hisses. "Only that Jimmy always knows everything. *Everything.* He'll find out that you did this. You're all going to die. And then he'll take the girls you love so much, and he'll fuck them and bury them too."

I hear distant laughter in my head.

I laugh to its cadence.

Grinning, I take a fistful of his hair. He howls in pain. The cigar drops from his mouth; the ash floating to the tiles. Holding him within the white ceramic tub, I drag the blade through the Mother Mary, opening her guts and spilling his blood straight into the drain. He flops around, gargling on the bubbling of warm tacky fluid, which paints the entire tub and my jeans in its bright crimson colouring.

After a few minutes, I let go of his hair. His head hits the bloody pool. Usually, I would call our cleaners to take care of this mess, but no one who bears any name apart from Butcher can be trusted with what I'm doing here.

So, I clean it myself.

After I separate him into plastic garbage bags and stuff him into two suitcases, I shower, washing him from my skin with hot water and chlorhexidine. I don't want a trace of him on me when I am with her.

Naked, I wander into the bedroom, my skin still burning from the water, steam rising from my skin. I stand at the end of the bed, staring at her perfect body. She is more curvaceous than she was at sixteen, exceptionally so.

"THESE ARE THE BEST BITS. *I want them all.*"

AS I SLIDE in behind her, I pull the sheet up over us, thread my arms under and over her, and cross them at her breasts to hold her close. Feeling her breath through her spine, I squeeze my eyes shut, focused on the echoes of the peaceful existence she once offered me. "We leave in two hours, baby," I whisper into her ear.

CHAPTER NINETEEN

shoshanna

Present day

SWAYING, surrounded by darkness, my mind awakens to movement beneath me and the hum of a motor, but my eyelids are too weighted to rise. I try to lift my hand to touch the throbbing behind my eyes, but my limb feels heavy, as though stuck with glue to the soft sheets I have melted into. The elastic-like substance draws my skin and the fabric together, my attempt to part them seemingly useless.

I breathe meaningfully, feeling the inhale and exhale in a mechanical way that seems strange.

I open my mouth and my jaw aches as I work it, rolling the socket left and right in slow circles.

My body suddenly gyrates when the mattress lifts and drops. A bump, I think. My mind reaches for the answer through a strange fog that doesn't scare me but confuses me.

Realisation overwhelms me.

I'm in a car.

CHAPTER TWENTY

bronson

Present day

FOR THE PAST THREE HOURS, we have been on this red dirt back road. Nothing but a wasteland of small woody shrubs surround us. A plane so fucking straight, it feels as though just over the blurry horizon is the edge of the earth. I squint, focusing on the heat rising from the bitumen in the distance, on an impossible curve where the earth and sky collide.

Love it, but I can't wait to get back to them.

I miss my outlaw.

Miss my beautiful brothers.

I can feel the District in my bones; it's a part of me and my family. A city built with the bricks of our legacy and bonds, now prosperous only because the residents are revelling in the deals they made with the devil so many decades ago. With *us*.

"You crazy son of a bitch!" Shoshanna screams, and I wince. *Fuck*, she sounds pissed. I was coming to terms with my decision to take her, coming to peace with it, but the rage in her bark throws me straight back into that place of disdain.

I feel it like a knife dragging down my skin and yet, I'll do it again and again and again if it means I get to keep her. She'll laugh about it one day. I'm sure she will.

Steering the RV off the road, I mentally brace myself for what's coming. As I step outside and head to the door of the luxury motorhome, the quiet from within its sheet-metal walls seems unnatural given the screech from a few moments ago.

It would have been easier and quicker to fly her back home, but I can't get the fucking diamonds through customs, so that was out of the question.

"Calm down, baby," I say through the door. "Don't be mad." I wait with bated breath for her to respond. As I press my palms on either side of the door, I dip my head between them, straining to catch any hint of movement.

Did she fall back asleep?

I gave her two decent shots of ketamine and an antihistamine to extend her slumber, but she should be awake by now. I knock on the door. "Baby, you okay?" When I hear nothing more, I decide to go in and check on her, remembering that she gets *hangry* easily. "I'm coming in, okay?"

Just as I unlock the latch and swing the door open, something blunt hits me square in the forehead and I grunt from the shock of it. Gripping the throbbing part of my head, my vision blackens slightly, and I stumble backwards. *Damn, baby*. "Fuck," I mutter.

She flies past me.

Too quick for me to stop her.

Merely a blur of black as my vision tries to catch up with what I know in my mind is happening.

I hiss and bite back the shock, fight against the static behind my eyes, and leg it quickly after her, not wanting her to get dizzy and stumble. She shouldn't be running after that fucking trip.

"Where are you going?" I call out, slowly gaining focus on the woman sprinting into the wasteland. I feel relief when she slows down, her head darting from side to side, surveying the scenery. She stops dead in her tracks, looking out over the small twiggy shrubs that scatter the desert.

I stop too, watching her come to terms with the vast landscape. Above her, an eagle circles us. Clouds of dirt floats just above the earth in the wake of her feet.

"There is nowhere to go, Shosh," I mutter, and I can hear the remorse in my voice as though my vocal cords are all twisted. I approach her slowly, eyeing her small womanly shape surrounded by nothing but desolate space. Clutched tightly in her hand is a metal frying pan.

The culprit of my head lump.

Her long black hair dangles down to just above her backside, loose and wild and incredible. Bare feet covered in red dust shuffle with nervousness. Long shapely legs poke out from below the oversized black shirt she is wearing —my black shirt. "Did you really think I was going to let you go back to him?"

She twists to face me and my heart aches under her expression. Where I thought I'd see fierce eyes ready to go rounds with me, I see amber pools of sadness. Not what was I was expecting. "I'll never forgive you," she murmurs.

Her words snake through my veins, so I take a step towards her, feeling the urge to grab her throat and pull her to me. My jaw clenches, but a smile of optimism plays with my lips. "You will."

She shakes her head slowly, biding her time as she gazes at me with tempestuous sorrow. "*No.*"

Then she walks straight towards me. Past me. I turn my head, chasing the scent of her. She strolls casually back to the RV, climbs inside, and slams the door.

Fuck.

CHAPTER TWENTY-ONE

shoshanna

Present day

THE RV SLOWS after five hours of non-stop travel. Pulling the blinds aside and peering out the windscreen, I watch as we roll into a quaint but derelict campground still bordered by nothingness as far as the eye can see. Crossing my legs on the queen-sized bed, I drum my nails on my bare thighs.

I don't even have any clothes.

Turning back to the inside cabin, my eyes dance around the impressive space, taking in the sight of the obnoxiously elaborate furnishings, decorated with all the modern commodities anyone could ever desire.

Except a phone...

I need to check on Akila.

My stomach growls, heavily affected by the tranquilliser and empty for over twelve hours. Tightening my grip around the pan, I remind myself I have a weapon. Not that he'd ever hurt me. Not really.

At that thought, sadness swallows me.

What have you done to us, Bronson?

I wasn't there for him, there to show him he could be more. That a simple life with me was better than the one Jimmy had planned for him. I'm reminded of a conversation I had with Clay. We spoke about how Jimmy's world would seduce Bronson. How I could stop it... And here it is... His world of corruption and greed and taking what he wants... Drugging me. Kidnapping me. This is just a glimpse into what time and the likes of Jimmy Storm's influence can do to a passionate man like Bronson.

With his cool smile and indecently good looks, charming and deadly in nature, it is easy to see how Bronson has lived his life for the past decade. But he was always too full of love to become Jimmy. I thought he felt too deeply to take so cruelly what wasn't his to take. What was I thinking? That he would just let me in and then let me go... I was so stupid.

He fucked me, stripped me of my consciousness, and then robbed my freewill. *My Bronson?* And he doesn't know what he has done. Taking me away from Akila... What will Perry do? *God*, I shake my head, squeezing my friend, 'the pan,' again.

I look at the clock hanging above the closet and know that hundreds of miles away, Perry will be searching for me. I'm sure of it. How long do people have to be missing before the police are called? Days, I think.

Will Katie tell him?

Will she care?

A wave of nausea twists through my stomach.

Hunger flexes its claws inside me like a monster.

The door to the RV opens, and he steps inside, having to

duck his head and bend his large tattooed six-foot five frame down ever so slightly. Faded denim jeans and a brown belt sit low on his hips, while a black singlet hugs his defined muscular body. His tattoos lick up from beneath the fabric, wrapping around his muscles. And he's glistening with sweat from the West Australian climate.

Once standing inside, he straightens. His eyes train on mine, flashing for a moment with uncertainty.

"There are two floors," he says calmly, a grin lightly pulling at his lips. I stare at him deadpan. "You should see the stars from up there. It's like that day at the lookout —so clear you can almost grab them. You remember that day, baby?"

In absolute disbelief, I shake my head slowly.

Does he think this will blow over?

He drugged me!

"You drugged me! What did you think would happen, Bronson? Did you think I'd just jump into your arms, and we would fuck all the way back to the District?"

He raises a dark eyebrow and his lips twist, his intentions clear in his half grin. "A man can dream... but I have important business, baby. You have no idea what—"

"I have important business!" I screech, jumping to my feet, brandishing the pan in front of me to keep the distance between us. "I have a life! People who depend on me... patients. You got what you wanted; you got in my head! Why take me?"

He lowers his voice in warning, but it's strangled, as though he's drowning out his true passionate response. "Because this job is important."

"If it's so important, then why let me get in the way? Huh? Why kidnap me?" I bite out. "Just leave me alone. Go be the dutiful brother and son and heir."

A soft chuckle leaves him as he says, "You're not a kid, baby. I *lady*-naped you."

"Don't be cute." I sneer with derision, not letting that masculine, deep chuckle caress me the way I know it can. Stop it from flowing into my heart and curling my toes with its husky, deep melody and *fuck*...

Growling my displeasure over my weakness for him, I continue, "You could have just left me to miss you forever. Fucked me like I am the only woman on earth for you and left me to yearn for you, like I have for over a decade." My voice begins to wobble through weighted breaths. "I cried myself to sleep every night for years and years, hoping you would come for me. I gave up. I gave in. I thought you hated me." I bite back the memories but feel them swarming me like bees, their painful stings embedding in my skin. "You must hate me to have done this to me. Why do this when you knew I'd hate *you* for it? Is this payback? For what I did?"

"Because!" he roars, opening his arms wide. "I was angry! Because the thought of him touching you made me crazy, because it is worse than your hate and I can't concentrate on my job while imagining all the ways you were letting him fuck you."

My heart jumps into my throat.

Blinking at him in disbelief, my pulse now an erratic tattoo between my ears, I watch him tighten and shake. He's only ever yelled at me once before... And it reminds me of a dream I had recently... *No*, not a dream. It was the sound of his throaty cries from last night.

And his tears...

So many tears.

I suddenly remember the feel of them on my face as I drifted off. Looking at him now, my hands twitch with the need to hold him in his torment. The torment caused by the decision to violate my trust and *fuck*, I still want to hold him through it all. I fight that pull between us.

Taking a step backwards, I encourage further distance between us. His fixed stare drops to watch my feet shuffle. My rejection squeezes a tiny grimace from him, but instead of turning away like I thought he might, he takes large strides towards me until I am pressed between his chest and the wall of the RV.

I inhale sharply at the pressure.

As he removes the pan from my grasp, I glance down and see a distinct phone-shaped bulge in his pocket. I wonder... if I can get him to relax enough, if I'll be able to grab it. I divert my eyes before he notices where my attention is.

One of his hands moves to grip my hip while the other meets my cheek. Combing his fingers through my hair, he lifts the long strands up, touching them to his nose. He closes his eyes as he inhales.

They flash open again, and their intensity pins me to the wall. "Are you going to run outside and misbehave if another car pulls up to this campsite, baby?"

Yes. I shake my head slowly. My hands ball into fists at my sides, duelling between the urge to either caress his chest or slap his cheek. "No. They could be just as dangerous as you are."

A deep, gravelly laugh expels from him. Little nervous giggles burst from me, but I swallow them down, not liking how easily he drew them from me or how foreign they sounded.

"I assure you," he mutters next to my ear, the warmth of his breath blanketing the skin along my throat. "They are *not.*"

A long moment passes.

And I think about his phone. Think about who I would

even call and how I would explain what happened. How I would explain I don't want to call the police. That I just want to get back to Akila. To check on my patients.

And forget *he* ever came to Darwin.

Forget I love him.

"Baby," he whispers, drawing me to him. "You're hungry. I can tell. I'm going up to the top deck to make you something. I'd like it if you joined me up there."

"We are not on holiday together, you nutcase," I growl, arching my neck to glare at him. "We are—"

"Stuck here," he says with a smirk. "Stuck together."

"Forced. I was forced."

"I regret nothing."

Shaking my head slowly, I allow a knowing smile to pull at my lips. "I don't believe that for a second. I heard you crying last night."

"I wasn't crying because I took you, baby. Or because I drugged you. I was crying because I had to." Releasing me from the cage of his body, he pushes off the wall and steps back, eyeing me thoughtfully. "I'm barbecuing. And you are—" His phone chimes in his pocket and he beams brightly, his dimple creating a divot beside his boyish grin, and for a moment, he looks like my Bronson. "Sorry, baby. Gotta make a call first. I'll meet you up there. Or I'll come down and drag your sweet arse up those stairs myself."

I lean against the wall, watching him as he takes the ladder up to the top level with that bright smile on his face. And goddamn-it, if I don't take the bait, wanting to know what has the nutcase so pleased with life.

"*Fuck*," I grumble under my breath as soon as I decide to follow him up. Huffing out my irritation, I climb to the top of the RV.

My breath catches at the sight of the sky above, enclosing us in a dark, glistening dome. "*God.*"

"This is the closest you'll ever be to him," Bronson says, smiling at me with his phone pressed to his ear. I peer around the second level, my eyes scanning the barbecue, the telescope, and the hot tub in the corner. Steam rises from it. Bubbles simmer away.

What the fuck?

He is out of his goddamn mind if he thinks I am just getting in there with him as if we are on our fucking honeymoon or some bullshit.

"Outlaw!" I hear him say, pulling my gaze back to him. I watch as he dips to turn the gas canister on before lighting the barbecue. "In a few days. I have a present for you." He turns. Gazing at me, he grins. His eyes and the sideways curve to his lips both sing of mischief. "Yeah. You remember when we watched *Aladdin*?" He pauses for a moment and my eyes widen, locked on his. "Well," he says smoothly. "I bumped into Princess Jasmine. And let me tell you, she is ..." His stark, turquoise-coloured eyes soften on my face, provoking tears to swell within mine. I fight their invasion. "*Beautiful.* And frog me, she wants to meet you, Outlaw."

When I hear a little girl squeal through the phone, my heart nearly stops dead in my chest. Does he have a daughter? No. *No.* Shaking my head, I feel a cramp move through me. I swallow hard, forcing down the image of the future we promised each other all those years ago. A future he has with another woman. I suddenly feel light-headed, my legs buckling under the weight of this new information.

"WHY DO *you like this movie so much, baby?*"

"*How can I not? Jasmine is the only Disney princess who looks remotely like me. And she is so fierce. She just wants to run away from her life and be part of a whole new world. I get her."*

OH MY GOD.

I hear the girl squeal again. And I think about her mother... No. I can't. I have Perry. I left. I can't lose my mind over this. I grip the edge of the railing. Opening my mouth, I suck thick air in. Air that doesn't want to be inside me. My heart doesn't either, thrashing around, ready to explode.

Just breathe, Shoshanna.

I move to sit at the table while he hollers and laughs with the little girl on the other end of the phone, animated and annoying in his adorability.

My heart hurts so fucking much.

When my gaze lands on an outdoor fridge, glowing with internal fluorescents, I grab a bottle of wine and a chilled glass and pour myself a drink to numb the memories.

Nearly thirty minutes later, the bottle is half empty. Or half full, according to Bronson Butcher. I chuckle at that thought —the sound once again... strange given the situation I have found myself in.

My head feels a little fuzzy.

He finishes cooking on the barbecue; it seems he's been told to let the girl on the phone go to bed. Tucking the handset into his back pocket, he walks a salad and marinated chicken over to the table.

He is visibly calmer, and I'm in awe of him and her and that expression on his face right now. I always knew he would make a wonderful father.

I quell the sob that wants to move up my throat. "You have a daughter?"

He lets out a deep chuckle, shaking his head at me. "No, baby. Calm down. That's Maxipad's little girl."

Well, *fuck.*

Calm soars through me when it shouldn't. His admission to not having a wonderful life with a daughter he adores shouldn't bring me relief. I always was so incredibly possessive of him. I stifle my pleased sigh by sipping more wine. "What?" I force a light chuckle. "You mean Max Butcher let someone get close enough to have a daughter with him?"

"Only one person." Bronson slides in opposite me, eyes glued to mine, just like they always are. "Yeah."

"Wow." Ignoring his eyes on me, I peer out over the horizon, feeling a strange wave of something move through my stomach, settle there, sink in deep. Jealousy, I think. Jealous another woman is part of their lives, in the way I almost was. I glance back at him while he watches me with that thoughtful gaze. "What's her name?"

"Whose, baby? Cassidy is Max's wife," he says. "And Kelly is my little outlaw. She's three."

"*Kelly.*" I smile through a soft sigh. I sip more wine, needing it, needing it to numb the feelings as they spread with the warmth of the liquid inside me. "You named her," I state, and it isn't a question. I know he did.

"I WANTED *to name Xander after Ned Kelly. But Maxipad wanted to name him Xander, the defender of man."*

"*And you can't say no to Max. Ever. Can you?"*

HE SMILES ROGUISHLY. "She is excited to meet you, by the way."

I blink at him. The warm Australian breeze sweeps across

us like a caress. "That wasn't fair. The Princess Jasmine thing. You're not playing fair."

Looking at him now, I can tell he's proud of her —of Kelly. Of Max. I can see a sparkle in his eyes, a satisfaction, a level of peace.

Peace.

I remember that in his eyes, too.

There was a time when I brought him peace.

But of course, knowing Max has someone to hold him would bring Bronson just as much happiness as having someone himself. He is the most selfless person for his family. And I was his fucking family too. "I never thought you'd hurt me like the way you did last night. You betrayed my trust."

He nods. Just like that. "Eat your chicken."

Despite my discomfort and sadness, my stomach shifts around, rippling with hunger. So I do eat. And of course, it is amazing. We sit under the stars without a single sound besides the clicking of the crickets, the croaking of the frogs, and the bubbling of the hot tub.

As my mind falls into a nice, inebriated state, allowing for the quiet to ignite the world, bring it to life. It fills my ears with noise —subtle ones that are usually subdued. I like them. With no buzzing, shuffling of feet, or voiceovers, I think about poor old Gwen by the window, wishing for a bit of this active quiet. I think about Akila locked up inside while the nurse Perry hired watches television. I think about Perry looking for me... Think about him ignoring Akila. Think about him planning to have her put into a home in my absence.

I look at Bronson as he eats his food. His eyes are trained on me while I'm deep in thought. I know I should tell him. But if I tell him, then he'll know... then I'll know. I'll have said it out loud. That she is the main reason I am still with Perry. And yet, I don't trust him with her. To do what is best for her. Unless he has me. I'm the currency. As the truth swarms through me, I blink at Bronson. He has to let me go back to her...

"I have to go back," I whisper.

His smooth grin twitches. "To Dr Clean?"

"To Akila."

He chuckles. "Nice try. She'll be fine, baby. She doesn't enjoy being coddled if I remember correctly."

"No." I shake my head, the image of my fiercely independent sister before her accident crashing into my mind. Is she living in her own perpetual hell right now? Dependant. Half alive and half asleep. I blink at the stars, feeling waves of emotion wash over me, an immense crash of whitewash hitting me before I say the words. "Akila has brain damage, Bronson. She has corresponding paraplegia. She was in a car crash."

I tear up. I don't know why. Don't know why it is happening, given the real Akila was taken from me so long ago. I haven't shed a single tear in years, but now they begin to burst from me. As I try to stop the strangled sobs that tighten my throat, Bronson slides over to my side. He scoops me up and sits me on his lap, where I curl into him instead of fighting him off.

"Tell me what happened," he demands, tightening his hold on me, big, tattooed arms twitching with possessiveness.

I rub my tears against his chest, allowing my grief to seek comfort in his arms. Allowing the wine to inebriate the part of me that should slap him for touching me after the shit he pulled. "They hit a tree on a back road," I say. "Dad went through the window. He died. But... *Akila*. She was still belted in when people arrived at the scene. They say she hit her head on the window. I knew Perry..." I swallow hard, not wanting to tell Bronson we were already dating at this point. "I knew Perry already. He was my boss. My Attending. And my ... friend. I was a medical student then. It was too much for me...

"They all wanted to switch off her life support. But she was all I had. The last of my family. I couldn't. I couldn't do it. Couldn't be responsible for ... *more*. Perry supported us. He supported my decision to keep her alive even though I some-times wish... Sometimes I wish I had switched it off." Guilt seeps through me. Without her, I would be free to *be*... But mainly because I should have let her go then. Shouldn't have needed to keep her alive to satiate a part of me that couldn't be responsible for another death. I should have let her go while she was still *her*. No decision would have been without guilt.

His nose touches my forehead. "Why do you say that?"

"Because I had no idea what her life would be like... now," I admit for the first time. "It's not much of a life."

"Hers or yours?" he asks, and a pang of pain flares through me. *Both, you arsehole! Her disabilities have become my shackles. Are you happy? I am all she has!* I slide from his lap, my eyes darting to the phone in his pocket. When I look back up, he's staring straight at me.

I clench my teeth together. "I will get back to her."

He smiles, but it isn't nice. "To *him*."

Shaking my head, disappointment and sadness duel within me. "I thought you were angry at me. When I came to see you, I thought I was meeting that boy in the park. I used to have nightmares about him. About where he was. How he felt. I wanted to talk to him. To find closure. To cuddle him one last time... But he's gone. Isn't he? You are too far down

Jimmy Storm's rabbit hole to see that your actions aren't normal. That life isn't yours to stomp on. That you can't take people without consent."

I turn from him and climb down to the first floor. He doesn't follow me down or call out after me, so I settle into the bed and stare at the RV's wall.

CHAPTER TWENTY-TWO

shoshanna

Present day

WRIGGLING AROUND ON THE BED, I can sense the hour by the sounds of the lively quiet. The RV isn't moving. No lights flicker above my eyelids. It's night-time again.

Between the wine and the sleep deprivation I have found myself in over the past several years of living and breathing medicine, of caring for Akila, I have accepted slumber like an old friend. And why fucking not? Having nothing to do and nowhere to go, why not accept a place to hide from the contradictory emotions in my reality? Why not welcome the pull and escape of sleep?

Now, as my mind flickers to life, I can tell it's been an entire day since I told him about Akila. He didn't wake me up, but the two times my mind pulled me from slumber, there was food on the bedside table. My health is obviously important to him, but my freedom, not so fucking much. *Nutcase.*

When my body feels a kind of warmth move through it, I sense him close by. The scent of man and the prickling of my skin all but shout his proximity. I open my eyes to a dimly lit area and roll to my side; the blankets shift around my naked body as I do. Was I naked when I went to sleep last night? Yes, I decide that I was.

Squinting around the space, I find him sitting on the couch opposite me. A lamp beside him illuminates the RV. Leaning forward, he sets his elbows on his knees and clasps his hands beneath his chin. He watches me.

"Are you with him because of her or do you love him?" he asks, his voice low and steady. Pained.

The words beat our last conversation back into my mind, reminding me of my confessions and tears. *Sleep.* I wish I could just sleep again. Feeling awake, feeling his dangerous heat even at this distance, like a living thing circling me, I can't even pretend I'm still tired.

"He's a good man," I say, attempting to lift my heavy hand to rub my eyes only to find it... resisting? Pulled back? I reach my other hand out to grab my wrist but find that one restrained too. I tug at them, feeling one pull the other as I attempt to move.

Growling in confusion, I twist around.

Then it hits me.

The crazy son of a bitch!

"What the fuck have you done?" My breathing jolts and races and skips. The more I raise my arms, the more I feel how they pull each other apart. A rope threads under the frame and knots at each wrist, limiting my movement.

"You want my phone, baby? So you can call that good man to come rescue you from me. The bad guy, right?"

Shit.

I can't find the words.

He narrows his glowing green-blue eyes in a predatorial way, reminding me of the way he looked at me the night he drugged me. "I've changed in the last ten years," he says, looking at my wrists and smiling. "My tastes have changed. If it's any consolation, I would have tied you up even if you were here willingly. The rope would be fluffier though."

I sneer. "It's no consolation."

"I haven't had any complaints yet, baby."

For reasons unbeknown to me, I hate that sentence most of all. Hate the way it awakens that volatile little beast inside me that screams he is *mine*. "I'm complaining now," I lie. Wait. What? Not lie. I *am* complaining.

"Well, you always were the exception." Deep, turquoise-coloured eyes stay fixed on mine, every fleck inside them a definable shape and colour. "You're so beautiful, Shoshanna," he says. "You'll forgive me one day."

"I won't," I bite out. "I'll never ever trust you again."

His gaze bounces pointedly from my tight scowl to my bound wrists and back again. "*Baby...* you're gonna have to."

I blink at him. *Fuck.* No. I shake my head. I tug at the ropes again, even though I know deep into my soul that he would never hurt me. Fear doesn't stir me, but butterflies race around deep in my abdomen. "Would you let me leave if I cried? If I begged? If I screamed?"

A devilish grin engulfs his face. "Try me." Standing, he reaches for the hem of his shirt. Lifting it over his head, he slowly exposes taut tattooed abdominals. He tosses the shirt aside, leaving only a pair of jeans, which hang so low I can see the distinct V of his muscles at the top of his pubic hair.

My mouth waters at the sight of perfect masculinity. A

truly impure display that provokes my every cell to vibrate against my will.

The butterflies multiply.

My heartbeat intensifies.

My resolve becomes rickety.

Bronson watches me as he reaches back and retrieves a black handgun from the back of his jeans. I breathe in deeply as he places it flat on the cabinet. It makes a small clicking sound when the metal meets the glass.

I had no idea it was there.

Though, I'm not entirely surprised.

Maybe I can get the gun...

I track him as he strolls casually to the bedside. Pulling out a drawer, he grabs a lighter from within.

"Don't fight me, baby," he orders. "I know you're a lioness. I think he may have caged you. I don't want to cage you... I want my wild girl back. But I *really* want to spend tonight making my lioness *purr*. Making her remember."

God.

He moves around the room, lighting several candles; the flickering of the flame matches the ticking of my heart — both moving and dancing in the wake of his actions. He switches the lamp off, and the dim swallows my rational thoughts just like it swallows the light.

I can still see him, illuminated in an orange glow. As I tug on the restraints, he crawls up the bed, kneeling on either side of my hips.

The intensity in his eyes... *kills* me.

He grins. "I'm nothing if not a romantic... now, baby. Ready to purr for me?"

I nod...

What?

I fucking nodded!

Jesus Christ, Shoshanna!

Dragging the blankets away from my naked flesh, he lets out a long hiss as he stares at my exposed body. I'm panting now under his almost tangible gaze. I expect him to touch me, but he doesn't.

As he reaches down to unbutton his jeans and pulls out his cock, my eyes widen. Even in his big hand, it looks heavy and thick. "See what you do to me, baby?"

God.

He strokes his length in a long, slow rhythm, squeezing hard at the base and drawing upwards with a groan. The vision of his tattooed abdomen tensing and the sound of the rumbles from his throat, have me shuddering and writhing between his knees. I lick my lips.

His hand picks up pace. Scorching me, his eyes move around my nipples, drop to my belly, and back up to my face, where he snares me. "*Shoshanna.*"

"*Bronson.*" I breathe his name as my pussy pulses at the space within, wanting him, but all the while my mind fills with shame and despair over what he draws so easily from me.

Raw groans spill from him. "*Fuck*, baby. Look at my cock while I come. While I come all over your perfect tits."

I watch in desperately aroused awe.

The candles glow. The flames' silhouettes dance across his body. His eyes glaze over, losing focus as his hips jerk against his fist and its messy and primal and hot as fuck.

Then he slides up my torso. Thrusting his cock between my breasts, he squeezes each plump mound together with his hands. He fucks my breasts with virility and indecency and desperation that is so sexy, I fight the bat of my lashes, not wanting to miss a second. Shuddering within moments, he shoots cum across my lips and cheeks. The warmth hits

186 · NICCI HARRIS

me, but his grunts and growls of vulnerable pleasure hit me harder.

I moan with him.

As his hand slams into the bed beside me, he leans forward and pants through the sensation of his orgasm, making me desperate to feel that good. He looks so delicious, so erotic. I can almost taste him on my tongue.

When he gains enough composure to lean back on his heels, he gazes down at my cum painted face with that big wide Bronson Butcher grin.

"*Beautiful*," he mutters, before crawling down the mattress, his lips skimming the entire length of my body as he goes. I suck a sharp breath in when heat floats across my pussy.

My cheeks burn as I can almost feel his stare on that part of me. Knowing I'm dripping, I just blush harder. Fingers touch the swelling flesh and slide around. Moaning with neediness, my hips seek more.

"*Fuck.*" He groans, and then his tongue slides up from my arsehole to my clit. I buck at the sensation, so primed, so prepped, so ready for him that the slightest attention may send me spiralling into agonising bliss.

One more slow lick.

Another.

My back arches up and I let out a long-anguished moan. I roll around, my backside sliding in his hands. It's too much. Too little. *God.* It's perfect torture.

Another lick.

And another.

Then his mouth is on me, kissing and mouthing my pussy like he would my lips and ... *fuck.*

Fuck.

I try to reach for his hair, wanting to grab at the strands, gain some kind of control, but the ropes won't allow it.

Shifting his weight, he pulls his lips back and pushes two fingers inside of me. I stare down at him as he works them in and out. His gaze meets mine from between my knees, his lips a glistening smirk. When he makes a show of licking my juices from them, the soft muscles circling his skilled fingers contract and squeeze. *Fuck.*

"I want to hear you purr," he says. "And I won't let you come until you do. I want to see your back curve. Tits jiggle. Hips roll." I let out a moan. My pelvis lifts on its own accord. "That's good. Good girl. Give me more. I want your pussy in the shape of my fingers tonight."

My eyes roll shut as he massages the nerves throbbing within me. It is a battle for dominance. He is without a doubt winning, rubbing me so precisely, the stimulation is sending me out of my mind. My leg jerks as heat boils in my belly and tingles spread to my toes.

"Look at me, baby," he demands.

I lift my weighted, dazed eyes open to find heated green-blue flames within his. As a dark shadow of possessiveness moves into his eyes, he jolts up to grab my throat. His fingers twist against the pulsing rhythm of my pussy, setting me off completely. "No one can save you from me, baby, because—" He grunts with the onslaught of his fingers, puncturing me with each word as he growls, "You. Are. Mine. Even your breath. Mine. Say. It."

My world spins as I whimper, "*I'm. Yours.*"

He leans down and licks inside my panting lips, lightly squeezing the column of my neck, forcing my sounds of tormented bliss to vibrate within his grip —forcing me to *purr.*

I come hard around his thrusting fingers.

* * *

The night is long, while I slip in and out of a broken slumber, having slept far too long during the day. I lay on my back, arms out wide, still restrained. Bronson's head is tucked into my neck. He breathes heavily in his sleepy condition. His arms band my center, his leg bend over me so he can fit on the bed.

My misguided fingers twitch with the need to caress his hair, but I can't, because the crazy fucker tied me to his goddamn bed! I growl, but he is completely out of it, not even stirring. The world is no longer on his shoulders, weighing down his decisions. I look at the gun on the cabinet opposite us, considering my choices. Because they are mine. Not his.

I could pretend. Could feign forgiveness. Get my hands on that gun or the phone and call... *Perry.*

I run that scenario over in my head, bounce it around and feel Perry's disappointment like a lead weight, even in my own illusion. Feel him coddling me, treating me like a victim.

I've now cheated on him.

Twice.

And so he'll call it rape. He'll make me feel *dirty*... That is easier than accepting the fact that maybe I didn't resist with all my heart. That my consent was in every movement I made, every moan, every pulse of my pussy.

I peer down at Bronson in his gentle state. My gaze dances around his tattoos. So many. Overlapping. Colours splashed everywhere.

My eyes snag on the one on his side, the one I refused to let myself look at. A large colourful depiction of Anubis, the jackal-headed warrior, runs from his hip to just under his ribcage. Wings of colour in orange, red, and amber, paint the sun behind him.

It is beautiful.

"So why does he have our Anubis on his torso?" my inner Akila asks. *"It's larger than his Butcher bird tattoo. Larger than the word Butcher on his neck."*

Akila was obsessed with the god. Anubis wasn't just the God of the undead, but often painted as the guide for lost souls, living and dead. He specialised in helplessness. He took care of the fragile ones after they die.

I exhale on a sigh, wondering what meaning it has to him. Maybe something to do with death? Jimmy Storm and his Family. An Egyptian tattoo could represent me in some way. Maybe? Us?

Then I know.

My stomach contracts.

Helplessness... I squeeze my eyes shut at the memory of being dragged from my house. Of being thrown in my dad's car. I grind my teeth in my discomfort, fighting the images. But they beat through me anyway. I fight them while watching him sleep, knowing he is beside me now... *no longer angry at me.*

Eventually, slumber returns to my reach.

CHAPTER TWENTY-THREE

shoshanna

Present day

I WRING MY HAIR OUT, twisting the long dark tendrils until water seeps out and slides down my naked body. The RV is moving, but there is barely any jarring to its motion. I can feel the humming beneath my feet, but the drive itself is smooth and even.

Wandering back into the main area, I glance around the space before lingering on the bed. At the rope that lies beside it.

Warmth settles in my stomach.

I guess I like the rope too, Bronson, you nutcase.

Sighing, I think about how it wasn't wrapped around my wrists when I woke up. Think about how he wasn't beside me. I wish that didn't bother me. Scooping up the shirt he wore yesterday, I pull it on.

Sitting on the couch, I draw the blinds back and notice

we have left the rural outback and are moving through urban streets. I blow out fast, knowing my time to make a break for it looms, and for some reason I hate that I'm no longer without a choice.

But I need to get back to Akila.

All I have to do is hit him with the pan again, make a break for it, run to anyone in the street, tell them what happened. Then... well, then I call Perry. Shaking my head at myself, I sigh. Last night I truly accepted the burden of feeling trapped —tied to Perry by circumstance... not by love. The thought won't leave now, having made a nest deep inside my resolve, where it wants to fester. But I don't have time for it now; my sole focus needs to be on getting back to Akila not wallowing on what happens once I have. What does it all mean... Bronson and I and the Anubis tattoo and ... I force those questions back —*she* needs me.

The thought knots my stomach.

The RV pulls into a service station, parking alongside a small playground. I jump to my feet and rush to the kitchen, grab the pan and clench it between my fingers. I squeeze it so tight, willing myself to keep it held high, ready.

I think about the needle going into my neck.

That crazy son of a bitch.

Think about waking up bound.

That crazy son of a bitch.

Think about him... *think about the Anubis tattoo.*

I place the pan back on the counter, my hand slowly slipping from it. When the door opens and he steps in, I am still blinking at the shiny cooking implement that was my weapon.

When I turn, he is standing tall and cool, eyeing me knowingly with a sideways smile that melts my heart. I step in front of the pan, in a completely inelegant and obvious way.

When he moves closer to me, I crane my neck to keep his line of sight. My breath gets caught in my throat as he leans forward, his body temperature like fire, his hand disappearing behind me. I think he is going to grab me and pull me to him, and I wait expectantly, closing my eyes.

Then his warmth leaves me.

My eyes snap open to find him holding the pan.

He offers it to me. "You might want to keep hold of this," he says with a deep chuckle.

"I don't need a pan to hit you," I say straight away. My narrowed gaze is suddenly drawn to his torso. His broad masculine body is sporting a white t-shirt with a cartoon snowman with buck teeth and eyes too close together.

A Disney shirt.

Text scrawled across one chest says, 'Olaf you a lot'.' I cover my smile, but my eyes give the size of it away. "What are you wearing?" I say into my palm. I drop my hand, forcing my grin to yield. "Is he the silly little snowman from *Frozen?*"

His chin rises with pride, his lips tick at one corner. "This is my favourite shirt, baby. And don't call Olaf silly. He knows what loyalty is. What love looks like. And even though he might fucking melt, he still wants to know the warmth of the flame. He takes on an ice monster... Baby, the dude is a badarse."

I stifle my smile once again.

Bronson studies the shirt on my body, hanging loose just above my knees. "You can borrow any of my shirts except this one," he says, pointing at the 'Olaf you a lot' shirt.

He eyes me a little longer, the laps of his gaze like a tongue moving across my skin. I squeeze my thighs together.

He grins wider. "I like you in my shirts, but right now, I need you in something more... *appropriate*."

I lift a brow at him, my expression unimpressed. "I don't have anything *more appropriate*. I didn't exactly pack for my lady-napping."

He nods, his expression shifting instantly to one more serious. "I need you to ride up front with me. And I need you to behave. Wear what I tell you to wear. Do not speak. Do not look anyone in the eye."

A shiver rushes over my spine at his words.

His tone.

Fumbling for a reply, I come up blank. I simply follow him as he walks to the cupboard, watching as he pulls out a short black dress. Only it isn't quite a dress. Scrolling the boning and lace and silk, I figure the material covers every-thing but definitely balances on the cusp of too short. It completely stomps on the cusp of flashing half my breasts. I scoff. It's definitely not '*more appropriate.*'

"You're out of your goddamn mind if you think I'm wearing that!" I state, feeling anger wrap itself around my body, covering me better than that 'dress' will.

He says nothing.

With a smirk playing around his face, he lays the dress down on the mattress and pulls out a pair of knee-high leather boots with at least a six-inch wedge. As his silence stretches, furthering my unease, I scowl at him. He moves to a drawer where he retrieves a thin, sparkly black headband.

No.

Not a headband.

A necklace...

A fucking collar.

I see red.

Vibrating with rage, I hiss through locked teeth, "Who

the hell do you think I am to you, you fucking maniac? I'm not a goddamn dog!" *Where is my fucking pan!* I spin to search for it, but the words he uttered yesterday still me.

'I've changed in the last ten years... My tastes have changed'.

Suddenly, the image of beautiful girls willingly wearing that collar for him flash behind my eyes. Obedient girls. Girls who submit to his every whim. The vision of them and him makes me want to slap them and him and put the collar around his fucking neck, parade him around so they all know who *he* belongs to.

God...

I breathe out fast.

Exhaling my jealousy and disdain, hating the way it suffocates me, I say, "I am not one of your slutty, moronic girlfriends, Bronson. I am not here willingly. I am not your submissive. I am not a whore. I am not—"

"You're not, baby," he interrupts, eyeing me with amusement, making me want to slap that gorgeous face again. "I heard you. You're not."

"I'm a doctor," I say, as though that title holds weight despite his grinning face, provoking me to want to stomp like a child. I can't be a doctor and wear that.

He chuckles softly. "I know you are."

"Forget it," I say, shaking my head adamantly. "I'm not wearing that fucking dress or that" –I point to the leather band in his big hand– "*thing.*"

He gazes down at the collar fondly, stroking the leather sensually, the genuine sexuality in his touch and eyes resonating at the delta between my thighs. *Fuck.* My heart begins to beat at an erratic tempo. "This *thing*... is to protect you, baby," he says, looking up at me.

Trying to hold my resolve, I fight the fantasy of his fingers stroking me between my folds in a similar slow and meaningful way. I glance at his Olaf shirt but it does very little to dampen his sex appeal. In fact, it just makes him even more of an enigma.

Clearing my throat, I say, "Does that crap usually work on girls?"

I can see why...

He smirks, his dimple moving into the space above his soft, charismatic curve. His eyes move between the leather and my neck where he can probably see the racing of my pulse through the thin sheath of skin. "They don't usually *need* convincing."

I glare at him, feeling venomous jealousy boiling within me. "How is that going to protect me?"

He steps towards me. "Because where we are going, this means no one can speak with you. No one can question you. No one—"

"So," I cut in, "it protects you!"

"Baby." He tilts his head, his eyes a soft vortex of sensuality and intrigue and goddamn his level of hotness. "No one will care that I lady-napped you."

Shaking my head slowly, I take a step backwards. "How is that even possible?"

He moves until I am pressed against the wall of the RV, his body a dangerous frame crowding me. "Trust me."

I arch my neck to meet his scorching green-blue eyes. "Never," I whisper. As he reaches up, wrapping the leather behind my neck, I squeeze my eyes shut under the intensity of his gaze. I hear him hiss as he circles my slender column and fastens the collar together at my throat.

I open my eyes to find his full of hunger.

"You're going to have to," he whispers in my ear. And I almost melt into a puddle at his feet. Knowing I don't have a choice, believing I don't have a choice, ignoring the fact I may have a choice, I walk into the bathroom. Over at the mirror, I stare at the collar. I hate it.

I touch the leather.

Hate it.

He appears behind me and rubs his groin into my backside. I moan at the feel of his thick length between my cheeks.

"*This* is what that *thing* and you do to me." He dips his lips to my neck. His tongue lashes out to lick the leather, his breath heavy with arousal on my skin. Lifting his head to stare at me in the mirror, he says, "Will you wear it, baby? For your own protection?"

I stare at myself again, taking in my partly dry darkbrown hair cascading down my shoulders and the glow on my cheeks. I look a little wild. *Who are you?*

I'm surprised when my reflection nods. "*Yes.*"

He moves away from me and disappears into the rear of the RV. I fix my hair while in a trance of confusion, contradictory emotions mingling inside me. Uncertainty, yes. But also, happiness. Joy. I feel like I can play for the first time in years. That it doesn't mean I don't want to be a doctor. Doesn't mean I don't take life seriously. I take life very seriously... for the past eleven years, every decision I have made has been...constructive. Safe.

I glance down at my finger, bare without my engagement ring sitting heavy on it like a ball and chain, like the shackle I now realise it is and with Akila and a baby one day, I might as well be sinking to the bottom of his ocean. Looking back at my refection, I stare at the collar wrapped around tanned skin. It feels less controlling than the ring. God, I'm going mad.

He makes me crazy.

Always has.

Once my hair is done, I get the rest over with. As I slide into the skin-tight black dress, the boning frames around my torso and narrow waist, pushing up my breasts, accentuating my already generous mounds. The swell of each noticeably rises and falls with each breath. If I were to wear something like this with Perry, he would surely use it as a reason to undermine me. My actions. My feelings. My ability as a doctor. His actions always seemed to come from a place of support and kindness, of concern, but I often feel that he likes me best when I am low and confused or acting 'up'.

I am his damsel in distress.

He is our hero —mine and Akila's.

Perry likes boxes. Everyone should fit into a neat little box, sealed so the contents will never change or be tainted, then tied with a pretty bow. I can't possibly be a doctor and enjoy the adventurous sexuality of a man like Bronson Butcher. My dad's words the day before I broke Bronson's heart hammer into my mind. *'That's the worst part of all though... isn't it? What does this say about you? Loving a psychopathic boy like him.'*

Perry and my dad would have liked each other.

After sliding the boots on, I step out into the back of the RV to find Bronson wearing black suit pants, a white shirt, and suspenders like a 1920s gangster might. I don't fight my smile, feeling a shudder when his eyes heat at the sight of me.

A long, deep rumble comes from within his chest, forcing my lips to part and my knees to buckle. "This is going to be hard," he says with a smirk, reaching down to stroke his cock through his slacks. And where I thought I'd feel embarrassed and undermined, I feel strangely empowered in this outfit.

I step towards him, and he lowers his gaze to meet mine.

Getting within an inch of his lips, I breathe against them. "I will run the first chance I get."

"Well," he says, brushing his lips along mine, "I best not give you any chances then."

Slowly, I walk towards the door and smile when it opens. Heat scorches my back, informing me of his intense gaze. I step out of the carriage and jump into the passenger seat, crossing my legs, the leather from my boots rubbing together, the sound coursing through me in an uncomfortably arousing way.

He slides into the driver's side, and we take off. His gun is visible in the center console, and I wonder what would happen if I lunged for it. Wonder if I would have time to draw it on him before he simply snatched it from my grasp.

I expect the feel of his eyes on me, but he is oddly still. Focused. Even though his mien seems nonchalant and cool, I notice the tight grip he has around the steering wheel.

Nerves thrash through me.

As soon as we entered the District's streets, I feel a tidal wave of melancholy and sorrow hit me. As though the sixteen-year-old version of myself was left at the City's limits and is now back inside me. Intense feelings rise to the backs of my eyes. Pin pricks of heat tease behind them.

The last time I was here, I destroyed him and a part of us. I try to stifle my sobs, but when I turn to hide my glossy eyes from him, I catch sight of a black van tailgating us.

The tears dry up.

I watch the ominous vehicle following the RV for a few kilometres before I turn back to Bronson, who is calmly watching the dark road rushing between the tyres. I look at his fists, still trying to crush the wheel within them.

I swallow hard. "We're being followed."

"I know, baby," he says smoothly.

We travel for twenty more minutes; the van never leaving our rear. Obvious. Intentional. Unapologetic.

Finally, we roll through open boom gates and head down a long driveway. I exhale my relief, but then the van follows us in. I twist to Bronson, but he's still stoic. Stoic on Bronson seems so wrong.

It is dark around the grounds, but delicately placed garden lights illuminate hedges and a manicured, lush lawn. So many hedges. Ahead, an enormous palace of a house looms above the shrubbery. There are cars everywhere, rows and rows of them stretching into the darkness, but Bronson pulls into one of the first bays. An empty bay right beside marble steps that lead up to a grand portico.

My stomach stirs.

I try to speak with an even voice as I say, "We're not where I think we are, are we?"

"Yes."

Twisting to face him, I scowl. "And you have me in this!" Noting that the van has now disappeared, I unbuckle my belt and feel the need to throttle Bronson for making me wear this outfit.

"We are speaking Jimmy's language, baby," he assures softly, not a hint of unease in his lovely, deep cadence. "He doesn't take women. He takes submissives. And just like every aspect of his life, he likes rules, codes, and contracts. He respects them. Understands them. When it comes to him, you are safer in that collar than you have ever been."

The first thing that comes to mind is, *'do you take women or submissives?'* Then I bite back the words, remembering I shouldn't care. "Why wouldn't I be safe? Aren't you family?"

He raises a dark brow at me. "Yes. We are *family*," he confirms, playing with the word family in an odd way that hints at something distasteful.

I blink at him as he steps from the driver's side, stare at him as he rounds the back of the vehicle. *Family.*

Opening the door for me, he smiles at my outfit. "Out you pop, baby."

I frown at him, sliding from the front seat. My feminine wedges hit the exposed aggregate driveway. Bronson shuts the door and slides the key into his pocket. I think about stealing it and taking the RV back to Darwin, but then he places his hand on the small of my back, halting my thoughts. His fingers span out, nearly covering my entire lower back, while his thumb strokes the dimple above the curve of my arse.

Although very gentle, it is a possessive and dominant hold that makes my heart thunder and my palms sweat.

Guiding me towards an imposing set of doors guarded by two men in black suits, his fingers continue their exploration of my lower back, distracting me enough not to pay much attention to the scantily dressed lady answering the door.

"Bronson, my boy," I hear a voice boom immediately. I widen my eyes at the formidable sight of Jimmy Storm sashaying towards us with wide open arms and a welcoming smile. "I'm pleased you came by before going home, my boy. And you brought a friend. This makes me very happy. It's good to see you with someone. You know I worry about you."

Bronson laughs. "No need to worry about me, Jimmy. I'm golden. You know that."

The two men never glance my way, as if I'm invisible. A fly on the wall.

"*Se*! Always reliable. Come, let's talk... How do you feel?" he asks, moving in a way that doesn't allow for objection.

"It's just a scratch, mate."

As Jimmy walks us down a corridor and into another room, I can't help but take him all in. I've seen him many times on the news, but never in the flesh. Clearly Italian, his skin is tanned but weathered with age, and his once dark hair is peppered with grey. A black suit hugs his strong but trim physique and he is shorter and leaner than Bronson, but more regal looking, his presence seemingly potent in the air. Such a mass of confidence and power... his body moves ethereally as though God-like and untouchable.

But no one is untouchable.

My displeasure over the thought that he is actually handsome despite his age is only matched by my awe as we step into a room lit in a dim hue of crimson. A lounge of sorts. The air is thick with cigar smoke. Across the misty space, I see many other suited men conversing as well as girls in a similar attire to me.

Straightaway, I notice the ones with collars are politely ignored, whereas the ones without are intensely observed.

Anger cascades through me.

My feminist brain screams.

Why would he want to be here with me? Why not wait until tomorrow to report to his precious Jimmy and save me from this scene.

As Jimmy walks towards a door at the rear of the lounge, I lean towards Bronson and whisper, "Why didn't you just leave me tied up in the RV! I'd have preferred it."

He spins to face me with a cool grin and something like mischief in his eyes —*like* mischief, but the telltale green glow to his irises screams a threat. "Me too. I hate you being here. I'm dreaming about gouging every man in here's eyes out of their sockets just for being in this room with you in *that*."

I exhale raggedly.

He tries to stifle a low growl. "But." He lowers his cheek

until it touches the side of mine. "I couldn't leave you alone in the RV... Cause they're searching it right now."

I gasp, bouncing my eyes to the ground in case my shock can be seen within them. "For what?"

"Another time," he whispers, pressing his lips to my cheek, lingering there for a few minutes.

Casually, Bronson turns around and tails Jimmy into the back room with me in tow. As we enter, Jimmy settles at his desk with a tight smile. A petite girl with shiny dark hair sits on the edge, whirling brown liquid around in a short glass. The sheer fabric of her skirting is barely a frill, and the corset encasing her small torso pushes up her pert breasts.

She eyes me kindly, and although her demeanour is content —satisfied even —she is showcasing bruises and bite marks on her thighs.

My stomach turns.

Jimmy looks at the girl. "Miranda, leave us, *se.*"

She slides from the desk and glides towards me, stopping shoulder to shoulder for a moment to study me. She presses her shoulder to mine playfully and then disappears; it is the weirdest interaction ever.

Jimmy smiles at her back as she leaves, watching her every move, fascinated by her perhaps. "She is the most sensitive little thing," he says. "I don't like to bore her with shop talk. Yours likes it, *se?* An intellectual, maybe?"

Bronson slides into a chair opposite Jimmy, pulling me down onto his lap. I shuffle in close. Not that I can't take my own, but I'll pick my battles. This isn't one of them.

"She likes to sit on my lap, no matter the banter." Bronson smirks and Jimmy laughs from his belly. The vibe is pleasant and awkward at the same time. "Anyway, where's Clay tonight? Not allowed out now that he's a councillor?"

"He's in Darwin," Jimmy states, leaning back into his big,

looming black chair. I twist my head into Bronson's neck, hiding the surprise that consumes my expression. *Darwin?* Why? "Hunting down Salvatore," Jimmy says, answering my thoughts.

Bronson twitches beneath me. "*Hunting?*"

"Se. I know what happened."

"What do you mean, Jimmy?" Bronson asks, his voice even.

"The tattoo," Jimmy states plainly, and I try not to look back, fighting with my own resolve to not engage. "The one you described. It belongs to Dominic."

"Demarco?" Bronson asks, playing with the dimples at my lower back again, settling something inside me. I relax on a little sigh. Twisting back towards Jimmy, I steel my face and watch the interaction with as much indifference as I can muster.

"*Se.* He has also—" Jimmy considers his words. "*Disappeared.* So, I believe Sal is now dirt or the whole thing was a ruse."

"The gun-shot in my chest doesn't feel much like a ruse, mate," Bronson says with a chuckle, and I smile easily, because it seems more natural to chuckle when he does, rather than feel the chill and discomfort washing over me.

Jimmy's brown eyes watch Bronson, scrutinizingly, following every tic, each subtle tell. "No. I'm sure it doesn't. But Sal wasn't shot at by Dom."

Bronson's fingers freeze on my back. "What are you saying?" he asks smoothly.

The pause that follows near ignites the air. "He's betrayed me, my boy," Jimmy finally says.

"He wouldn't do that, Jimmy," Bronson states, circling my lower back once again. "That kid idolises you. Loves you."

"*Yes.*" Jimmy nods. A dark and distrusting shadow moves across his eyes. I look away, the phantom of that sentiment uncomfortable to behold. Like if I can see it, maybe it can see me. "Yes," he agrees again, his tone almost a hiss, "he does... But the missing diamonds. Sal. Dominic... *You.* Someone is trying to get to me, *se?*"

"I don't know about all of that, mate." Bronson leans back a little. "Seems like they just wanted the diamonds."

Jimmy considers him for a moment. "Perhaps." He taps the desk and stands in one smooth movement, a big smile engulfing his face. "No more of this tonight. Go take your *bedda* girl to the sauna. I am sure she will like it. You must be stiff from all that travel."

We leave Jimmy's office.

Bronson's circling fingers become more of a massage on my lower back, moving in a needy way.

And I'm still unsure about what just happened.

CHAPTER TWENTY-FOUR

shoshanna

Present day

AFTER WE RE-ENTER the dimly lit lounge, Bronson grabs a drink from the bar, steering me around as he does. My eyes bounce around the room. Guests seem to offer us a quick look before lowering their eyes. I wonder if they are afraid of Bronson. These men don't appear the type to be afraid of much, but they are clearly wary of his presence.

There is a larger-than-life aspect to him, always has been. I used to revel in the fact I was the one standing beside him. To a sixteen-year-old girl, there was something about not knowing what he'll do or say that was... *exciting.*

But to a twenty-seven-year-old woman, I can now see it's just danger sitting out of sight. Perhaps twenty-seven-year-old Bronson has a reputation that proceeds him. I never really noticed it before, but I suppose people are legitimately afraid of what he may do on a whim.

The conversation we just had with Jimmy shuffles around in my stomach. Questions about Clay in Darwin, Salvatore, and the missing diamonds all mingle together. I need to know what they are doing in Darwin. *My Darwin.*

What business did Bronson have there?

Is he in trouble?

Fucksake.

He's always in trouble.

Part of me wants to go back to the RV, bide my time until I can make a break for it, then leave him with Jimmy Storm and the bullshit surrounding him. The other, though, feels an intense pull to stay with Bronson. To be the person by his side. To wring information out of him, sort it all out, and keep him safe.

Bronson passes me a wine before leading me outside and around towards an external building illuminated with a warm orange light at the front door. As we wander through glass double doors, we enter a small cloakroom with a coffee table and clothing rack.

When his hand moves away from my lower back, the spot feels instantly colder. The beer clicks on the coffee table as he settles it down, making his silence obvious and unnatural.

"Are you going to tell me what happened in there?" I ask, watching him slowly undress. "Or why we are still here?" Ignoring my questions, he turns his back to me and pulls his suspenders down until they hang around his legs.

I hate his silence.

It's ominous.

I try to wash the knot forming in my throat down by, sipping my wine. I can tell it's expensive from the way it slides down my oesophagus with ease. Placing the glass down beside his beer, I decide the best thing to do is read the room and stay quiet.

Bronson unbuttons his shirt and slides it off his muscular shoulders, revealing an intricate family tree that ripples as his back muscles contract. I've seen it many times before. The trunk and branches were his first ever tattoo.

I remember the day well.

He made jokes the entire time as if he was being tickled by a feather rather than carved into by a needle. The sixteen-year-old me swooned the entire time.

He was my dream boy.

We have lost so much time, Bronson.

Where did it go?

My heart squeezes in my chest at the memory.

As he removes his pants, I observe the recent additions to his vast ink profile. The tree is now an intricate piece that traces the full length of his spine and across his broad shoulder blades. Seeing the names 'Cassidy' and 'Kelly' alongside Max's, I find myself smiling. For a moment, I forget I am here against my will; I'm just excited to meet them.

The more I look, the more I see. Along his side and up the underside of one arm, I think I see scars. It's hard to be sure, as they are covered in ink that methodically follows the contours of the raised skin, hiding them from obvious identification.

Who did that?

I make fast work of removing my boots and dress until I stand in my underwear. Before he finishes, I push the doors open and walk into the sauna. The steam hits me like a draft of hot, wet air, followed by the smell of wood and oils.

My body instantly softens.

Muscles go lax.

Bronson strides into the sauna completely naked, sits

down on the wooden step, and stares straight at me with the most beautiful and arresting green-blue eyes. I press my thighs together, a torturous ache beginning. He watches my discomfort with a grin playing with his lips.

He taps his knee.

The little demanding action should annoy me. It doesn't. It *thrills* me.

Jesus Christ, Shoshanna.

Get a grip.

Heat rushes up my spine as I slowly approach him. I'm snared by his narrowed eyes as they crawl all over my thighs and stomach, stopping to watch the sway of my breasts. I can almost see the memory of his cock thrusting between them, playing in his perverted mind.

When he reaches down to give his thick erection a few strokes, I follow each drag of his fist. Opening my mouth, I pant at the sight, overwhelmed by his hot and dangerous mien.

God, he radiates sex appeal.

"Sit on my lap, baby."

I reach him. Sliding my knee on to the wood beside his thigh, I straddle his lap, settling my bum right over his cock. I rock on him once, needing to ease the ache between my legs. He lets out a slow hiss as my pussy pulses against him. It is excruciating and wrong how much I want to feel him fill me. Thickening inside me. Kneading the muscles that beckon for attention.

It's the heat.

Fuck.

It's the whole scene.

The sweat sliding down our bodies. The silence. *Him* —in every way made to fuck a woman within an inch of her sanity, leaving her a puddle in his arms.

Nerves thrash through me, but I have no idea why. We were intimate only yesterday. But today. *This*... This is different. I'm letting myself get carried away in the scene, in the role he has cast me in. And I'm not tied up or drunk or misled. Can't lie to myself about my consent.

I want him.

Laying my trembling arms over his shoulders, I press my cheek to his. His tongue slides out to slick the hot drops of sweat beading on my skin. He groans with each lick.

"Talk to me," I whisper in his ear.

"Something's not right," he mutters, rubbing his nose and lips in the crook of my neck. He brings his hands up to massage my back, arching me so I press my pelvis and breasts into him. "He's searching our clothes."

I don't know what Jimmy knows. I just know I don't want him to know it because Bronson's heart is beating like a battle drum and it scares me. Terrifies me. I don't want to lose him again. *No.* I mean, I just don't want anything to happen to him. "What is he expecting to find?"

"Diamonds."

My breath stops in my throat. "*Fuck.* Bronson, what have you done? You're in danger."

"*Baby.*" He kisses down my neck. His erection presses up between my legs, rubbing against the silk of my underwear. "I was in danger the moment I was born."

His words hurt my heart. "Will he find them?"

"Maybe," he murmurs smoothly. "They're in the wedges of your shoes, baby." I suck a choppy breath in. "Calm down. It's fine. I won't let anything happen to you."

I try to steel my face, feeling tingles move along my spine. "Are there cameras in here?"

His breath hits me hard. "*Yes.*"

Sweat slides down my chest, slipping between my

breasts and into the fabric of my bra. "What is he expecting to see? What would any other girl be doing right now?"

"Riding my cock."

Jealousy lashes out and wraps itself around me. I peer across the sauna. The thought of Jimmy watching us, our actions and affections on display while our secrets are whispered from cheek to cheek, sets a boil within me. A reminiscent feeling of being the one beside him, being his partner in crime and life when no one else is welcome to be. I feel shameful too, for a brief moment, but I ignore it. Excitement and the thrill of danger have a stronger hold on me. Seventeen-year-old Shoshanna with all her wildness and anger and crazies is still part of who I am.

Eagerly, I reach between us, my hand gliding through our sweat as I reach my pussy. Lifting onto my knees, I slide my knickers across, baring my folds. I lock eyes with Bronson, feeling a glimmer of bashfulness move across my cheeks as I offer myself to him. His face is sweaty and tense, his pupils dilating, leaving thin green-blue rings that stare at me, dark and daring.

I grip his shoulders tightly as he positions his steel-like cock, his crown nudging at my pussy. Lowering myself onto him, we both moan instantly as his girth pries my muscles apart while his length moves up into me until my bum meets his thighs. Panting at the pressure inside me, filled to the hilt, I undulate against him.

For a moment, pain flares through my core.

But as I grind slowly, the discomfort of being so full subsides. My body accepts him. And all the nerves inside me are awakened.

Pressing my cheek back to his, we breathe together as I lift again. Closing my eyes, I revel in the feel of every thick, pulsing inch of him drawing out of me. Then I sit back down, taking him all in again.

"Yes, baby. Like that," he hisses, the sound wisps through clenched teeth. His body tenses, his arms band my back tightly, his hips move steadily up and down with my rhythm. We create a pace together. A flow where our slick bodies move as one.

It's slow.

And I want to kiss him.

But that would mean something else.

He massages the length of my spine, before stopping to caress the thick swell of my arse and then gripping both cheeks. I feel his fingers spanning low, touching us both where he enters me.

I reach around to unclip my bra, but he leans forward to bite the top of my breast, causing me to fall forward. His mouth moves to my ear. "No," he growls low, strained. "I don't want him to see your beautiful nipples. Nothing more than he already has. Stay deep. Keep your bra on."

I move my hand back to grip his shoulder. Focus on the dance of our hips. I keep him deep. Close. Agonising bliss builds inside me as I pick up speed, riding him with brazen need.

"*Yes*, baby. Use me. Take what you want," he growls, teeth grit in restraint as he allows me to ride him at my own pace. I roll and adjust my hips in the exact way I like, using him like a toy to chase the peak of a building sensation.

"*Bronson*." I pant, throwing my head back, arching my body more. My thighs burn as I continue to lift and slide down, lift and slide. The entire time his arms twitch around me, wanting to throw me down and fuck me; I can tell. But he doesn't. And now, the tremors hit me hard. Wave upon wave of warmth and pleasure rush to my pussy, igniting it.

"*Bronson. Yes. God.*" I come apart, still riding him. Shaking. Unable to stop. The sensation continues, and I don't want it to relent because it's him and me. This feeling. It's *us.*

His hand finds its way into my hair, wrapping the dark strands around his fingers, yanking my head back. My throat arches so he can eat at my skin. His other hand grips my hip, pressing me down as he pumps upward.

My head spins.

Through a deep strained groan, he comes, filling me fiercely.

He releases the death grip he has in my hair. I flop forward on to him, wrapping my arms around his neck as though we are lovers. My body is so hot and wet, my muscles melt against him. He twists his face until the corners of our mouths touch, our heavy long exhales fusing together.

A pang hits my heart.

I wish things were different.

Perspiration slides down my brow, pooling at my upper lip. His tongue ducks out to lick the bead. Swiftly, he stands, his cock squeezing out from inside me. He cradles my weak, warm, lethargic body against him.

I cuddle his neck, relaxing as he walks me from the steam and out into the cloakroom. The fresh air hits me like a bat to my senses. Awakens me. Guilt and shame engulf me as the sparse cool air surrounds me, chilling me, reminding me that I live with another man.

That Perry has Akila.

And Akila needs to come first.

He slides me down to the ground, perhaps feeling my body tense up with discomfort.

So while I can still feel him inside me, between my legs and in my heart, I am consumed by the guilt betrayal brings.

Betraying Akila. By being here and risking her happiness for a moment of my own.

I can feel Bronson's eyes on me as I quickly get dressed. As I pull the wedges on, I give them a subtle inspection. The heel is still in perfect shape, the stitching as it was... *I think.* He follows suit, pulling his clothes on and finally his suspenders. Around us stirs angry energy.

He grips my elbow, pulling me with him.

I near jog to keep up, my heels feeling strange, like the fate of our very lives rest within them. And I could swear the heel below my left foot slips, wanting to open and pour the diamonds out. I swallow hard, wishing I was ignorant of their presence, wishing I never asked about them. *"Bronson."*

He ignores me as we enter the lounge again.

CHAPTER TWENTY-FIVE

bronson

Present day

MY BREATHING RAGES through my chest, but I hide it well. Hide it behind my epic grin. I wipe my sweaty palms down my thighs, feeling fire in my heart. I love the way the last twenty minutes made me feel.

It was a moment of rhapsody. Of acceptance. A moment where I thought she'd stopped fucking fighting *us*.

Then she fucking tensed up, seemingly regretful. Well, fuck. She hasn't stopped fighting. And she is fucking lying to herself if thinks she can just shut me out.

I'm in her soul.

Been inside her in ways no one has.

And I'm not known for giving up what I want. Not when I felt our connection swallow her as she shuddered around my cock. It was fucking beautiful.

The hairs on the back of my neck stand on end, sensing her proximity and all the space around her

When we enter the lounge, I notice Jimmy's dipshit friends have pissed off, which isn't good. It's barely ten; they normally stay late. Fire thrashes through my veins. My hands twitch in preparation.

I grin.

Reaching behind me, I touch the gun tucked into my pants, reminding myself it's there, playing with the idea of ending it all now and putting a bullet into Jimmy Storm's heart.

But I'd never make it out alive.

The Family would come for my brothers.

They would come for my girls.

For Kelly, Cassidy, Shoshanna...

I glance back to see Shosh's beautiful amber eyes dance around the room, the empty room seemingly unsettling her too.

Clever girl.

Don't worry, baby. No one will touch you.

Realisation swarms me.

My spine steels.

Did he fucking find them?

I know Jimmy fucking Storm. He suspects everyone down to his own blood and we are more than blood to him because we share the vows and ancestry oaths that he cherishes more than religion or life.

Missing diamonds.

Missing Nephew.

Missing associate.

That's got to hurt his ego.

'Someone is trying to get to me, *se*?' Yeah, Jimmy. They fucking are. *Me.* I already expected that he would search the

RV, but our clothes. Didn't see that coming. That was a bold move for the man to make, obvious and unlike Jimmy. He doesn't show his hand until it's the last one he has, which means the fibres that hold him are fraying. I chuckle lightly as I stride towards the door, knowing he'll stop me soon.

Fucking ay, he's unravelling.

I just have to hope he's smart enough not to fuck with me tonight while I have Shoshanna with me. Smart enough... hesitant enough because he needs me. Needs my brothers. Needs Clay. The ghost of that name will stop him —*Clay Butcher.* His heir...

But I'll go down fighting if I have to. If I have to, I'll fucking kill them all and she won't have a goddamn scratch, or I'll burn his house to the ground, burn his name, his legacy.

Nearing the exit, I survey the room quickly to count the guards. *Four.* I wander casually, but my mind and body are sparking with anything but casual response. At the sound of a gun shots, I barrel around to protect *her.*

One thing on my mind.

One objective.

Feeling my whole body detonate, I throw myself in front of her, knocking her to the ground. Stepping over her, I plant one foot on either side of her body. I guard her, my gun now gripped tightly in my fist, pointed at the person who shot... *Jimmy?*

What the fuck?

He smiles at me.

JIMMY NODS. *"Offer everyone your smile, my boy."*

My brows draw in. "But what if I don't like them?"

"Smile harder. They'll never know what hit them."

. . .

I SHAKE the reverie from my head. Glancing from him to the man lying on the floor, moaning, and rocking back and forth with his calf in his arms, I feign an amiable smile.

It was one of his guards.

A flesh wound.

I lower my gun to my side.

Quickly, a smirk moves across my face. "Jimmy, you loose cannon. What's the occasion?" I laugh, stepping from either side of Shoshanna's trembling frame. I lean down and pull her to her feet, evading her eyes because they might crack me open, tear down my practised smile and calm facade.

Make me homicidal.

She's scared.

I don't need to see those beautiful amber eyes glowing with fear to know this. I feel it in every inch of muscle that I plan on using to carve any man who hurts her up.

I imagine slicing Jimmy's neck open and pulling his tongue through the incision. For scaring her. For his bullshit lessons about smiling. For his lies. I shake the murderous thought, tucking the gun back into my pants.

He looks at me deadpan. "Do you remember when I told you to hide your vulnerabilities behind your smile? *Se?* You are very good at doing this." He tsks. "But not today."

"How much have you had to drink, old boy?" I smirk, heat moving over my whole body. Ready to fight. Ready to kill.

He puts his gun back in his harness. "Your girl–" He nods behind me, towards Shoshanna. "Doesn't like blood? That seems odd given her occupation."

Fuck.

He clasps his hands in front of him, bouncing his eyes to

Shoshanna, breaking one of his own rules to not engage with another man's property. But he knows she isn't my submissive. "I think this man is in need of a doctor, *se?*"

My blood sets to a boil.

My smile twists, but I hold it still.

"You have been lying to me." He takes two steps towards us. "Playing the girl off on being someone she isn't. I know who is important to my boys. I care. This is the lovely *Shoshanna Adel...* "

Fuck.

Stay calm.

"Why are you lying to me?" He sighs roughly. "Now, if you weren't like a son to me, *se?* I might be angrier. I wasn't sure what I was seeing when the girl walked in with you. She looked very... *affected* by you."

I can feel Shoshanna right behind me, can smell her, but I won't take my arrowed eyes off him. "I hope I affect her. What are you getting at, mate?"

"I needed to see for myself," he says, knowing eyes zeroing in on me. I hold the fucker's stare. "Now I have, and well... the girl is either, an excellent performer... *very* sensual. I very much enjoyed it. Or if I didn't know any better, I'd say she loves you, my boy." He smiles widely, opening his arms. "And I'm a romantic. So that makes me very happy. Of course, you should keep her. But that means we need to tie up loose ends, *se?* Not good for business."

Her breathing gets heavier behind me.

I let this play out.

This isn't about the diamonds.

Dominic's words feed through the distant laughter I hear in my head. *"Jimmy knows everything. Everything."*

"You know she has a fiancé, *se?* He claims that you kidnapped her. Now, luckily for you, your uncle Jimmy has been... *watching* the whole situation. I've been keeping an eye on her for you. It is a good thing, *se*. This could have been very bad for the Family. For Clay. This attention. It's not good for him. It's not good for us."

Keeping an eye on her for me... I force my smile to linger, a tight-lipped curve that hides a snarl. "You, sly old dog." Shaking my head with feigned amusement, I force out, "Mate, she's here willingly, aren't you baby?"

Silence.

Then a small voice breathes, "*Yes.*"

At the sound of that small voice, rage slashes through me like a fucking machete. I hate her voice small. I lower my head, staring at Jimmy through my lashes, shaking violently with restrained rage. But I smile. *I fucking smile!*

"*Bellissimo,*" Jimmy coos. "I want love for you, my boy. I want to see you happy."

I grin harder, ready for anything. I know you, Jimmy. *What the fuck do you have planned?* My eyes dart back around the room, calculating my first kill and my second.

Last will be him...

The man who taught me everything I know.

Jimmy eyes me quietly and then signals a guard. My gaze moves from him to a door as it slowly opens.

My smile falls.

Shoshanna's gasp sails through the air behind me.

Entering alongside one of Jimmy's hired help, is Dr Clean. He walks up to stand beside Jimmy, as though he knows the man and my blood runs scorching hot. He has no idea.

Looking Shoshanna over, he sneers in disgust at her outfit, and my hands convulse with the need to slice those lips from his face.

"I saw you in the sauna with him," Dr Clean hisses. "Your poor sister won't like where I send her."

I don't turn to see her expression, can't turn. But fucking ay, I'm going to finish that mother fucker right now.

"No more secrets, my boy. No loose ends," Jimmy says, looking straight at me, the message obvious. I nod, knowing what comes next. I lunge for Shoshanna, smothering her head against my chest, squeezing my arms around her ears, feeling her trembling within my protective grasp.

The Glock goes off.

Jimmy puts a bullet, point blank, between Dr Clean's eyes. Blood paints the back wall in an elegant spray of bright red as he tumbles to the floor.

She shoves me away. The room bellows with her violent screams when she sees him. My muscles tighten painfully at the sound of it. She rushes towards his slumped corpse, dropping to her knees by his side. All I can do is watch for a moment, as she tries to understand he's gone.

Tries to save him.

He has the perfect, wholesome appearance of a doll, skin, white, brown eyes, hollow, and lips, blushed. A tiny round hole between his brows leaks small tracks of blood down his lifeless face. The rest, I know, is spilling from a crater in the back of his skull.

I grab her before she is exposed to any more bloodshed. To anymore of my world. And the laughing in my head won't stop as I pry her from him. "Baby, baby, he's gone... let him go." She has his blood all over her, the crimson colour on her hands and thighs, and I hate it.

My soul boiling.

"*No.*" She sobs.

I wrestle her from the ground, drag her arms from him.

She kicks and screams and claws at me. I take it all. Need it, even.

"Get her home," Jimmy orders and heat strikes my temples as I flash him a murderous look that in any other situation I would mask. "This is a nice neighbourhood," he says. "*Se?* We don't need to wake anyone."

I see red.

See it.

Blood.

And I can't do a thing about it. With that, Jimmy leaves the lounge and the body now bathing in a red pool. I don't care that Jimmy killed the fucking doctor. Hell, I wanted to do it myself. But... her pain. Her cries...

My body vibrates with venomous rage.

You'll kill him, Bronson.

Words break from her, but they are ravished by her cries and groans. I throw her over my shoulder. As though she is stalling, caught in a perpetual state of frenzy, of despair, she keeps fighting me all the way to the RV.

"I'm sorry, baby," I say, throwing her on the bed, before storming out and locking the door on her, enclosing her screams. "I'm so fucking sorry."

CHAPTER TWENTY-SIX

bronson

Seventeen years old.

RESTING my elbows on either side of her hips, I walk my newly tattooed fingers from her pubic-line up to her navel, circling the cute little hole. She breathes through her palms, stressing out about stuff that doesn't really fucking matter. Stuff we can sort out.

Shifting, I rest my head on her belly, pressing my ear against her skin.

I can hear sloshing.

That's what he'll hear too.

Or she...

Nah... it's definitely a boy. Butchers don't have daughters. I knew she was going to have my babies the moment we met, and now here she is... having my baby.

My baby is having my baby.

I grin, feeling my whole fucking world shift and tilt and

change for them, feeling my heart pulse for them, my existence now... all about *them*.

I love you so much, Shoshanna.

I love you so much, little boy.

I kiss her stomach, and she groans into her hands. She thinks I'm nuts. But I think... *I think you're smiling behind your palms, baby.* That roguish smile that shows her true feelings because she is bat-shit-crazy. Just like me. Rubbing my face against her stomach, I feel her smooth, tanned skin beneath my cheek. I can't fucking wait until she is swollen and has those badarse tiger stripes pregnant girls get. Her body is amazing. It's a fucking gift. She is wondrous, and I'm in awe of everything she is.

"What about medical school?" she grumbles, her words muffled, but I can still decipher them.

"I'll stay home with him," I say, the idea making me smile so hard I want to cry. I've never cried from happiness, but I've seen her do it before. I think I want to, thinking about him hanging out with his daddy... Teaching him about the world. Life. How things work and go together. "I wanna be home with him, baby. You can still go to medical school. Make us proud."

She drops her arms, flopping them to the mattress. Peering up at her from her stomach, I grin at her beautiful face, which is tense with apprehension.

"And money?" she asks with that half-arsed tight smile of hers.

I laugh. "I have plenty of money." Chuckling, I lower my face to meet her stomach again. "Hear that?" I whisper to him, having our own private conversation. "I'm going to spoil the shit out of you, buddy. You and your mummy."

"Where will we live?"

Glancing around my room, at the overly boyish décor,

and I know she can't live here. Don't want her to either. Not with my mum. "I don't care," I admit, looking back up at her. "We can buy a house somewhere. Just the three of us. Maybe in Brussman? I'm eighteen in two months, baby. I'll sort something out."

"Where will we—"

"We made a life, Shoshanna!" I laugh, bouncing to my feet, planting them on either side of her body. "We made a life. And he won't be angry or sad or broken." I can feel the heat behind my eyes now. I let my grin break my face, too consumed by happiness to stop the tears. "He'll be perfect. Cause *you* are. And I'll learn to be, baby. I swear it. I'll be better. A good citizen. Pay taxes and shit. I'll get a part-time job or whatever. Fuck, I'll work on bikes. I'd like that." I stare into her big amber eyes as they gloss over too. She *is* happy. "I'll cook dinner for you every damn night. We'll never eat in front of the TV. We'll sit at the table and talk about our day. I'll sit at the head, and you'll sit beside me, and he'll make a mess on the floor, but the dog will clean it up—"

"The dog?"

"Yeah. A staffy. And it'll be fucking *perfect*."

Excitement fills my every cell. I feel light, like I could fly. Swallowing, I plead with my eyes as hers bounce around with uncertainty. They are teary and unsure. I wait for a sign she is with me. That she agrees we can do this...

"What if someone doesn't let us? What if someone tells us we're too young? We're underage."

I just grin. "Then I'll kill them."

She chuckles through a little sigh because she's crazy and I'm mad and we love it. "Okay, nutcase."

"Fuck yes!" I get to my feet, accidentally knocking my head on my ceiling fan. She giggles. As I jump on the bed like a child, her body bounces above my blue sheets. "We are having a fucking baby!" I expect her eye-roll, and when she does, I beam harder. Beam and tear up like a fucking man who loves his girl and baby and isn't afraid to fucking show it.

Laughing with puddles in my irises and peaceful silence in my mind, I drop on to the mattress beside her. Pulling her body into the larger frame of mine, I cocoon her tightly and protectively. As I hold her against me, a wave of trepidation casts a shadow over my happiness. Just for a moment. I squeeze her tighter. "You know... good things don't happen to people like me."

My baby and our baby nestle deeper into me. "What about me? Aren't I a good thing?"

"You're the best," I state. "But this means I get to keep you forever. And him. And more babies. So many babies."

She scoffs on a laugh. "Fuck off. What about my body?"

I laugh and kiss her crown, her dark hair like silk beneath my lips. "I want you plump with my babies. You'll never be hotter to me than you will be then."

She shakes her head in the crook of my neck. "You're so fucking crazy."

"I don't think you should swear anymore, baby. You're a mummy now." I laugh because she instantly scowls and everything about her makes me smile. Even her scowls. "It's all good anyway. I got this, baby. I'm going to take care of you. I actually got what I wanted, and I'm never fucking letting you or him go."

CHAPTER TWENTY-SEVEN

shoshanna

Seventeen years old

A HORN BEEPS.

I rush from my house, halting when I see Clay Butcher's Chrysler parked at the curb. I expected Max's Range Rover or the Ducati. Not in a million years did I expect to see a city vehicle. I peer around for the Ducati but see nothing, just the big black looming presence of the District's newest and youngest board member's entourage.

Slowing, I close the gap between me and Clay's vehicle, moving to gaze through the passenger's panel of glass, knowing he can see me even though I can't see him.

I tilt my head, plucking a dark brow at him —an obvious demand for an explanation. I wait. The window winds down, revealing his clear-blue eyes. Of course, he's wearing a tailored black three-piece suit. He's always 'on'.

There is a refined kind of confidence to him. One that teases others with a lingering indifference. He's got emotional walls the size of the goddamn Himalayas. I couldn't even guess how he actually feels if my life depended on it.

He smiles softly. "The boys are going to be late today. I'll take you to school."

I smirk at him, leaning back on the heel of my black ankle boots. "I don't get into stranger's cars without lollypops. It's just slack. You should have come prepared."

He holds his hand up as his driver says something to him. "That's an inappropriate joke," he states, looking deadpan at me.

I smile nervously. "Yes. But a *joke*."

Clay slides over the two leather seats to push the passenger door open for me. "Come on, Shoshanna. I don't bite. And I'm sure I can find a mint if that is a requisite for your company."

I blink at him as he moves back to his seat. I'm a little thrown by his attempt at humour. Suddenly feeling prickles hit my neck, I peer over the black roof to find several of my neighbours in their gardens, pretending to trim their twiggy rose bushes. I get it. He's in his early-twenties and Clay Butcher is already a household name. 'He'll be the premier of Western Australia one day, running the entire state', people whisper.

Sighing, I step in, dragging my heavy school bag with me. I drop it on the leather seat between us.

Clay leans back, comfortable in his space while I feel anything but. It's *his* space. I scoot closer to the door, leaning against it.

"To what do I owe the pleasure?" I ask, trying to not feel

the beat of my heart in my ears. I can't remember ever being alone with Clay Butcher. Not once in the four years that Bronson and I have been dating. I like him, but he's definitely not the kind of man you let your guard down around.

Twisting his torso to face me, he lifts his knee on the seat. A casual position he might offer a friend.

That's weird...

Staring at me with that smooth, rich Clay Butcher smile, he says, "Don't be nervous. You're very important to my brother and to my family."

I nod. "Your family is very important to me."

He lets out a deep chuckle. "Did you know I wasn't around much when the boys were young? I never really had time to protect them. From—" He considers his words. "Our lifestyle."

As the car begins to roll, I feel butterflies move inside my stomach. "There's a big age gap, so I bet they annoyed you," I say, trying not to appear nervous. I just don't know the direction of the conversation, and since he is unreadable, I can't pre-plan my answers.

He eyes me with calm confidence. "Belt, Shoshanna. Mark is an excellent driver, but he's not used to carrying such precious cargo." I fumble for words while my hands search for the belt and drag it over my shoulder, doing as I'm told. I doubt Clay often *asks*. He commands.

"No," he says, after I have clipped the belt in. "They never annoyed me. I didn't see them enough for them to annoy me because Victoria had me young. When she was your age, actually."

He knows. I speak through a sigh. "Bronson told you?"

He clasps his hands in front of him, resting them on his lap. "Yes. Congratulations."

I scoff once but clear my throat to mask it. "But you think I'm too young. That we're too young. That I'm ruining his life?"

His clear blue eyes measure me up with the slightest of amusement. "I think you are in love with my little brother and you *are* going to be very happy."

Woah. I smile tightly because the way he played with the word *are* makes my butterflies dizzy. I'd murder all the fuckers if I could; they have no place in my stomach. "Wow... Well, thank you?"

"Shoshanna." He speaks my name in a serious tone. "It is important you understand what this means. What your part is—"

"Did you pick me up to interrogate me?" I cut in, gazing at the driver as he navigates the streets of the District. He doesn't turn to look at us, and I wonder what it would be like to know these powerful men's secrets and dealings while pretending to be ignorant and uninterested.

"No, not at all," Clay assures me. "Let's start here. When I was born, Butch was a newly made man in his twenties. Just starting out. Jimmy and this life kept him very busy. Boxing and the business... kept him *very* busy. So they sent me away to boarding school."

"Is that why Butch is with Victoria? Because she got pregnant?" I ask. What is he implying? That I am like her? Bronson is not with me out of obligation. "That's not what's happening here, you know that, right?"

"I know that," he says. "My brother breathes for you." I sigh my relief, not wanting anyone to think that. "It was a business deal," he says, correcting me. "Victoria and Butch, that is. Through all her faults as a mother, she makes a very skilled and loyal partner in our business."

My stomach flips. Why is he being so candid? "Why are you telling me this?"

"Because," he says, unclasping his hands and resting one along the back of the seat, "I don't want that for you. Bronson is in too deep. It's been his identity since he was a kid. He's falling in love with Jimmy and the Family. But, luckily, he loves you endlessly more."

I smile at that. "I know."

"Butch married for business," he presses. "I will too."

And I know he is referring to Aurora —Jimmy Storm's daughter. They have been a celebrity couple for years. I honestly thought, well, I thought they were in love. They sold it to the District well. "That doesn't seem fair."

He smiles softly, a world of power in his eyes but also something genuine and raw. I like this side of him. A side I doubt many people see. Perhaps only his family. Is that what I am now? "We take what we have and we make it our own," he says. "Fighting it does nothing but leaves us exhausted and exposed. But I don't want this life for my brothers."

I let out a dubious sigh. "Too late." The car slowly pulls up alongside my school. Kids in all directions freeze like bunnies in headlights at the eldest Butcher brother's entourage. They know who he is.

"It's not," he declares, ignoring the outside world, seemingly unaffected by the attention he receives. I relax in the private sanctuary of his car, invisible behind tinted black windows. I look back at Clay. "When I marry Aurora," he says. "My brothers will be able to marry for love. Don't get me wrong, Aurora is my closest confidant. I am very fond of her. But she is the eldest daughter of the most powerful man in the state, and you don't grow up in our world with misconceptions about your role in this legacy... But let's just say, we will have a slightly different managerial style than Jimmy... Until then, though, you keep my little brother occupied and out of trouble. Be his distraction from our business. And I give you my word, I won't be absent again. I will protect you and my brother... my nephew...from this *lifestyle*. You will be safe and happy together."

I nod in acceptance.

CHAPTER TWENTY-EIGHT

shoshanna

Present day

THE RV ROLLS SLOWLY to a stop. But I just stare at my hands, trembling and covered in his blood. They remind me of a night in ED when a car crash victim came in. A girl my sister's age. Panic took over me as the girl's hair turned from blonde to black, her irises from blue to amber, and she morphed into Akila right before my eyes. There was so much blood and screaming and I wanted so desperately to save her.

In the end, I couldn't.

What will happen to his body?

"Your poor sister won't like where I send her."

I close my eyes and see his, staring at me from across the smoke-filled room, standing beside Jimmy Storm with the comfort an old friend might. Did they know each other?

I can't get Perry's face out of my head, twisted in disgust, eyeing me like dirt. Like filth. Then his eyes switch from hazel to dark brown. His blond hair turns black, his face distorts, and suddenly my dad is staring at me with his lips curled in contempt.

My body vibrates with anger and sorrow, both emotions racketing through me, shaking me back and forth. With both men, I was so weak. I allowed them to make me feel less... Less of a person, of a doctor. Less knowledgeable. Less worthy. Less clever. Less sane.

Less.

Less.

Just fucking less.

I glare at the door as it opens, feeling wild with pent up madness. Pent up craziness. Bronson steps inside and I lunge from the mattress, needing to unleash it all. It's his fault! If he had have just stayed in the District. Stayed away. Perry would still be alive, and I would be blissfully ignorant of the lies and deceit around our relationship. Ignorant to his connection to Jimmy Storm... *Fucking Jimmy Storm.* My mind rolls with anger. He ruined my Bronson and murdered Perry.

As I hit Bronson's body, he goes to grab my hands, thinking I'm trying to slap him, but I reach behind him and pull his gun from his jeans. We topple over. Tumbling to the floor, his big body rolls, pinning me beneath him.

Then I press the nose of the gun to his temple.

Time stands still.

Breathing rapidly, we stare at each other, eyes mere inches away, noses brushing, bodies merged completely.

He blinks a few times at me as if for the first time, his expression the same puzzled one he had that first day at the pool.

"*Hey,*" he says on a breath.

Hot tears blanket my face. "This is your fault! You did this!"

He nods, his nose sliding over mine. "I know."

"You took me! This is your fault!" I cry, tears blurring my vision of him.

"I know, baby," he says calmly, feeding his hands up into my hair, his fingers circling through the strands reverently. As though I don't have a gun to his head, ready to blow his brains out.

"I wanted him because he was good!" I gasp for air, my breath hitting his face hard. "I'd never lose what we made together. I'd never lose him because he was respectable. He was good. You made him bad like you! Like Jimmy!"

His brows pinch in together, and he tilts his head, a ghost of sadness shifting through his gemstone eyes. "I didn't make him bad, baby," he says, with a remorseful shake of his head. "I'd love to play the villain for you. But... he just was bad. We all are."

I splutter all over him, open-mouthed and sobbing. The black handgun in my fist shakes, vibrating against his temple. He doesn't seem bothered that it's there. He looks at me with loving empathy. "Why didn't you kill Jimmy?" I yell, hating his loving, understanding gaze. A gaze without a glimmer of condescension or disdain. Not a shadow of disapproval.

"If I had, we'd both be dead," he says.

"You won't kill him because you're just like him!" I scream. "You took me away from Akila. You got Perry killed. After all we went through. After all we shared! You took me! You were my choice, Bronson! I chose you! I wanted you. Then you do this. You ruined it all." The truth swallows me whole. "They used what matters to me to control me. And now you are too. Just another handler to organise my life for me. It's my fucking life. Mine!"

I look at the gun, my finger twitching on the trigger.

Reaching up, he quickly disarms me. My mouth flaps with uncertainty while he studies me, that same infatuation dancing through his gaze.

The crazy son of a bitch is smiling.

I nearly blew his fucking head off.

"Were you actually willing to shoot me?" he asks, his grin twitching to grow larger, to let a laugh expel.

I nod slowly because I was, but then shake my head violently because I also wasn't. Unable to move or glance away from his piercing eyes, I stay frozen beneath him. So unsure what he'll do or what I should do. What even happened?

"Oh God," I manage to say on a rough exhale. "*Oh,* God."

He traps me with his intense gaze. The freckles in his eyes mimic burning green embers. As the gun in his hand moves slowly down my body, I inhale sharply.

I'm suddenly paralysed when he presses the cold metal to the fabric covering my pussy. My thighs clench around the hard barrel, trying to fend off the invasion, but that innate movement only works to increase its ominous presence. He uses the barrel to rub and part my folds. The material of my knickers moving into me with each stroke.

"You wanna play with my gun, baby?" he growls against my gasping mouth. I try to breathe, but it is as though he has a fist around my throat, a phantom feeling he controls with his mere presence. "He wants to play with you." His other hand goes to the side of my face, his thumb resting just below my eye and his forefinger just above. "Keep these beautiful eyes on me. I want to watch them shine when my Glock makes my fierce baby purr." I hold his gaze, words held captive alongside the air in my throat. "Remember to breathe, baby."

I quickly release the breath inside me.

Moving the gun faster, he rubs the barrel back and forth through my folds. The cold metal is demanding and if an inanimate object could be angry, it is. Desperate whimpers leave me as I rock my hips up and down, joining the motions of the Glock.

Bronson growls as I press back against it, inclining my pelvis, feeling dizzy, feeling as though I am plummeting over the edge. Looking at him, at his mouth open and panting with excitement, at his eyes infatuated with me, I envelop the nape of his neck, holding him to me. His forehead meets mine, our lips brushing but not kissing.

"I was fucking selfish," he whispers. "I want you. I want you slapping me across the face, hitting me with pans." His voice is coarse and uneven while his arm moves between our bodies, keeping his rhythm. "I want you to be my beautiful distraction from this goddamn chaos I've managed my entire fucking life."

I roll my head against the floor of the RV, moaning. "*Bronson.*" I'm reminded of that night at the lookout. Of how I seek pleasure when bad things happen.

Holding on to him, I let myself come apart. Every muscle inside me contracts, tightening and shaking all at once. My pussy clenches around nothing while the painfully aggressive shaft of the Glock continues to rub until I can't take it. I release a loud, agonising cry, coming hard, my orgasm ripping through me to his unrelenting stimulation.

He pulls the gun away.

All my adrenaline drops away.

And my mind is suddenly mush.

Now, I look at him, not sure what to say or do. Not sure how I feel. It's as though I am watching another person being pulled to their feet. Pulled from the RV. Lifted into the air. Cradled against a beautiful warm body.

I look around to see where we are. Straightaway, I recognise the house opposite and know we are at the Butcher residence. The manicured lawn is a blur of green as he strides forward, but I can tell it is different. Not wanting to think, not wanting any memories of the past few hours, I hide my head at the base of his throat.

"Afternoon, boys," Bronson says as he passes two men. Butcher guards, I presume. They have always had them. Two at the front. Two at the back. One across the street.

When he steps inside, I'm taken aback by the white tiles that used to be black. Nothing seems familiar.

"Bron! Are you—*Holy shit*! Is that who I think it is?" I hear the unmistakable voice of Xander Butcher.

"Can't stop to talk, little brother," Bronson states, taking the steep steps two by two. I tighten my arms around him in case he loses his footing and we both tumble down them.

"What is she doing here, Bron?" Xander asks, a hint of concern in his voice, and that is so like him. "You didn't do anything stupid did you?"

Bronson laughs softly. "Define stupid?"

"Kidnapping your ex-girlfriend," Xander states, calling up from below us, his voice just finding us as we turn down a hallway.

Bronson quickly yells back, "Lady-napping. Talk soon. You good? Good boy. *Love you*."

He is all smiles and easy-going conversations, but the

firmness of his hold on me and the speed of his heartbeat sing a different song. My heart isn't fast, though. It feels slow, like my mind. Lethargic. Not interested in action, but merely keeping me alive.

Confused, I lift my hands to touch my face, feel it's still there, still mine. My palms feel rough and strange. I pull them away and stare at blood caked on to parts of my skin. I know whose blood it is. The information isn't missing. I know what happened. I just don't feel anything about it. Nothing at all.

Perry.

Bronson lowers me to the floor, my boots land on tiles. I chant his name in my head —*Perry, Perry, Perry* —trying to invoke a stronger response. I turn to watch Bronson fill up the bathtub.

The ensuite is large.

Polished Carrara tiles run down the walls and across the floor. Gold tap ware. Freestanding bath. It's modern and not the bathroom I remember from childhood. Bronson said Max is an architect, perhaps he designed them a new home.

My eyes land on Bronson, who is now standing in only black pants. He walks towards me. I back up, my feet moving away from him as he closes the gap between us.

"*Shhhh.*" He cups my cheeks when the wall behind my back halts me from moving any further. Tears mist over my eyes. "You're in shock, baby." He steers me towards the tub. "Lift your arms." I do as he asks, watching him as he removes my dress, my bra, my knickers.

Our eyes stay locked.

He unbuttons his pants and slides them down. I am in his arms in an instant, and we are stepping into the bath. Sitting down in warm water, he positions me onto his lap. I can feel his length below my arse, slightly hard. He starts to wash me, his gentle big hands lifting the water up to my shoulders and pouring it over them. Little streams rush down my back and over my breasts.

"Everything is different, baby," he says smoothly. "I want you to know. I'm not *with* Jimmy... I'm against him."

I register his words, lifting my head to look into his eyes. They soften at me. My mind fog still moves between us, between the words, making them hard to completely understand. Why were we there then? Why was Perry?

Perry is dead. Dead. *Dead.*

He's been lying to me...

A surge of fury hits me, and I twist to face Bronson fully, planting my knees on either side of his thighs. His cock presses against my pussy. A groan vibrates in his throat as I slide my folds along his length. The warm bath water sloshes around my body. His pupils dilate as his gaze drops to watch my breasts sway, his thighs tensing beneath my rolling hips.

I move my lips to his, hovering over them. I can kiss him now. I can do anything because it is all over. The past eleven years. Everything I built with Perry. Lies. All the lies. And Akila, she's already dead inside. I weep, feeling my entire life falling down around me.

Cupping his neck, I mash our mouths together, using him to self soothe. He hisses against my bruising lips, his hands massaging up my back, arching me into him. His tongue lashes out, entering my mouth as I try to breathe and sob.

I hate Perry...

I hate every night that I let him fuck me and all the while he was lying to me. Hate every time he threatened to take Akila away. Hate that I loved him once. Hate that he might have loved me. It doesn't even matter. Not anymore. He's dead. Dead. *Dead.* God, stop it! I start to pant as we kiss, panic swallowing me, consuming me.

"It's all lies," I say into his mouth. I break our connection, blinking at him, lost in thought. "I'm alone. There is no one left. I'm alone." I cry softly. *"You won't like where I send your sister,"* I hear the echoes of his words moments before Jimmy shot him. "You won't like where I send your sister," I say, letting his betrayal move through me.

A dark shadow drifts across Bronson's eyes. He lifts me from his lap, turns me to face the wall, and places me on my knees in front of him. I grip the bathtub, the cold ceramic hard within my crushing grasp. I try to break it anyway.

Break it apart.

My head is suddenly yanked backwards, causing my neck to lengthen, raising my chin to the ceiling. He bends me to his desire. His fingers slide up between my legs, stroking between my folds.

"Hard," I whimper, pushing back on them.

The growl he releases is one of agony. As he grips my hip with his other hand, he drives his cock into me. The full length of him from this angle steals my breath. I let out a long cry. He doesn't wait for me to adjust to him, to catch up with his motions.

His hips drive into me hard and fast.

I gasp and moan, yelp and cry, with each slap of his pelvis to my arse. The rawness of his fast pace keeps all the messages, lies, and questions out of my mind.

Out of my reality.

"I. Am. Here!" he grunts, fisting my hair tighter, curving my spine further, fucking me harder with his powerful body. "Can't you feel me, baby?" he hisses, tugging on the long dark strands in his unyielding fist, causing a sting to race across my scalp. "Feel. Me. Fuck.

You. Deep inside you. You're not alone. You'll never be alone again."

My body starts to shake with fatigue, holding myself up on weak, exhausted limbs, keeping myself from falling forward with each thrust of his hips. I'm so full. Then so empty. And it is brutal love-making that hurts in the best mind-numbing way.

When he releases his death grip on my hair, I nearly collapse into the water, but he threads a hand around my waist, holding me up. My knees slide around the bathtub when he presses his chest to my back, but he holds me to him. Feeding his other hand through my fingers, he braces himself.

Then he takes me again, his virile body sliding over me, his hips bucking into me, his fingers squeezing mine as he starts to tense up.

I come apart just like my life has, trembling as wave upon wave of blinding pleasure lurches through me.

As I mewl through my orgasm, he speeds up further for a few more puncturing thrusts. Holding himself deep, he comes into my clenching pussy, using me to pump every drop of cum from him.

He stills, and all I hear are his heavy breaths.

Tears hang in my eyes. My body aches from being taken so hard. But then he peppers kisses along the nape of my neck. A chaste sensation that whispers an apology. An apology for what, I don't know. I wanted it like that. Hard and overwhelming. "You're not alone. Neither of you. I'm going to take care of you. You just have to fucking let me."

His words from when we were kids come crashing back.

. . .

"IT'S ALL GOOD ANYWAY. *I got this, baby. I'm going to take care of you. I actually got what I wanted and I'm never fucking letting you or him go.*"

I DIDN'T LISTEN to him then. If I had, If I had truly believed he could take care of things, I wouldn't have left. We wouldn't have lost so many years together... This time, I'm going to listen to him. Going to believe in him.

CHAPTER TWENTY-NINE
shoshanna

Seventeen years old.

NO.

My room has been completely upturned. Every drawer is out, stacked neatly in the corner, all their contents organised beside them. Every book is piled up on my bed. Every bag is open and emptied on to the mattress. My clothes are all neatly folded in a suitcase. And my dad... he is sitting on the edge of my grey and purple sheets, flicking through my diary with a pained expression etched onto his face.

He lifts his head, brown eyes full of disappointment and disgust, finding me standing in the doorway. I drop my school bag with a thud, my breath suddenly shallow. Dad is a relatively stoic man, but today his disdain soars through my room.

"What are you doing?" I say, my voice like a mouse's

squeak. My body, unable to move, stays frozen with utter dread.

"I had no idea," he mutters, slowly shaking his head.

I look at the diary. At the page that is open. "*No.*"

He exhales through his nose, his dark brows weaving with anger. "It's not my fault," he declares. "Your mother had mental health issues. I really shouldn't be at all surprised that you do too."

Oh God. I fight to breathe. "Dad."

"But I just had no idea." He waves the diary in his hand, laughing once with derision. It's not nice, and I feel a roll of terror whirl through me. "I thought my girls were angels."

Bile moves up my throat, seemingly affected by the surrounding energy. It is thick with guilt and revulsion.

Looking at the diary, he says, "I guessed you might have a boyfriend, but I never knew..."

I stare at the book, wanting to lunge for it, rip it from his hands and swear at him for invading my privacy —our privacy, mine and Bronson's —but we are past that point now.

It is too late.

"Is this all true? Or is it fiction? A game you play with him?" he asks, glancing back at the entry that should have never made it to print. I feel like a colossal fool for writing such a thing —a fool who has condemned herself.

Less than a fool.

Naive.

Ignorant.

Swallowing hard, I force myself to speak. "It's fiction." My face is suddenly cold. My cheeks feel numb. "I made it all up."

He studies me, measuring my expression carefully. "So you're a liar now, too. You lie for him."

"No."

He taps the page. "This young boy came into the hospital. Did you know that? He drove his car off the Stormy River bridge. He drowned, but his body was beaten and bruised. He must have been thrown around a lot. Yet, the car didn't have any damage to show such a thing. The coroner wanted to do an autopsy to confirm the cause of death, but the family stopped us. They didn't want his body disturbed at all. Strange... isn't it? It was as though they feared what they might find. Feared... something."

Tears burn the backs of my eyes. "I don't know."

"You knew a boy died. That he was beaten. What does it say here—" Dad peers down at the page, reading the words aloud. *My words.* "'Bronson feels so guilty, but I don't care about the boy. I just want him to find peace.'" When his eyes meet me again, I see absolute hatred blazing through them. As they repel me, piercing into me, I take a step backwards. He sneers as he says, "Then you let him touch you so that you both felt better about what happened? About murder. Is this all true?"

I cover my mouth, shaking my head slowly. The night at the lookout connected us in a way nothing else could, but the way my father simplifies it makes it feel vile. Feeling vomit growing, ready to release with my panic, I try to steady my breaths. "*No.*"

"You let him touch you that night... and then, you let him put a baby inside you?"

My heart hammers behind my ribcage as my eyes burst with tears. I sob softly under his gaze. "No."

"So you're not pregnant?"

My shoulders heave while emotions consume my entire being. Filled with fear, I just nod hesitantly. I touch my lower stomach, thinking about the potent excitement Bronson felt.

It was undeniably the most peaceful he ever looked. "I'm keeping him."

Dad glares at me, his features twisting into a dark mask of disgust. "No, you won't be." He stands up and walks towards me, tapping the book on his palm. "You'll be getting rid of *it.*" He spits out the word as though it is poisonous. *Dirty.* "Or this goes to the police."

No.

Shaking my head frantically, I try to comprehend his words. No, I don't understand what he's saying. That can't— I can't—"No, please. No," I whimper, breaking down completely in front of him. My heart starts to tear. I reach for his arm, clinging to him with utter despair of his words. "Please don't make me do this to him."

He sneers. "Him?"

"He's finally got something he wanted," I cry. "You don't know the kind of world he was born into. I can't take this from him. He is his." I touch my stomach again. "He wants him. He wants *us.*"

"He has no idea what he wants! You are children!" He shakes me off; his own daughter disgusting him to the point he no longer wants her hands on his clothes. "You're just like your mother. You could go to prison for withholding information. And that boy, he *will* go to prison for half his life if you don't pack your suitcase."

My suitcase? I try to control my fear and grief, but it swallows me whole. Where are we going? When are we going? For how long? "*God.* Please, don't make me do this. I love him."

I sink to my knees, and my dad steps around me. "That's the worst part of all, though... isn't it? What does this say about you? Loving a psychopathic boy like him." He peers down his nose at my crumbled form. "Your appointment is tomorrow. Pack so we can leave straight after."

Leaving me on the floor, sobbing and cradling my stomach, he disappears down the hallway. Akila is suddenly on her knees beside me, holding me to her chest. She rocks me back and forth, kissing my forehead. She doesn't fill the gaps between my heaving breaths and violent sobs with words and lies and hope. There is nothing to say.

No hope to offer. I am utterly *hopeless.*

As my lungs ache, I wince at the pain in my chest.

The tear in my heart severs it in two.

But when Bronson finds out, his heart... his will just die.

CHAPTER THIRTY

bronson

Present day

THE NEXT MORNING, I leave her to sleep the pain away, to give in to fatigue and welcome the mindlessness slumber can offer her. I hope for nothingness for her right now as I leave my bedroom. Hope it's peaceful and black behind her beautiful amber eyes.

As I descend the stairs, I think about her playing with my gun. Her anger. Would she have killed me? Would she kill Jimmy if she could? She is beautifully dark when she lets herself be. I missed that side of her. Images of her mouth open, breathing through her orgasm while my gun slid around her wet pussy, roll around in my mind. My cock stirs.

Then I think about the bathtub. Her screaming that she's alone. Fucking alone?

Where the fuck am I then, baby?

I grin as I picture her body gyrating as I fuck her hard in water stained with her fiancé's blood. I'm glad the fucker is dead, but I still feel venomous towards Jimmy for the spectacle. If I wasn't already planning on killing him, that would have been enough to seal the deal.

And Perry and his familiarity.

Those fuckers know each other...

"I've been keeping an eye on her for you." Jimmy's words hiss through my mind.

I'm going to find out exactly what that means, old boy, and if my girl wants to shoot you in the face, I'm going to show her how.

I'm still not sure what he knows, what he presumes, what he thinks is going down, but he's unpredictable and that isn't usually his style.

Feeling a pull to go back to her, I fight it. If I could stay with her all night, maybe fuck her slow while she sleeps, maybe lick her skin, or just hold her close to my chest to remind her she isn't fucking alone, I would.

My phone buzzes, distracting me from my thoughts. Knowing it's my old man summoning me, I take the hallway towards Dad's office.

When I enter, he rises and approaches quickly. My Dad looks so much like my beautiful Max —same disapproving scowl, same beefcake physique. He's just an old beaten version with badarse scars from years of professional boxing. He's still scary-as-shit, but in a tailored two-piece suit, he could easily be a self-important CEO on his way to a job in the CBD. "You ever get shot again, you better damn tell me or I'll break your nose for disrespecting me. I had to find out from Jimmy that my own son got shot."

I open my arms, offering the grumpy old man a cuddle. "I missed you too, Dad."

He stops an arm's length away, ignoring my outstretched

hands, and stares at my chest with a demand screaming from his concerned face. "Show me what happened."

A light smile hits my lips as I tug my shirt off and tuck it into the back of my jeans. He looks at the wound, hardly distinguishable against the backdrop of an inked red diamond. "I thought we agreed you would say you got away after the shootout? You dumb fuck! What if you had died? What do you think your brothers would do? They'd burn Darwin to the goddamn ground."

"That would be a waste of a beautiful holiday destination." I chuckle, but he eyes me like he's about to make good on his threat. "I knew exactly where to shoot. I'm fine," I say, which is half true. What I didn't expect was how long it would take the ambulance to get to me and how much blood I would lose in the meantime. "There is no way I would've let anyone shoot at Sal and not gone after them," I state adamantly. "I'd never leave him to be picked off. Jimmy knows that. It was the only way. I did what I had to do."

Dad's eyes dart over my shoulder as the office door opens. I twist and grin at the sight of my little brother Xander, who is sighing roughly and shaking his head. He's a pretty fucker, my little bro —still boyish even at twenty-two. "Don't shake your head at me. Come give your big brother a fucking cuddle," I order as he approaches. I know I should be in a worse mood given the night that just past, but I can't seem to settle on anger alone, being home with my family and knowing my beautiful distraction is upstairs in my bed.

Xander bands his arms around me, and I squeeze the little shit hard. Not so little now, really, having been bulking up with his daily boxing obsession.

"You're going to get yourself killed one day." He tightens his arms around me. "I'm not going to survive that, Bron."

"You're going to outlive all of us, buddy. So you'll have to survive it." I release him and move over to Dad's bar, in need of a coffee, before serious discussions commence. "More important things to talk about. Sit down." I look at Dad, who is red faced and ready to pummel me. I chuckle to myself, saying, "You too, old man. Sit down."

Dad moves over to sit behind his desk. He leans back and waits for me to speak. His forehead is tight, brows furrowed —he's unimpressed. I'm cool with it. It's just because the big softy loves me. Xander sits on the chair opposite him while I sip the coffee I poured. Pressing my shoulder to the wall, I eye them both. "It's done," I confirm. "I have the diamonds. Sal is out of the way."

Xander looks down, trying to hide the pain he feels at the loss of his cousin. He knew the deal. It doesn't make it any easier for the kid. "It was quick, buddy. He got laid right before. We had a great send off for him," I say reassuringly, but he doesn't feel things the way I do. I've known that for a long time. I can compartmentalise with ease. He can't.

Dad doesn't flinch, evermore the fixed-faced man I grew up with, but I'm certain that deep inside that scarred heart of his, he feels pangs of grief for the boy he watched grow up alongside his own.

My little brother presses his palms to his face, shaking his head into them. I hate that my actions cause him sorrow, feeling heat in my veins at the sight of it. He doesn't fill the room with his grief, but nor do we disregard his feelings. I feel it too. I'll miss him, but we can't have Sal in the picture when taking down his uncle. It had to be done. Xander knows this. "Demarco is dead too." I pause as Xander raises his head, wide eyed with uncertainty. "I've sent the tattoo on his neck to his boss as a gift."

"What?" Dad leans forward on his desk. "To Dustin?"

A grin spreads across my cheeks, and a flutter begins in my chest. Thinking about the threat Demarco made on my girls, I grin wider still, but it doesn't feel nice at all. It feels manic. "It's being couriered by boat to the docks at Stormy River," I continue. "It's where he's been hiding out. He'll get it in a few days."

"*Jesus Christ,*" Xander mutters. "What if he suspects us?"

"He will. He does. It's why I had to take a bullet. But Demarco let slip that Jimmy isn't happy with Dustin. That Dustin isn't happy with Jimmy," I say, staring at Dad. The look of disapproval has slipped from his face, replaced by intrigue and something else entirely. Something I can't read. "I suppose Jimmy didn't like the spectacle at the auction after all."

Dad offers the roguish of smiles. "Dustin loves his place beside Jimmy, boys. I bet he doesn't enjoy being put on the side-lines like this."

I share a smirk with my dad. "I bet he doesn't."

"What will sending him the tattoo achieve?" Xander asks, looking between us questioningly.

"I want him paranoid, beautiful brother," I state, looking into his wide blue eyes. "So when he receives his oldest friend's skin, he'll know someone means business. But I'm not entirely sure he'll go to Jimmy with this information, given their issues with each other. One man down. One man weaker. I want them all suspicious. At odds. I want them all to fuck up. Just like Jimmy did last night."

Dad tenses. "How so?"

"He showed me his cards," I state, amusement moving through my voice. "He's nervous. I'd say... he's *very* fucking nervous. The stupid idiot flexed his muscles yesterday and showed me he doesn't trust me. And that... he never has." I continue the story, recounting what happened with Shoshanna. With Perry. He's been watching her ... the extent of which I will find out. These are secrets and lies he's had locked up for decades, and I'm cracking the bitches open.

One by one.

I recall what he said last night. *"Do you remember when I told you to hide your vulnerabilities behind your smile? Se? You are very good at doing this... but not today."*

"All these years," I say through a bitter chuckle. "That sly bastard hasn't missed a thing. He's been watching all of us. I don't know what he has on you, Xan, or on Clay, but he's been keeping our vulnerabilities at his fingertips."

I fix my eyes on my dad, who is reining in his anger. He'll head straight for the gym soon, beat the bag until his knuckles shift and ache more than they already do because of serious arthritis. "Konnor was yours," I say to him. "Shoshanna... is mine." I mean that last sentence in more ways than one.

Dad stands up at his desk. "If Jimmy is coming apart, I need to see it for myself. To assess the danger. We have too much to lose now. Jimmy knows it. We are no longer impenetrable. We have Kelly. Cassidy. We are in fact far more vulnerable than we have ever been." He presses the button on his phone for the intercom, speaking into it. "Get Carter to call me. Contact my son, tell him we need him here as soon as he gets back from Bali. Bring the girls too."

He shifts his gaze back to me, and I see his eyes blaze. The flames excite me. I take a step towards him, waiting with bated breath for his approval. I want Jimmy's blood on my hands. I want to see fear in his eyes for the first time... and the last. Dad nods at me, seeing my blood lust shift across my face. "Soon, son. It will be soon. We don't act without

Clay. Jimmy has sent him to Darwin. He's meeting members of their city and appearing to be searching for Salvatore. He'll be back in a few days."

So we wait.

Until then, I have my beautiful distraction.

CHAPTER THIRTY-ONE

shoshanna

Present day

WHEN I OPEN MY EYES, there are three seconds when everything is as it was the day before. Average. Normal things fill my senses: my stomach growls with hunger, my body writhes on the soft sheets, a hot hard wall of muscles holds me from behind... Then the fourth second comes and with it, reality crashes down on me. Images of what happened mere hours ago assault me. I squeeze my eyes shut, fending them off, but that only makes it worse. I open my eyes again and look at the unfamiliar wooden floorboards and white blinds. In the corner of the room is a small teepee displaying the characters from *Frozen*. A large television hangs on the wall directly opposite the foot of the bed. The furniture is a light oak and adorned with scribbles and stickers.

A kid's handiwork, for sure.

It is all too strange.

And the emptiness in my stomach and rip through my heart, remind me again why... I grip at the thick, fully tattooed arm draped over my waist. I squeeze harder, silently begging him to wake up because I'm awake and aware, and I don't want to be alone in this state.

Perry is dead...

"It's okay, baby," Bronson mutters, his voice gravelly and deep in his sleepy condition. His fingertips trail the length of my side, provoking little goosebumps all over my skin. I spin to face him, to find his beautiful, turquoise-coloured eyes batting back from slumber.

He leans in and draws little circles on my nose with his. My heart aches. Eleven years apart. Eleven years wasted. "It'll be okay. Don't think about it." He crawls down my body slightly, bracing my breast in his palm, licking at the tight bud on top. "I missed your tits." I feed my fingers through his hair. The dark-brown strands are exactly what I want coiled around my fingers. The colour I want.

He mouths my nipple softly. "I was rough yesterday," he says between breaths and kisses, loving my body worshipfully.

I breathe the words through a moan. "I needed it."

"I want you now. I want you slow." He rubs his face between my breasts, groaning as the soft flesh jiggles. He rubs his rock-hard cock into my thigh. "I want you bound to my bed. I want you writhing beneath me. I want to take my time."

I sigh through the emotions he brings. "But it's not okay. I'm not okay, Bronson. I'm not okay with anything that happened."

Continuing his reverent caresses of my breasts, he speaks against the soft, supple flesh. "We'll work at it. Work through it together. Remember? You said that to me at the lookout that day."

'THEN YOU LET HIM TOUCH YOU," *Dad spat out. "So that you both felt better about what happened? About murder. Is this all true?'*

THE VISION of him fingering me after he killed that boy comes back. Of him making me come with his gun moments after Jimmy shot Perry in the head. Of us in the bathtub in blood-dyed water. I cover my face, escaping into my palms. "There is something very wrong with me."

His lips still on my nipple. Shifting until his hands cup my face, his tattooed fingers knotted through my hair, he stares at me. "There is *nothing* wrong with you. Trust me, I see you."

I exhale in a rush, lost in the tempestuous waves of green and blue pinning me to the bed. "Okay, Butcher. Tell me... what do you see?"

His palm moves to cover my face, his fingers stroking the contours and curves adoringly. I close my eyes, holding them like that, still feeling his gaze moving around my features with a scorching intensity. "You are *perfect*. My perfect Shoshanna. I've seen the bitch and angel in you, baby. I've seen you crazy. Sexy... Kind. I know *you*. And you know what you are... someone who *tries*. Someone who *fights*. No matter the obstacle. No matter the damage. You *fight*."

He moves his hand back into my hair, and I open my eyes to find him staring down at me. Dipping his head, he takes my lips softly, sucking and pulling on the top pleat. I slide my tongue out and into the gap between his mouth, licking his as it moves out as well. It's slow and sensual, and sailing through every motion are our feelings for one another. His fingers make circles in my hair while his legs cage me between them. His long muscular body presses down on top of me, stealing a tiny bit of air, enough to warn me of his strength, his possession... of *him*. And his cock is hard and pulsing between our mashed bodies. I lift my hips into him, my breath skipping around between our kisses.

His mouth leaves mine in a slow, teasing way, drawing down my lower lip until he releases it. He moves to my chin, his tongue leading, licking me in an animalistic way that no other man has ever done before. No one has ever *tasted* me like Bronson Butcher has.

I can't get swept away. Can't allow myself this moment of pleasure until I know what to expect when I get home. "Akila," I whisper. "Akila."

He braces himself on one elbow, his eyes connecting with mine again. "Your phone is on the bedside table."

I blink at him. "What?"

A slow, sweet curve moves across his lips, his dimple setting into his left-cheek. "Call whoever you need to. My dimple and I comply."

I smile a little. And not wasting any time, I scoot to the side of the mattress and grab my phone. As I unlock the display, Bronson rolls onto his back and I glance over to see his cocky, relaxed position. Lifting his hands, he cups the back of his neck. The entire length of his naked tattooed body is on display beside me, his cock a long thick ridge slung across his thigh, his ankles crossed casually.

Jesus Christ.

I try to concentrate on the phone, having saved her details even though I've never actually used them before.

"Hello?" I hear Mary's hesitant voice say through the speaker.

"Mary," I say her name with a sigh of relief. "It's Dr Adel. Is Akila—" I stop before I say anything that could cause alarm. I have no idea what Perry has told them, but I doubt he would draw unwanted attention, given his respectability and the web of lies around it. I clear my throat. "How is Akila today?"

"Where have you been?" she asks, hinting at unease. "Perry said you needed a break. Are you okay?"

I breathe out fast. "Yes. I'm fine. I'm just having a little time off. A bit of *me* time." *God*, that sounds dumb. I would never usually say anything like that. "Has Brenda started doing full-time night shifts?"

"Yes. Akila has twenty-four-seven care at the moment, but..." She pauses and my heart hits the back of my throat.

"But what?" I ask, my voice a high-pitched, uneven cadence. Bronson slides in behind me, his long muscular legs frame mine, hanging down the sides of the mattress.

"Perry mentioned before he left that he plans on putting her in a home. That you two need more alone time. And that you agreed. I know how you feel about that, so... "

"No," I grind out. I lean against Bronson, finding comfort that I never realised I was missing... this entire time. "He has changed his mind." I think fast, think of what to do from afar. "I'm going to send a," I internally groan at the word, "*friend* around to see you with all the details. And to collect a few things and spend some time with Akila for me. Her name is Katie. When she gets there, can you let her in? She's a registered nurse at my hospital, so she'll be fine with Akila."

Mary lets out a sad little scoff. "Dr Adel, I've been looking after Akila for two years. I am very fond of her. She is such a beautiful, fiery spirit. Perry once said you think she is still in there. But he doesn't. Well, I do. I have wanted to tell you a few times, but you always seem... uninterested in talking to me. When you get home, her eyes flare with happiness. But I want you to know that it isn't because we haven't had a wonderful day together; it's just because she loves you so much."

I suck a wobbly breath in, her words filling me with so much emotion it takes me a few seconds to force the tears down. "Mary, I have never said—"

"You have never said anything," she interrupts. "You're right. But your body language makes it perfectly clear that you don't want me looking after your sister."

I deflate. "That's not—"

"I know you want to look after her yourself," she says persistently. "*God*, I think that is so wonderful. But I've seen this before, and if you don't find a happy medium, you'll resent her. You don't need to prove anything to anyone. Of course, you can look after her. You can be a good sister and live your own life too."

I shake my head and sigh. "It's not you... I just..."

"I know," she says with wisdom and understanding moving through her tone. "Just let me do my job. I would never let *anything* happen to her... I'll let your friend in to see her, of course, Dr Adel."

"Shoshanna," I say, guilt lacing my voice for judging her so quickly without even giving her a chance. "Please, just call me Shoshanna."

"Okay," she says, and I can hear her smile. "Enjoy your *me* time. Akila will be fine. I promise."

"Oh, Mary?" I jump in quickly before she can put the phone down. "Can you read her the magazines that come in the mail?"

She laughs softly. "I already do."

Tears sting the back of my eyes, clinging to the corners, ready to overflow and release with them all the drowning weights of my self-inflicted responsibilities. My adamant viewpoint to be the only one capable of understanding my sister's needs. Of caring for her. "Thank you."

"Talk soon, Shoshanna."

"Bye," I say, lowering the phone from my ear. I stare straight ahead, feeling waves of guilt and stupidity hammer down on me. I never even gave her a chance. I wanted to prove to everyone that I could be her guardian. I still felt like a child when she was in that car crash... I never considered my attitude towards the nurses was driven by pride and stubbornness and jealousy.

Big, tattooed arms cross over my chest, pulling me backwards and locking me against the wall of his hard body. Bronson's head rests on my shoulder, and I tilt my forehead to meet the edge of his. I sigh. "I think Akila is okay."

"Want me to send someone to get her?"

He's always diving straight in, never scanning the area for danger, assessing the room, just throwing himself into what he wants. I'm not ready to involve Akila in this mess. In this world. I look down at the phone, my fingers unenthusiastically calling the only person left to call, the only person who is close to a sort of acquaintance of mine.

She picks up the phone. "They have fired you," Katie says straightaway, her tone dripping in amusement.

I force the truth out, past my pride and need to be levelheaded and pristine. I've been fired anyway, so what the hell. "You know the guy...*The* guy, well, he drugged me, kidnapped me, and dragged me back to our home city." I breathe out fast. The rumble of Bronson's laughter vibrates against my spine. I clutch the phone harder, as her silence both annoys and concerns me. "Katie?"

She clears her throat. "Well, um, that's quite a week you've had. Do you need—"

"You were right," I blurt. "I was stuck up. I was rude to you—" My voice breaks on the honesty. "I treated you like you were beneath me. I might have even believed it. You don't have to listen or care, but there it is."

She sighs. "Who is looking after Akila?"

I pause, surprised she knows my sister's name, even more surprised she cares. Apparently, I'm silent for too long because she says, "Your sister?"

I scoff. "I know who Akila is."

"*Sorry.*" She clicks her tongue. "Guess I thought maybe you had *Cockheimers.*"

I reach up and rub my temples. "What?"

She laughs. "Memory and mental abnormalities from the excessive consumption of cock."

I shake my head, fighting my reluctant smile, my dark satirical side chuckling. "That's seriously inappropriate, Katie. That's a really terrible disease."

"Yes. So is *Cockheimers.* It kills ambitions. Motivations. *Elasticity...* I knew you weren't as boring as you acted. *Fuck.* I might actually like you... no wait, false alarm. So you want me to check on Akila? Where's Perry?"

His name moves into my throat, lodging itself in deep while I struggle for a response. "He's not around," I finally say. "I think he... *left* me."

"Do you wanna be my BFF?"

I groan. "Oh my God, I hate you."

"No, you don't," she sings. "You fucking like me, which is why you called me. Are you going to go to the police?"

Bronson's lips touch my shoulder, and a shiver rushes the full length of my body, curling my toes. "*No...* it's not really like that."

"You fucking hussy."

"Fine," I submit, my tone void. "I'm a hussy."

"Jesus, you could sound happier about it." She breathes out with exasperation, disappointment moving through the sound. I'm just not up for a verbal sparring match. "I'll go see your sister."

Relief embraces me. "Thank you." After giving her the address, I kill the call, feeling overwhelmed. I wish I could switch it off again, slip into another quiet, sleepy place and wake up when Perry's memory is distant and painless. "She is going to check on her," I say to Bronson. "Katie is a really excellent nurse."

"Oh yeah. Hot blonde," he says, locking me tight to him. I cringe at his admiration for her appearance, especially seeing how she is my complete opposite. His hand moves up to my throat, where he circles the column and squeezes softly. "Stay with me," he murmurs, and my pulse thunders on the other side of his fist. "Stay with me. I'll do anything, everything for you. I'll do whatever you ask."

I smile at the thought. "Don't call her hot again."

"Done."

"Are you giving me the choice to stay?" I ask, my breaths laboured from the air deficiency his fist causes. "What if I say no?"

"Try me," he growls by my ear, suddenly releasing my throat. He shuffles from the bed. I twist to face him, following his movements across the room as he pulls a pair of jeans and a shirt on. Perving at him, I realise I've never done that with another man before. I like the way he moves, like the smoothness of his strides, the confidence in each gesture.

"What did I say about looking at me like that?" he says,

pulling me out of my head. I smile a little at him, not feeling good but not feeling terrible either.

"Are we in danger?" I ask because last night may be as normal as breakfast to him. I want to ask him again what is going to happen to Perry's body, but I think I know the answer.

"*You* are not in danger," he assures me, and my heart twists at the thought of something happening to him.

Unaffected by the topic, he pulls his bike jacket on, looking so much like *my* Bronson. The black leather stretches around his manly body and I feel like I want to smile at him again, but it also feels wrong to smile too much today. "I'll take care of everything. You just need to trust me." His eyes roll over my face in a thoughtful way. "Will you come for a ride with me? Clear the shit out of your head?"

"If I cleared all the shit out, I'm not sure what would be left," I admit, because the *shit* is so heavily wrapped around every memory I have. Dad. Perry. Akila. *Him.*

"Don't clear it then, baby. Just organise it... Come on, I have something I want to show you." He grabs his helmet from on top of a chest of drawers. Ducking quickly into the walk-in robe, he reappears with a spare bike jacket and ... *my helmet.* I take a quick breath in at the sight of it. It is silver with purple glittery swirls. The perfect helmet for a sixteen-year-old girl.

"She's been waiting for you," he says with a smirk. "I've got plenty of spares, so I didn't let anyone else wear her. I did feel sorry for her, though. It's not her fault I can't stand to see her on another girl's head."

Tears threaten to fill my eyes, but I force them down. I stand up and walk over to his drawer, aware that I'm naked, aware of his eyes as they blaze trails across my skin. I pull out a pair of black sweatpants and one of his t-shirts.

"In the top right drawer," he says, nodding towards it. "You'll find some clothes."

I glance at him sideways, dubious. "I'm not wearing some other slut's clothes."

A slow grin moves across his face. "I like it when you're jealous. Reminds me of good times... But don't worry, baby. They're Stacey's. She leaves a heap in Xander's room. Some might fit you."

"She's still always here, hey?" I ask, remembering Xander's best friend from high school. "Have her and Xander finally got together?"

"No, actually." He moves closer to me, leaning his shoulder on the wall. "She's gay."

"Oh." Opening up the drawer, I see a tiny pair of jeans and leggings. I spin to face him, my brows knitting together. "These will be tight."

He hums his satisfaction. "I was hoping so."

After I pull on a white singlet and squeeze into the dark denim jeans, I grab hold of my old helmet and we head to the garage.

I want to smile again when I see the Ducati. The same red one he had eleven years ago. With all his money, I have no idea why he wouldn't buy a new one. He's sentimental, my Bronson. He helps me into the jacket, buttoning it up for me and checking the fit; it's way too big.

"I'll get you your own soon," he says, swinging his leg over the Ducati. When he ignites the engine, he ignites something inside me, too. The roller door shudders to a start, disappearing into the roofline. I walk slowly over, feeling my heart growing and my lungs wanting to breathe deeply.

Sliding on behind him, I band his waist and lift my shoes onto the footrest. He takes off, the growl of the engine not painful to hear like I thought it might be. The last time I saw his bike, heard his bike, it was screaming away from me in a manifestation of his rage. Today though, the growl is thrilling and soothing and *us*. We are so much more than that day.

We fly around the District streets as if we never left, as if we never lost all this time together. And I decide that I was right all those years ago; the sound of freedom is the growl of his Ducati. Holding him tightly, I watch the streets pass, some with familiarity and others seemingly foreign. It's my city. It may be corrupt. And I may have not always loved it, but my memory of it involves a sense of invisibility and youth. Of possibility. Of eternity. I felt like he was the king of this town, and I was his queen.

No one could have convinced me otherwise.

That is, not until the day my dad found my diary. Until he showed me what little power I had. What reality really looked like. I sigh, thinking about the past years with Perry. Tears build in my eyes for him. Maybe he had no idea what he was getting into with Jimmy Storm.

I'd like to think he was led astray.

I'd like to think that, but I don't believe it.

As we curve around a cliff and head up a steep sandy road, I steady myself. Bronson revs the engine, and the bike soars around like a young vehicle, not like the well-used machine it is. We get to the top of the cliff, slowing down to a stop. My breath is taken away by the view of Connolly, over the rooftops, and in the distance, the ocean —a waving blue abyss stretching to the end of our reality.

We jump off and Bronson helps me with my helmet, his hands taking the opportunity to stroke my jaw and neck. Within my pocket, my phone vibrates. Bronson watches me closely as I retrieve the handset and open the notification. As a selfie of Katie and Akila pops up, my chest tightens. My sister looks the same, vague but beautiful, lost somewhere behind her amber eyes or not there at all. I don't know which.

I snap a quick selfie before capturing the view. Sending the pictures back, I ask Katie to show Akila where I am.

Where I am...

Home.

I breathe in the air; it smells familiar and like rebellion.

"Recognise any of this?" Bronson asks, pulling me back to him. He leads me over to the edge. The wind whips my hair around, so I collect it all up and pull it down one shoulder.

Peering across the tops of houses and over what looks like a light industrial area to the west, I try to recognise something specific. "I don't recognise this area... I mean, I recognise the ocean."

"Well done." He chuckles, standing behind me, shielding me from the wind as it whirls up the hill. "Top marks. You really are a scholar, baby. That *is* the ocean."

I shake my head, wanting to smile but still feeling sadness circling all my other feelings, keeping them in check. "Cute."

"Yeah." He positions my shoulders to the west and wraps his arms around my middle, resting his chin on top of my crown. Pointing, he says, "Recognise that tree?"

I blink at it. It's a Norfolk Pine. "Is that *our* Norfolk Pine?" Suddenly desperate to see the lookout or anything familiar, I search harder. The sadness circling everything inside me shifts into my stomach, forcing it to drop. "It's all gone. They developed it."

I feel his chin move on top of my head as he nods. "Yeah. They developed it four years ago. The whole reserve is gone. It's all light industrial businesses now."

"I hate that," I spit out. "Why industrial? Why not at

least cafes or houses? Can I see it from here? Where was it?" I ask, and I know he doesn't need further context. He lowers his head to beside mine, cheek to cheek. I shiver as his warm breath collides with my skin.

Lifting his arm, he points to a silver roof. "It was right there, baby. Our palace." I let out a stained sigh. "I watched them tear it down from here," he says.

I turn to look at him, long dark strands slithering out from my fist and whirling around my face. Craning my neck, I search his perfect face, remembering how annoying I found his beauty the first time I saw him. "What did you do when they demolished it?"

His eyes stay glued ahead as he says, "I watched and got very *very* drunk."

My heart twists. "Alone?"

Releasing a small, sad chuckle, he looks at me as if I should understand this. Should have known. "Who would I've been with?"

A tear slides down my cheek. "That isn't real," I say, shaking my head adamantly. "That kind of love. Even people who love each other to the ends of the earth still find love again if it ends. They put that person in a special place inside them and move on."

He says nothing and his silence is like a poker to my heart. Bronson has been alone all this time. Never quite letting anyone in. I envision him up here, watching the bull-dozers flatten the trees and shrubs. Watching the wooden planks from our lookout falling apart and rolling into the dirt. My throat tightens and I try to swallow down my grief, but it's uncomfortable. "Did you find no one else? Ever?"

His eyes soften and he lifts his hand, his fingers spanning out to touch my face. I close my eyes as he traces my features the way he likes to do. "I've been with plenty of girls, baby," he admits. "I *care* about a lot of them. But *you're* my girl."

His hand drops from my face, leaving my skin singing about the love he has for me. Love like that of a fairy-tale. Unrealistic. Dangerous. Intense. Wild. But how else would I expect Bronson Butcher to love other than that?

I open my eyes and he's grinning at me, his dimple set into his left cheek. "Let's watch Disney movies for the rest of the day. You should just let that beautiful mind relax."

And it actually sounds perfect.

For the first time in as long as I can remember, I'm not worried about Akila. I'm not desperate to prove myself at work. I have no next step... Or responsibility. I just feel lost... And I'm okay with it because when we are lost, we are forced to look for ourselves. "That sounds good."

CHAPTER THIRTY-TWO

shoshanna

Present day

THE NEXT DAY, I'm still fighting the visions of Perry on the floor. Covered in blood. The sound of the gunshot. I wish I knew what to do now. I've always had a goal. A direction. A person to go home to... first my dad, then Akila, then Perry... Now, my direction is unclear.

In any normal situation, I'd be going to the police. Go back to work. Hope time heals the loss. But it isn't a normal situation. I don't feel the loss of Perry as the more I think about him, the more I hate him for the lies. The more I feel residual shame for letting him touch me. I do feel *loss*... but it is the loss of the false reality he painted. Loss of the future we started to build around his lies and deceit. And it isn't a normal situation because Jimmy Storm owns the police... But I hold on to Bronson's words. *"I'm not with him. I'm against him."*

It feels wrong to wish for a man's death.

Nevertheless, I wish for Jimmy Storm's death.

We spend the morning riding around the District again. Now Bronson has something he wants to show me. Given the last trip. I'm convinced this one will hit me with just as much melancholy. So, while observing the roads he takes, I become pretty sure we are moving through the light industrial area the reserve once occupied. Breathing deeply, I emotionally prepare myself to see the silver roofed building. As I'm sure that is where he is taking me.

We turn the corner and as we pull up the drive, my heart expands even more at the sight of what is ahead. We ride past rows and rows of motorbikes before he circles the building, heading towards a large dirt track. Kids stand on the side, looking a few bikes over. Two others race around the track. We park-up alongside a black Harley and within seconds, four dirt bikes approach us. The kids on them yelping excitedly at Bronson, competing to get his attention.

"I changed the drive sprocket from a fifteen to a fourteen tooth!" one of them yells.

"He didn't. He's full of shit! I did it," another insists.

"You fixed the chain, I fucking changed the sprocket!"

They couldn't be over twelve-years-old. I find myself in awe of them as I jump off the Ducati, Bronson quickly following me. "Boys, boys, we have a lady present. Watch your language," he says with cool amusement as he pulls his helmet off and hangs it on the handlebars.

He approaches me, helping me remove my helmet like he always does, and all the boys fall into quiet anticipation, watching and waiting. I can't take my eyes off them as they vibrate with excitement. They remove their helmets, revealing sweaty wet hair that sticks to their foreheads. They grin at Bronson, admiration glowing within every set of eyes. I wouldn't be surprised if they have a Bronson shrine here.

I shake my hair loose, and the boys are now staring at me. "Hi, I'm Shoshanna," I say, bouncing my gaze between them and their bikes. "Cool bikes. Are they yours?"

"He owns them," one boy says, pointing at Bronson but grinning at me, his lips curving to the side in a flirtatious way. He feeds his hand through his slick black hair, saying, "But we fix em."

"You break em," a boy with blond hair laughs.

"Are you flirting with my girl, Callum?" Bronson teases, entwining our hands and guiding us towards the track. "Show us what you boys have been working on."

As we make our way over to the dusty, hilling track, the boys swarm around us. They look like puppies tumbling at our heels, desperate for a pat. It's adorable.

We join a few more boys, and they all show us their bikes. They laugh amongst themselves; the commotion and their hollering are enough to finally cause my smile to beat the sadness. I watch them banter, and when Bronson clips one kid over the back of the head for cursing, they all laugh.

I do too.

"Take her out. She's so fast," the boy I now know is Callum says, his eyes darting eagerly from Bronson to the bike. "She'll be a smoother ride than your grandma Ducati."

I gasp in mock horror. "Oh, man. That's fighting words."

"Well well." Bronson climbs on the dark green dirt-bike, kick starting her. "I best defend my girl's honour and prove you wrong. Let's see how she goes."

"Here," I hear a feminine voice say from behind me as Bronson speeds off around the track. Some boys jump on their machines, racing after him, while others run over to the side, hooting and teasing.

I spin around and a woman my age is holding out a beer for me. She's tanned with dark-brown hair and eyes, perhaps an islander —Samoan or Maori. Her button up blue shirt is covered in oil and dirt, but she still looks attractive.

"Thank you." I take it and use that opportunity to peer over at the building. The far side looks like a motorbike mechanic's workshop, a few men kneeling, working on fancy looking machines. The other side looks like a motorbike massacre, parts everywhere, bits and pieces and half-built vehicles. A bit of formality and a bit of anarchy. It's a large area. Noisy with both machinery and music.

The vibe is playful.

I like it a lot.

"They love it when he visits. It's not often enough," the girl says, moving in next to me, looking across the yard. Out of the corner of my eye, I see her tilt her beer to me, so I tilt mine to hers. They clink in greeting. "I'm Juliette."

"Shoshanna," I say, unable to tear my eyes from Bronson as he takes the jumps, getting air, pushing the machine to its limits.

"He's never brought anyone here before," she states, her voice husky and confident. "I know who he is. The whole District knows. But... I have never met his brothers."

I turn to look at her. "You're friends?"

"Not really." She turns to face me, raisin-coloured eyes meet mine. "He owns the place." She shrugs. "I manage it." A little smile hits her lips as though she knows our history — our secrets —but before I can pry, she walks back towards the workshop. "Nice to meet you, Shoshanna," she calls out over her shoulder.

In my own company again, with the view of him and those boys, the lovely district breeze that smells like our lookout and my past, I realise something that becomes hard to swallow. Something that makes the empty place in my stomach retch, turn, and sting.

Our boy would have been about their age...

So, while I watch Bronson pull the bike up alongside the eager boys and jump off, patting Callum on the back encouragingly, I get a front row view of what life could have been. Of what my life with Bronson *should* have been. With our son. His words from years ago soar around me. *"I'll be better. A good citizen. Pay taxes and shit. I'll get a part-time job or whatever. Fuck, I'll work on bikes. I'd like that."*

Tears begin to bubble, but I swallow them down with the knot in my throat. I want this picture with him. He was my choice. All those years ago, I chose him. In that moment, Bronson looks at me from the side-line, a small grin hitting his lips.

A grin just for me.

He says something that makes the boys sulk before striding towards me. I take a step towards him, craning my neck to meet his green-blue gaze.

He nods at the workshop. "Do you like it, baby?"

I let myself smile at him; it's sad but still a smile. I just wish I could fall in love with him all over again without the weight of what happened a few days ago, making me feel as though I shouldn't be happy. "I think you're something special, nutcase."

Sitting heavily between us is the truth about what this means, why he did it, who he did it for. But neither of us can manage to say it aloud in case it is the catalyst to this dreamy state I am in willingly.

His hand moves to my neck, cradling my head from below my chin. "Well, my evil plan is working, then. Isn't it? You ready to head back?"

I grab his helmet off the Ducati and stand on my tippy

toes, raising it to his head. He dips so that I can put the helmet on him, smirking with a satisfied curve to his lips.

And in those few seconds, a tiny bit of the *shit* in my head organises itself. What happen to Perry wasn't his fault. It was Jimmy's and... maybe even his own for believing he could trap me using borrowed power from the likes of Jimmy Storm. He lied to me about who he was. Something Bronson would never do; he has never pretended to be anything other than exactly what he is. I used to be the same. I'd like to be that again. I tap the side of Bronson's helmet with my palm. "Let's go, nutcase."

During the ride back, I think about how much I need to talk to him about that day in the park. It's a dangerous entity whirling around us. I don't want to get swept up in it, but I do want to acknowledge it.

After we arrive at his house, we eat and then shower. I sit on the mattress, naked and drying my hair with a towel, wondering how long I'm going to pretend I don't have a house and a life in Darwin. Am I staying with him? Should I bring Akila here? I know the answer, even though it seems completely crazy. I know I'll never want to leave. We can pick up where we left off. We can...

He slides his naked body in behind me, taking the towel from my hands, drying my wet strands.

"You said you wanted me to stay with you." I sigh, feeling his fingers massaging my scalp from the other side of the material. "Did you mean—"

"I meant *stay*," he murmurs by my ear. "Be with me. Bring Akila home. I'll take care of both of you like I always wanted to."

And that's just it. I've had enough of people taking care of me. "I think I should take care of myself from now on."

"Fine." His breath hits my neck. "Take care of me too."

A small smile tugs at the corner of my mouth, but he can't see it. I look out the window at the canals behind their house, at the rooftops on the other side. Memories flow back. "I need looking after, baby." He licks the shell of my ear, mouthing it and taking it into his mouth. "Ever think of that?" he says, kissing from my ear to my neck. "That maybe...maybe I needed you much more than you ever needed me."

I think about how painful it was without him. Going through that again... I don't think I can. "I'm scared."

"Me too."

"Do you think we can just pick up where we left off?" I sigh, the concept impossible after everything we have been through. "Just... I don't know. Move forward."

"We can try—" Quickly he pulls me backwards with him, rolling me onto my stomach. My damp dark-hair fans out all around the sheets. I inhale quickly as he mounts me, his cock slapping the crease of my arse. "You wanna pick up where we left off? Well, do you remember the first time we made love, baby?" He places a hand on either side of my head on the pillow.

Of course, I remember, Bronson.

Twisting my head, I peer back at him. *"Yes."*

"Remind me," he teases, looking down at me like the boy I fell in love with at thirteen but with the body of man, skin adorned with ink and muscles and stories. "How did it happen?" His eyes grow heavy as he strokes his cock between my arse cheeks, jerking himself off with my body. I watch him, licking my lips at the vision of how indecent and delicious he is. "You snuck into my room on my seventeenth birthday." I smile. "You brought me red roses. You told me you didn't want to buy them. That it was a copout. You wanted me to have roses that were never meant for anyone else. So, you picked wild ones and sliced the thorns off with the knife you kept in your boot. Your blood was on the stem of one where you cut yourself and I thought nothing was more romantic than that."

He crawls down my body, reverently kissing every inch of skin along my spine. I roll my face around the pillow, close my eyes and just... *feeling him.*

"You wanted our first time to be special," I say. "You waited so long for me. Max was already having sex, but you weren't. You never made me feel bad about it, either. But I knew you needed it this night. I saw it in your eyes and was so nervous. I didn't know what to do with my hands. So ... you pushed me onto my stomach and told me to grip the sheets."

Bronson runs his fingers up my sides, little shivers rushing along their path. He moves my arms up and feeds our fingers together, moulding mine around the sheets and blankets, just like he did all those years ago. Lifting my pelvis off the mattress, he tucks a pillow under my hips.

"Keep going," he whispers beside my ear.

"You knelt either side of my thighs and played with my pussy," I say as he follows my words like a command, sitting on his heels, his thighs either side of mine. I moan when his fingers touch the wet swelling lips between my legs.

He hums in a deep, raw cadence. "You have a perfect pussy, baby. Smooth. Tight. Your beautiful pink inside is hidden from me until I part these lovely, tanned lips."

Jesus christ.

I moan at his words. At his touch. His fingers are worshipful in their slow and skilled exploration. I rub my hips into the pillow, tilting my pussy to him. Writhing and humming, I struggle to think or form thoughts, let alone words.

"Then I licked my fingers," he says for me, because I'm too intent on giving myself over to the soft sensual torture he is subjecting me to. "I wiped your juices on my lips so I could taste you while I made love to you for the first time. I wanted all my senses to be full of you. My entire being to be absorbed by you. Only you." His hands leave my aching, needy core. I twist my face further to watch him coat his lips with *me*. No man has ever made every part of me seem like a meal. Like a treat. He closes his eyes as he licks at his fingers, forcing me to moan my arousal.

Opening his eyes and staring down at me, a glimmer of sadness shifts through his eyes, but then it's gone. Before I can think more about it, he drops to his elbows, his hard body stealing my air, labouring my breaths.

His forehead presses to my hair, lips touching my ear. "Then I sank inside you." Reaching down, he manoeuvres us both. Slowly, he pushes inside me, squeezing my legs together with his thighs, tightening the hole he's dipping into. I whimper at his excruciatingly slow speed.

"I told you I loved you. I told you how good you were doing," he says around deep rumbling groans, his voice coiled and near breaking. "I love you, Shoshanna. I love you. You're such a good girl to me... You take me *so* good."

"*Bronson*," is all I can manage; my voice is trapped in my throat with all my sorrow and happiness and melancholy. Feeding his hand beneath me, he presses it to my lower abdomen, and I nearly break on a sob. His palm rests right over the spot our baby was growing.

"I love you," he murmurs, but I don't know if he's talking to me this time. Tears build inside my eyes as he cradles my empty womb, reminding me, reminding us, who we are and what we have been through.

His breaths become strained, gruff, as he starts to move inside me, deep and meaningful and with a painful amount of sentiment. Sliding his face over to mine, he kisses me. Our mouths dance and moan at a collective pace.

He is so gentle with each thrust and withdraw that every pulse of his cock ripples through me. The movements slow and rhythmic.

Time passes by, and he keeps himself close, deep, keeps his lips caressing mine and his hand protectively over my abdomen. My heart aches, and I hope one day... I hope that one day it doesn't still hurt like this.

As I feel my orgasm building through my muscles, forcing my body to tighten in preparation to unravel with sensation, he speeds up slightly. And I know he wants to come *with* me. I let out a loud groan, so he eats at my mouth, enclosing my sounds within our kiss.

I come hard, shaking and tensing, and as I do, he suddenly loses a bit of control, his own climax consuming his movements and confusing his pace. My pussy clenches around his cock, wringing his release out. The palm holding my abdomen presses up harder, and I know he can sense his cock pressing on the other side as he comes inside me.

When he lies on my back, letting most of his weight press on me, he says, "He can still have siblings. A bit of you. A bit of me. We'll give him siblings." At those words, at the way they were uttered with a hoarse, strangled tone, I erupt, sobbing without restraint. Now he has acknowledged the thing that broke us up. And he doesn't know... he doesn't know that I can't fix it. Can't give his boy a sibling. I gasp for air around my fitful cries. "I'm so sorry," he says, peppering kisses all over the nape of my neck. "I'm sorry I wasn't there for you, baby. I'm sorry you went through that alone. I'm sorry you thought I blamed you. All these years. I didn't blame you."

Shaking my head against the pillow, I weep.

I blame myself.

Because I can't give him siblings.

I can't give you what you want, Bronson.

CHAPTER THIRTY-THREE

shoshanna

Seventeen years old.

THE PARK IS empty today and I'm glad. Trees sway gently in the breeze, but the sun is out, bright and happy when it has no right being so. Its heat doesn't reach me either.

Hugging my knees to my chest, I bat my arid eyes slowly. They burn, the hours of crying have left them rough and dry. The tears now caked on my cheeks, the salty streams pinching at my sensitive skin.

I look like hell.

I know I do.

Broken capillaries dot my eyelids from the violent sobs and I'm cold. Colder than I can remember ever being. Goosebumps race across every inch of my skin as I rock back and forth on the grass, just focused on breathing, on the air entering me and then leaving my body.

My hollow body.

My empty body.

Inside my abdomen, cramps and spasms take over. The flesh having been disturbed—violated. Wincing, I squeeze my eyes shut to the feel of the punches of pressure inside me. Between my legs, I bleed out the little bits that protected him for nearly three months. It couldn't protect him though.

I couldn't.

Dad confiscated my phone yesterday, but I found it a few hours ago in his overnight bag, with several missed calls from Bronson. And now, it vibrates in my clenched fist with a call, but I don't dare answer it.

I don't have much time.

The truck is at our house.

I snuck away, but he will surely be looking for me. The growl of Bronson's motor bike echoes in distant streets, the sound racing towards me, soaring through the air like a warm protective coat of armour no one can break through.

My armour.

My bottom lip wobbles.

It doesn't sound like freedom today…

Within seconds, the Ducati is screaming into the carpark. The bike doesn't even completely stop before he kills the engine and leaps from it, sending the heavy machine into the ground where it slides a few meters along the bitumen. He races towards me, throwing the helmet from his face. His movements, desperate and riddled with fear.

Slowly, I stand on shaky legs and when he reaches me, he swallows me up in his arms. Holding the shaky, cold frame of me so tight, I might burst.

"What's going on? What happened? Is it the baby?" he asks, and a lump fills my throat. I wrap my arms around his warm, hard body. A wall of muscles.

They couldn't protect us this time.

And I had to choose.

I had to choose you, Bronson, over our boy. I couldn't bear the thought of you in prison for most of your life.

He's going to hate me soon, and so I can't bring myself to tell him right away. Nuzzling into his chest, seeking comfort in the broad wall of his body, I fist his shirt with desperation, sobbing tearlessly against him.

I breathe him in, trying to bank the scent of my first love into my memories. *Forever.* I wish I could bottle it. Bottle Bronson Butcher. The way he makes me feel so precious. Beautiful. Interesting. Unique. The one for him. And the way he accepts all my crazies.

That *is* what love is.

He pushes me out from his chest. His green-blue irises whirl with concern and discomfort and something else, something dangerous, a brewing storm of volatility. He searches me, every inch of skin, mapping my cracked lips and ballooned eyes. He lifts his hand to stroke down my face, forcing me to close my eyes, exhaling heavily. His warm fingers soothe the dry cold skin that is spotted in broken blood vessels. "What. Happened?"

"Just hold me," I squeak out and he pulls me back into his loving embrace, holding me so tightly. As though he alone can protect me from every darkness in the world.

But he can't.

"My dad found my diary," I croak, my voice fucking shuddering out between choppy sobs.

He pushes me out in front of him again, gripping my shoulders with a protective firmness. "What does that mean?"

I look straight into his eyes. "I'm so sorry."

His brows pinch. "What?"

"He knows what you did?"

"What does he know?"

"You killed that boy," I say, my throat raw from crying, my voice a hoarse, raspy melody that hurts to hear. "I'm so sorry, I wrote about it, Bronson. I'm so sorry. He said he was going to go to the police."

His shoulders relax on a big exhale, and I don't understand why he's suddenly so relieved. "Fucking hell, baby. Don't do that to me," he chuckles softly, shaking his head. "Is that all? Fuck. Jimmy owns the police, baby. Don't stress. Let him go to the police. He'll end up in a lot of trouble."

I freeze.

All the blood now rushing from my body, leaving me a weak, useless excuse of a human. "*No.*"

He smiles at me, and I can't stand it. "Baby, I thought something happened to *you*. To the baby." He pulls me against his chest once more and holds me as I start to break down all over again, realising I let them suck our baby from inside me. For nothing.

For nothing.

The truth like a sinking hole inside me, drawing into its depths the promises, future, the love and laughter, all the happiness we ever had.

"He made me!" I wail against his chest, clinging to his shirt, fingers aching through the intensity of my grasp. "He made me!"

He tenses beneath my hands.

Air leaves me in a rush, and I can no longer draw any in —my lungs paralysed. I press my head harder into him, hiding my face. His hands come down and circle my wrists, prying me from his shirt. As my fingers release it, I curl in on myself, shaking and standing alone without his warmth.

He takes one step backwards, putting further space

between us, the tether of our love stretching the distance. I look up at him, finding his eyes are so still, so wide, and it's terrifying. It's as though he is afraid to blink.

"Do. What?" he asks, his voice low with warning.

"He said you'd go away," I admit, my voice shaking out as the tether between us starts to fray. "For half your life, if I didn't."

"Didn't. What?"

I touch my abdomen.

He starts to shake with rage. He looks down at my hand spanned across the place he likes to talk to, to kiss, then his body shakes even harder—frighteningly hard.

I take a steady step backwards, the tether snapping like a physical thing, leaving us separate. For the first time in four years.

"No, baby. No," he mutters, his voice breaking with each word. "*No.*"

"*Bronson.*" I step to touch him, but he surges away from me as though I am a snake. Just like my dad did, pulling away from me in disgust.

"Don't touch me right now." He shakes his head, his ominous fury seems to build in his face, his eyes bright green and thin like slits, his body taut and vibrating.

My pulse thrashes around in my neck and ears, alerting me to run away from him but Bronson would never hurt me.

Would he?

"FUCK!" he suddenly roars, gyrating his body around as though he can't control the violence within himself. "*Fuck.*" A force that wants to claw out through his stomach or mouth and incinerate everything.

He bursts into tears, growling and sobbing at the same time, and the two pieces of my heart turn to ash within my ribcage. "*My boy…*" he mutters, sorrow wrapping itself around each letter in those words. Tears roll down his broken face, falling into his mouth as he sobs. I can't bear it. It is the most gut-wrenching sight to behold. "Where did he die? Where is he now?" Suddenly, he turns and strides towards his bike.

"Don't! Don't ride like this," I say, struck by panic. I run after him, but my body hurts. "Don't ride, *please*."

My cries fall on deaf ears.

He is too focused on leaving me to retrieve his helmet. Dragging the bike up from the ground, he starts the engine with an aggressive rev. He jumps on and speeds off; the motor growling up the street, leaving an echo of aggression and pain and heartbreak in its wake.

I watch him disappear.

Helpless.

Sobbing softly, I drop to my knees, the ache inside me now moving through all my cells. From the empty bloody spot in my uterus to the embers and ash of my heart.

I shudder.

"He's taking me away from you, Bronson," I whisper to the cold air, hoping it will carry my love and message to him. "Happy eighteenth birthday for next month. I love you, nutcase... for all your crazies."

CHAPTER THIRTY-FOUR

shoshanna

Present day

"A GIRL!"

I'm awoken by a bang from the door hitting the stopper and a little girl squealing those words. I pull the covers up quickly, hiding my nakedness beneath them. Bronson groans, his body weighing me down, a heavy leg and arm slung over me, a seemingly protective measure. I guess he wants to ensure I don't go anywhere. He slowly rolls to the side, his leg still hooked around mine, his mind wrapped up in slumber.

I sit up, holding the blue sheet to my chest. My dark hair is mussed around my head and down my shoulders.

"Hi," I say to the little girl staring at me with wide grey-blue eyes. "You must be the famous Kelly."

"Oh my God. I'm *so* fricking sorry." A pretty blonde appears behind Kelly, quickly scooping the little girl up to straddle her hip as she tries not to look at me sitting up in Bronson's bed. "Kel, you need to knock." She turns away from the room, her beautiful wavy blonde hair swaying around her slim frame. I presume this is Cassidy. She doesn't walk off though, but rather shuffles nervously, like she is fighting with what to do. She finally says, "I can't wait to meet you, Shoshanna. I'm really excited. *Frick*, I'm sorry. We'll go now."

"Her name is Jasmine," Kelly says as Cassidy closes the door behind them.

Falling back on the mattress, I exhale hard. *Life is a peach, Akila.* Fuck me. Memories of his words whispered in my ear, of his desperate choked tone when he all but begged me to give him another baby, of him wanting to start where we left off, crash down on me. How am I going to tell him that I may not be able to have children? Will he still want me? What if this feeling he has, this insane, beautiful, intense feeling he has for me, is a mask to rewrite history? To take away that day?

"Was that my outlaw?" Bronson murmurs, his voice husky and deep. Propping himself up on his elbow, he stares down at me, assessing my expression fondly. "What's going on in your impressive mind, baby?"

"Yes, it was. And Cassidy. She's... *really pretty.*"

He grins at me, pride flittering across his face. "I know. She's perfect"

I arch an eyebrow at him, and he sets his mouth in to his typical smirk. "Perfect?" I ask, pretending I don't already know what he's implying.

"For him," he confirms, and I attempt a smile. Moving his hand up, feeding his fingers through my hair, staring at the strands coiled around them, he says, "You up for playing with me today?" His eyes and hands awaken the butterflies that seem to hang out in my stomach these days.

"There is no word more ambiguous than *playing* when it comes from your mouth, Bronson Butcher. It could literally mean having a tea party with dolls and teddy bears, shooting something, or fucking, so I'm going to need you to be more specific."

His dark brows furrow in contemplation. Several long moments pass between us. "Alright," he finally says, jumping to his feet, the entire length of his masculine physique bared to me. "That's a great idea."

Swallowing, I try to focus my attention on his intense stare, not on his cock as it hangs between his thick tattooed thighs. Not on that. "I'm sorry, what? What part?"

"The whole idea." Moving over to the robe, he grabs his clothes and pulls on a pair of torn faded jeans and a long-sleeved black shirt with a pink bowtie printed on it.

He's a fucking nutcase.

Studying the bowtie, I say, "Like we are going to have a tea party, shoot something, and then fuck?"

A wicked grin slowly spreads across his lips. "And *that* is why you're my girl." He reaches back into the robe, pulling out a black top-hat with a red silk band. Tucked into it is a card with the impossible fraction, 10/6.

I smile through a long, slow exhale, sensing the person he is today. The person he is to *them*. The clown. The one who brings them nothing but easy fun times. But I know that tightly wrapped within that facade is the weight of responsibility, the burden of possessiveness... and his own *madness*. I sigh, realising he is the one looking after them all the time, which is why he needs me. He pulls his hat on and he's what they need him to be —their big brother.

"I bet that little girl adores you," I say through a soft exhale.

He winks at me. As if he's Casanova in that hat rather than a complete dork. "Feelings mutual," he states. "Get ready, baby. We have a party to attend."

* * *

As we take the wooden staircase down to the bottom floor, I steal a moment to appreciate the view through the floor-to-ceiling windows. The horizon is in sight, beyond the canals and rooftops of Connolly. It's striking.

The entire house is classy.

I look down. The denim shorts I have on are once again a half-size too small, stretching around my arse and thighs like rubber. Tucked into them is a white shirt. My dark waves hang loose and natural down my shoulders, and I doubt that anyone who looks at me would consider me *classy*. And they definitely would never guess that I'm a surgeon.

Bronson feeds his hand through mine, walking me out towards the little girl playing with her mum on the grass. They race around clutching bubble makers —big loops that careen through the air —a stream of detergent bubbles trailing them. I glance over at the outdoor lounge to find Max and Luca conversing.

Luca looks the same —salt and pepper coloured hair with a strong build that seems capable of snapping a man in two. Max, quite frankly, is giving off the same intimidating vibe as he did as a kid, but now with the added support of muscles. He's a polar opposite to his petite wife dancing on the lawn with their daughter. Kelly's yellow tutu flaps as she tries to copy her mum, spinning and fumbling but smiling as though she is nailing the moves. Cassidy is clearly a dancer, showing her little girl how to turn and use her hands to guide her movements. Max can't seem to keep his gaze on his dad while they talk; every few seconds it moves to the grass, and he holds his wife and daughter in his line of sight, snagged on them. And I know Max Butcher, and *that look*... is completely new —enchantment, I'd call it.

I smile at the family he has made for himself.

My feet suddenly slow, thinking about what I did to them, to their family, all those years ago. He was their blood... And Clay knew, so they all must have known. Suddenly, my heels dig into the white tiles, grounding me.

Bronson stops as I do, turning to study me as my cheeks drain, pale, and cool.

"Shosh*anna*," he says in the tone only he uses when saying my name. "Don't be nervous, baby."

I take a big breath in, forcing down my shame, and let Bronson lead me out into the alfresco. As I step outside onto the hardwood decking, I hear a squeal soar through the air.

He squeezes my fingers between his before releasing my hand and squatting down low. Opening his arms wide, he accepts the eager little girl who is barrelling into them.

"Outlaw," he sings. Standing with her now fastened to his hip, he beams brightly.

She tilts her head, blinking at his hat. "Hat. It's funny."

"Yeah, it's my tea party hat," Bronson boasts, quickly turning her attention to me. "This is Shoshanna."

"Not Jasmine?" she pouts, and I grin at the way her freckles bunch on her nose.

Bronson smooths a piece of hair behind my ear. "Well, *I* think she is, but you know, she has to disguise herself when she leaves the castle, cover up, so people don't recognise her." He wiggles his brows at me, and I roll my eyes.

I hold my hand out for Kelly and she takes it, kissing my knuckles. A royal greeting. "Are you Bronson's friend?"

I nod, saying, "Yes. His old friend." She measures me up,

and it makes me stifle a chuckle, seeing a little Butcher in her blue-grey eyes, taking the new person in, assessing whether they are worthy of her company, of her uncle's company.

"Just a friend," she declares. "Not a girlfriend because I'm going to marry him when I'm bigger."

I beam at her. "Wow. Can I come to the wedding?"

She ponders my question seriously. "Um, yes."

"Let me get a moment with the princess, will you, sweetheart." I hear from over my shoulder, turning to see Luca. "Pleasure to see you again, Shoshanna," he says, taking my hand in his. "Your absence has been a great loss to this family. I hope you know ... we all feel that way."

Max scoffs from behind me, and I turn to glare at him like I used to do, but he rises from the lounge and walks over to us. Kelly's face lights up when she sees him approach, immediately waving her arms out for him as Bronson passes her over to her dad.

Max lifts Kelly onto his shoulders, and she squeals, "Daddy Robot," while pretending to steer him by his ears. They wander down the bank towards the canal.

"Ignore Maxipad. I'll beat the shit out of him later," Bronson says, taking my hand in his again, lifting it to his mouth and pressing his lips reverently to my knuckles just like Kelly had done.

I exhale a big breath, and Luca pats me on the shoulder before squeezing it lightly. "Max noticed your absence, too. He just has an eloquent way of saying it." Heading in through the sliding door, he says, "Welcome home, Shoshanna."

I look back at Max. I knew he'd be the one to hold a grudge, as he never liked me in the first place. In the corner of my eye, I see blonde hair bounding towards me. I compose myself to meet the girl that has moved into their hearts.

Into Bronson's.

I smile at her in preparation to say a genuine hello when she engulfs me in her arms, humming her enjoyment.

"I am so glad you're here." She squeezes me with her surprisingly strong little arms. "This is so great. It's meant to be, and I know there is history, but he's worth it, and he loves you so much." She pushes me out in front of her, her hazel eyes then widen as though she didn't have control over her own mouth just then. "I should shut up. I'm sorry. I'm just nervous. Please forget, like, *everything* I just said. Bronson doesn't share this stuff with me, it's not like we have been talking about you or anything." She looks at Bronson, picking at her nail polish as though she can escape through the film. "I'm sorry." He just laughs. "*Frick*," she says, I think to herself. "Sorry... again. I'm, you'll get used to me."

I can't help but smile at her, even though she might not be so eager to welcome me back if she knew 'the history' she speaks of. "You must be Cassidy. And..." I chuckle softly because her candid outburst is pure and totally endearing. "You are not at all what I expected when I heard Max got married."

She giggles for a moment before taking a handful of her wavy blonde hair and pulling it down her slender shoulder. "I get that a lot."

I nod, wanting to say something like, 'it's as if the wolf caught a deer,' but I don't want to offend her because she is clearly a wonderful presence in this house.

She brightens. "Let's have a drink?"

Peering at Bronson and then down at our joined hands, I feel unwilling to let him go. He strokes my forefinger with his thumb, watching me attentively as he says, "I can't take my eyes off you if I tried."

His way of saying he'll be close. "Well, you are such a perv," I say, grinning at him.

Cassidy makes a *naw* sound, drawing me back to her as she bounces a little towards the dining-room door. "This makes me so *fricking* happy. What do you drink? Mimosa?"

"I'll have whatever you're having," I reply, twisting to follow her in, letting go of Bronson's hand.

"Max said we'll be alone a bit later. The guys have..." Her smile slips slightly, but she hides it well —the smooth motion practised. I know that kind of smile, and it makes me very aware that although she may appear sweet and whole-some, she is still Max's wife, which means she is probably clever, cautious, and protective of everything *Butcher*. "*Business*," she finally says. "It'll be me and you tonight for a while."

I wonder if she was told to babysit me while he is with his brothers and dad. She leads us into the kitchen, heads straight to the large chrome fridge, and begins making our drinks. I glance through the glass window at Bronson, noticing that he has joined Max and Kelly at the foot of the canal. Kelly is entertaining them, performing little spins between the two brothers, her blonde hair whirling through the wind. The men are conversing, but both dart their eyes up to us every so often.

I sigh, breathing out what feels a lot like loss. Looking at the boys I grew up with but haven't seen for half my life, now fully grown men in every way, I feel like I'm in an alternate reality. The one I often dreamed of but didn't come to fruition. When Bronson and I were only kids, and hoped for a future together, willing to let go of everything else to obtain it. I didn't let it go for years... So why am I not reaching out for this picture, taking my second chance with him?

I lean my hip on the edge of the breakfast bar, watching Cassidy move around the elaborate kitchen with complete ease and confidence. "How did you and Max meet?" I ask.

"I stalked him." She releases a nervous giggle. "Not really. I just forced him to love me, really. He had no choice."

"It was quite an embarrassing thing to watch," a woman says from behind me, forcing an immediate shiver to rush down the length of my spine. Cassidy freezes up ever so slightly, but then turns with a soft smile placed on her face.

"You didn't have to watch," Cassidy says as I turn around to find Victoria Butcher sashaying towards me, her red pencil dress moving with her as though glued on. Bronson's mother stops within an arm's length, tilting her head at me.

With her presence, she brings enough poisonous energy to literally surround us in the kitchen. I feel my blood start to bubble in my veins. If the boys were in here, she never would have said that to Cassidy, but we don't need them here.

I'm here.

Her eyes do a quick perusal of me, dropping to my feet and then up to my narrowed gaze. I don't even feign a smile for the cold-hearted bitch.

She raises a blonde brow at me. "Shoshanna, you look the same."

"You don't. You look older," I say, deadpan, and Cassidy spits out her drink before biting her lip to stop from any further outbursts.

Victoria levels me with her blue eyes, a spiteful shadow crossing over them. "*Children* make you age... Do you have any?"

I straighten, eye to eye with her, feeling nothing but unadulterated hatred for this woman, for every time she hit her sons, for all the nastiness she bestowed upon them. For hating them when they needed love. For scaring everyone away from them as though she owns them, as though she wants to be the only female constant in their lives. *How she must hate Cassidy.* I wonder what hardships she has put the poor girl through. "No. I don't."

She looks down at my stomach, hammering a message home. She knows. "You're lucky, young lady."

"You're a bitch," I spit out, loving the honesty. "Everyone else might pretend you're not a vapid cunt, but I won't. And you can't scare me away from him. So get out of my fucking face."

The red line of her mouth twitches, and I'm surprised she doesn't take a swing at me. I know how much she likes to hit people, but we're not children anymore and I'm not afraid of her.

She hums before saying, "Well, I suppose it's a good thing then that you cut that bastard baby from your guts. It would have shared blood with this vapid cunt."

My body ignites, but I clench my jaw instead of clawing at her face like I want to. "Stay away from me," I hiss. "Stay away from him. They might not want to tell Butch what you did to them because they know he'd *kill* you. But I'll tell him. I'll tell him everything."

Glaring at me, she takes a step back, and the energy between us stretches, thinning and allowing me to feel Cassidy's presence behind me. Victoria turns and meanders towards Butch's office. I remain fixed on the red material of her dress, searing a hole through it, feeling a million things on the tip of my tongue, grappling for release.

"Oh and *Vicky,*" I call out, knowing that casual term will strip a bit of her prowess. She turns with an almost impressed look on her face, plucking an eyebrow at me. "I'm not going anywhere." As I say it, I also accept it.

I'm not going anywhere.

I'll bring Akila home.

She smirks, saying, "That is yet to be seen." As she disappears down the hallway, her heels echo off the white tiles.

The rolling sound of the sliding door catches my attention. I glance over to find Max standing there staring straight at me, and I wonder how long he's been watching us. I'm not surprised though. His grey-blue eyes bounce over my shoulder to his wife and then back to me again.

"You're not going anywhere?" he repeats my words as he strides the short distance over to Cassidy. Taking her into his arms protectively, he leads me to believe he may have heard Victoria's tone at the very least. She squeezes his waist and presses her chin to his chest, peering up to watch him as he stares with his notorious Max Butcher scowl over her head at me.

"That's what she said, Max," Cassidy says, her tone gentle and soothing. "It's not all she said either. She just dropped the *C-bomb* and scolded your mum. She's kind of a badarse." She chuckles a little, reaching up to smooth the lines between his brows, provoking him to instantly soften beneath her caress. I can see how they work now. The effect she has on him is like magic. But his fixed stare tells me he is waiting for my answer. My eyes dart through the glass window and land on Bronson, who is flat on his back with Kelly perched on his stomach, chatting away. He cups the back of his head, his large, tattooed arms framing his face, and I'm not sure I could dream of a more beautiful view. He makes a stupid face at her. She erupts in a giggle. You would think they were having the most interesting conversation, given the enthusiasm in every gesture.

I let myself smile. Looking back at Max, I say, "Yeah."

He lifts his chin and kisses Cassidy's finger until she lowers her hand with a little giggle. "Okay." He nods at me; a corner of his lip twitches with a hint of a grin. "Good."

"Yay!" Cassidy sings, turning to cuddle me before instantly being pulled back into his arms again. "You made up."

"Did we?" I ask, taking the champagne flute and sipping the mimosa she poured for me. I eye Max with a smirk. "I didn't even know we were fighting."

His cutting grey-blue gaze leaves me and softens on his wife's face, scrolling over her with absolute infatuation. The kind of look I genuinely never thought I would see on him. He lifts her until she is wrapped around his waist and then walks with her outside.

"I'm talking to Shoshanna," she protests half-heartedly while he completely ignores her reluctance to leave me.

Leaning on the counter again, I watch as he slides Cassidy to one side so he can scoop his daughter up with his free hand. He tucks her under his arm as she squeals and laughs. My heart feels every sweet giggle like a warm caress.

Sighing at the sight, I head to find a bathroom. The only one I know of is in Bronson's room, so I jog up the stairs towards it. With the door in sight, I meander down the hallway.

Footsteps suddenly thunder behind me, and I gasp when someone grabs the nape of my neck. My shoulders rise with the uncomfortable feeling, muscles tense under the firm dominant hold. When I'm twisted around, I inhale panic until his lips meet mine and I exhale with relief. I hum my enjoyment for a moment before my senses settle and I want to kick his arse again.

Agitated by his dominance, I attempt to slap his chest, but he catches my arm with his free hand. When I try with the other, he catches that too and then holds them together with one hand. He squeezes the top of my spine; the feel of his unyielding grip, overwhelming and authoritarian, almost causes an ache to rush through my limbs.

"When I couldn't see you anymore, I nearly fucking lost my mind." He growls against my lips before licking inside my mouth. The need in his frantic movements send me spinning, and the tumble in his tone twists the nerves between my legs as though the sound has form and strength and precision all of its own.

Sliding his hand to the front of my throat, he forces me against the wall of the hallway and leans his heavy, long body into mine. I whimper in both fear and delight at the pressure. My pulse hammers away on the other side of his palm. He releases my wrists to place his hand on the wall above me, and his leg rises between my thighs while his lips make a meal out of mine

I try to breathe between his demanding kisses, try to speak. "You. Were. Busy."

He pulls back and presses his lips to my forehead, breathing roughly. His palm pulses around my throat, squeezing lightly and releasing at the same rate as his heavy breaths hit my face. His fear of my absence startles me. His energy is desperate and dangerous, causing his words to swirl back into my mind. *"Maybe I needed you much more than you ever needed me."*

My hands find their way up his back, rolling over his tense muscles, provoking them to ripple in response to my touch. "I'm not going to just disappear without saying anything, nutcase." I breathe the truth out and his whole body relaxes around me.

He lets out a heavy exhale. "Okay, baby."

Reaching between us, I circle his wrist and pull his hand from my throat. My lips find his knuckles, kissing the ink-laced skin while his mouth brushes my forehead.

"Come with me," I whisper, pulling him towards his room. My mind races with thoughts of his volatility. One moment he's peacefully lying on the grass, the next he's pinning me to a wall, shaking with discomfort over the idea I may have bolted. It won't work between us if he doesn't trust me.

And I him.

We enter his room, and the light from the sun sits high in the sky, casting a shadow over his sheets. He positions himself on the edge of the bed, eyeing me with a smirk that twitches with mischief. I arch a brow at him, reading his mind, which seems to be in a perpetual state of perversion. "You mentioned that your tastes have changed," I say. Walking slowly over to the drawer, the one that I know has this item in it, I inhale strength, finding it easy when he's quiet and not manhandling me. I retrieve the collar, and he sucks a rough breath in. "And *this*, you seemed quite taken by it," I say, pivoting to face him straight on.

He studies me like I'm something to eat. Leaning forward, he rests his elbows on his knees. "Go on, baby. What do you want to know?"

"The whole scene at Jimmy's... " Images of girls in negligees and dressed scantily appear in my mind as I say, "Is that what you like? Do you have submissives instead of girl-friends?"

He chuckles, a deep rumbling sound that spreads through me in a wonderful way. "No, baby. I have no interest in any permanent female presence in my bedroom... if she's not you."

I exhale relief, my shoulders dropping and loosening. I would never wish loneliness on anyone, but Bronson Butcher is mine, and the jealous being inside me screams this fact. "But you like it when girls wear this? You seemed to—"

"I like what it represented when *you* wore it," he cuts in. "That you belong to me. I liked that every man there was too afraid to spare you a glance in case I saw. I liked that a lot."

I look down at the collar and feel my lips curve with a small smile. Not because I want to wear it but because I understand that level of possessiveness. If I could have paraded him around in a collar in front of the girls at school, I would have. Waves of warmth course through my stomach. "I wouldn't just take off, okay? I know that might be hard for you to believe. And to be honest, I don't trust you because you keep proving to me that you'll assert your dominance at any given moment," I say, just as his phone comes to life with a call; I hear the buzzing coming from in his jeans.

Digging it out, he gives it a quick once over before stuffing it back into his pocket. "I have to go, baby."

Cassidy's knowledge of their plans for this afternoon settles in my stomach like envy. Because if I'm staying, this is my business too. I need to know where he is. If he is safe. I don't want to be in the dark. Running my fingers through my hair, I say, "You have business with your brothers?"

He gazes at me. "Yes."

He moves forward, but I step back, needing space to ask the next question. "Are you going to kill Jimmy Storm?"

Stopping just before me, he grins, excitement and something sour, like resentment, flittering across his turquoise-coloured eyes. It should scare me. But it doesn't. I understand why he feels that way. "Yes."

"When?" I ask, anxiously.

"Soon."

"Soon?" I square my shoulders. "That's it? Since when are you the one-word man?"

He chuckles. "Since I don't want to worry you with

family issues. We'll sort it all out soon...Then we can bring Akila home... Do you want that?"

If he still wants me once I tell him that I may not be able to give him more children of our own. Then yes. My heart screams yes. My mind whispers it. "Yes," I admit, sentiment playing with each letter. "I want that."

"What about being afraid of the pain?" he says, and then smirks. "Asking for a friend."

I release a soft sigh that holds all my fears and uncertainties. Trying not to cringe, I say, "Because even though I might fucking melt... I still want to know the warmth of the flame." I repeat his words, shaking my head at how silly I feel referencing a cartoon snowman.

"Fuck yeah!" He fist pumps the air, and I can't stop the giggle that erupts from me. "I won't be too long, baby." He takes the two steps needed to stand so close that I can feel the heat from his skin. Even enclosed in his silly bowtie shirt, his body is a wall of muscles that I want to explore more of, to circle every tattoo, to trace every line. "The girls are waiting for you in the living room."

Bouncing my eyes from his chest, I crane my neck to meet his gaze. "Yeah," I say contemptuously. "Cassidy is babysitting me."

As his hand rises to caress my face the way he loves to do, he says, "*Lady*-sitting. Don't worry, she'll let you stay up late. And she'll probably give you two desserts."

"Cute," I mutter against his palm before nipping him, an attempt to get him to lower his hand, but instead, he pushes his fingers into the depth of my mouth and holds my jaw in a vice-like grip. My eyes widen, and his narrow as he holds my gaping lips. I pant around his fingers.

"You always did think so," he says in a deep, gravelly voice that forces shock waves of blissful anxiousness into my veins, forcing my blood to pump fast and my pulse to quicken. "Keep the collar out. I'm putting it on you the moment we walk back into this room. Then you're going to drop to your dainty knees and let me fuck this pretty mouth. And you'll be swallowing what I give you, so don't fill up on dessert."

He releases my jaw and steps backwards, watching my reaction to his words. I glare at him, feeling a playful burst of retaliation settle into my mind.

I place the collar on top of the chest of drawers.

And he disappears through the door.

CHAPTER THIRTY-FIVE

bronson

Present day

"YES," *she said. "I want that."*

Playing her acceptance on loop in my mind, I navigate my way towards Dad's office, dead set on getting this meeting over with so I can enjoy the rest of my night —the culmination of which will include her on her knees with the leather collar around her throat, restricting her breaths as she swallows my cock.

I adjust myself.

I pass Carter standing at the double doors to the lounge room. The big lug is guarding that entrance. Inside, I hear Cassidy and my outlaw picking out a movie to watch tonight. I wrinkle my nose, feeling ripped off that I can't join them and my baby. It's a pretty picture—Shoshanna, Cassidy, and Kelly. I want more people in that picture—more children.

Suddenly, the weight of my own half-truth burdens me. *We'll sort it all out soon,* I told her.

Soon.

I can't guarantee that. I have no idea how long it will take for Jimmy to break. To do something so stupid, we can overthrow him without retaliation from the Family.

When I enter the office, I find my dad and brothers already waiting.

"Afternoon, darlings," I sing, walking over to the drinks cabinet and helping myself to a glass of the hard stuff.

Max is in the exact same position as Dad, leaning back in his chair, his arms folded across his chest, seemingly impatient to get started. Xan is looking at the black phone on Dad's desk as though the person on the line can see him.

"I didn't win the last fight." Xander speaks to the intercom as I lean against the wall, watching over them all while sipping my whiskey neat. "I should have, though. I don't know what happened."

"You didn't set the pace, buddy," Clay says through the speaker and I grin hard, having missed the big dickhead. It's the first chance I've had to speak with him about Dustin and the shipping yard and whether he knows. A fist encloses my heart at the thought of one of my brothers betraying me —*us.* I can't imagine a more painful experience. As my mind explores that possibility, I decide it's not possible. He doesn't know. He'd never keep something like that from us. I set my empty whiskey glass down on the cabinet, deciding not to refill it given the echoes of laughter in my mind —a warning for me to stay in control and present.

Xander looks at Max, rolling his eyes slightly. "Yeah, that's exactly what Max said."

Max clears his throat. "Let's start."

"I went to see Jimmy," Dad begins, unfolding his arms

and reaching for one of the neatly wrapped port cigars he leaves on display to the left of his desk. "I told him that I wasn't happy he shot the doctor in front of the girl... No reason to hide such a thing. Long conversation short, he'd had a bit to drink and thought he was looking after his boy..."

"I'm touched," I say with a wry smile. "And the fact he's been following her. Knew Doctor Clean? What of that?"

"It doesn't matter what he said, son," Dad states. "He was lying to me. I can tell. Which, for the first time in over twenty years, means I have no idea what he's planning."

Xander looks at the phone. "Why don't we frame Dustin for his murder? Kill two birds with one stone."

"We need him to make mistakes. We need the family to deem him incapable of running things here," Max states.

"The Family needs to approve the hit, Xan," Clay says through the speaker, his voice level and smooth —unaffected. I narrow my eyes on the speaker, unable to shake the lingering shadow of his possible betrayal. "We can't just kill Alceu's grandson and not expect them to come for us."

"We've sent the skin to Dustin. Let's send Jimmy a present too." Xander says, glancing between us, before he reaches for his whiskey and takes a sip, perhaps needing a use for his idle hands. *Boxers*, so fidgety.

"We need Alceu on our side. Starting a war between Dustin and Jimmy might mean we can't handle things discreetly. They will come out and send someone who they believe is capable to take over the head. They paid for Jimmy to come out here all those years ago, remember?" Dad sucks on his cigar, the smoke hanging around him, thickening the air. The scent wafts over to me, singeing my nostrils in the best way with its port and sandalwood clouds. I want one of those bitches. Making my way to Dad's desk, I grab one and spark it up as my old boy continues, "I left Sicily on my own, many years before. I thought I was free from that world. But it followed me. They wanted him to make something of this place, and they wanted me by his side. They still own him. They own his men. We need to be in control of this situation. Jimmy needs to look like the liability we need to clean up."

Xander scoffs. "We are Alceu's blood. Let's go to him."

Dad looks at the cigar, tapping the column with his forefinger, dislodging ash and embers into a crystal tray. "We are his blood, but Jimmy is Paul's son and Alceu's grandson."

"Adopted grandson," Xander says, spite wrapping itself around each word. I watch Xander as he takes this all too personally. Does he feel entitled because we share Alceu's blood? Then the kid hasn't been paying attention. The name Butcher is all that matters. Just because we share traces of DNA with him from his mother's side doesn't mean he'll choose us over the boy he helped raise back in the old country.

"It means nothing to Alceu," Dad says again.

"When was the last time you spoke with him, Dad? Maybe it does mean something to him," Xander spits out.

"Xander, quiet!" Max barks, and my little brother slumps back into his chair, defeated and disgruntled by Max's tone, as though he doesn't know that he pokes the bear.

I chuckle at them and straighten, standing at my full height. "He took a vow. He lied to you. He took your son." I stare at the phone in all its ominous silence, and say, "He took your little brother, Clay."

When I find my old man's blue eyes again, he's fixed on me as though he can see my suspicions ghosting across my face. "I don't need reminding," he states. "But we only have the words of a dead man and—"

"Me," Max says because he is the only one who heard it

from the fucker's mouth. The arrogant son-of-a-bitch who took our half-brother Konnor and locked him in a basement all those years ago admitted to Max that he'd been paid by Jimmy Storm to do so.

I inhale my cigar, smiling around the puffs of white vapour riding my breath as I exhale. I'll never get tired of hearing that story. Of how it ended with Max draining the prick into a toilet bowl. But although I trust Max's word above anyone else's, it is no secret that he isn't an admirer of the Family or Jimmy. That fact will play on everyone's mind if his word is the sole reason we give for Jimmy's assassination —the mother fucking head of our firm in Australia.

Dad nods. "Yes. It won't be enough."

"Bron," Clay says through the phone, and I take a step towards it. "You mentioned that Jimmy seems to be nervous, correct?"

"Yeah, I reckon he's paranoid as fuck," I admit, putting out my cigar in Dad's ash tray.

"Stay together. Let's leave this conversation until I get back in a few days. I want to get a good feel for Jimmy's state of mind before we plan anything," Clay says, and I hate not being able to analyse the movement of his mouth and the shifting of his eyes. More than that, I hate the beast at my back screaming that he knows more than he is letting on. I want to decapitate that fucking monster.

Because it can't be true.

"Big brother," I hiss at the phone before I can stop myself. "Dustin is in the District. Did you know?"

Max unfolds his arms, the information obviously new to him. I move to grip his shoulder reassuringly. After the attack on his wife, no one wants Dustin's head more than him. We glare at the phone, awaiting an answer. A long pause electrifies the air, and the echoes of laughter in my mind brew.

Finally, he says, "If Dustin were in the District, I would know about it."

"He is. Demarco confirmed it and I—"

"Dad already mentioned this to me yesterday. This concern has not been overlooked. I sent men out to the docks to search for him, but found no trace. Demarco lied," Clay states with a strange edge to his voice. "*Trust me*, Bron."

The laughter in my head dwindles.

'*Trust me, Bron.*'

And I do. I have to.

Okay, big brother.

Dad stands, a way of ending our meeting. With that decided and the monster of suspicion in my mind seemingly quiet, I grab Xander. Putting him in a headlock, I scuff his brown hair, trying to make the grumpy kid crack a smile. He does. I kiss his forehead and chuckle my way out of Dad's office, flanked by Max. We both head towards the living room to find our girls.

CHAPTER THIRTY-SIX
bronson

Present day

TRUE TO MY FUCKING WORD, as soon as we wander back into my room, I stalk straight to the leather collar. The whiskey and beers I consumed at dinner slosh around in my mind, reminding me I'm not in peak physical or mental condition. I don't care. I snatch the beautiful leather band from the top and turn to face her.

She holds up her hands. "Wait just a minute, Butcher. I want to know what happened in the meeting with your dad."

I lower my chin, staring at her through my lashes. My heart beats hard, pulsing between my ears and throbbing in my cock. "I've been waiting for hours to get this on you and now—" I reach down and grip my erection, squeezing until a small amount of the aching ebbs. "He needs to be stuffed inside your pretty body. You can choose which hole."

She parts her lips, her chest rising and falling, trying to keep her calm. I know that look on her face. Releasing my cock, I walk over to her. My eyes snare on her lips, on the pink hole between them. As I reach for her, she shuffles backwards, but that only makes me hotter to catch her. Lunging for her wrist and pulling her towards me, I capture her against my chest. Dropping her wrist, I band her middle, holding her close.

"Bronson—" she pants.

Her hot, thick curves and the alcohol in my stomach warm my blood. A grin moves across my lips as I lift the collar. "Put it on. Now."

She bats her lashes at me. There is a sultry slant to her eyes that is new and intriguing, throwing me off guard.

"Okay," she purrs, and her smooth voice fucks with me further. My baby takes the collar from my hand and brings it up between us. I don't know what she is playing at, but I'm willing to take part. I just hope she knows the rules. Shoshanna slides one of her fists along the length of the leather, making a show of the motion. She hums, and the sound forces me to stiffen.

Then she stands on her tippy toes.

And when she reaches around behind me, wrapping the collar around my throat, I hiss. My cock damn near wrestles its way out of my jeans. Like that alien in *Alien*. *Fuck me.*

"Naughty girl," I rumble.

"Naughty boy," she counters, and I'm both aroused by this switch and eager to fuck her until she can't walk. She takes a steady step back, and I loosen my hold around her, letting her slip from my arms.

"Now," she says, sashaying over to the mirror, "let's get something straight, Butcher. You are not the boss of me." Facing her reflection, she undresses.

The cords in my arms contract as I refrain myself from grabbing her. I'm fixed on her as she leisurely removes her shirt, exposing her slender shoulders, her little waist, the swell of each hip, and the two dimples above her round arse. Her skin is olive and flawless. I lick my lips. In the mirror, her breasts heave with nerves, but I pretend not to see the subtle slip in her cute play at dominance.

She unclasps her bra, letting it slide from her shoulders and puddle at her feet. My eyes burn into her soft flesh. I'm so fucking hard it hurts.

Slowly, she slides her shorts down, bending over to free her feet from them. Her round arse and the pretty folds of her pussy flash at me. I lift my fist to my mouth, biting down on my knuckles and groaning my arousal out.

She spins around, swallowing hard when she sees my flaring eyes, my fist between my teeth. For a split second, she looks wary. I fight the urge to study her pussy, anchoring my gaze on her nervous amber orbs.

"*You're mine,*" she whispers to me, her words so soft but their meaning so fucking loud.

Fucken, ay, baby.

I agree.

I am.

She struts her hourglass body over to me, her dark hair spilling down her breasts and back. I drop my gaze to study her naked physique in motion, study the bounce of each breast, the rise of each hip, the sway of each thigh.

She reaches me, standing so close her light brown nipples brush my stomach. Lowering my fist, I peer down at her through hooded eyes. I curl both hands in tight, willing them not to open and grab her. She smiles at me and a little slice of peace slips into my heart. Into my mind.

Where it's strangely quiet.

Peaceful... yes.

Her hands slide under my shirt, over the ridges of my abdominals, and I groan to the feel of each gentle touch. I help her remove my shirt; my baby's not tall enough to do it alone.

I clench my teeth together when she drops to her knees. Fuck, she's beautiful. She unbuttons my jeans, sliding them and my boxers down my thighs. As she releases my cock, it bounces up against my abdomen, and I groan my approval; my buddy wanted out a while ago.

She gapes at it, and I watch her wet her lips with uncertainty. I chuckle at her expression.

He's a fucking meal, right, baby?

I grip the base and drag my hand up the full length, squeezing my pre-cum out until it beads on top. "Lick it off," I order, forgetting that she wants to be in charge. She does as I command. Leaning in, her warm wet tongue laps at the cum on my slit. My legs nearly buckle. "Swallow him, baby. I'm wearing the collar. He's yours to take care of."

Shoshanna takes my erection from me, her fingertips unable to meet around its girth. I throb in her palm, bucking my hips towards her lips.

"Open."

She parts her lips to accept my cock, slides it through her warm wet entrance, along her tongue, and to the back of her throat. Her lips close, creating suction. Shifting my weight, I watch her head bob to take me deeper and then draw back when her throat contracts around me, activating every nerve along my shaft.

"*Fuck,*" I growl through a strained breath. She always did like to suck my cock. She likes to bring me to my knees with the swipe of her tongue. Feeling my arms shaking with stimulation, I realise how much I want to fist her hair and take her sweet mouth like I would her pussy.

She works me into a state. Her tongue undulates beneath the head of my cock while her fist squeezes the base, the part she can't quite fit inside her.

Watching her eyes gloss over, I begin to rock my hips in and out of her hot mouth. The view of her kneeling body, her thighs elegantly pressed together, her physique curvaceous but gently toned, her attention on my cock, is perfection.

Unable to hold my hands at my sides any longer, I frame her head with my palms, holding her still. My vision closes in on me as I fuck her mouth. I tilt her head back, stepping over her slightly to watch the show from a new angle.

I groan as my cock meets the back of her throat. Her tongue protests, flipping around, making the sensation even better. Watching every second, I use her sweet mouth, slowing down when I feel too good, wanting to savour the experience.

After a while, her lips swell, her cheeks glow and flush, and I know she's getting overwhelmed, so I give my good girl what she wants. "Swallow it all down, baby. You worked so hard for it." She moans around my cock, setting a boil inside my abdomen.

A deep rumble fills my chest as pounding heat wraps around my balls, rocketing my climax from me. In awe, I watch it spill out, filling her pink cheeks. Her eyes widen, the light above us illuminating the metallic freckles within them. I don't let her go until her throat rolls, swallowing every drop I shot into her warm, wet depth.

My hands stroke her cheeks as I release my grip. Grinning at her, I stumble backwards, my satisfied cock sliding free. She beams, her perfect teeth peeking out; she's proud of herself. *You should be, baby.*

Reaching down, I help her climb to her feet, relishing the fact she is completely naked. I want her naked whenever we are alone. Her hair is wild around her face, so I smooth it down her head and neck. "Well, *fuck*." I brush my finger along her red puffy lips that are still slick with moisture.

This face...

I kiss her lips, hums rumbling from both of our chests. I want more of her. Want my fill. Lifting her up and wrapping her legs around my waist, I sit her sexy arse on my hands. I stride to the bed, then throw her on it. A gasp leaves her as she bounces on the mattress right before I crawl up her body, intent on licking every inch of her lush olive skin. She drops back, allowing me to hover over her. "My turn."

Lowering myself to her breast, I lick the erect tanned nipple on top, flicking it and drawing it into my mouth. I cup the outer swell, massaging the flesh, plumping it, and feeling the soft, lithe mound, the epitome of femininity. Everything I like about a woman. She arches her back on a gentle sweet moan, offering me more to take. Deep hums vibrate in my throat as I mouth her and think about nothing but her.

Her lightly salted skin.

Her gentle mewling sounds.

I trail my fingertips down her belly, and it quivers. Stopping at the little black strip of hair between her thighs, I play with the strands. She lifts her pelvis off the bed, titling, begging me to push my fingers inside her. I grin around her nipple, not doing as she silently commands. I may be in the collar, but she has my scent all over her, has plump red lips from sucking me dry, and the remnants of my cum in her mouth. That all screams *mine*.

All mine.

With that thought, my cock tingles. Unable to pull my lips away from her perfect tits and the slight dewiness of her skin but needing to fill her pussy more than she needs me to, I dip my fingers lower. Her hands slide into my hair, my scalp rippling as she strokes through the short strands with her nails.

I slide my fingers along the length of the most perfect lips before pushing them open and stroking the pulsing inner folds. Her hips pivot up and down; her pussy is greedy as all fuck, but I want to feel every inch of her. I want this. This is for my pleasure just as much as hers.

After a few minutes of playing with her, I push two fingers inside, curling them and twisting them, duelling with the muscles that react and squeeze me. I groan from deep within my chest, the feeling so beautiful. So female. Her body is incredible.

And I'm lost in it.

In my beautiful distraction.

She sucks me in, her essence like a mist that surrounds us, making every other part of my life hard to see and easy to forget. And thank fuck for that. It's been years since I've felt this kind of peace.

My hand releases her breast, my mouth slides her nipple free, and I crawl down her flat, soft stomach to get to my personal brand of drug. I can smell her juices before I even taste them, hot, salty, feminine.

I'm a big guy, so my legs hang from the bed and fuck that. I grip her thighs, dragging her along the mattress until her backside hangs just off the edge. She gasps, and it is hot as fuck. Her plump arse shuffles, her legs bending further to keep her feet firmly planted on the mattress.

"Beautiful." I breathe out the word, staring at the slit between her legs, the cute little hole below. "If you could see what I can see, baby. Fuck me."

Dropping to my knees in front of her, I trail my tongue

along her leg until I reach her lips, kissing them straight away, unable to tease myself and her any longer. I pull the soft skin into my mouth, sucking on it, then trail my tongue inside the valley between. She groans, shuffling her arse around.

I thread my hands under her arse so I can feed her to me and lick her single-mindedly. Bringing all her flavours into my mouth, I swallow them because they are mine. I tongue her opening, dipping in and out. In and out. Fuck me, she tastes too good, it's almost dangerous.

Addictive.

While I kiss her, taking my time, slow and steady licks that have my cock thrumming against my abdomen, I forget everything else. She really is a distraction. Consuming me. My entire body awake, hard, quivering, wanting, needing, her.

Only her.

Nothing else. My only responsibility is to her. But I don't lose myself... It doesn't feel like that... It feels like I find myself in her, in the gentle tilt of her hips, in the clenching and pulsing of her pussy, in her beautiful flavours, in her broken feminine moans.

I find what I want —*her.*

Time passes by and I kiss her, licking her orgasm from her lips each time I make her break apart, open, and in the throes of it all, I am in utter and total peace.

Hours later, we lay in silence, side by side, our legs entwined, our breaths heavy. My mind... *settled.*

So fucking *quiet...*

She shuffles until her head is on my bicep and her small gentle hand rests on my chest, her fingers tickling my hairs. She moves them over my torso, investigating my ink. *Do you want to know what they all mean, baby?*

Her palm presses over my Anubis tattoo and a rough sigh leaves me. Her eyes widen like saucers, darting up to my face. She feels them. As her fingers roll over the hidden uneven skin, her amber irises pool, tears clinging to the corners. I hate her tears, but they are mine, too.

His and mine.

I'll share her with him. Him with her. No one else.

The tips of her fingers skate along the small valleys and bumps of the scars I love so much. Five years ago, they faded, and I couldn't fucking stand it, so I needed colour and form. Needed a constant reminder of the flames that had burnt me and him when I had said goodbye.

"What happened?" she whispers, cupping the spot between my hip and arm as if she can apply enough pressure to smooth out my skin.

To heal the memory.

To be a part of it.

But it was just me and him that day.

"I cremated him."

CHAPTER THIRTY-SEVEN

bronson

Seventeen years old

I SEE BLACK.

I hear only maniacal laughter ringing between my ears, but it isn't from my lips, and today I know, I know it's in my deranged mind. It followed me on my bike over here —the ghost of a little boy who nearly drowned, invisible but everywhere. He followed me all the way up to the doors and now he's settled inside me, waiting to be unleashed.

Staring straight ahead, I sway with emotional weakness. Emotional fatigue. My fingers —numb from the death grip I have on my gun. My mind —swarming with evil and indifference.

My heart...

I stumble through the glass sliding doors, trying not to sob and snarl at the lady behind the desk. She jumps up with a start, shuffling backwards towards another door. I slowly lift the gun in my hand, the metal piece vibrating in my fist.

Raising her hands up by her head, she says something, but I can't hear her words or voice through the laughter wrapping itself around my soul. I blink at her.

She is nothing.

Shoot her!

My eyes sting from shedding too many tears. Arid. Painful. Hard to hold open. "Where is my boy?" I mumble, my head heavy and full of blistering hysterics. "Where did you put him?" I don't want to kill them. I need to. I need my boy. I need... "My boy!" I roar, the gun shaking so hard in my clenched hand. Shaking almost as hard as the woman staring death in the eye.

She is crying now.

I can see the tears bursting from her eyes, coating her cheeks, dropping onto her wobbly lips, but I don't care. Don't care that she's scared. She *should* cry.

I point the gun at the roof, firing it once, the gun pulsing in my fist, and the lady hits the deck. In the corner of my eye, I see a man slowly walking through a white door beside the desk.

My Glock slides through the air to line up with his face.

With his hands held in sight, his brown eyes widen, and he clears his throat. "Take what you want. We don't keep cash on the premises."

The laughter gets louder. I go to speak, but my throat is so rough, I barely can. I clear it and force the words out, "Shoshanna Adel. My boy. Where is he?" The man's eyes dart around and then he blinks, realisation moving through his face like a dancing demon, taunting me with the truth and pity and bullshit.

Shoot him, Bronson.

I tilt my head, knowing he's reaching for words, but I've had enough of waiting. "Now!" I howl. "Tell me!"

"I'm sorry, young man." The man swallows, and I concentrate on his words, not on the laughter. I squint at him. "We put all the bio-waste in the freezer. Together. I mean, we... we cremate them. Together."

The laughter dies.

"*Bio waste.*" I drop to my knees. My hand presses on the floor, the gun tightly clasped inside resting on the tiles. My body hangs hunched and weak. Tears I didn't know I still had inside me spring from my eyes as my shoulders gyrate with violent sobs. "*Bio waste...*" Vacantly, I talk to the floor, hissing, "Leave. Now."

I will myself not to look at him as he quickly shuffles past me, followed by at least five more sets of feet. I will myself not to gun them all down, will myself not to lay them in a freezer. Bio waste. To be cremated. *Together.*

I climb to my feet, stumbling further into the clinic where my girl lost her baby. Where I lost my future. Where I can be closer to him. *"Good things don't happen to people like me."* I can hear sirens in the distance as I search for the freezer.

When I open a white door and step into a surgical room, my eyes become trained on the gurney. I imagine her laying there. Alone. Scared. I wince. As I turn my back on the room, my eyes get snagged on something.

I stare at an ISO tank.

At an oxygen tank.

Cremated.

I back up until I am outside the room, thinking about my boy and how his daddy will be the one to cremate him. Only a Butcher is allowed to send off a Butcher. His daddy will be the one to do it, knowing he never even took his first breath...

I snarl, point the gun at the first tank with the image of my face by her belly, her fingers in my hair, and I shoot.

The canister explodes.

An angry vortex of sparks and metal and gas swarm the room. I shoot the other before the air is too thick with white clouds that I can no longer see the tank.

Flames come at me.

I fall back.

The inferno howls around me. Heat. Roaring. The entire room billows with flames and smoke, and my skin suddenly stings. I crawl along the floor, coughing and whispering, "Daddy loves you. Daddy won't forget you."

I crawl along the ground, through the sliding door. The grass under my knees suddenly stills me, and I register that I'm outside. My lungs are scorching, filled with heat and ash and gas.

I roll on the lawn as heat climbs up my back and arms, moving through my leather jacket, real and painful and everything I deserve for all my sins. At the sound of another explosion, I sit up on my heels and watch as the building bleeds. Slowly, piece by piece, it crumbles. Debris spits out. The walls and roof crack. And I watch my peace swallowed up and incinerated.

Peace.

Hope.

Bio waste.

CHAPTER THIRTY-EIGHT

shoshanna

Present day

I LET MY SORROW FLOW, let the tears drop onto his chest, let myself wallow in his grief and mine.

"I spent two nights in hospital, chained to the bed. Under arrest." His fingers comb through my hair. "I knew I still had you. That was all I thought about. Dad stayed with me the entire time, the fucking big softy..." He pauses, swallowing hard, the next memory seemingly too painful to say or hear. "Jimmy came for us. He sorted everything out. The courts deemed me unable to stand trial for reasons of mental health. Then he drove me straight to you." Bronson's fingers freeze in my hair, and I still my worshipful exploration of the scars marring his side. "We watched all your furniture being hauled out and put in a truck. Jimmy sat with me for an hour. In silence. I've never seen him that way before, and I never fucking did again."

A whimper escapes me, a curdling sound that mixes with the tears tightening my throat. "I'm sorry."

"Don't," he admonishes, pressing his lips to my forehead. "It was *my* fault. I left you alone in that park. We promised each other a future, that we would go through life together and I broke my fucking word to you."

"No." I sob, peering up at him as he stares straight ahead. It's as if he's seeing the memories projected on the white ceiling. Or seeing nothing at all.

"Yeah. That night, I took my vows. I sliced open my palm, swore on Saint Jude. The saint of fucking lost causes." He chuckles coldly. My heart twists, because it's not true. He is so many great things, my Bronson Butcher. Strong. Loyal. Generous with his time. Nothing about him is a lost cause. "And I became the youngest made-man in history. I wasn't going to break another promise, baby. Not to anyone. So I've spent the past decade keeping it. I gave my entire life to Jimmy. And now, well, fuck, now I'm going to kill him."

I trace the scars under Anubis. They are smooth and defined —*thin*. This part of his skin forever weakened.

I feel weak too, imagining how I almost lost him to those flames as well, how I nearly lost both my boys the same day. Grief makes me frail, consuming my mind and body, stripping me of power and strength, leaving my entire being unwilling to work.

Unwilling to work...

Did my years of grieving the loss of him and our son cause my body to break? Too frail, too weak with sadness to give me another chance at making life. I know that's not true. Not medically substantiated, but not all things are...

I swallow hard. "I'm not sure I can have another baby, Bronson." He sits up, staring straight at me, caught completely off guard by my declaration. I sit up too, forcing down the shudder in my breath. "They told me a little while ago." Uncertainty flitters through me. I feel as though I'm putting a fresh flame to the foundations of our new relationship, to the pretty picture he has in his head. "My body just isn't producing enough eggs."

Slowly, he reaches for my throat, circling it. He pulls me down beneath him so he can lean his body weight on me. The intensity of his glowing green-blue eyes commands my breath. Leaning in until his lips touch my ear, he rumbles, "Are you okay? Have you checked for other issues?"

I blink at him, confused by the question. "Yes. I'm fine. Don't worry about me, nutcase."

He nods, his brows set seriously above penetrating eyes. "So, are you saying you want to have kids with me?"

I breathe out fast. Smiling through a few gentle tears as we agree to a life together, as we make our first new plan, our first new promise, as adults, I say. "*Yes.* I'm just not sure that—"

He squeezes my throat, sealing my words within the slender column. "We'll try everything. I'll be fucking you until you can't breathe, baby. And then we can try IVF or *fuck*... you want to have a baby with me! We're going to give him a sibling. A bit of you. A bit of me. So close to him in every way."

"We're going to try," I promise him.

A mischievous grin spreads across his cheeks, a provocative curve that threatens me with indecency and all kinds of rough and fun things. "Let's start right fucking now."

CHAPTER THIRTY-NINE
shoshanna

Present day

MY MIND IS CONTENT, the sheets are soft and smooth beneath me and I'm happily between two states, floating somewhere between reality and a dreamy sleep.

Dreaming about our closure.

Dreaming about our future.

An explosion...

I sit up, reality reaching in and dragging me from my slumber. The noises are real, deafening and everywhere. My heart lurches, awakening every cell in my body, provoking my pulse to thrash violently around within my ribcage, the sensation near bruising.

I scream, but the sound of my own voice is drowned out by the endless gunfire. This is real. This is really happening.

Squeezing my eyes shut and covering my ears, I continue to cry and scream through the bellowing racket.

Within seconds, I'm dragged from the bed. My body hits the floor, but the feel of the drop is numb. It's unable to compete with the perpetual roll of ammunition penetrating the walls and windows.

I'm shoved beneath the bed, the mattress and metal frame surrounding me —a cave of feigned security.

I tremble with fear.

Glass breaks, the shattering cadence warning me of the ominous metal bullets propelling through the space. Through the walls. The window. *In the house.*

My brain isn't working the way it should. I reach for action in this situation but come back with nothing. Only the need to make myself small and hold my ears through this torturous chaos, wish it away, wish for life.

Alone. I'm alone under the bed.

Then I realise.

No. *No.*

He's out there in this.

He didn't hide under the bed with me.

I wail, tears rising violently to my eyes, breeching my face like a downfall of hopelessness, washing away all his peace and mine. The small slither we were allowed before the world ripped it from us —again. Cradling my head, my palms to my ears, I shake violently. Tears, saliva, my soul — they spill from me as I wait helplessly... We are helpless again. I picture Anubis in my head, almost feel him around me, watching me.

I inhale sharply, but my fitful sobs make it hard to draw air in along with something else... the air is thicker.

Tastes funny.

Then there is silence.

I try to draw air in again, hearing my own breath like a drone between my ears. Do I lower my hands? A tiny bit of adrenaline drops, allowing me to feel. Consider. I pry my fingers from my face, open my eyes, and scoot back further under the bed. The air is thick with smoke or... gas. A kind of fog.

Blinking through it, the thick clouds float into my eyes, making them sting. Panic sets in as reality soars through the gaps my adrenaline has left in my consciousness.

Bronson.

The boys.

Kelly.

Cassidy.

I know what I have to do. I have to crawl out. *Crawl,* I scream in my head. My limbs feel useless and heavy in my shock, but I have to find them; I could save them.

My fingers find the hem of the oversized shirt I am wearing, reminding myself that I am naked underneath. It doesn't matter. Heaving in and out courage, I claw myself from under the bed. Staying on my stomach, I move over glass and pieces of debris —brick and plasterboard, I think.

Crawling through the bedroom, I can decipher footsteps and the static from two-way transceivers, leading me to believe they are from the Butcher guards. I hope. *God, I hope.*

The fog seems to rise around me as I move across broken rubble and out into the hallway. I peer in both directions, seeing nothing but a dense grey abyss.

Shattered glass from the blown windows shreds my flesh as I crawl along the floorboards, my elbows and knees sliding around in my blood. I hear two gunshots sound somewhere below me.

I freeze.

My heart hammers, threatening to burst out. And while a part of me screams to stay put, to get back under the goddamn bed, a louder part orders me to make sure no one needs me. I could save someone. I could save him.

I need to save him this time!

"I have her." I hear the echoed voice of a speaker. The fog illuminates around me, and I'm hauled up into a man's arms. "It's okay, Miss Adel. Stay calm."

My hands fumble around a gas mask as he pulls one over my face. I breathe into it. Deep breaths that allow my focus to steal some moments away from the hell of my mind. Of my frantic pulse. Blood rushes to my ears as I let him carry me through the house, trusting he is a Butcher guard and not someone I should fight off.

Black figures fly past me.

Two more gunshots.

The man carrying me starts to jog, so I clutch at him, sobbing and vibrating in his arms. Suddenly, I'm passed to someone else, and then I can see clearly in this room before I'm lowered to the ground and the door I came through shuts. But my legs don't hold me, so I'm guided further to the floor, until I no longer need to find the strength to stand.

I push my mask up just as I'm taken into small but strong arms. Her hands are in my hair and she's kissing my cheeks, her blonde hair curtaining us. I realise in this moment that I'm bawling hysterically. Another set of arms find me, and I glance across to see wisps of golden blonde hair. Both Cassidy and I open our arms to take Kelly in between us; we all cry and huddle together.

"It's going to be okay," a man says from beside us and his voice is so loud, I wince. The room is in a state of eerie silence. My ears no longer ring with the remnants of gunfire. Instantly, I loosen my hold on the two girls, raise my head, and investigate the quiet space. We are in a windowless suite, furnished much like a hotel room might be, with a modern kitchen and a sunken living room. Three men guard the door, kitted up in full length black gear and holding semi-automatic rifles. Two open doors appear to lead to bedrooms.

A shiver rushes along my spine as I realise that I'm sitting on the floor of some kind of bunker.

A man with burns etched into his face drops to his haunches beside me and holds a black vest out. I recognise him from when I was younger. "Put this on." Carter says. "You're going to be fine."

But I'm not worried about myself. Frantically, I search the room again, the door, the kitchen, the bedrooms, desperately hoping I find them sitting in a corner conversing, planning, allowing the guards to secure the property while they are safe with us...

The boys aren't in here.

My world tilts.

I circle back around to Cassidy, and my heart contracts painfully in my chest. As my teary eyes focus on her hazel pools, we connect, sharing our fears and sorrow so deeply they become a tangible entity uniting us.

She swallows hard. "They'll be fine," she mutters, fear strangling each word, but she tries hard to stifle it. To hide it from her daughter, who is curled in her lap, tightly enveloped in the protective hold of her arms. Glancing down at Kelly, Cassidy silently pleads with me not to alarm her further. To stay calm. To pretend. I wipe my tears away, forcing a straight face.

"Of course they will be. They're like superheroes," I find my voice enough to say, a little strained but clear. "I hear Max has super strength."

Kelly slowly lifts her head, looking up from her mummy's

arms. Tears glide down her face, rolling over the freckled arch of her nose. "Daddy? Like, in *The Incredibles*?"

I nod, fighting the need to cry at her sweet innocence. "*Yeah*. Didn't you notice how strong he is?"

Feedback from Carter's receiver draws all of our attention to him. I jump to my feet, followed quickly by Cassidy.

"They're coming," the man on the other end of the phone says. The door swings open, and dust and remnants of fog creep in around the silhouette of a man. Max strides over to Cassidy, and I step back from her as she rushes to him.

"*Max.*" His name soars desperately from her lips as he drops to his knees in front of her, taking both his girls into his arms. Tucking Kelly into his torso with a protective hand banding her head, he focuses his attention on his wife, using his other big arm to hold her close. He presses his forehead to her lips, breathing roughly, strained. Her petite hands cup his face as she whispers things against his skin that only he can hear. Tears build behind my eyes, feeling the sudden sadness shift through the air, the information not being uttered moves like a phantom through the room.

Hearing the stomping of boots, I dart my gaze to the door, taking a little step forward when... Luca appears. I deflate. He quickly scans the room, finding me immediately and stopping as though I'm the person he was seeking out.

I suck a wobbly breath in, shaking my head as his brows weave and he releases a splintered exhale. A sound that on a woman might be considered a whimper. Stepping away from him, not liking the look in his eyes, I refuse to acknowledge the message on his face. *No.*

"Where is he?" I demand, my body slowly losing all strength, my stomach twisting. The energy surrounding the Butcher men is nauseating in its grief. "Where is he!"

Luca approaches me. "We can't find him."

My breathing becomes fitful. My head jolts from side to side, as I stammer, "No. He's just..." I reach for something to hold on to, to keep my body straight, at my normal height — I feel like I'm shrinking. "He's just... *joking,* or did you look for his bike? Maybe he went after them. That's something he would do. Yes. Yeah, that's—"

"We looked everywhere." Luca catches me as my knees give up. A strangled sob forces its way up my throat. "They have him." He cups my cheeks, but my eyes bounce away, dropping to the floor, losing focus. "Look at me."

No, I won't. I don't want to exist without him anymore. I won't. I tremble in Luca's arms. "Look at me, Shoshanna. We will find my son. You have my word. We will bring him home."

"The police and ambulance are in the drive," a man says through the receiver. "Xander is with them."

"Copy that, we're heading out now," Carter replies.

I suddenly can't hear anymore. Words become inaudible as I drown in all the things unsaid —like I love you, like I want to be with you, I won't ever leave you again. I never told him he is my world, that my mind finds peace in his madness, that his madness allows me to be me. That without him, I was just half of a person. Half a heart.

Allowing fear to weigh me down, I sink deeper and deeper into hopelessness.

"I'LL PROTECT YOU. *Never leave you alone to fend for yourself.*"

THEN IT ALL FREEZES.

I widen my eyes and straighten, knowing what I have to

do. Protect him. Like I used to. *Together.* That's what we promised one another years ago when we had no idea what love and life were all about, but still understood the depths of loyalty, of commitment.

Pulling myself from Luca's arms, I stare at him, resolute in my decision. I clench my teeth, talking through them. "I'm going with you."

"No—"

"I. Am. Going!" I square my shoulders, not allowing any slip in my resolve. "I want to help. I can help."

Luca's brows weave. "If something happens to you, my son won't survive that either. Your safety might just keep him fighting. Keep him going."

Craning my neck, I level him with my stare. "I'm coming with you. There is nowhere else for me."

CHAPTER FORTY
shoshanna's poem

Eighteen years old.

Bronson,

Losing you is the closest I will ever feel to death. For feeling this pain means I am indeed alive. And so, to feel death is worse than the absolute of death itself.

It is a lonely place. For the loss is so personal, as no one is like you. Like me. Like us. No one will fill the emptiness that seems to occupy so much space inside me.

You were a big presence.

The gaping hole filled up with emptiness is a

desert where you used to live and thrive and be my guide.

I hold on to the hope that eventually my emotions will die. Or I will.

CHAPTER FORTY-ONE

bronson

Present day

FIGHTING TO LIFT MY CHIN, feeling an ache in the back of my skull, I wrestle with the weakness in my mind, in my muscles. The humming of a fan overhead alerts me to where I might be.

Well, this isn't good.

I shake the fatigue as it wraps around my thoughts, creating a haze of events that are hard to organise... Fucking... gunfire. Shoshanna... I picture her under the bed, covering her ears with her palms, screaming, and crying. I wince through the image, hearing my own deranged mind laughing... I fend the noise off, needing to concentrate. Reaching further for understanding... I see Kelly...Cassidy, they were in Max's arms. And Xander was... *Fuck*, I can't remember. I lost him. I growl at my own confused conscious, fighting to find the proceeding memory —what the fuck happened next?

A metallic liquid slides down my throat as my head finally agrees to rise, and given the throbbing in my face, I'm guessing it is blood pissing from my nose and lips. I spit the shit up, but in my clumsy attempt, droplets of the sticky mess land on my face. Opening my eyes, I squint at the back of a thin blindfold. The dim hue of an orange light shining in through the gap at my brow.

I stretch open my jaw, working it in circles, attempting to alleviate the tension behind my skin.

"Mother fuckers," I grunt.

Flexing my arms, I fight against restraints, twisting them behind the chair I'm sitting on. My ankles are bound too. I shuffle my weight, sliding the chair along the ground. The scratch of metal on concrete gives me a sense of what it might be made of and whether I can break it apart.

A low hiss soars through my mouth when I hear a heavy door slide along a concrete floor. I know the sound. And now I know what room I'm in. Usually, I'm not the sad fuck bound to the fucking chair, though. Ironic, really.

Two men laugh with deep, snarly tones that set the laughter in my head to mayhem.

"What's that around his neck?" one of them says, but I don't chase the voice with the tilt of my head. I keep my body relaxed, my face square on. I don't know his voice, but I know where he's standing —at least three metres from me. Perhaps my bindings don't give him much sense of security.

Smart man.

"Is that a fucking collar?" another voice about three steps from my right says. He's much closer than the other, but I don't humour him with any movement. "Are you a faggot or something like that?"

The grin that creeps across my lips is so manic the swelling below my jaw and cheeks bunch and ache. "Come over here, give me a kiss, and find out."

My ears twitch as the one closest to me takes a step. Staring down the bridge of my nose, below my thin black veil, I can see dark shoes and the lower part of his leg. His breath hits the side of my cheek, but I keep my head stationary. My smile softens and relaxes while images of a bloody massacre flash behind my eyes.

"I don't know what you think is so fucking funny, *Butcher*," he spits out. "He told me you're a bit fucked in the head. You're being executed, you dumb fuck. And I get to do it."

Sounds like a challenge to me. I launch myself sideways, knocking him to the ground, crushing him beneath my much larger body and the chair. The blindfold slips to my nose, revealing the room, the bitch in the corner advancing on me, and the dipshit below me.

I buck in the chair, worming my way up his body towards the base of his throat. On contact, I maul him, sinking my teeth into the soft flesh covering his trachea. He howls in horror and pain. Flailing around, he beats me with his weak fists. Holding the cord of his throat captive in my jaw, I shake my head like a dog, blood pissing into my mouth. His roars and yelps of panic are suddenly cut short when I squash his airway.

A blow to my chin snaps my head back.

Black engulfs me.

But my mind is far from silent.

CHAPTER FORTY-TWO

bronson

Present day

"I WANT YOU TO KNOW, this will pain me." Jimmy sighs. I open my eyes to find my blindfold removed and Jimmy sitting across from me within arm's reach.

Chilled.

Unreadable.

Just like my Jimmy always is. His ankle rests on his knee, his pristine black slacks rising slightly to reveal polished black shoes and folded black socks. And a pretty knife strapped to his calf. I quickly survey the cold concrete room —the killing floor. In each corner is a guard, ready with a bulletproof vest and a handgun held in front of him. I wonder if any of those fucks were at my house earlier today.

"I care for you, my boy," Jimmy states, leaning back in his chair. "I've worried for a long time about you, *se?* I think you may be sick in the mind." He tilts his head, offering a quick glance to the body on the floor —the sad fuck who thought he'd execute me. I grin, tasting his blood in my mouth, the dried fluid coating my teeth, making them rough. *Fuck*. What must I look like —as crazy as I feel, I suspect. "You see. You chewed out his windpipe. I might have been impressed once, but now..." Standing up, he walks over to a table in the corner. "Now my ways are more elegant. You love your brothers, *se?*" he mutters to the table and then turns, his hollow brown eyes finding mine. "I am doing this for them. For my family. You will get them killed. You will affect our whole operation. Trust, it is important to have trust in a fami—"

I cough up a bit of blood, a mist of crimson floating in the air, cutting off his sentence. "Jimmy, spare me the narcissistic bullshit, will you?"

His lips twitch, and I grin wider. The old boy hates it when his insightful monologues are interrupted.

"I did a lot for you, *se?* I looked after your girl. I knew that day when I sat with you while you grieved that she was your soul, *se?* I knew I had to watch over her. And Perry owed me a great deal of money, but I took a loss *for you*. To keep your girl happy." He strides over to me, stopping in front, forcing me to lift my chin to keep my eyes on the sly prick's face. My mind howls with hysterical laughter, my muscles burning with the need to rip his head from his spine. A slow smile pulls at the left side of his lips, and I fight my own grin to stay steady. "I made sure she was warm at night. Well cared for. Well *fucked*."

Fuck, I'm burning everywhere, my mind frying in the heat of pure rage.

He sighs. "But the girl is exquisite and as smart as a woman can be. So, of course, he fell in love with her. I may have too if I were him. If I was inside her every night."

Amusement engulfs his face as he measures my response to his words, as I begin to outwardly pant with restraint. He smiles, he fucking smiles, and I flare my eyes, seeing only a corpse.

A dead man.

A man who I love.

A man who I hate.

"That's good news, *se?* It wasn't all a lie. His love for her wasn't. He wanted her for himself, to make decisions for her without me interfering and so, in exchange for his compliance in a... *medical* project I'm investing in, I gave her to him." He pauses, making a pyramid with his hands, pressing his fingers to his lips. "I gave her to him by having her father and sister driven off the road. She was so young. She needed him so much more after that."

The energy is charged.

I can't think of anything except his death. His eyes are pinned on me. "Nothing to say now, my boy? No jokes? You think I'm the enemy, don't you? Your own—" He reaches for the word. "*Misguided* mind has confused you, my boy. It's a dangerous thing, your illness. You don't even realise what this is, do you, my boy?"

My face begins to tic. Years of listening to him preach and guide me, I consumed all his advice. Lived it in my bones. In my core. Used it to protect my brothers. *Fuck*, I believed in it.

He sighs with derision. "Clay found Salvatore's body."

My grin drops.

"You are a liability to this family. To his family."

The heat in my veins freezes over.

"He will run the District one day and you're a burden to his campaign."

The laughter in my head slowly sinks to a cold dark place in my mind, to being alone and having the weight of Max's life in my young hands. I shake my head, dragging myself out of the bathtub and back to the ominous abattoir killing floor. Forcing sanity, finding rationality in my confused bloodied state, I tell myself that he's full of shit. Has to be.

My brother would never betray me.

He's a Butcher.

"Trust me, Bron."

Then the door opens.

Tears flood my face when Clay steps inside, his eyes sympathetic but cold —schooled and controlled and ever more my beautiful, unreadable big brother. My heart wilts. It was all for them. Everything I ever did. All for my brothers.

And Jimmy...

Jimmy's respect.

"Here he is. Did you just get back?" Jimmy coos, his voice dripping in adoration for my big brother. I used to feel the same way about him; funny, really.

Clay stops in front of me. "Apparently not soon enough."

I slump in the chair, my mind and muscles unwilling to fight anymore. This time, I'll just let myself drown.

Staring at the cement floor, I lose focus as I accept defeat. I think about my son, my boy, a smile twitching at my lips. If there is a heaven, I'll finally get to hold him.

"I'm sorry, Bron. But Konnor isn't worth this fight. He isn't our brother. Jimmy has made us what we are. And Dad... he broke a vow first when he fucked Dustin's wife."

My mind screams. I want to slap the words from my consciousness. *Stop, fucking make it stop. Kill me.* I can't listen to this betrayal. It's like a knife slicing through my entire meaning of life. Through everything I hold dear. Through what it means to be a Butcher. I wish I'd died before I saw my brother standing in front of me, ripping apart my name.

This is my own form of hell, of torture.

Squatting at my feet, Clay tries to catch my line of sight. He pulls a handkerchief from his pocket, wiping the crimson liquid leaking from my lip and left eye. I keep my gaze low, concentrating on the small puddle of blood leaking from the dipshit's neck as it slowly dries and crusts over. "Jimmy saved Konnor, Bron. He'd be dead if it wasn't for him."

"I did Luca a favour, my boy. He's like a brother to me, and Konnor is his blood. Dustin wanted the boy in the ground, *se? I* saved him. This entire vendetta, my own nephew's murder, it's all been a result of paranoia in your sick mind, *se?* We can't have anyone going rogue. I was never your enemy."

Clay lowers his hand from my face, placing it on my knee. "I never wanted it to go down like this, but believe me, brother, this is the only way."

"Se, this hurts us both. This vendetta ends today. Clay will tell Luca that this was Dustin's doing. You killed his man, sent him a present, *se?* We'll take him out as a *family.* Maxwell will get his revenge, and with both *liabilities* having been taken care of quietly, there won't be any further issues arising between our families... Isn't that what you want? To leave them with a sense of peace?"

The shootout...

Clay knew we were all together.

What if he killed my girls...

I raise my head and train my eyes on the clear blue ones close to me. I tug on my restraints to inch closer, getting to a place where I can feel my brother's warmth. More tears trace the bloody tracks on my face. "You could have killed my girls," I spit out, feeling venomous.

Clay blinks once. "What're you talking about?"

"The shootout," I snarl, scrutinising his apathetic face, a mask of calm and sophistication and bullshit. My brother is so beautiful... I'll skin his beauty from his bones if I make it out of here alive.

His jaw muscles pulse as he says, "We had it all under control." The sound of a phone buzzing catches Clay's attention. His eyes drop to his side to acknowledge the vibrations. Surely there is nothing more important than sending his little brother to an early grave.

Clay leans forwards. Pressing his lips to my forehead, he lingers there to whisper, "It's over, brother. It's all over now." I look up at him as he straightens. Reaching into the left breast of his jacket, he retrieves his Glock. I decide to smile at him, noticing a shift in his stance. A tiny shuffle that makes no sense.

ONLY A BUTCHER IS ALLOWED *to send off a Butcher.*

THE GUN'S nose touches my forehead, and I push against it, wishing I had more time with my baby, dreaming about an alternative reality where I never walked away from her that day in the park but instead, held her, kissed her, told her I was there. Swore my devotion to her. With or without our son. Gave her my heart. My time. My everything. Lived for *her*. Watched her become a doctor or not. It wouldn't matter. Just watched her become something that made her happy. Then, when she was ready, we would have another boy. I would be so proud to be his dad because he'd be a hell of a lot smarter than me and just as cute as her.

I squeeze my eyes tighter, clutching at that false reverie despite feeling the cold nose of my big brother's gun between my brows.

Bracing myself.

Waiting.

Smiling.

The cold metal leaves me and I exhale fast as its absence stokes further anticipation. I'm ready...

Opening my eyes again, I become fixed on Clay as he points the gun at Jimmy. A wild grin creeps across my face, and I both want to beat the shit out of Clay and kiss him. Jimmy glares at him, radiating disappointment, shaking his head on a low, gruff sigh.

"What are you doing, my boy?" Clasping his hands in front of him, he waits for an answer.

"I have a gift for you, Jimmy," Clay states.

Jimmy is steel faced, but his gaze shifts quickly around the room to the guards, who are still and unresponsive to the gun pointed between their boss's brows.

"Do you think you can kill me and walk out of here alive?" Jimmy says, his tone dripping in amusement, and I fucking laugh. The sound echoes around the room. I have no fucking idea what is going on, but I was ready to die, to have my brains blow across this room, to see my boy... but I'm pretty fucking glad I didn't die before seeing this scene. "My son-in-law and his brother have forgotten themselves. Draw your weapons," he states to the men in the corners.

They don't move.

Clay lowers his gun to his side. "Draw your weapons," he orders smoothly, and all four men retrieve their guns, aiming them at Jimmy.

Jimmy shifts his gaze across the cold concrete room, narrowing his brown eyes in contempt and... *pride?*

Casually, Clay steps closer. Reaching into Jimmy's jacket pocket, he removes his boss's Glock from its harness. Strolling over to the intercom attached to the wall, Clay speaks through it. "I have disarmed him." He turns back to Jimmy, who is watching him like a shark biding its time, circling the situation with cunning and consideration before it lashes out. "You said it yourself, Jimmy. Trust is of utmost importance. We can't have any liabilities. We can't have anyone going rogue. Did you advise Alceu about taking out Bronson, about using us to avenge him and take out Dustin? And all those years ago when you locked Luca's son in a basement, my half-brother, Alceu's blood, did you ask if you could use five million dollars of The Family's money?"

The metal door opposite me swings open and in walks a hunched old Sicilian man, but I'd know that face anywhere —Alceu. Flanking him are four guards.

What the fuck is this beautiful scene?

He might be white-haired, and slow moving, but his presence hasn't lessened with his ever-aging body. He's still a killer through and through. The ghosts of all the men he's killed have darkened his eyes, making them dark pools of indifference. Of boredom. He's seen it all by now.

Stopping at Clay's side, he smooths down his black lapels. The scent of mint and cigars hangs around him like a low grey cloud. "My boy," Alceu says to Jimmy, his tone hoarse in his old age and yet undeniably commanding. "It's been a long time. Your guards, they don't speak Sicilian? Australians everywhere. Such a beautiful country other than the language... The women, though... You have been keeping them all to yourself, *se?*"

"*Alceu,*" Jimmy coos. "I didn't think you could fly. What a wonderful surprise this is." He opens his arms, and they embrace, kissing each other cheek to cheek like the polite snakes they are.

I tug on my restraints, darting my eyes to Jimmy's calf, remembering his blade.

Alceu steps back. "You left me no choice."

"Perhaps we should discuss any issue without the boys, *se?* There is no need for the theatrics. It's not long now and I'll be stepping down anyway. Clay is ready to lead with my guidance, aren't you, *son?*" Jimmy says, rolling the word *son* around his tongue, showing possessiveness. Like he owns my big brother even now, even as he's taking his place.

Clay moves over to me. Dropping to his knees, he unties my ankles as I keep watch over his shoulder. "Well, hello to you too, darling."

"I'm sorry for the show, buddy." He frees my legs and grips my shoulder, staring up at me. "I came as quickly as I could, but I needed to get the boss myself. *Fuck*, this is not how I planned this. I didn't know about the shootout. I didn't know he'd take you like this. Believe me."

"All that bullshit you just said to me. About Konnor. About Dad..." I clench my teeth, eyeing him warningly. "What purpose was that?"

"I needed him to admit to knowing Konnor was Dad's biological son. I'm sorry, buddy. Alceu needed to hear all of this from his lips. And that Jimmy was willing to kill you."

He removes the bindings around my wrists, and I spring to my feet, shaking out the fatigue and pain in my muscles.

"Jimmy was willing to kill you."

I have no idea why, but hearing those words spoken with sympathy and regret causes a sharp sensation in my chest. I saw for myself what he was willing to do, but... that's business.

I bite back the churn of my stomach.

Business.

It's why I killed my cousin. It's why I kill. For him. *For business.* Feeling a sharp sensation in my chest, I clench my teeth, wishing the word *business* was adequate enough to separate my feeling for Jimmy, slice them off at the head, and spill them out, let them go. There is no place for them inside me and yet, I idolised this man.

Wanted to be like him.

"The boy murdered my nephew." Jimmy's voice drags me to him, and I allow it to pull me right over there. Lurching forward, fuming, running on blood boiling hatred for the man who stole over a decade from me, I slam my fist into his face. His nose breaks. So does the skin on my knuckles.

Fuck, why do I feel so sick?

Alceu holds his hand up. "Enough of this. This is distasteful. I don't need it. I'm tired. I've been travelling for the past two days."

Jimmy stumbles back, hissing low before touching his nose as blood gushes from it. "The boy is wild, *se?"* Attempting to stop the bleeding, he pinches the arch of his nose.

Grinning at the fucker, because I'm exactly what he taught me to be, I reference his teachings as I say, "Jimmy forgot himself."

Clay pulls me backwards, and I let him. Flicking my body around, pain and confusion ebbing in my mind but still firing through my veins, I try to regain control. But anger and betrayal are chasing me down, bubbling to the surface.

Alceu waves dismissively. "The boy was tied to a chair. His muscles are... *twitching.* This happens. Let me get a good look at you, boy." He hums as he scrutinises Jimmy. "You still have that fire in your eyes. Your father had it too. It is that fire that brought me here. I came all this way to hear you speak. To hear the truth from my grandson's mouth. I'm impressed with what you have created here, *se?* I'm very proud. Not many men would have me travel across the world at my age to hear them speak. I gave that to you. I gave you that honour." Alceu points at us. "These boys. Luca's boys. *My* blood. They are your operation. Have you told them how important they are to us?" Sighing with strained disappointment, he eyes Jimmy thoughtfully.

I drop my gaze to watch Jimmy's fingers twitch by his side, and I wonder if he is picturing the blade strapped to his leg. "*Luca*'s boys," he repeats, spite filling his deep, smooth tone.

Clay steps away from me, positioning himself on Alceu's right-hand side. "My family. Your men. They don't trust you anymore, Jimmy. And you have been operating as though you have no one to answer to. As though you are, the boss." He looks at Alceu, drilling in his message. "We're a family first. Have you forgotten that? *Cosa Nostra. Our* thing. Family. What are we if not family men?"

A slow smile moves across Jimmy's face as he measures the situation, moving his knowing gaze from Alceu to Clay. "Do you know how my saint died?"

Alceu turns and places his hand on Clay's forearm. "I'm glad I came to see you both. I'll retire for the day. Boys," he says, signalling the guards. "These three need some family time. Leave them." I grin as all the guards shadow Alceu into the heart of the abattoir. The metal door slides shut behind them, enclosing us inside together.

"Yes," Clay states adamantly, tucking his hands into his pockets. "He was killed by his son."

"*Yes.*" Jimmy nods slowly, respect sailing back into his eyes. "I'm proud of you, my boy. You will kill me now, take my place, and run this city with my grandchildren. Another great achievement of mine."

"I'm not going to kill you, Jimmy." Clay takes a few steps backwards with a calculated smooth grin. "I don't kill men with my fists anymore." Reaching inside his jacket, he pulls out a silver knuckle duster. The shiny piece flashes under the overhead orange light as he passes it to me. Taking it, I notice the cracked dried blood on my hands. The feel of it on my face, like clay, forces my awareness of its presence almost everywhere. I must look as mad as he believes me to be.

I grin from ear to fucking ear.

He made me mad.

He wants mad.

I can give him mad.

With my heart beating like a war drum, excitement rushing through my veins, I say, "How many men have I killed for you, Jimmy? I'd put the count in the fifties. Twice as many as any of my brothers." I look down at his ankle as he shuffles his feet. "Get your knife out, mate. You can fight me like a Sicilian does, and I'll kill you like a Butcher does."

He reaches down. Pulling the thick, shiny blade out, he lowers his head and glares through his lashes at me. The reality of this moment hammers down on me.

I'm going to kill Jimmy.

"DO YOU RESPECT ME, MY BOY?"

I nod, gripping the bloody blade in my hand. "Yes."

"Tell me why?"

Glancing at the corpse on the floor, I say, "Because everyone else does."

"Do they?" Jimmy leans down to meet my eyes. "Or are they afraid of me? Do you know the difference?"

I shake my head because I don't. "No."

"That's because there isn't one."

. . .

I MOVE IN, jabbing him in his cocky mouth with the metal duster, spilling pretty rich red fluid from it. Hissing, he swipes at me, but I jump back just in time. The blade grazes my shirt, leaving a tiny slice in the material. We circle each other. Jimmy goes in again, connecting with my side, drawing a bloody stripe along one of my ribs.

A daring smile curves across his lips.

"OFFER EVERYONE YOUR SMILE, MY BOY."
My brows draw in. "But what if I don't like them?"
"Smile harder. They'll never know what hit them."

STIFLING a violent sob at the reverie, I force a smile to match his own. Lunging forward, I jab him in the right eye, step back, jab, step, jab, step.

He falls to the floor, and I pounce on him, kneeling on either side of his body. A sharp sensation shoots through my hip, drawing my focus to the pain. Gazing down, I see a black handle bobbing, the blade completely embedded in my flesh.

"HE WAS YOUR FRIEND," *I say, staring at the smoking hole between the man's brows.*
"Se. And now he gets to remain one."

LAUGHING LIKE A MADMAN, I draw strength from the agony. Hovering over him, I revel in knowing I'm the last thing he'll ever see. The mad Butcher, the pawn, takes down the great Jimmy Fucking Storm. My friend... My idol.

He spits blood at my face. Looking at me, he laughs, his laughter mocking mine. His eyes taunting as he mouths, "*My boy*," and nausea and fury engulf me.

"MY SON NEEDS *to go to university," Dad says, butting his cigar out, the smoke moving between the two men.*

I shake my head, look to Jimmy for support. "I don't want to go to fucking university. I want to work for my family."

Jimmy grins. "The boy knows what he wants, Luca."

He places a hand on my shoulder and squeezes.

GROWLING at myself as tears rip violently from within me, I force my body into action, force my muscles to take his life even as my heart splinters and opens up. One metal fist. One bare. I beat the life out of the man I idolise, beat the bullshit advice, the manipulative support, the lies and deceit. I beat him for Shoshanna, beat him for sweet Akila. I beat the mouth that says, 'my boy,' knowing I'll never hear it again.

I beat him raw like a fucking Butcher.

With my fists.

With my muscles.

With my brother at my side.

.

CHAPTER FORTY-THREE

shoshanna

Present day

THROUGH THE BARBED-WIRE FENCING, I run towards the abattoir under the watchful eyes of Luca, Max, Xander, and several Butcher guards. Summoning all my strength to face whatever is behind those imposing doors. Cattle and livestock graze in the surrounding paddocks, a peaceful lining to the grisly centre where evil operates.

The thick riot gear they forced me to wear restricts my movements, making my body heavy and sluggish. Several guards separate from the main group. Rounding the perimeter of the building, they disappear into the dark fields.

Max moves in first, his gun raised and ready. Behind him Luca and two other men follow while Xander flanks the rear. A line of Butcher guards separates each of them, a seemingly well organised formation. My pulse races around in my throat, but I can't let the moment overwhelm me. This is where I belong.

With him.

At the sight of Jimmy's guards, several red dots arrow in on their chests. They raise their hands, and we slow down, wondering why there is no retaliation. One man approaches Luca and I rush over to hear the conversation.

"You can move freely," he says to Luca as crackling feedback comes through the speaker on his vest. Xander darts his eyes around in confusion, his body vibrating, ready for a fight. Max slows and stands by his dad, gun rested by his thigh, steady and prepared.

I don't need any further explanation. Darting into the abattoir, I catch Luca's gruff order to his guards, "Follow her." Moving straight through the doors, I push past guards, heading to a room at the end of the hall. He's in there. I know. My lungs burn. The entire space is cold and hollow — heartless. I want to puke. As I pant and draw air in, my nostrils singe with the presence of chemicals. A stench only lightly masking the rancid smell of death and blood. Of raw meat. Of shit.

Legging it into the room, I search the area. I come to a dead stop. My heart contracts, skipping through my veins with relief when I see Bronson is very much alive.

Then it sinks into a black hole in my stomach.

He's on his knees, covered from head to toe in blood. Too much blood to be entirely his own. In a heap on the floor in front of him, is the bludgeoned corpse of Jimmy Storm. A few metres away, another body lay, his neck skin flapping open.

Standing beside Bronson, Clay is still and solemn, gripping his little brother's shoulder supportively.

Completely ignoring the gruesome scene inches from my man's knees, I rush over to him. Dropping to the cement floor, I fling my arms around his blood-soaked shoulders, clutching with desperation. He buries his head into my chest, hunching over and bursting into violent sobs.

Oh, God.

Nutcase.

Vibrating with emotion, he is letting me hold him in his trembling state. Pulling his head to my chest, I comb my fingers through his wet hair, not caring about the blood all over me.

Glaring at the corpse on the floor, I realise I couldn't care less about Jimmy Storm's death. But I feel Jimmy's betrayal seeping through Bronson and into my soul, feel his broken heart as though it were my own, tearing down the middle, just like it did at the park.

This time we are together.

I tighten my hold, clutching at the seventeen-year-old boy who wanted to be something else, who wanted to be a stay-at-home dad, a good person, who wanted to be *better.*

Better than this!

"*Shh.*" I burst at the seams with sorrow, begging to go back in time, to have another chance at the park, where I didn't leave, where I saved him from this world.

Where I was his distraction.

From all of this horror.

I try to soothe him with my hand, with a gentle voice, but my body shakes, and he's far too overwhelmed with torment to hear me.

His tears fall down, mingling with mine, his breath and moans and growls all mix, and it's the worse sound in the world. Yet, he's letting me hold him, letting himself be vulnerable with me.

"*Bron,*" Xander mutters from over my shoulder, and Bronson's arms tighten around me, as though he can't bear being seen. Wanting to disappear into my arms, he shuffles in closer. He's so much bigger than me, but I try to make him feel secure.

I wish I could hide him.

In my peripherals, I see my medical bag being placed beside me.

"Leave them," Luca orders, but I don't look up. Hearing the door shut, I cup Bronson's cheeks, searching and scrutinising the damage to his beautiful face. He sobs into my palms, unable to hold himself together.

Slowly, he opens bloodshot eyes, swollen and utterly defeated. He clenches his jaw, trying to rein in the fitful emotions. I catch his attention, anchoring him to me.

Then he stops crying.

He breathes out hard.

His eyes tormented pits of turquoise.

I wince at the deep gash by his brow, the open split in his lower lip. I lower my gaze, rolling over a thin slice by his abdomen. At the sight of a black handle, swaying from his hip, the blade itself inside him, I break.

"Oh, *God*." I burst into tears, covering my mouth and eyes. He leans forwards and kisses my hands, so I drop them to desperately accept his lips on mine. "I love you."

"Don't cry, baby."

I nod, forcing myself to focus, to not get dragged under with my emotions. Leaning back, I inspect the wound. The blade shouldn't have hit anything vital, but it could have clipped his Iliac artery. If so, when we remove the handle, it'll need immediate work. A theatre. More than I can offer here. Despair wraps around me, suffocating me, making it hard to breathe.

I ignore it.

This time, I can be what he needs. I push on the skin,

watching the flow of the blood that leaks out. Noting the angle of the handle, I'm almost certain the blade is about an inch away from the primary artery.

Steeling his body, he whispers. "You shouldn't be here."

I frown up at him. "Where else would I be?"

His hand moves to my face, cradling my cheek fondly, and the look in his eyes is full of horror and fear but also undying affection. A sad affection that begs for something, pleading to be healed. "Shosh*anna*. You going to fix me, baby? You going to save me again?"

"You saved me first," I say on a whimper, reaching into my black case, rummaging through it until I find what I need: gloves, fentanyl, gauze, sutures, scissors, bandages. Passing him the fentanyl, I say, "Suck on this."

He takes the tube, actually doing as he's told for once. From here, I take a big breath in, pull my gloves on, and get to work. Clenching my jaw, I draw the blade from his flesh. When blood spills from the channel, slow and controllable, I relax on an exhale. "Press here." I use Bronson's palm to apply pressure to the site, leaving small gaps where I can suture. Making my way up the wound, inch by inch, I wince with vicarious pain even though he barely flinches.

After I've finished with it, I reach into my bag, ready to clean and care for every scratch, big and small, on his beautiful body. Wishing I could do the same for the ones in his mind and heart. He reaches for me, his large muscular arm covered in tattoos, still splattered with blood.

A gruesome but raw vision.

He grips the curve of my neck, pulling my lips to brush along his. "You came for me."

Feeling the intensity in his grip, my throat curving towards him under the pressure. "You let me care for you," I whisper. "You need me."

Pulling me into his lap, his body still tight, he says. "I do need you, baby. But not just now, always. You're it. You're my peace. My quiet place."

"And you're my life," I murmur, my voice strangled. His grip relaxes, and I lean my forehead against his, feeling his breath fan down my skin as he exhales his emotions, exhales his tension. "I'm bones, blood, muscles, and movement, but nothing else, nutcase. With you though, I'm loved and loving and aware and awake. And I can be, me. Crazy. A bitch. An angel. Me." I close my eyes, dipping to kiss his lips, to seal my bleeding honesty in a physical way. "I love you."

He groans as we roll our mouths and tongues together, every stroke a message of commitment. I can taste blood and salt and sweat, but I don't care. It's *us*, seeking pleasure, accepting each other for all our crazies.

Dragging my lips to his forehead, I press them firmly against him, quick, chaste, before pulling his face into the crook of my neck, cradling him there. Long, powerful arms go around my back, crossing over at my spine, holding me possessively.

"We'll get through it *together*," I say with a reminiscing sound, a promise echoed from when we were young and did not know what life or love was all about.

What the world would throw at us.

How his madness would shake me to life.

How my distraction would bring him peace.

Burying his face further into my embrace, he whispers, "Okay, baby."

THE END

Shoshanna

Twelve months later

I RACE into the workshop under a cloud of nervousness, knowing he'll be devastated if he misses Clay's ceremony. Dodging old parts of machines, I call out to him through the ruckus. No one even turns. I step over an old engine and weave my way through the people. They must be having another 'play, pimp, or pay' day because the entire shop is crawling with people and the noise is wild and chaotic. Fuel by Metallica is blasting from the speakers. Poor, organised Juliette will be pulling her hair out right now, trying to maintain a sense of professionalism amid Bronson's playful anarchy.

Heading straight for his station in the back corner, where

dozens of teenage boys gather, shoulder to shoulder, to get a front-row view of the elegant or beastly machine my nutcase is building, I can't help but smile.

When I get to the front of the crowd, I lean on one hip and fold my arms over my breasts. Raising an eyebrow, I take him all in. He's squatting by a black Harley Davidson, playing with something at the rear that has all the teenage boys peering over in awe —they are far more focused on him than on me in my tight black dress.

Which is a refreshing change.

His shirt is tucked into the back of his jeans, swinging as he works. Following the movement of his sweaty tattooed bicep as it flexes, pulling on something —a bolt, a chain, I don't know —trying to get it to move or wedge, I know nothing about bikes, I hum my enjoyment of the view. He's a beautiful work of art, my Bronson Butcher. Dark. Fun. A killer and a clown. Crixus notices me immediately, leaving his side and barrelling over. Jumping in the air, springing off his back paws, he's a stocky dog-shaped jack-in-the-box.

I squat down, letting him lather me in soggy kisses. "Your daddy needs an alarm clock," I say to him. Standing, I project my voice out to Bronson. "Nutcase!"

His head pops up, his eyes narrowing on me from over the leather seat. Jumping to his feet, he opens his arms. "Baby!"

The crowd turns to stare at me, but I grin straight ahead. "Are you forgetting something?"

His eyes roll over my body, obvious and meaningful, caressing me with each slight narrow and flare. Then his face drops as he seemingly remembers why I'm wearing this pretty black dress. "Oh, fuck!"

I nod, saying, "Yeah." I laugh as he leaps over the bike,

the crowd parting for him instantly. Crixus scurries after him, near hitting his heels.

"Don't touch my bike, Callum." Bronson laughs, turning to point two fingers at his eyes, then pointing them at Callum. "I'm watching you." He peers down at Crixus. "Crixus boy, you stay here, buddy."

Callum grins, taking a little step back from the Harley. "Crixus, come here, boy," he calls. Crixus rushes over to Callum. Grabbing his collar, Callum grips it as our little staffy attempts to follow us. "Can I fix the left wheel alignment for you?"

"Not if you want to live," Bronson says as he darts into the office, grabs his wallet, and then reappears. Spinning on my black wrap-around heels, heading towards the sleek black van out front, I'm suddenly halted by a big warm palm around my throat and hot lips pressing to mine. The boys hoot and wolf whistle, and I close my eyes, breathing him in.

I kiss him. Trace his tongue with mine. Lean my body against his —the love between us is palpable.

He smells like oil and sweat.

And if freedom had a scent, it would be that of Bronson Butcher when he is working on bikes. When he has grease on his tattooed arms and chest instead of blood, when he is shirtless and wild, when he has dirt under his fingernails.

I fucking love it.

"Slow down," he whispers, his breath skating along my parted lips. "Don't flaunt this sexy body in front of me and not kiss me or I'll throw you over my shoulder. Take you into my office. Bend you ove—" His eyes drop to my breasts, and he groans, a deep rumble that forces my pulse to run rampant in my throat. He licks his lips, indecency illuminating the green freckles in his eyes. "You're leaking, mummy."

A little smile ticks at the corner of my lips. "You're such a pervert."

"Isn't it great?" He entwines our fingers, guiding me outside where our van idles. Our driver, Henri, waits by the front passenger door. He's formal today, in a black suit and tie.

It's an important day.

"Henri, you handsome fucker." Bronson lightly slaps his cheek. "You don't dress up like that for me."

Henri chuckles. "You have never taken me out on a date, Mr Butcher."

Laughing, Bronson jumps into the back of the van. Moving to the rear where Akila's wheelchair is parked, he says, "Hey sis," before planting a kiss on her cheek. "You look fucking beautiful. I think I'm with the wrong sister."

I smirk, rolling my eyes as I climb into the back with them. Tugging out the soaked nipple pads, I retrieve new ones from my satchel and line my bra with them. Bronson makes his way to the front, sliding in next to me. On my other side, our son sleeps in his baby seat. Bronson reaches over my lap, stroking a tattooed finger down the porcelain cheek of our sleeping baby boy.

Bronson's tanned skin is a stark contrast to our fair baby boy. Stone doesn't look like either of us; I exhale, the reason riding my breath.

He is probably not Bronson's.

"*It doesn't matter,*" Bronson's words float into my heart and head.

Feelings of reluctancy and subsequent guilt followed my pregnancy. But they are gone now. Dissolving in the hospital room when Bronson took Stone into his arms after my caesarean. I remember the way our baby—so tiny and fragile

—seemed to disappear into the mass of Bronson's ink-laced embrace. A sense of truth wrapped around me as Bronson studied the boy's flushed face, which to me was clearly not akin to his or mine.

It didn't matter.

Bronson grinned and said, "Yeah. He's a fucking Butcher alright."

And that was that.

His boy.

***

After we park at the hall, Henri grabs Akila, Bronson grabs his boy, and I climb out with the same smile that often plays on my lips now.

Gathered together, the media line the walkway, and both casually dressed young interns and formally dressed politicians engage in interviews and speak with Connolly residents. Above the hall, hanging from the roofline, is a fifteen-foot banner with Clay Butcher's face on it.

He's smiling charmingly. Practiced. Clever. I knew this day would come, but at thirty-five he's climbed the ladder faster than any other young politician in the state.

As soon as we enter, we are instantly greeted by ushers who guide us towards the private area alongside the stage. The District flag, the Australian flag, and the Aboriginal flag act as a backdrop for the platform ahead while in front a band waits for instruction. Already drifting around us is the rhythmic sound of a man playing the didgeridoo.

I spot the Butcher men with ease, all three towering over the rest of the congregation, looking smart in slacks and button-up shirts. Xander is in a heated discussion with another man I don't know, and Max has no interest in anyone besides his wife, who has her back pressed to his chest, held within a cage of his arms. Kelly shoves through the boys, diving towards Bronson and Stone. "Can I see, Stone?"

"Outlaw!" Bronson drops to his haunches, cuddling her to his side and giving her a chance to speak baby-talk with her cousin. He does too, both coo exaggeratively.

I beam at them.

I spin around to check Akila is close. Not too far behind, Henri is pushing her over to us. Gazing at her lovely amber eyes, I have come to accept that there is not much life in them. Know that I should have let her go. The next time she is ready, I will make sure I am, too. Still, her face can be expressive, and I hold on to those fleeting moments.

A man's voice soars around us as the speakers in each corner become active. On stage, a council member begins the ceremony by thanking the traditional owners of our land, and a group of children sing the national anthem in Noongar.

It doesn't take long before the speaker is welcoming Clay Butcher on stage. The new Mayor of Connolly.

The room ignites.

From the side of the stage, he strides on with slow, confident movements. Smoothing down his graphite-coloured two-piece suit, he grabs the microphone from the stand and stops in place. As the crowd chants his name, Clay, Clay Clay, he nods his appreciation with a cool smile.

"I'm here," he says smoothly. "I'm here. You have me." The crowd keeps going. "Thank you. Quieten down. Behave..." They laugh, their voices and bustles dwindling with respect for his wishes.

"We are the fastest growing city in the country," he states with a reverent nod. "Did you know that? This city is more than just the place you sleep, and eat, and play. It breathes. It's alive. With a body made up of buildings and parks, streets and canals. With exceptional qualities, our architecture, our talented citizens, our beaches. With personality, our arts, culture, the guy on the corner of Mills Avenue who throws the pot-pourri in the drains to make our pipes smell nice." They all burst into knowing laughter. Clay threads his fingers together, resting them in front of him, his face serious now. "With flaws... I don't want to just talk about the good. My first promise to you is to see this city —all of it. Not just the parts that shine, but also the parts that don't. I will pay attention to all aspects of her. I will take her seriously. I will treat her morally. And I will do a great deal for her."

The people detonate.

Clay continues, but Bronson appears behind me, stealing my attention. Wrapping his arms around my middle, he places his chin on my crown. I peer across to see Stone in Max's thick arms; he's rocking the tiny boy back and forth and Cassidy looks like she's about to melt into a puddle on the floor.

Thinking about the life I live now, I smile. It's my resting smile. It's a small smile, a still one. One that plays on my lips softly and without effort.

It's contentment.

And Bronson worried that I'd find a world away from the hospital slow-paced and boring, but I enjoy my new role with Akila, with girls just like her. It's definitely slower, but it's in no way boring.

And I have many origami roses to show for all the gossiping I do with them... apparently, women are never too old to swoon over boys —over men.

And I still only ever speak about one boy.

He's twenty-eight now.

And although he was always perfect to me. My perfect nutcase. It matters how his soul feels. How he feels about himself... and he tells me he feels *better*.

"HE'LL BE PERFECT. *Cause you are. And I'll learn to be, baby. I swear it. I'll be better.*"

his pretty little burden - book four

Chapter One
Clay

SITTING IN THE FRONT PEW, under the stained-glass windows crowning the District's oldest church, alongside the daughters of the man in the polished mahogany casket before me, I feign my attention. My eyes set ahead, but my muscles tighten as vengeance rolls through the room.

It's not that I do not grieve this man.

I do.

I grieve alongside his family—my family—the council officials, and hundreds of members of the city who saw Jimmy Storm as a kind of philanthropist.

Grieving him was always a certainty.

My jaw clenches in a solemn smile as I feel something is amiss.

I stare respectfully forward while behind me the presence of my father, brothers, and their partners is ripe with sadness, bitterness, and betrayal. Jimmy would be proud he still affects them so.

Despite the fact my brother and I executed him ourselves, it isn't problematic grieving with his admirers as we shared a kind of affection for this man.

He was a second father to us.

But that is the way it goes.

His time was up the moment he betrayed the *Cosa Nostra*. Stole one of our own. Lied to another made-man. Spent money he had no right to spend.

Greed and hubris were his biggest sins.

Still, he had loyal followers...

In the adjacent pew, the Family heads from Sicily listen like devout Catholics as the priest recites psalm after psalm, their conscience is as clear as mine, their minds without shame, but surely, they too feel the electrified air. See the side-eye glances.

Usually, I am the most powerful man in the room, but today, I'm matched by many. This is the first and last time this number of Family members will be in Australia.

Caporegimes and Bosses from Sicily and from across the country are spread throughout the room. Between these four walls is the most dangerous place in the world; a gathering like this rarely happens. The last time was probably back in '57 at the Apalachin meeting, where my American Family was raided and arrested by the feds. It's bad business bringing everyone to one location, but for Jimmy Storm's funeral... they came anyway.

We stand to pray.

The fact my six-foot-five frame towers above most is not lost on me as right now a shot to the back of my head would be child's play. Even so, I stay at my full height. They wouldn't dare. If someone did, they better aim true because I'll have him gutted while his heart still beats.

Aurora, Jimmy's eldest daughter and my wife, stands quietly beside me, her whiskey-coloured eyes misted over but not a tear to be seen—for she is no fool either. She is *Cosa Nostra* royalty. So, her father's death came as no surprise to her. I've never kept a secret from my wife, and she has never made me regret that stance.

When we sit again, Aurora holds her hands in her lap, and I tear my eyes away from the priest at the altar to watch her worry her wedding band around her long, elegant finger. A piece of jewellery equal parts a platinum shackle and a crown. We do not have a traditional relationship—nor a sexual one— our union is based on business. Being my wife is the last claim she has to this empire now that her father has been overthrown.

Still, she is my partner.

Exhaling hard, I reach for her hand and hold it, stilling her nervous fidgeting.

She squeezes my fingers.

Beside her, her younger sisters share muted sobs while wafting black silk hand fans at their flushed faces. Despite the millions we give this church, air-conditioning doesn't seem to be a priority in the midst of a scorching Australian summer.

The ceremony runs for hours.

Each time we stand to pray, the back of my neck prickles under the eyes of Jimmy's beloved citizens. The narcissist in him was very skilled at playing Gandhi, disturbingly so. A skill I have honed as my own, but Jimmy still sails through this procession like a phantom. Even now, the guests that idolised him breathe life back into his corpse.

Jimmy Storm was the heart and teeth of the District,

enlightening and adoring his followers while gnashing and shredding those who challenged him.

He and my father built this city from the ashes of poverty. They nourished it. Fed it. They cleaned the streets and secured previously unattainable tenders for employment. They saw our residents hold gold and green in their fists. Jimmy and my father are businessmen, and they sank their claws so far into the heart of the District that if anyone was to rip the *Cosa Nostra* from it, the entire city would bleed to death.

Alceu and my father deliver speeches and condolences as the heads of the Family in the District.

Solemn nods.

Tight smiles.

Grief thick in the air.

The procession ends. But the eerie current coursing through the very fibres in the air does not dissipate as the bodies filter from the pews. I clasp my hands in my lap, waiting. My father and the four most formidable men in the world also linger to speak with me, alone in this house of God.

Aurora leaves my side, knowing the ritual to be had is not for her to witness. As members of the city leave alongside her, she takes her time to console them in a flawlessly elegant manner. Pride moves through me. She is just like Jimmy.

The church doors echo as they shut. The silence surrounding us is woven with superiority and expectation.

With tension.

I'd know it anywhere.

I sigh roughly, the sound breaking the quiet.

"Rest in peace, my boy," Alceu states, his words projected towards the corpse of the man he raised as his own back in the old country. I stare ahead at the garlands and polished wood of his coffin, my attention not straying from the stage.

"Now is the time, Clay," he says. "We are all here to see you take your place."

The most dangerous man in this room by my measure— my father—waits respectfully quiet behind me. Significance moves through my bones. I've been bred for this moment my entire life, and now that it is here, I'm ready.

I dig into my pocket, retrieving the card I have carried with me since I was twenty-one. Spinning it in my hand, I approach the coffin.

The priest hovers nearby.

I still when he moves. Quick. Jerky. Pulling a gun from his robe, he points it between my eyes, his hand shaking violently.

I slide the card between my newly growing smile; my instincts are very rarely wrong. Darting from his line of fire, I draw my Glock before he can take a breath and blow the priest backwards into his pulpit, the gun still braced in his rigid right hand. I don't look behind me at the four men on the bench.

I approach the priest, my shadow creeping up his trembling form as I tower over him. *So, it was you.* The man whimpers, hisses, gurgles on blood and saliva; the helpless sounds of a dying man fill this sacred room.

My heart pumps hard. Steady. Strong.

The gaping wound at the priest's stomach puddles and pools. His hand vibrates around the poorly held gun; the other clumsily holds the hole while viscous fluid, stomach contents, and toxins bubble through split flesh and infect his whole fucking nervous system.

A stomach wound means a slow death. Sepsis first. Then his organs will shut down.

At least he is in *His* house.

Humidity gathers in the air, causing my skin to mist, for sweat to slide down my forehead. The shift is immediate. Control seeps through me as the threat that hung in the air now dwindles with the man choking on his own fluids. I expected a final present from Jimmy.

The priest was a nice touch.

Dropping to my haunches, I stare indifferently into the wide haunted eyes of God's representative, wondering how much Jimmy paid for his soul.

"*Please,*" he begs, his voice rattling in his throat. His eyes drop to the gun, as he tries to lift it to his temple. He wants me to show him mercy. Blow his brains out. His crooked fingers twitch around the gun, before finally weakening, dropping the metal piece to the stage.

Reaching for his mouth, I enclose it, silencing the gurgling and sobbing beneath my iron-tight grip. He flails around. My bicep twitches as I hold him still. Hold him until the life leaves his fearful grey eyes. *I am merciful.*

I wipe the card on his wound, smearing Saint George— my saint—with holy blood spilled—*desecrated*—at *His* altar.

Standing, I approach the coffin and casually flick the card on top before slowly making my way down the aisle, the sound of my father and the four Dons from Sicily flanking me as I do.

So, it begins.

Get book

his pretty little burden

Sweet little Fawn is the daughter of a boss in The District Cosa Nostra.

The daughter of the man who betrayed my family.

Not only is she a burden—barely eighteen, naïve, the epitome of a little deer in headlights-
But she is too damn pretty.

Too pretty to have clawed her way through life, merely surviving.

Too pretty to be so utterly vulnerable, alone, and asking for help from the deadliest man in the city—me.

Christ. She is too pretty to be walking my halls at midnight.

Too damn pretty... to not be mine.
My pretty little burden

Get book

dear reader

Stop. Please. I want to talk about Baby Stone. I want to discuss my decision to have him not be Bronson's biological son.

I didn't do it to be 'mean.'

This was an important aspect of Bronson's character and journey. The principal theme in The Kids of District series is *family*, and I like to explore this concept thoroughly. Bronson is by far the most unapologetically loving of all the Butcher pack. He just loves so hard with his big crazy heart. His love is without prejudice. It is without conditions.

And Stone needed a dad. Bronson couldn't love him any more than he does. The fact he isn't his blood is insignificant, and this aspect of the story shines a light on Bronson's character even more. On this amazing man who genuinely and wholly loves and accepts. He was never disappointed. So, you shouldn't be. He got his boy. A perfect, healthy boy.

Be happy for them both.

Secondly, a few very close friends of mine have struggled

with fertility. And even in this modern world, they are often met with ignorance around their family unit. A family pulled together with love and fight and desire, not a decision quickly made nor a chance, but unyielding dedication, a marathon to have a family. And yet, it is still not enough for some people. Even though they have a beautiful child by their side, they still endure comments like, "Maybe one day you'll have one of your own."

This hurts my heart.

So, after discussions with one of these friends (also a writer), we both envisioned Bronson holding a boy in his arms that wasn't his own blood and saying, "Yeah, he's a fucking Butcher alright."

And nothing else matters.

Just try and tell our Nutcase that Stone isn't his.

But, I didn't make this decision lightly. I made it for every father who loves his wife's biological child(ren), even though they aren't his own blood. For every couple who adopted, who truly understand how trivial biological ties are. I made it for Bronson, who would burn the world to the ground for the people he loves: his sister-in-law, his brothers, his dad, his outlaw, his beautiful distraction and their beautiful son, and everyone else who makes his loved one's smile, them too.

He never, not even for a split-second, doubted that Stone was his. Some readers have reached out to me and said that Bronson and Shoshanna deserved 'their own' child... to which I say, "Stone *is* theirs." I feel as though they are missing the point. Why would that make any difference? I know Bronson wanted a "little bit of you and a little bit of me." That is part of his journey, too. Stone will be very much like the man who loves and raises him —he will be 'a lot of Bronson Butcher,' not just a little.

On a final note, this isn't the end for Bronson and Shoshanna. I can assure you, Bron will never stop wanting more children. Adopted. Surrogate. Biological. IVF. Whatever.

They will have a big, happy family.

our thing - book one & two

Blurb:

The city's golden girl falls heart first into a dark underworld.
I want two things in life: to be the leading ballerina in my academy—
And ***Max Butcher***...

A massive, tattooed boxer, and renowned thug.
And my very first crush...

I may be a silly little girl to him, but he's intent on protecting, possessing, and claiming me in every way—his little piece of purity.

But there is more to Max Butcher than the cold, cruel facade he wears like armour. I know; I saw the broken boy inside him one day when we were only children.

So, even as I stand in the shadows with him, as people get hurt... *as people die...* I refuse to let him believe he's nothing more than a piece in his Family's corrupt empire.

There is good inside Max Butcher, and I refuse to let him live in the dark forever.

Get book

facing us – the prequel

Have you read Konnor & Blesk's story?

Blurb:
He is desperate to remember.
She will destroy everything to forget.

Konnor: Up until now, my life has been a mirage of sorts. Of dark, lonely places. Of bourbon and women. I don't care. I think I'm pretty happy really.
But then she happens...

Blesk: He wants me. He'll do anything, drop everything, to have me. But when he uncovers who I am and what I've done, he'll rue ever facing me.
I've already buried everything he loves...

We both have secrets. Mine are harrowing. His, heart-breaking. Just merely being together threatens to expose everything we have tried to escape.

Will finally facing our past bring us peace or... spark chaos?

Get Book!

the district -
origin story

Jimmy Storm —1979
Controllare le strade; control della citta
(Control the streets; control the city.)

MY FATHER WAS a *ladder-man* in the late 1940s. In the old country—Sicily. He was the boy the Family trusted with their money, for he was the one with the clearest vantage point. The expression *ladder-man* had come about back in the early gambling days when young men would stand on ladders on the casino gaming floors, watching and waiting for misconduct.

My father was the most trusted and feared man in Sicily —a complete oxymoron, I know. But it all depended on who was doing the trusting and who was doing the fearing.

The Family paid him ninety lira an hour, which was good money back then, and so of course, the crooks of the club — the ones on the gaming floor pocketing chips, counting cards, and winning too much of the Family's money —found death quickly. There was very little chance for rebuttal once my father had them in his sights. He was an adolescent then and rather engrossed in the power bestowed upon him, as would any young man be with the strength of many at his beck and call.

Things were irrevocably simpler back then. If there was a misdemeanour, it was handled quickly, quietly, and strictly; very few people lived to talk about it. Which is how it should be.

According to gossip, my grandfather was a 'likable type' and had no knowledge of his son's activities. Luckily for us, my grandfather had died when my father was sixteen, leaving him without any relations. *Luckily?* Yes, because there is little I can learn from a 'likable type' of man.

After three years of being the boy up the ladder on the most notorious gaming floors in Sicily, my father became an orphan. And an orphan he was for exactly two days before the Family picked him up and officially made him their own. They bought my father. They owned him then. It wasn't until then that he really understood what he'd signed up for.

He had married the mob.

When you marry the mob, as when you marry a woman, you are contractually, spiritually, legally, and emotionally bound to them. The key difference being, there is no such thing as divorcees —only widowers. That is where it all had started —humble beginnings and a life of servitude to the Family.

When I was a young man, my ego was larger than Achilles', rivalling my father's in every way. It would be fair to say I flexed my muscles every chance I could —at the boys at school, at the people on the sidewalk offering me less than obedient glances... at everyone. I was a *sfacciato* little shit, and partly because of that cheekiness, I learned to thrive on the sensation people's submission gave me. I'd usually be hard as a rock beneath my trousers in the midst of a power play.

I am Jimmy Storm, son of Paul Storm, and my name is legendary. Storm is not our real name, of course. My father named himself when he became a made-man.

Half of Sicily owed the Family money, which meant we owned half of Sicily and her people. We managed people with ease, for their lives were worthless to us and priceless to them. I grew up around the cruellest, slyest, dirtiest bastards in the country and they set the benchmark for my behaviour as an adolescent; they were my idols.

When I turned twenty-seven, my *zu* Norris and I left Sicily, taking with us blessings and funds from the Family, with our sights set on a new place of profit. We flew to an area of Australia renowned for its wealthy residents —a secluded section on the coast consisting of four towns: Brussman, Connolly, Stormy River, and Moorup. I recently learnt of an Australian idiom for this kind of unmonitored and isolated area —'Bandit Country'.

I was out to prove myself at any cost.

Which brings me to today, and the reason I have my shoes pressed to a man's trachea.

"I am *Jimmy Storm!*" I state. The rubber of my heel presses very slowly on his windpipe, and when he tries to buck away, I know I have found the *puntu debole*. He tries desperately to claw at my foot, attempting to relieve some pressure. He can't, but that doesn't save my shoe from getting covered in fingerprints, and *that* is just so inconvenient.

My *zu* and I have been in this miserable part of the world for three god forsaken weeks and have found nothing short of disorganised, disrespectful, and inferior versions of la Cosa Nostra. The young man whose trachea I'm currently crushing is Dustin Nerrock, and he is 'the name' about these parts. A slightly hostile *parràmune* has taken place and I am simply establishing my dominance.

We'd met under casual terms, but this disrespectful man forgot his manners along the way. I've been told, 'What the Australian male lacks in brains, he makes up for in brawn' and I truly hope so. Since being here, we have found a lack of connections, a lack of muscle due to scope —all of Sicily is smaller than this area of Western Australia —and far too many new legalities to... manipulate without consultants to advise us. Despite my indelicate means of conversing, the end game is to get Dustin Nerrock and a few other big-name families in this area to work with us.

For us...

Dustin's father died last year, leaving him with businesses scattered throughout the area, but with no idea on how to utilise them. Money and dominance are the game. The man under my shoe has more money than sense, an ego that rivals my own, and a name people know. And soon, here, people will know mine.

"Do you have any idea who—" Dustin chokes, struggling to force words out while my boot is pressed to his throat.

Pity...

"*Oh scusari,*" I say, feigning concern. "Did you say something?" His face looks so feeble; I want to crush it 'til it goes away. Men who bow are ants, small and helpless, but infinitely useful when put to work. I've been told my temper is an issue. Apparently, it is obvious when I'm irate; I speak a mongrel version of Italian, Sicilian, and English, and my accent seems to thicken... *Personally, I don't hear it...*

"*Madonna Mia,* are you going to cry like a *paparédda,*

Dustin. You're the man about these parts. Stand up!" I yell, and then press my heel further into his jugular... so he can't. "*Alzarsi!* Stand up!" He can't. I won't let him, and the whole idea of that makes my dick twitch.

I find myself tiring of his weak attempts to fight me off. I remove my shoe from his neck, allowing him to gasp and drag some much-needed air into his lungs. And he does, sucking like a man possessed. His palms meet the pavement under the dimly lit street lights and I take a few steps back to allow him room to stand. His pushes off his hands and climbs to his feet, a scowl firmly set on his face. Dustin all but growls at me and then spits blood to the side, his body shuddering slightly while he regains air and stability.

I mock, "Are you okay, *paparédda?*"

"You're in deep shit," he hisses, coughing at the pavement.

The bitterness in the air is tangible, an entity apart. It is time to switch the play and lead the conversation in a more mutually beneficial direction. I've humiliated him, and now I shall woo him.

"Let's talk like gentlemen, Dustin," I begin, removing a handkerchief from my pocket and offering it to him as he coughs and clears his throat. "Please oblige me?" I wave the folded white material in front of him, a feigned gesture of a truce.

He takes it and uses it to wipe away the little pieces of gravel pressed to his cheek. "Talk..."

"Perhaps we can start again. *Se?*" This is my favourite part of conversing —switching the play, manipulating the conversation. "You know who I am now, and I know who you are. You also know what I do, *se?*"

He stares at me, his brows drawn together, his eyes narrowed. "Yes."

"Well," I say, clapping my hands and grinning widely at him. "That's an excellent start. May I recommend we take this little *parramune* to a more appropriate place? I know an establishment not too far from here... Will you join me for a drink? Put this *little* and unfortunate indiscretion behind us..."

***

It didn't take long for me to gain Dustin Nerrock's favour. In fact, it took less time than I'd imagined. The man is hungry, power hungry. I recognise it in him. It is indeed a trait we share. After three hours with Dustin, I'm even more convinced that this area holds infinite possibilities. To start with, there is a high crime rate, which, of course, is a huge benefit to my cause as protection comes at a cost. There are strictly governed gun laws, which, of course, means demand, and I am happy to supply. There is a vast class division, which means two things: an opportunity to clean up the riffraff at a cost, and addicts —I love addicts.

My father once told me to never choose a side, but to rather find out their motivation(s) and make them beholden to you. 'Control the streets; control the city.' I share this philosophy with Dustin. The final and most tantalising piece of information is that this country is bursting at the seams with minerals and is far too big to secure thoroughly. There is gold, diamonds, and unsealed access roads.

"I have never met a rich man I didn't like," I declare, clinking Dustin's glass with mine.

A grin stretches across his face. The grin of a man whose eyes are suffused in dollar signs. "Well, that said, there are others we need in on this..."

"Yes." I raise the glass to my lips and the smoky whiskey fumes float deliciously up my nostrils. "A man who my *Capo* told me about. *Big* pull in the old country." I use my hands to talk. My Sicilian mannerisms are hardwired. "*Big* pull. But he seems quite the enigma. I could not track him down. He has recently married some beauty queen from England and is probably just... How do you Australians say it? *Fucking* and *fucking*. No time for business when there is pussy. *Se?*" We both laugh and I play the game of equals; that is what I want him to believe. "So this man," I continue, "he is a half-Sicilian, half-Australian, mongrel. *But* the Family... They seem to love him. The name I was given was Paul Lucchese."

Dustin's gaze narrows, his amused expression slipping. "I know who you're talking about...We can't trust that bastard." And I'm immediately intrigued...

"He is very important to the Family." I feign a sigh, but I'm eager to meet the man who has inspired such a reaction. I have never liked 'likable people'; it is the unlikable ones I prefer. They have attitude and spirit. They make excellent soldiers.

Dustin seems to study my expression. "He will never agree."

"He will. I assure you—" My attention is redirected to a clearly inebriated character as he swipes a collection of glasses off the bar; the sound of them smashing rudely invades my senses. I tilt my head and watch from our booth as he begins to yell and threaten the bartender.

Well, this is a pity.

I was having such a peaceful drink, and I have my favourite shirt on. The inebriated man's grasp of the English language shocks me, and it makes me wonder whether it was his mother or father who has failed him so profoundly; perhaps both.

"Listen, 'ere," he starts, pointing a shaky finger at the bartender. "I ain't sellin' nufin. I'm just 'ere for a drink."

Interesting...

I shuffle from my seat and excuse myself politely. After walking slowly over to the man at the bar, I lean beside him and smile.

"Wah you want?" He lowers his voice. "I ain't sell nufin'." His mouth opens and expels words only vaguely fathomable. It is a damn pity about this shirt.

"Scusa." I motion across to my table. "I was drinking over there with a very important colleague of mine and you're making it rather hard to concentrate. May I suggest finding a different establishment, *se?"*

It has been a long time since a man dared strike me, and it is apparent why over the course of the next few seconds. He stumbles backwards and then jolts forward, throwing his fist into my face. The smell of his breath knocks me harder than his knuckles do. My cheek burns for a short moment.

I shrug apologetically to the wide-eyed bartender and jab the bastard beside me twice in the throat. *Jab. Jab.* His knees meet the floor with a thud. My knee rises to connect with his chin. *Crack.* A guttural groan curdles up his throat. My knee rises again. Another groan. The back of my hand collides with his cheek. How *irrispettoso.* I can't stand disrespect in any form. As I stare down at his swaying body, I notice a small stain on my shirt.

"*Madonna Mia. Fare le corna a qualcuno,*" I hiss at him. "Look what you did."

***

Dustin's brawn most definitely comes in handy as we relocate my new friend to a more private locale —an old building Dustin inherited. He doesn't look quite as lively laying bound on the cold concrete floor. Although, my dick does like the bindings...

I can already tell that after this exchange, I'll be in dire need of a lady's company.

"Will you drag Mr...?" I stare questioningly at our bound captive.

"Get fucked ..." He chokes on his own words.

"Very well, will you drag Mr Get Fucked so he is sitting against that wall just there, *se?*" I smile calmly in my new partner's direction, pointing at the rear brick wall. "Thank you, Dustin."

This disused warehouse would make an excellent abattoir; perhaps I will recommend a new business endeavour to Dustin. I ponder this as I remove a few items from my bag and set them down on the wooden workbench behind me: a blade, a bottle of aqua, and a Luna Stick. Pouring a small amount of water onto my shirt, I gently wipe at the stain. The chill from the liquid sends shivers down my spine.

"Such a pity," I mutter to myself. When I tilt my head to watch Dustin manoeuvre our intoxicated captive to a more suitable position, I feel serenity wash over me. These are the moments where I truly shine. In the grit. When others usually waver, I am at my most contained. Perhaps, it also has to do with my new partner's eager and obedient behaviour; after all, I did nearly squash his throat into the pavement a mere few hours ago. A sly grin draws my lips out. Who said money can't buy happiness? Money can purchase the most loyal of comrades, and fear has no limit. Empires have been built on the foundations of both.

"I am Jimmy Storm. You know me?" I query, though I know the answer.

"No," our barely coherent friend snaps, pulling away from Dustin's grip.

"Well, this is Dustin Nerrock. You know him?" I ask, once again knowing the response. Our inebriated friend glances up at Dustin and nods, appearing to exhibit a suitable level of unease. "Well, now you know me too. Jimmy. Storm. I would like to know who you work for."

"I'm not fucki—"

"*A-ta-ta-ta.*" I wave my finger at his rude interruption. "Before you say no, we found ten grams of heroin on you. Now, don't lie to Jimmy. Tell me who in this town supplies you... And then I will give you an offer you can't refuse."

"I'm neva snitchin'. He'd fuckin' kill me."

"I see." I sigh and turn to my assortment of items. "I respect that." As I pick up the switch knife and feel the cold metal in my palm, I run my finger over the blade, the rigid edge grating my pad. The excitement of what's to follow forces blood directly to my groin and I find myself in a state of impatience, eager to show Dustin how I assure success.

I spin on my heels and walk directly to my captive. I lean down. The blade slices through his flesh like a zipper parting fabric. The knife ruptures the nerves within. The deed is done. His eyes widen and his hand grips his left wrist. Blood trickles through his fingers and drips onto the concrete.

"Shit," he cries. "Wha tha fuck? You said you respected tha."

"I do, very much," I state adamantly. "I hope you live. Loyalty is my favourite virtue."

"*Christ,*" Dustin mutters from behind me. *Yes,* this is how we interrogate in *my* Family.

"You will die from exsanguination within ten minutes." I squat at the man's side and grin, watching his face pale and his head bobble on his neck as nausea floods him. I have seen this look many times. "I am a spiritual man. You would not know, but I am a Catholic. And I could swear to Mother *Maria...*" I stare at him as he struggles to hold his head up, narrowing my eyes to better study his. "I could swear you can see death take a man. The seconds just before... in his eyes... you see death enter him."

Something akin to a whimper splutters from his throat and panicked tears burst from the corners of his shallow eyes. This poor underprivileged street rat will not be missed and without any evidence, his disappearance will be stamped as drug related. Which, in a way, it is. "Now, tell me where I can find your boss and I will help you live."

"What? How?" Dustin asks me.

I laugh from deep within my abdomen; I just can't help it. "I told you, I'm a spiritual man."

My weeping captive tries to speak, "He is... he owns..."

"Can you feel that chill?" I ask him, moving so close my lips brush the shell of his ear. "*He* is near, my friend."

"He owns Le Feir. The bakery." He passes out, seven minutes before closing time. The smell of his blood, metallic and tangy, hits my nose. It pools around his outstretched legs, creating small glistening puddles. *Yes,* I think to myself, *this warehouse would make an excellent abattoir.*

Deciding to keep my word, I stand and walk briskly over to the workbench, retrieve the Luna Caustic nitrate stick — one of my favourite tools. While I roll up my sleeves and wet the stick's tip, I think about what a real shame it is that my captive won't be conscious to feel the burn. I hear it is quite a unique sensation. My dick is throbbing like a stubbed toe below my zipper as I approach my captive and squat by his side. I begin to cauterise his slit wrist. The blood makes it rather difficult, however, not impossible, and I've had plenty of practise. "So young Dustin," I call over my shoulder, my eyes unwavering as I work. "We will pay Mr Le Feir a visit tomorrow, make a deal. We don't want any product besides ours hitting these streets. This is now our *quartier,* our *District.* Why is this?"

"Control the streets, control the city," he replies, his nerves stammering through his voice. A chuckle escapes me. I think I may have scared my new partner; how quaint. It appears Dustin Nerrock doesn't get his hands dirty; he must be a proficient delegator. But as my father once told me, 'It is the dirt that makes the man appreciate the sparkle'.

"More importantly than Mr Fier," I say, "is organising a meeting with the man my *Capo* spoke about...You know him. Where will we find him?"

I hear Dustin release an exaggerated breath. "He doesn't go by Paul Lucchese anymore. His name is Luca Butcher and he lives in Connolly."

nicci who?

I'm an Australian chick writing real love stories for dark souls.
Stalk me.
Meet other Butcher Boy lovers on Facebook. Join Harris's Harem of Dark Romance Lovers
Stalk us.

It's taken three years into my author career to write a biography because, let's face it, you probably don't care that I live in Australia, hate owls, am sober, or that my husband's name is Ed—not Edward or Eddie—Ed... like who names their son 'just' Ed? (love my in-laws, btw). Anyway, you probably don't really care that my son's name is Jarrah—not Jarrod or Jason—to compensate for his dad's name *Ed*...

I ramble...

Here's what you really want to know. I'm a contradiction. Contradictory people are my jam. I am an independent woman who has lived her entire life doing things the wrong way, the impulsive way, the risky way... my way. I'm not from a rich family but I've taken wealthy people chances... I'm my own boss. I'm a full-time author, an Amazon best-seller, all despite the amount of people who said I couldn't, shouldn't, wouldn't... I'm that person.

So while I live a feminist kind of life... I write about men who kill, who control, who take their women like it's their last breath, pinning them down and whispering *"good girl"* and *"mine"* and *"you belong to me"* and all the red flag utterances that would have most independent women rolling their eyes so hard they see their brains.

I write about men who protect their women. Men who control them because they are so obsessed, so in love, they are terrified not to... Do I have daddy issues? *Probably.* Did I need to be controlled and protected more as a child and this is my outlet? *Possibly.*

So... if you don't like that... if you don't see the internal strength in my heroines, how they are the emotional rocks for these controlling *alphahole* men... then don't read my books. You won't like them. We can still be friends.

But I want both. I want my cake and to have a six-foot-five, tattooed, alphamale eat it too.

facebook.com/authornicciharris

amazon.com/author/nicciharris

bookbub.com/authors/nicci-harris

goodreads.com/nicciharris

instagram.com/author.nicciharris

Made in the USA
Las Vegas, NV
10 March 2024

86998989R00246